KILLING ME

KILLING ME

ME

MICHELLE GAGNON

G. P. PUTNAM'S SONS

NEW YORK

PUTNAM
— EST. 1838 —

G. P. PUTNAM'S SONS
Publishers Since 1838
An imprint of Penguin Random House LLC
penguinrandomhouse.com

Library of Congress Cataloging-in-Publication Data

Names: Gagnon, Michelle, author.
Title: Killing me / Michelle Gagnon.
Description: New York: G. P. Putnam's Sons, 2023.
Identifiers: LCCN 2023004703 (print) | LCCN 2023004704 (ebook) |
ISBN 9780593540749 (Hardcover) | ISBN 9780593540756 (Ebook)
Subjects: LCGFT: Thrillers (Fiction) | Humorous fiction. |
Novels. Classification: LCC PS3607.A35862 K55 2023 (print) | LCC PS3607.A35862 (ebook) |
DDC 813/.6—dc23/eng/20230208
LC record available at https://lccn.loc.gov/2023004703
LC ebook record available at https://lccn.loc.gov/2023004704

Printed in the United States of America
1   3   5   7   9   10   8   6   4   2

BOOK DESIGN BY KRISTIN DEL ROSARIO

To everyone who's had to pick themselves up, dust themselves off, and start all over again.

You better run.

—PAT BENATAR

KILLING ME

CHAPTER ONE

YOU ONLY LIVE ONCE

The worst part was that I felt stupid.

Well, that's not entirely true. The *real* worst part was that I was tied up in the back of a van with a hood over my head, and based on recent news reports, something truly horrific was about to happen.

But feeling stupid was definitely second worst.

I'd followed every campus safety alert and obsessively read every news article. Johnson City, Tennessee, wasn't the kind of place where anything of significance ever happened, and then—whammo! It was the hunting grounds for a serial killer. The population of sixty-six thousand seemed to have doubled overnight: satellite news vans lined Main Street (yes, there was an actual, honest-to-God Main Street); the Holiday Inn was fully booked, which never happened outside of college reunion weekends; and the *Johnson City Tribune* finally had articles that didn't involve the school board or city council. The killings were all anyone talked about in the Foodtown checkout line, over drinks at the Crow Bar, heck, even at the local strip club (suffice it to say, I've explored the local adult entertainment options).

Like me, the victims were all petite brunettes in their early twenties. Those similarities had elicited a tingle of excitement—the "it could've been me" awe of someone who missed a flight that crashed. Although I was equally certain that only a real idiot fell victim to a serial killer. That sort of thing happened to wide-eyed innocents who offered to help a guy with a fake cast load something into his van. I wouldn't fall for the old "Can you give me directions?" or "Help, I'm on crutches!" tricks. Not me, no way.

Well, ha ha. The joke was on me. Because it turns out I'd been exactly as dumb as those other girls.

Will I be his fifth victim, or the sixth? It was a strange thing to focus on, but while I lay on the floor of the van (of course it was a van), rocking from side to side as we drove along a bumpy road, that number seemed terribly important.

Calm down, I told myself. There was an FBI task force dedicated to the case; the *Tribune* claimed they'd basically taken over the Johnson City Police Department. An intrepid agent was probably already on my trail, they'd surely find a critical clue just in time to save me—

Except there were no clues; we hadn't scuffled, and I hadn't dropped anything. *Stupid*, I chastised myself again.

The bastard hadn't even done something clever to trick me. Just past dusk I had been walking back to my crappy apartment in the University Edge complex, so named because it was inconveniently located at the campus's farthest reach. I'd been mulling over the meager contents of my fridge, wondering if putting strawberry jelly on leftover rice qualified as dinner. Consequently, I'd barely registered the white van pulling to the curb fifty feet ahead. A guy in a delivery uniform got out and lumbered around to the side panel, completely ignoring me. I considered crossing the street, but when he grabbed a vase of flowers from inside and turned toward the house, I figured I was just being paranoid. So I continued toward him.

Then he literally butted me into the van. For a second, I thought it was an accident. I was opening my mouth to chew him out when the panel door slid shut and he was *on* me. I struggled, but within seconds he'd slapped a piece of duct tape across my mouth and jabbed me in the neck with a needle. When I came to, I was bound up like a sushi roll.

If it hadn't been so terrifying, it would've been downright comical. Imagine a surveillance video (not that there were any in this podunk town) of me getting catapulted into a van by a guy's ass. If serial killers put out blooper reels, that would be on it.

I was about to chuckle when my brain helpfully reminded me, *You're going to die.*

I started hyperventilating, which, trust me, is not fun when you're gagged, hooded, and barely able to breathe through your nose. I was still getting over a cold, too, so survival depended on my marginally less congested left nostril.

Calm the fuck down, panicking won't solve anything. I was trying not to think about the other victims, but good luck with that when a spare tire is digging into your back. Horrific images kept intruding. (I hadn't seen anything, obviously, but you know how that can make it even worse?) Their heads had been shaved. No problem there, I'd done that back in high school. The FBI had been a little vague about the next part, but apparently there had been other shaving, too (*don't think about it*), and then their entire bodies had been painted to look like Pokémon characters.

Seriously. Pokémon. Like, lizards and shit.

The FBI was also vague about how the women were killed, but

it involved strangulation. Hopefully super quick and painless strangulation.

After they were killed, the Pikachu Killer (yup, that's what they called him) dumped the body somewhere weird—like a mall parking lot, or a high school football field—then sent local news networks a GPS link.

Get it? Like they were playing Pokémon GO. That's the kind of asshole who was about to kill me. Someone obsessed with an app no one even used anymore.

Not me, I thought, gritting my teeth. When this dickwad opened the door, I'd fight like hell. I'd escape and lead the FBI back to him. I'd be a hero, the woman who took down the Pikachu Killer. Every talk show would want me as a guest. I'd smile bravely as they questioned me about the ordeal. Maybe even write a bestselling memoir. Eventually, this would just be an awful memory that I'd get past with the help of a fancy therapist.

The van abruptly lurched, hurling me sideways. Then it slowed down. My heart pounded faster—this was it. We were arriving at the creepy cabin/warehouse/underground lair, or whatever he used for a kill room.

Sweat broke out on my forehead. I desperately tried to remember the women's self-defense class I took last year. Was I supposed to go for his eyes first, or his balls? I should've paid more attention, but there had been this really cute girl who distracted me—

The brakes squealed as we lurched to a stop. My heart was racing so fast it felt like I might pass out, which wouldn't be helpful at all.

I might not remember self-defense, but I'd always been a good planner, and escape routes were my specialty. *So come up with a plan, genius.*

My hands and feet were also bound with duct tape, based on the gross sticky feel. I dimly recalled seeing someone on TV split duct tape bindings, but I'd been super stoned at the time and hadn't thought I'd ever *need* that particular nugget of information, so I couldn't remember how it was done. I tried everything I could think of, but the tape didn't budge. If only he'd used handcuffs; I'm a pro at getting out of those.

So: using my hands and feet was basically out. Which was far from ideal.

I had my head, though, which I knew from unpleasant past experience was unusually hard and concussion-proof. If I slammed it into his torso, I could knock him down and then I'd—what, hop away? Well, yeah, if I had to.

Five. He's already killed five girls who looked like me. I experienced a bizarre surge of satisfaction when that number popped into my head; then the van's door popped open, ushering in a blast of chill air.

Okay, Amber, I told myself. *It's now or never. The minute he grabs you, you've gotta—*

A sharp jab in my ankle made me scream against the duct tape. God*dammit*, he was drugging me again.

On the plus side, when I awoke I no longer felt stupid. Unfortunately, that emotion was replaced by utter, abject terror, so it wasn't exactly an improvement.

The hood was gone. I was in a dark room lit by a bare bulb. The floor was concrete, and the walls and ceiling were covered in bumpy noise-canceling foam. The periphery of the room was cast in shadow, but the illuminated circle contained enough to inspire nightmares for the rest of my natural life. Which, judging by how things were going, was probably not going to be very long. It looked like the set of a low-budget horror movie, and would've been campy if it weren't so gruesome.

Directly beneath the lightbulb was a steel worktable with leather bindings for hands and feet; it was covered with streaks of blood (was a tidy serial killer too much to ask for?). Beside the table stood a rolling surgical tray cluttered with sharp pointy things, including a buzz saw with an extension cord.

I was duct-taped to a chair a few feet away from all of that, which, when I thought about it, made very little sense. Why not just start with me on the table? Clearly organization wasn't this guy's strong suit.

A wave of nausea swept over me. I fought it back—my mouth was still covered with duct tape, and if I threw up, I'd choke to death on my own vomit. *Focus, Amber.* How long had I been out? Hours? Days? The drugs had left my head feeling swollen and sluggish. By now, maybe someone had noted my absence and reported it to the FBI. (My renegade agent was developing features now; she was a raven-haired beauty in her early thirties who favored pantsuits, with a no-nonsense demeanor that concealed her true sensitive nature.) They had an entire unit dedicated to finding this guy, right? Once I was reported missing . . .

. . . except it was Easter break. My roommate Joanie was with her family, and campus was empty. No one was expecting me anywhere. My best hope was that the pizza guy would find it weird that I hadn't ordered anything in a few days; but he'd probably assume I'd gone away, too.

Man, I'd kill for a slice of pepperoni right now.

My stomach rumbled. The last thing I'd eaten had been a stale donut swiped from the faculty lounge that morning. Was that really going to be my final meal? It hadn't even been a good donut, it was mealy and had no frosting.

That sparked another flood of tears. *Christ. Now you're crying over a bad donut.*

A loud *thump* from above. I stared at the (also soundproofed) ceiling, listening hard. There was a heavy tread that gradually receded. He could return at any moment; I was running out of time. I scanned the room frantically, struggling with my bonds. In movies this was always the point where the heroine found a way to save herself with a bobby pin or something . . .

The plastic chair was child-sized, so small that my knees were bent to an uncomfortable angle. My arms were taped to its back legs, my ankles and calves to the front. Must've been a big sale on duct tape at Home Depot, because he certainly hadn't skimped. I couldn't shift my limbs at all.

Still, this wasn't exactly the sturdiest piece of furniture, so maybe I'd get lucky. I rocked back and forth on the chair, pushing off hard until it tilted past the balance point and dropped to the ground. My back bore the full brunt of the fall, knocking the wind out of me.

The chair didn't break. I hadn't landed on anything critical, but it hurt like hell and now I was stranded on my back like some sort of turtle.

A door creaked open on my left. I froze, every muscle reflexively clenching: even my heart seemed to stutter to a stop. *Breathe, Amber,* I reminded myself. *And get ready.*

There was a long pause. I strained my eyes, trying to make sense of the shifting shadows. It was completely silent but I could sense him there, watching me. I felt powerless and hopeless. I started to hyperventilate, my stuffed nostrils flaring to draw in air.

The killer stepped into the square of light.

Approaching the van earlier, I'd clocked him as a stooped, middle-aged guy with a bit of pudge around the middle. He was wearing white coveralls, a ball cap, and sunglasses. Seemingly harmless, totally forgettable.

Not anymore. He was easily six-four, maybe even taller. He had broad shoulders, a barrel chest, and powerful hairy legs.

I could tell all that because he was basically naked, aside from a tiny leather apron strapped around his waist. Two thoughts popped into my head. One: Why bother? I mean, an apron that size wouldn't keep him from getting dirty (or bloody). And two, where the hell did one even buy such a thing?

This fearsome spectacle was mitigated by the only other thing he was wearing.

It was a Pikachu mask.

Like, the kind a little kid would wear on Halloween.

It was too much for my mind to process: terrifying and absurd and hilarious, which added up to me lying on my back thinking, *Huh*.

The killer stood there for a few long beats, as though inviting me to revel in whatever the fuck he was supposed to be. Then he strode forward purposefully. I wriggled frantically, trying to shift the chair, but all I succeeded in doing was scraping the back of my arms. He acted as if I were an annoying fish who had flopped out of a net onto the deck of his boat. Bending over, he grabbed the back of the chair, then set it upright with a hard yank that threw my head forward.

He was behind me, so close I could feel his breath on my neck. All the hairs on my body stood up. I craned my head, trying to see what he was doing, but he was out of my sightline.

He trailed a finger from the top of my scalp all the way down to my upper back. It was a creepily intimate, possessive gesture that made me shudder. Tears flowed down my face, and I sobbed against the duct tape. Fear drove every coherent thought from my head. When I felt the prick of a needle in my arm, I embraced the darkness it offered with relief.

This time when I woke up, my scalp was unnaturally cold, and I was lying on my back. The pounding in my head was a million times worse; it felt like someone was thumping my skull with a mallet. The light seemed brighter, too, but that might've just been the migraine. I was shivering; it was either much colder in the room or . . .

My eyes finally adjusted, confirming my worst suspicions. I was naked. He'd strapped me to that disgusting table, and the overhead bulb glared directly in my eyes. My hands and feet were bound so tightly by the leather restraints that I couldn't lift them at all.

I could raise my head, though, enough to see that my entire body was bright blue. Intricate swirls on my skin looked like scales; they were actually kind of pretty and had clearly taken some time to paint. *Christ, how long was I unconscious?*

And what comes next?

I realized abruptly that the duct tape had been removed. I flexed my jaw a few times, reveling in my newfound ability to breathe like a normal human being. Then I opened my mouth to scream . . . but hesitated. That would just bring him running, and if the tape was gone, there probably wasn't anyone close enough to hear, right? Not to mention all the soundproofing. He clearly wasn't sloppy when it mattered.

The surgical tray was by my right elbow. I craned my head higher—the room seemed empty. Maybe Leather Apron was having a snack before getting down to it.

Ridiculously, the thought made my stomach grumble. I would seriously murder for a sandwich right now.

Murder. Ha, that's funny. I yanked at the restraints again, but they just cut into my flesh. My hands were so numb that I probably wouldn't be able to use them even if I were free.

This is it, I realized. *Victim number six, all teed up and ready to go.*

An odd sense of calm settled over me; there was a strange sort of peace in simply accepting my fate. Relief, even. I hadn't had an easy life, and I'd made some terrible mistakes along the way. People had been hurt. Someone had even died. Maybe this was fate's way of balancing the scales.

And he might've made a mistake this time, somewhere along the way. One of my neighbors could've spotted the abduction out their front window; my money was on the creep across the street who mowed his lawn in jean shorts. It was too late to save me, but other petite brunettes would be spared the same fate, and my sacrifice would mean something.

The door creaked open again. He was back.

I closed my eyes and said a short prayer, asking for the end to be as quick and painless as possible. Then I lifted my head to glare at Leather Apron.

As he stepped forward, my confusion grew. No apron, no Pikachu. This person was smaller, too, dressed entirely in black and wearing a ski mask. They held a long, thin stick.

"Who the hell are you?" I croaked.

They ignored me, which was pretty darn insulting under the circumstances.

"Um, hello?" I finally said.

"Shut up," the figure growled. I frowned. The voice was definitely female. This must be one of those sick couples who killed together instead of having a normal hobby, like bowling or *Star Wars* cosplay.

"Where is he?" she demanded, stepping closer to the table.

"Seriously?" I choked out a sharp laugh. "How the fuck am I supposed to know?"

The woman scanned the room, her eyes bright blue behind the ski mask. I watched her, then said, "Just out of curiosity, I'd love to know what happens next."

"Christ, you really don't follow directions," she hissed. "Keep your damn mouth shut."

This was the part where I should've begged for my life, but I truly didn't care for her tone. "Listen, you bitch, I don't care—"

She lunged forward, jabbing the end of her stick into my belly. Recognizing it as a cattle prod, I gulped. "Fine. I'll shut up."

"If you don't, I'll tape your mouth closed," she threatened.

You mean tape it closed again, I almost retorted, but just then the door swung wide behind her, flooding the room with light.

And that's when a lot of things happened in rapid succession.

Leather Apron charged into the room with a roar. Ski Mask leapt out of his path and he crashed into the table, shifting it back enough to rock me against the restraints. As he came around again, meaty paws swinging, Ski Mask dropped low and executed some kind of acrobatic move that landed her behind him. It was hard to make out exactly what happened next from my limited vantage point, but the end result was that Leather Apron ended up sprawled across my (naked) chest, his bulk crushing my lungs and probably cracking a few ribs in the process.

That was when I saw the cattle prod lash out. Before I could protest, Ski Mask jammed it into the thickest part of his neck.

The surge coursed through him and right into me. My whole body seized up. The pain was indescribable, like every nerve ending had caught fire simultaneously.

I almost passed out again. Fighting to stay conscious, I struggled to breathe around the weight on my chest and gasped, "What. The. Fuck. Is. Happening."

Ski Mask had stepped back into the shadows, holding the cattle prod like it was a sword. The guy on top of me wasn't moving, though. He didn't even seem to be breathing.

"Is he dead?" I choked out.

Ski Mask stepped forward again and poked Leather Apron. He shifted slightly but otherwise didn't react. Keeping the tip of the cattle prod on his neck, she reached out and carefully checked his dangling wrist for a pulse, then groaned. "God*dammit*, that's the second one this year." She examined the cattle prod. "Maybe I should replace this."

"The second . . . what?" My drugged, zapped brain was having a hard time keeping up, and the lack of oxygen wasn't helping.

Acting like she hadn't heard me, the woman pulled off the ski mask. She was probably in her midthirties. Blond hair cropped in a pixie cut. Disarmingly pretty, despite the fact that her sharp features were twisted in a deep frown. She sighed. "I hate when they die on me. Fucks up the whole plan."

"What plan?" I choked out, mystified. Wasn't she working with Leather Apron? And if not, what was she doing here? "Listen, if you're not a fucking serial killer, could you get this piece of shit off me?"

She raised an eyebrow. "You've got quite a mouth on you."

"I'm painted blue, tied to a table, and there's a fucking dead maniac lying on top of me. So, yeah, some strong words are called for."

"Noted." Her right leg shot out, sweeping his legs. Slowly and gracelessly, Leather Apron slid off the table, leaving the mask behind as he landed with a *thump* on the floor. Staring down at him, she wrinkled her nose distastefully.

"What?" I asked, gratefully filling my lungs with deep draughts of sweet, stale air.

"His apron came off. I'm never going to be able to unsee that." Looking annoyed, Ski Mask briskly undid the straps binding my hands and feet.

I carefully sat up, wincing at the pain sparking all over my body. My very naked, cold body. Teeth chattering, I crossed my arms over my chest and asked, "So . . . I'm not going to die?"

"We all die," Ski Mask said blithely, bending to check the pulse at his neck. "But you're fine for the moment. Unless you walk out of here and get hit by a bus or something." She straightened. "Crap. He must've had a heart condition."

It was only then that the reality hit. I'd escaped—well, I'd been rescued. It was over. Overcome by emotion, I leapt from the table and threw my arms around her neck. "Ohmigod, you saved me! I can't thank you enough, I just . . . I . . ." I burst into sobs, tears and snot flowing down my cheeks.

Ski Mask pushed me away, distastefully eyeing the smudges of blue on her clothes. "You can thank me by not ruining my outfit." She jerked her head toward a pile of clothing in the corner. "I'm guessing those belong to you?"

"Oh, yeah. Great," I mumbled, hurrying over. Everything I'd worn to the library that morning was still there, and relatively intact except for the duct tape remnants stuck to my sleeves and pants legs. I swiped at the blue paint with my camisole but only succeeded in smudging it. Giving up, I pulled on my sweatshirt and jeans. I'd honestly never been so happy to get dressed in my life.

It was taking a long time for my brain to reboot; whatever he'd drugged me with lingered, and everything seemed to be happening at half the usual speed. I watched my savior prowl around the perimeter of the room. "What are you doing?" I finally asked.

"Making sure I didn't forget anything," she said.

"Like what?" I asked.

"Evidence."

"Um . . ." I gestured to the dead naked guy. "Pretty sure that ship has sailed. Hey, do you have a phone? We should call someone— unless you already did?" I couldn't stop staring at Leather Apron. Even in death he was intimidating. Probably early forties, with a farmer's tan and a shaved head. Big and meaty, with enormous hands. His open eyes gazed off to the right as if there was something puzzling past my shoulder. Hollowly, I said, "He was going to kill me."

"Definitely," Ski Mask agreed. "He spent hours strangling the other victims. He'd bring them to the brink of death, then stop right before crushing their larynx. Over and over, until the hypoxia became so extreme their bodies simply couldn't recover. Then he stabbed them. The paint job is impressive, don't you think?"

"What?" Despite being fully clothed, I started to shiver. If she wasn't working with him, how could she possibly know that? Nothing she said sounded right or made sense. I shook my head to try to clear it, and a wave of dizziness nearly brought me to my knees.

Noticing, she said, "You're going into shock."

"Yeah, probably." Trying to rub feeling back into my arms, I asked, "So, are the cops on the way?"

She waved a hand at him dismissively. "No point with the dead ones. They'll find him eventually."

"*No point?*" I repeated, dumbfounded. "Are you serious? You saved my life and got rid of a serial killer. You're a damn hero."

"I didn't intend to kill him," she said with irritation.

"But . . . we should tell someone, right?" My mind was groggy, but I was pretty sure that was what people did. Not that I was a big fan of the cops, but still . . . this sort of thing was their specialty.

"If you want to, be my guest." She checked her watch. "Dammit, I was supposed to be on the road an hour ago."

And with that, she turned and walked away.

CHAPTER TWO

THE STRANGE WOMAN

gaped after her, then scrambled to catch up. "You're leaving?"

She didn't answer, continuing down a dim hallway. I realized we were in a basement. The rough concrete walls were painted black and covered with oversized, glow-in-the-dark emoji stickers. They leered and shimmered in the gloom. It was the creepiest, most ridiculous decorating job I'd ever seen. Ahead of us, rickety-looking stairs rose toward a lit doorway. I was seized by a sudden, irrational fear that the door would slam shut, trapping me forever. It took considerable self-restraint not to shove past her and bolt for the opening.

I managed to get a grip, barely. Everything still felt unreal; this had to be a nightmare, right? Part of me wondered if I'd wake up on my bed in a flop sweat.

Ski Mask stopped abruptly, and I crashed into her back.

"Try respecting personal space," she said. "And if you do call 911, I'd appreciate it if you didn't mention me."

"What?"

"There's a landline in the kitchen. Just tell them he was torturing you with the cattle prod, and one of your hand restraints came loose, so you managed to grab it. Got it?" She flipped the prod around and offered me the handle. "Apparently I need to invest in a new one anyway."

"Um, can we . . . can we talk about this up there?" It felt like the walls were pulsing, edging closer to me. "I really don't like small spaces."

"Fine."

She trotted up the stairs and I hurried after her. We emerged in a brightly lit room. I squinted against the glare; it was like walking out of a cave into the sunlight. Like being drawn up out of a well. Like—

"Yuck," I said as my eyes finally adjusted. We were in a kitchen. Mounted on the wall opposite was the promised landline, an ugly brown corded model circa 1982. It appeared relatively clean, but everything else was disgusting. Stacks of pizza boxes, Chinese take-out cartons, empty cans, and filthy plates tottered perilously on the counters and table. Flies swarmed everywhere. I covered my nose, trying not to gag.

"Most of them aren't this messy," Ski Mask said. "Wait five minutes before calling."

The light provided a better look at her. She was much taller than me, with a general demeanor that took "resting bitch face" to a whole new level. A black turtleneck and dark jeans clung to her whip-thin frame. Passing her on the street, I would've pegged her as a Type A Pilates mom who'd traded in a fancy corporate job to reign over the PTA.

She tapped my arm with the electric cattle prod. "Hello?"

"Uh . . . what?" I gazed at her blankly.

"Wait five minutes, then call 911," she said, enunciating like I was an idiot. "When they show up, tell them you got lucky and managed to shock him. Or just leave. Your choice." She held out the cattle prod again, more insistently.

Numbly, I took it. "But . . . I don't get it. Where are you going?"

"Nowhere that concerns you. Good luck." She turned away again and marched into the next room.

"Jesus Christ, hang on!" I scampered after her through a maze of newspapers stacked nearly to the ceiling. She wove through confidently, like she knew exactly where she was going. "Please, just wait!"

"Why?" she asked without stopping.

"Because . . . because . . . I mean, I almost died down there! And I don't know who you are or how you found me."

"I was tracking *him*. You were just . . . there." She waved a hand dismissively.

"But . . . why?" I wrinkled my forehead. "Why didn't you just call the cops, or the FBI—"

"I've tried that. It doesn't work."

Catching movement out of the corner of my eye, I startled. *Just a mirror*, I realized with relief, trying to process my reflection. I'd forgotten about the blue paint, but that wasn't the most alarming thing. I was completely bald—and I mean everywhere, even my eyebrows had been shaved off. I ran a hand over my head, feeling unfamiliar bumps and valleys. Cautiously, I pulled the waistband of my pants away to check *down there*: nothing. I'd been in such a rush to get dressed, I hadn't even noticed.

Out of everything that had happened, this felt like the biggest violation. I'd spent all day afraid. Now I was pissed off. "That fucking asshole. I look like a Smurf after chemo."

"Hair grows back. You'll be fine," she said over her shoulder, still walking.

"Hey!" I followed her onto a wobbly porch. The house was pretty much what I'd imagined, a ramshackle cabin that looked like a stiff breeze would turn it into kindling. Ski Mask tripped lightly down the stairs. The fake florist van was still parked in the gravel driveway at an angle; seeing it, I shuddered. My backpack was probably still inside. It held everything I owned of value: my phone, laptop, and house keys.

But the thought of climbing in to retrieve it was terrifying.

Just do it fast. I hurried over and slid the van door open. The floor was littered with a spare tire, wilted flowers, slashed duct tape, and a black hood; I spotted my battered backpack against the far wall. Taking a deep breath, I lunged forward and grabbed it, then crabbed out as fast as possible, barking my shins on the running board. The backpack was still zipped shut; I hefted the familiar weight over one shoulder and slid the door closed.

Ski Mask was already halfway to the trees. I broke into a jog to catch up. Slightly out of breath, I gasped, "Where are we?"

"The police will tell you when they get here," she said, striding down the driveway. "Go back to the house."

"But . . . where's your car?"

She stopped and held up a hand. "Look, I know you've had a challenging day—"

"Challenging?!" I gaped at her.

"You're in shock, so you're not thinking clearly. Listen very carefully. You're okay, aside from the"—she gestured toward my head—"bald thing. He's dead, you're safe. So just do what I say. Wait five minutes, call the cops, and you'll be able to go home. All right? Come on now." She made a shooing motion with her hands. "Back to the house."

Following her gaze to the gaping front door, I quailed. "I won't go back there. Not ever."

"Well, that's melodramatic." She sighed. "It's a long hike back to civilization, but I can point you in the right direction."

"Can't you just give me a ride?" I hated the pleading tone in my voice, but the thought of walking anywhere alone in the dark sent my heart skittering in my chest.

Ski Mask was already shaking her head. "No."

"Why not?" I demanded.

"Are you always this annoying?"

"Are you always this much of a bitch?" I retorted.

She raised an eyebrow, then turned and kept going.

"Hey, wait! I'm sorry. Really, I didn't mean—"

"Don't care."

"But—"

"Enjoy the rest of your life. Goodbye."

She got another ten feet, the crunch of her heels loud on the gravel, before I called out, "I'll tell them."

She stopped but didn't turn around. "What?"

Her tone was icy, filled with warning.

Screw it. I was the one holding a cattle prod now, defective or not. "You want me to keep my mouth shut? Give me a ride back to town."

Turning to face me, she said with exasperation, "Johnson City is in the opposite direction."

"Wait, how'd you know where I live?" Off her stony silence, I said, "Never mind. Honestly, I don't give a shit where you drop me, as long as there's a phone and maybe some food. But I am not going back in there"—I stabbed a finger toward the house—"and I'd really rather not spend the rest of the night walking alone through the woods. With my luck, I'd get abducted by another freak."

"Looking like that? Unlikely. It's a very particular kink," she said dryly.

"Please. Just get me back to civilization."

She sighed and pulled a face. "Fine. As long as you get out when I tell you to. Understood?"

"Yes. Absolutely. Thanks."

Looking put out, Ski Mask kept walking down the driveway. I followed, letting the cattle prod bump against my shin as I walked.

We tromped along a winding dirt road for nearly a half hour. Ski Mask didn't say another word the entire time. I, on the other hand, couldn't stop babbling. It felt like if I stopped talking, the final threads of my sanity might snap. Nightmarish images kept intruding on my consciousness: the guy in the apron, the tangy funk of his body odor so strong I could still smell it. Lying in the van. The sight of my bald head in the mirror.

To beat those memories back I chattered about everything from past girlfriends to favorite bands. I couldn't shake the feeling that maybe we'd been wrong, and Leather Apron wasn't actually dead. Maybe he'd regained consciousness and was watching us right now. This was exactly where the jump scare happened in horror movies; I kept waiting for him to leap out from behind a tree and finish what he'd started. I could practically feel those beefy hands wrapped around my throat; swallowing hard, I stuck close to the middle of the one-lane road.

Ski Mask's car was tucked into a small break in the trees, covered by a green tarp and bushy branches. Clearly, she'd come prepared. The brisk early-spring air was clearing my head, and as my brain sputtered back to life it produced a slew of questions. I cleared my throat and asked, "So what's your name? And how'd you know where I live?"

She stopped dead and I almost walked into her. It didn't seem to have anything to do with me, though. She scanned the surrounding trees, eyes narrowed.

"What is it?" I asked nervously. "Do you think . . . was he working with someone else? Are they still out here?"

"No," she said curtly. "He was definitely alone."

"Then what is it?"

Another long beat while she continued to peer into the forest. Under her breath, she said something that was hard to make out but sounded a lot like "Motherfucker."

My heart started pounding again. I tried to swallow, but my throat felt like it was full of sand. I braced, ready to drop my pack and run.

Ski Mask simply shook her head, looking annoyed as she said, "Let's get out of here." She started pulling branches off the tarp. I tried to help, but she waved me away. "You'll get paint on them. Can't risk forensics finding anything this far away."

"Okay," I said in a muted voice. I didn't want to give her a reason to ditch me, especially if there was someone else out here. She yanked the tarp off in one fluid motion, revealing a dark midsize sedan.

"I'll pull out, then you can get in," she said curtly.

I nodded and stepped back as she carefully tucked the tarp on top of a large duffel bag in the trunk. Then she climbed into the driver's seat and backed the car out slowly until it idled beside me.

I quickly opened the passenger door and climbed in, clumsily tucking the cattle prod into the slot between the seat and the door. The headlights flared to life, illuminating impenetrable foliage. I flinched, imagining all sorts of terrible creatures out there . . .

Stop it, I chastised myself. *You're safe now.*

But deep down I knew it would be a long time before I felt safe again.

Ski Mask eased onto the road, crunching over the discarded

branches. We drove for ten minutes in complete silence, and then the woods suddenly opened before us and the gravel ended in smooth pavement. She put on the right turn signal and checked the road in both directions before pulling out. A giggle escaped my throat at the absurdity of the gesture.

"What?" she demanded.

"Nothing. Just . . . nothing," I said. Her car stood in stark contrast to Leather Apron's hovel; it was immaculate and had stickers indicating that it was a rental. The clock read four a.m.; unless I'd lost an entire day, I'd been taken less than twelve hours ago. Which didn't seem possible; it felt like a lifetime had passed. I cleared my throat and said, "Nice car."

"Hardly. But it's functional. There's a towel on the back seat. You can use it to wipe off."

Awkwardly, I grabbed it and used the visor mirror to rub off as much blue paint as possible. Whatever he had used was thick and pasty; it would take soap and water to make a real dent, but I did the best I could. The woods gradually ceded to farmland on either side of the car. I didn't recognize any landmarks. Granted, I hadn't spent much time exploring. I was only here for senior year and barely went anywhere aside from home, work, and school.

With each mile that passed, my muscles unclenched a bit and my breathing came easier. I settled back against the seat and said, "I'm Amber."

"I don't care," Ski Mask answered, reaching over to flip on the radio. It was tuned to an AM station. And of course, of all things, they were taking calls about the Pikachu Killer.

"I can't even play the game anymore," said a woman with a thick nasal accent. "Totally ruined it for me."

"Yeah, the company lost a ton of money on this," the host agreed.

"A serial killer is bad for business, amirite? 'Specially if you're selling things to kids—"

I reached over and flicked it off. "You said 'when they die on me.'"

"So?"

"So you've done this before," I said, connecting the dots: her oddly blasé attitude, the cattle prod, the fact that she'd shown up when she had. "You said it was the second time this year."

She didn't answer. The fields were broken up intermittently by small buildings; we'd reached the outskirts of a town. Night was starting to fade, shifting to pale blue at the horizon. We passed a sign that read **BURNSVILLE: 15 mi.** I was pretty sure that was about an hour south of my college.

Everything was running through my mind on a reel: the van, the table, the way she'd taken him out. She'd been so calm through it all, almost nonchalant. Like it was just another day at the office. *Christ, my head hurts.* Rubbing my temples, I asked, "So is this, like, your thing? Tracking down serial killers and saving their victims?"

Ski Mask abruptly slowed and pulled to the side of the road, shifting into park. "This is far enough. Get out."

"What? No!" I protested, my heart rate kicking up again. The thought of standing alone in the dark on the side of the road was terrifying to contemplate. As panic clawed up my throat, I begged, "Please! You promised me a ride to town!"

"No, I said I'd take you back to civilization, and this is close enough." She gave me a pointed look. "And you agreed to get out when I told you to."

I crossed my arms and sat back. "No."

She rolled her eyes and bent forward, retrieving something from under her seat. "I really didn't want to have to do this." When she straightened, she was holding a gun. Pointing it at me, she said, "Out."

"Seriously?" I shook my head. "You won't shoot me."

"Try me."

"If you had a gun, why didn't you bring it in there?"

"Christ, what is it with you and the questions? Someone should drive by soon, you can catch a ride with them." Off my look, she added, "The chances of it being another serial killer are negligible."

"Sorry about this," I said.

Her eyebrows raised. "Sorry about what?"

Instead of answering, I swept the cattle prod across the space between us and pressed the tip of it to her thigh. As her eyes widened, I pushed the button.

CHAPTER THREE

NO QUESTIONS ASKED

We were approaching the Burnsville city limits when she came to. "Oh, hey," I said. "Sorry about that."

She glared at me. "What the fuck did you do?"

"Well, well, well. Look who's full of questions now." I imitated her snort. In the rearview mirror I watched her wriggle in the back seat.

She must've cranked the voltage to compensate for the size of Leather Apron because when I zapped her, her eyes rolled up in her head. For a second, I thought I might've killed her. As she went limp, the gun fell into the footwell. I dove to grab it, shoving aside her feet. Holding it against her temple, I checked for a pulse and allowed myself a second of relief when I found one. Then I took the car keys out of the ignition and hurried to check the trunk.

She'd been considerate enough to stock the duffel bag with rolls of duct tape, along with other things; there was a regular hardware store in there. It took considerable effort to drag Ski Mask out of the driver's seat and reposition her in the back; she'd definitely have some bruises to thank me for. Binding her arms and legs gave me a twinge—it felt way too close to how Leather Apron had treated me. But I had to do it. Or so I kept telling myself.

And like she said, I'd been drugged and was probably in shock. Which meant I definitely wasn't thinking totally clearly and couldn't be held responsible for my actions.

"You bitch," she snarled. "I should've shot you."

"Funny thing is, I checked the gun. It wasn't loaded."

In response, she brought her knees to her chest and kicked the back of my seat.

"Ow!" I protested. "Relax! I just want some answers." A car pulled up behind us. High beams flared, and then it swerved into the oncoming lane and sped past.

"Fuck you."

"I guess I'll just keep driving until you're in a better mood." I eyed the road. "There must be a place to turn around . . ."

"Jesus." Grunting, Ski Mask struggled up to a seated position. Her hands were behind her back, forcing her to lean forward. "I could bite your ear off from here, you know."

"You could, but then we'd probably crash." I pressed down on the gas and the car leapt forward, thrusting her back against the seat. She yelped. "I've got the airbag, but you'll go right through the windshield. So maybe just chill and leave my ear alone."

"You ungrateful brat."

"Oh, I'm super grateful, actually. I just wasn't up for a long walk."

"Where's my gun?"

"Somewhere safe." I'd stashed it in the trunk, inside the spare tire. "Don't worry, you'll get it back."

"When?"

"When I decide." I had to admit, part of me was enjoying feeling in control again. Not a very nice part, but there you have it.

She stared daggers at me. Pulling a card out of her playbook, I ignored her. "Do you know that guy's name? The asshole in the apron?" A long beat passed. "C'mon, I'm going to find out anyway. I bet it's super redneck. Am I right?"

"Beau Lee Jessop," she finally said.

"Figures. And how'd you find us?" Ski Mask shifted to face the window, her jaw set in a hard line. "I mean, your timing was perfect. Any longer and I'd probably be dead."

"I won't make that mistake again," she muttered.

I frowned but decided to let it slide. Besides, I had bigger questions. A pretty significant chunk of my life had been spent studying people, and this woman was . . . puzzling. Which intrigued me.

Also, thinking about her helped keep me from remembering him. And right now, I needed that. "Are you, like, a vigilante who hunts serial killers?"

After a beat, she grudgingly said, "I suppose you could say that."

"Huh." I turned that over in my mind. No one puts themself in that kind of danger without good reason. Revenge, maybe? Like a superhero origin story? "So are you former FBI? Or a cop?"

"Do I look like a cop?" she asked in a voice dripping with disdain.

"Not really, no." I glanced back at her again. "You kinda give off a corporate lawyer vibe."

"I'm not a lawyer."

"Then what are you?"

No answer.

"Fine." I sighed. She was more withholding than my last girlfriend, and that was saying something. "Why do you do it?"

"Why do you care?" she shot back.

"Just seems like a weird hobby," I said. "Pretty dangerous, too. Doesn't it scare you?"

"It really doesn't end with you, does it?"

"Well, I spent hours thinking I was going to die, and then you burst in like some sort of ninja—"

"I did not 'burst in.'"

"Whatever. And then you kill the guy—accidentally," I said, raising a hand to stave off her protest. "Although if it was up to me, it would've been slower and much more painful. Then you just up and leave, which is super weird. *And* you want me not to tell the cops about you. So, yeah, I've got some questions."

Ski Mask didn't say anything for a few minutes. The first rays of sunlight appeared, tinting her skin golden. "If I answer your questions, will you give back my car?"

"Absolutely," I said. "And I'll keep my mouth shut."

"There's a diner up ahead and I need caffeine. Pull in and untie me."

I tried and failed to repress a satisfied grin. "Great."

"You really are a pain in the ass, you know that?" she grumbled.

"So I've been told. Many times."

Ten minutes later we were sitting in a booth across from each other. Apparently the Blue Moon Diner took the term *greasy spoon* literally; even the menus were disconcertingly sticky. A long counter flanked by swivel stools ran down the right side of the room; a row of booths with cracked vinyl seats and faded tabletops lined the left. The waitress was a middle-aged woman with a ratty French braid and the gravelly voice of a chain-smoker. Aside from an old guy dozing in the farthest booth, we were the only customers. I hoped that was due to the early hour and not the food; it would be just my luck to die of salmonella after surviving a serial killer.

The waitress (*Bea*, according to her name tag, which was uncomfortably close to *Beau*) sloshed coffee into two mugs before taking our order: the farmer's breakfast for me, because I was not about to count calories after the night I'd had, and toast for my erstwhile savior/captive. Plain toast, mind you. No wonder she was so skinny.

Bea didn't blink at my shaved head and residual Smurfy skin tone, which made me think she must encounter some weird shit on a regular basis.

"You should try to wash the rest of that off," Ski Mask said as Bea shuffled away. "The restroom is over there."

"I wouldn't want you to get lonely." Her car keys were tucked in my pocket, but for all I knew, hot-wiring cars was her side hustle.

"Fine. Let's get this over with." Ski Mask pulled back a sleeve to check the time again; unless I was mistaken, she was wearing an actual goddamn Rolex under beige surgical gloves.

"Um, aren't you going to take those off?" I asked, gesturing to them.

"And leave fingerprints? Absolutely not."

"You're going to eat toast with gloves on?"

"Ask your questions," she said impatiently.

"Okay, fine. Sheesh." I hesitated, then asked, "What's your name?"

"It doesn't matter. Next."

"Seriously?" In response to her blank stare, I sipped my coffee, then made a face and added sugar to try to salvage it. As I stirred it in, I said, "I'm guessing it's something fancy, based on your accent. Old money, not flashy even though that sweater you're wearing is St. John and easily set you back five hundred bucks. Am I close?"

"Hardly," she said, but judging by her expression, I bet I was right on target.

"Reading people is kind of my hobby." More like my superpower, actually, but I wasn't about to tell her that.

"Yes, you did a marvelous job reading Mr. Jessop."

I squirmed at the reminder. "I didn't exactly get the chance."

We both shut up as Bea slapped plates down in front of us and refilled our mugs. The smell of runny eggs and bacon and hash browns almost reduced me to tears—it wasn't the prettiest plate of food I'd ever seen, but it was easily the most beautiful. Much better than yesterday's stale donut. The realization that I had an entire lifetime of stale donuts ahead of me produced a surge of emotion.

"You're crying." Ski Mask pulled a couple of napkins out of the dispenser and handed them to me. "Here."

"Thanks." The strange thing was, I hadn't even realized it. I wiped my face, turning the cheap napkin an alarming shade of blue, then blew my nose in it. Ski Mask eyed me with distaste as I self-consciously tucked it in my pocket. "So how did you find me?"

"I already explained that I was following him, not looking for you."

That was kind of insulting, but whatever. "Why were you follow-ing him?"

"He was the most likely perpetrator."

"Perpetrator, huh? Sure you're not a cop?"

"Absolutely sure. Next question." Another glance at her watch. She sighed. "I really do have somewhere to be."

"Where?"

"She's watching us. Eat," Ski Mask said in a low voice as she cut her toast with the knife and fork and took a delicate bite.

Looking up, I saw Bea openly staring from the kitchen door. Obediently, I shoveled a few bites of food into my mouth, then threw Bea a thumbs-up even though I'd gotten better hash browns from a box. She went back into the kitchen. I slugged coffee to wash them down, then asked, "How did you find him?"

"Computer algorithm." Off my look, she shrugged. "I'm good with computers. That's *my* hobby."

I ignored what was clearly intended as a diss. "Okay, so you developed an algorithm to catch a serial killer. That's . . . cool, I guess." (More like insane and creepy, but whatever.) "And that told you it was him?"

She cocked her head to the side, as if debating whether to answer. Then she said, "I wasn't only following him. There were a few candidates, it took time to narrow it down."

"How much time?"

"About two months."

"Two months?" I nearly choked on my eggs. "But the FBI only got here a few weeks ago!"

"They're not the brightest." She nibbled at her toast and wrinkled her nose. "This bread is stale."

"Okay," I said, trying to sort through everything in my mind. "So, your hobby is hunting serial killers using a computer algorithm. Then you zap them and save whoever they took."

She cocked her head to the side. "Technically, you're the first one I've saved."

My skin crawled at that. "Guess I was lucky. Do you usually get there too late?" I wanted to take the words back as soon as they left my mouth—they sounded judgey—but she seemed unperturbed.

"Not necessarily."

Meaning what, exactly? I thought. That she usually *left* the victims there? The fact that she could talk about all this while daintily eating toast was unsettling. "Was it just a coincidence that you showed up when you did? For me, I mean."

"Oh, no. I witnessed the abduction." She pushed her plate back. "That confirmed it was him."

I gaped at her. She'd actually seen me get pushed in the van? And hadn't raised any alarms? "But . . . why didn't you call the cops?"

"I prefer not to involve them until it's over. They're too likely to make mistakes."

"And you don't?"

"Rarely."

The cold, clinical detachment in her voice was getting to me. "Wait, so . . . you just left me with him? For *hours*. You let him shave me! He could've killed me!"

She sniffed. "Unlikely. Based on past victims, he preferred to take his time. And I had a few loose ends to tie up. You know, before I *saved* you." She threw me a pointed look.

"Loose ends?" I snapped. "Like what, picking up your dry cleaning? What if he'd hurried this time?"

"Then you'd be dead." She shrugged. "And I'd still have my car keys and would be enjoying a much better breakfast right now. Are you done? Because I really do need to get going."

This was easily one of the more surreal conversations I'd ever had. There were a million things I should ask, but my mind had gone blank. The wave of adrenaline I'd been riding was abating, sapping the last of my strength. Ski Mask looked tired, annoyed, and impatient. Judging by the set of her jaw, even if I came up with more questions, she seemed unlikely to answer.

And did it matter, really? Sure, everything about her was odd. The way she'd saved me was bizarre. But I was here. I was alive. That was the important thing, right?

Suddenly, I just wanted it to be over. To go home, take the longest shower of my life, and crawl into bed. Deciding, I tossed her keys on the table. "Here."

She looked surprised but quickly scooped them up. "Thank you."

"No problem. Thanks for saving me. And sorry about that." I waved my hand toward the car. "I don't normally take people hostage."

"Well. You did have a rough night," she conceded.

As she reached for the bill, I put my hand on it. "I've got it. Least I can do."

"Thanks." She slid out of the booth. "By the way—"

"I'll wait five minutes before calling." I hesitated, then added, "It'll probably be an anonymous tip anyway."

"Will it? That's an odd choice." She examined me curiously. "Not a fan of the police?"

"Let's just say I've had some bad experiences," I mumbled.

"Apparently." After a beat, she added, "I'm glad you're okay, Amber."

"I am, too." Tears misted my eyes again and I drew a deep, shuddery breath. "Be careful out there, okay?"

She nodded. "You too."

The bell above the door was still jingling when Bea came back. "You need anything else, hon?"

"No, I'm good." I watched the Toyota turn left out of the parking lot, headed north. Once it was gone, I turned back to Bea and asked, "Can I borrow your phone? It's a local call."

I left my backpack in the booth to reassure her, then took Bea's phone outside. It was old school, an actual flip phone; I didn't know they even sold those anymore. I stared at it for a second, debating what to do.

Here's the thing: there were certain elements of my past that the FBI might not look kindly on. In fact, there was a not-insignificant chance I could end up in a cell, horribly unfair though that would be. Explaining my escape without mentioning my savior also seemed challenging. I could just sell her out, but that struck me as ungrateful. And the way my life was going, I really couldn't risk any more bad karma.

I could just not call, but based on what I'd seen at the cabin, Beau didn't entertain regularly. He might never be found, and I'd be left wondering if he'd somehow survived. I had to be sure.

So I blocked the number and dialed 911. Mimicking Bea's raspy drawl, I said "There's something strange goin' on at Beau Jessop's place. Think it might be 'bout those dead girls."

Then I hung up fast and went back inside. I paid in cash and left the phone and a decent tip for Bea, then hiked back to the nearest crossroads. A police car tore past as I walked; I kept my head down, covering my baldness with my sweatshirt hood.

I walked to the nearest bus stop, then cobbled together the most direct route (which wasn't very direct at all). It took nearly two hours to make my way home. The whole time I stared out the bus window, numbly trying to process everything that had happened.

The nearest stop was a block from my apartment. I stumbled down the bus's stairs, feeling like my legs might give out. Bleary-eyed, I forced myself to put one foot in front of the other, fighting the temptation to just curl up on a neighbor's lawn. I couldn't help but shudder as I approached the spot where Beau had grabbed me. Giving it a wide berth, I made my way to the rundown student housing complex where I lived.

Opening the door to my apartment felt like walking into a stranger's house where everything was oddly familiar. The door to my roommate's bedroom was ajar, displaying a tangle of clothes piled on the bed from her rushed packing job.

Had that only been yesterday? It hardly seemed possible.

I dumped my backpack on the floor, then took the most thorough shower of my life. Long after the water had run cold, I still didn't feel clean. My skin was shiny red from scrubbing, every trace of blue washed down the drain.

I wrapped myself in the biggest towel we had and shuffled back to my room, then collapsed on the bed and slept for a full day.

When I awoke, it was just past dawn. I lay in bed staring at the ceiling. It was Good Friday, and even though I wasn't religiously observant, the fact that I was alive could be considered a goddamn miracle.

Thanks to the holiday, I hadn't even missed anything important. Classes would start up again on Monday. And since I was one of the few people left on campus, I was supposed to work an extra shift in the research library that night.

I laughed out loud. It was utterly bizarre to even contemplate going to work like nothing had happened. But the wildly unpredictable childhood I'd suffered through had prepared me for something like this, right? It was a dubious upside, but I'd take it.

I sighed and checked my phone—there was a text from an unknown number. Frowning, I opened it.

> Went back 2 the scene and got rid of your fingerprints
> even though u r an asshole

There was a Smurf emoji beside it.

"Guess she really is good with computers," I muttered, discomfited. How the hell had she gotten my number when all I'd told her was my first name? It was a little spooky. I was grateful, though. Now that my head was clear, the last thing I wanted was any further involvement in this. If I could reach into my brain and slice out the past thirty-six hours, I would.

I pulled the sheets all the way up to my chin. Could I really just act like nothing had happened? Or would that be impossible, even for someone like me?

"Only one way to find out," I muttered, pushing back the covers and staggering to my feet.

CHAPTER FOUR

I LOVE TROUBLE

The headline popped up on my phone as I shoveled dry, stale cornflakes into my mouth: FBI CONFIRMS PIKACHU KILLER FOUND DEAD.

I choked as a mouthful went down the wrong pipe, then hit my chest with a closed fist to force it back out. My finger hovered over the bulletin, but what could the article tell me that I didn't already know? I could practically picture my imaginary hot FBI agent frowning as she bent over Beau's corpse, taking in the smears of blue paint and utter lack of fingerprints (hopefully), trying to suss out what had happened.

I chewed my lip. Maybe I'd made a mistake. What if coming forward had bought me goodwill for past crimes? Maybe they'd even believe my side of the story. I could get on with my life without constantly looking over my shoulder.

Or they'd just throw me in jail.

Stay out of it, I decided. I'd worked hard on crafting a new persona for myself and wasn't keen to do anything that might jeopardize it. FBI lady would just have to deal with the uncertainty.

I spent the rest of Friday lounging on the couch flipping channels; focusing on anything for more than a few minutes was beyond me. Then I called in sick to work; after my ordeal, I decided that spending the night alone in a creepy, deserted library probably wasn't the best idea.

On Saturday, I practiced penciling in eyebrows and ordered a wig online that matched my old hair. Then I did a repeat of Friday, but with pizza delivery (damn guy didn't even seem to have missed me).

I should've spent Sunday working; originally, I'd planned on finishing two major papers. But after staring at a blank screen for an hour, I conceded defeat and went back to the couch. I was on season three of a dumb reality show, and it felt really important to get to season four by Monday.

I was dozing off when keys in the lock startled me. I shot to my feet, pulse racing. The front door swung open to reveal my roommate Joanie, who I'd somehow forgotten was coming back. I'd never had the apartment to myself for so long; it was hard to suppress the sense that she was an interloper.

"The fuck did you do to yourself?" Joanie asked, dropping the handle of her wheelie bag.

My hands instinctively went to my bare head; the wig wasn't coming until Tuesday. I'd worn a baseball cap for the pizza delivery but took it off because it made my scalp itch.

"It was . . . an internet challenge. For . . . a disease," I explained lamely.

Joanie cocked an eyebrow. She was a nice, normal girl from Louisville who didn't know what to make of me even before I turned up completely hairless. Based on the framed photos crammed onto every spare inch of table space, she'd enjoyed the kind of childhood I'd only seen on TV: split-level ranch, cheerleading squad, quarterback boyfriend named Dylan who was now a senior at Florida State. She was finishing up a teaching certification, after which she'd move to Florida to join him. Like a lot of people at school, she was raised Evangelical and regarded me (and my "lifestyle") with more than a little wariness. We were a marriage of necessity, both seniors who'd transferred in from community colleges. Consequently, our conversations centered on groceries and cleaning and not much else. Which was fine by me; I wasn't here to make friends. Although as I watched her unwind her scarf, I felt a little pang; it would be nice to have someone to confide in. Maybe I should've made more of an effort.

"I wouldn't shave my head for anyone," Joanie declared, throwing her coat on the couch; it landed close enough to make me flinch. "Did you hear they caught the guy? Dylan didn't want me to come back. If they hadn't found him I might've stayed home, swear to God." Joanie plopped down on the chair across from me.

"Yeah, I heard," I muttered. "It's great. I've gotta finish a paper, so, um . . . good night."

"I've got a couple of scarves if you want to borrow them," she offered, eyeing my baldness.

"I'm good. But thanks."

"Sure," she said, picking up the remote and switching back to Netflix. "And it's your turn to clean the bathroom this week."

"Right. Will do." I shut my bedroom door and leaned against it, closing my eyes. Having someone else in the apartment should've been comforting; Joanie wasn't my bff, but if I screamed, she'd call 911 (if only for her own protection). But somehow, I felt more alone than before.

I'd been putting it off, but Joanie had sparked my curiosity. Steeling myself, I did a search for Beau Lee Jessop.

Thanks to my anonymous tip, the police had found Beau late Thursday morning and alerted the FBI. (Apparently they hadn't raced there immediately. Although, in their defense, there were probably a lot of wack jobs calling in.) I scrolled through a flood of news reports, both local and national (serial killers being as much of a national obsession as baseball). Over the weekend the media had dug up reams of information on Beau's fucked-up childhood, the dark chat rooms he frequented, everything. No one who'd known him was surprised; a former high school classmate even claimed he was unofficially nominated "Most Likely to Become a Serial Killer."

By the time I looked up, it was past midnight. The living room light was off; Joanie must've crashed out. I got ready for bed and climbed in, drawing the sheets to my neck, trying to repress the shivers that had started up again.

As a psychology major, I knew that there were three stages to trauma recovery: establishing safety, retelling the story of what happened (preferably to a trained professional), and reconnecting with others.

Problem was, I couldn't even conceive of making headway on number one. The fact that I had been abducted right outside my home didn't help, but I couldn't afford to move since my student loan only covered this shitty apartment (without Joanie, I couldn't even have afforded that). And regrettably, I'd sworn off other alternatives for raising quick cash. So I was going to have to spend the next couple months walking past the spot where I'd been grabbed. That didn't exactly foster a sense of safety.

Rationally, I knew that Beau was dead. But my subconscious didn't care. I barely slept that night. I got up multiple times to check the locks on the front door and windows. Unexpected noises made me bolt upright in bed, startling me into a cold sweat. By morning, it was clear that Beau Lee Jessop had stolen something precious from me. I'd left part of myself behind in that hideous basement chamber—a part I was probably never going to get back.

T he next day, I almost fell asleep in Abnormal Psych and dragged through my afternoon shift at the library. Thankfully it stayed busy, so I didn't have to shelve anything in the creepy stacks that lined the interior of the building. I was the beneficiary of a lot of pitying looks for my shaved head; people probably figured I was a cancer patient. In another life, I would've taken full advantage of that.

By dinnertime I was completely wiped out. I plodded home, keeping to the opposite side of the street from where I'd been grabbed, warily eyeing every car that passed.

Without that hypervigilance, I might not have spotted the guy in a navy FBI windbreaker strolling out of my building. He was tall, well over six feet, wearing a ball cap pulled low over his eyes. As he looked up, I turned away and held my phone to my ear. Instinct kicked in, and my adrenaline started pumping. My parents hadn't given me much, but they had instilled one core tenet deep in my psyche: when you see the cops, run.

Steady, I reminded myself. I walked purposefully toward the nearest apartment building, digging through my bag as if searching for keys.

I could feel his eyes on my back. *Fuck. Act normal.*

I was almost at the front door when it swung wide and a guy in sweats trotted out. I hurried forward and caught it, ignoring the weird look he gave me (although to be fair, he probably didn't see bald chicks every day). I ducked inside, heart hammering, then chanced a glance back.

FBI guy was climbing into a nondescript sedan that screamed rent-a-car. Maybe it was just paranoia, but I could swear he was watching me. I hurried up the stairs to the second floor. A girl came down the hall in yoga pants with a mat slung over her shoulder. She frowned at me. "You don't live here."

"Chill, I'm visiting someone," I muttered, scurrying past. I climbed all the way to the roof exit and sat on the step below a sign that read **OPEN ONLY IN EMERGENCY / ALARM WILL SOUND**.

I put my head in my hands and tried to catch my breath. I really needed to get in shape if I was going to be dodging serial killers and cops for the rest of my life. Joanie was always telling me to try Zumba; maybe it was worth a shot. *Wait ten minutes*, I told myself. *He should be long gone by then.*

My phone buzzed with a text from my new best friend Un-known Number: FBI is on to you.

"Yeah, no shit," I muttered. "Thanks for the warning."

The phone rang. I immediately picked up and said, "If we're going to be text buddies, you should unblock your number."

A man's voice said, "Amber Jamison? This is Agent Cabot from the FBI."

Fuck. I cleared my throat and tried to sound casual. "Oh, hi. How'd you get my number?"

"Your roommate gave it to us. I'm calling because your name came up in the course of one of our investigations, and we were wondering if you'd mind coming in to talk."

"To talk?" I parroted stupidly.

"Shouldn't take long," Agent Cabot said. "How does tomorrow work for you?"

"Um, I have class."

"We can work around your schedule."

I squeezed my eyes shut. He was making it pretty clear that this was not optional. "Sure," I said, feeling faint. "Of course."

"Excellent. Why don't you swing by the police station on Main Street tomorrow afternoon? Does five o'clock work?"

"Yes."

"Great. Just give the desk sergeant my name and he'll bring you back to us."

"Uh-huh." I swallowed hard against the dryness in my throat.

"See you then, Miss Jamison."

I hung up and put my head in my hands. How the hell had the FBI found me? And what did they know? I toyed with the possibility that they wanted to give me a medal, but that seemed like the kind of thing he would have led with. And this wasn't some small-town cop; the FBI could probably dig up everything down to my bra size in under five minutes.

Crap. I'm screwed. I checked my watch: six p.m. Which meant I had less than twenty-four hours to get out of town.

Luckily, this wasn't my first rodeo; compared to other times I'd had to cut bait and run, twenty-four hours was practically an eon.

I'd hoped all that was behind me, though. I felt a flare of rage—even though I'd survived, that bastard Beau had managed to derail my life anyway.

But I didn't have time to dwell. Taking the stairs two at a time, I hurried back to the street. Hunkered behind the bushes flanking the door, I surreptitiously checked in both directions: all clear, at least for the moment. At a pace just short of a jog I hurried to the next block. Most of these homes were single-family bungalows with peeling paint and tidy lawns. Cutting through a backyard, I emerged in the alleyway behind my apartment building and snuck in the emergency exit. The entire time, an imaginary clock was counting down in my head. There was no guarantee that Agent Cabot would wait until tomorrow, and if he started investigating my past, it wouldn't take long to uncover something that spurred another house call.

I needed to hurry.

I slipped into the apartment without running into anyone on the stairs. Joanie was standing at the stove stirring a pot, an apron over her sundress, hair piled on top of her head. The room was steamy and smelled of pasta, and Taylor Swift twanged from the portable speakers set on the counter. Joanie's eyes were bright with curiosity as she spun on me and said, "Ohmigod, the hottest FBI guy was just here asking about you!"

"Really?" I managed to sound surprised. "Weird. Did he say why?"

She eyed me. "He just said it was important. Do you think it has anything to do with that Jessop guy?"

I repressed a flinch at his name and coolly replied, "How would I know anything about that?"

Joanie cocked her head to the side, looking pointedly at my scalp. "I mean, it's pretty weird, you shaving your head right when they caught him."

"I told you, it was an internet challenge."

"Right. But you always told me you weren't into that. Like, you don't even have an Insta page."

"Well, I got bored over break, okay?" Joanie wasn't an idiot, and I knew my explanations were coming off weak. Better get a move on. "I've got a lot of work to do. If there's any extra pasta, I'd love some," I tossed back over my shoulder before closing my bedroom door.

She called after me, "I'd share, but there's barely any food left. *Someone* ate most of it while I was gone."

On the plus side, no more bickering with Joanie, I thought as I shoved things into a bag. Luckily, I didn't own much and wasn't very attached to what I did have. It only took ten minutes to fill two duffels with toiletries, clothes, and a few keepsakes. I stood back, hands on hips as I ruefully eyed my textbooks. *There go the rental deposits.* I bit my lip in frustration. I'd been so close to finishing my degree, just two months to go. And now I wouldn't even be able to apply the credits to another school; that would be too easy for the FBI to track.

Beau Lee Jessop: the gift that kept on giving.

Saying a silent prayer of thanks that our apartment was in the back of the building, I leaned out my bedroom window and carefully dropped the duffels into the bushes below. I dug out the Glock stowed on the top shelf of my closet. (God bless America for not having a rigorous background check system.) Making sure it wasn't loaded, I tucked it in my backpack along with two boxes of ammunition.

And that was basically it. There were only a couple hundred dollars in my bank account, well within the daily limit for withdrawal. I'd stop at an ATM in the next town to get it. Then I'd figure out next steps.

"Where are you going?" Joanie demanded when I stepped back into the living room, the fork pausing halfway to her mouth.

"Library," I said. "I forgot something."

"Uh-huh." She took a bite, then said around it, "I saved you some pasta. Even though you don't deserve it."

"Thanks," I said, surprised. Sharing food (willingly, at least) was very out of character for Joanie. Suspiciously so. Maybe she'd informed the hot FBI guy that I was home and was trying to stall until he arrived. "I'll be back soon."

The door closed behind me before she replied. I hurried downstairs, then eased open the alley door: no one in sight. I dug my duffel bags out of the bushes and walked quickly to where I'd parked. My shitmobile started on the second try, and I carefully drove toward the city limits, following every traffic code to the letter.

Ten minutes later, Johnson City was in my rearview mirror. There was no sign of anyone following me. My shoulders relaxed. I'd done it. At least for the moment, I'd gotten away.

Now what?

CHAPTER FIVE

ONCE A THIEF

Except for an ATM drive-by to clear out my account, I didn't stop until I hit Kentucky. I parked in a nearly empty Waffle Barn parking lot and sat for a minute to collect myself. It was coming up on eight p.m., and the lack of sleep had caught up with me. Exhaustion was starting to have a serious impact on my driving skills; I'd nearly swerved into the oncoming lane twice over the past hour. Plus, my stomach throbbed with hunger. I'd decided that this was far enough away to risk grabbing a quick meal.

The Waffle Barn's interior made the Blue Moon Diner look high end. Instead of booths, rickety tables with chairs better suited for AA meetings were scattered around the room. A handful of senior citizens hunched over syrup-smeared plates. The lighting was dim, adding to the general defeated ambiance. But like every other Waffle Barn it was clean, there was a restroom, and the food would be reliably tasty and cheap.

Plus, no security cameras.

I ordered, then used the bathroom. When I came back, a huge

stack of waffles with a side of fried eggs was waiting for me. I spent the next five minutes focused on transferring the contents of the plate to my stomach. Then I sat back and inhaled deeply.

An elderly woman at the next table smiled at me. Her wig was crooked, and penciled-in eyebrows gave her a look of perpetual surprise. Not that I was one to talk, my own were probably looking pretty ragged. "Best waffles in Kentucky."

"I believe it," I said, automatically matching her drawl. Internally, I smacked myself. Mirroring was a bad habit, one I'd done a pretty good job of breaking over the past few years. Funny that I backslid the minute I went on the lam.

"What type you got, sweetheart?" she asked kindly.

It took a minute to realize she wasn't asking about the waffles; I kept forgetting I was bald. I should've paid overnight shipping for that damn wig. I hesitated, then said, "Leukemia."

She shook her head and tutted. "Lost my friend Carol to that last year."

You're a terrible person. Don't lie to her. But I was already chirping, "Oh, that's such a shame. My doctor says I'll be fine. This was my last round of chemo."

"Good for you." Waving over the waitress, the woman said, "Sally, put this nice young lady's food on my tab."

"Oh, no, I really couldn't," I protested.

She winked. "My pleasure, sweetheart."

Sally was whip-thin and had teeth that showed more than a passing familiarity with a meth pipe. She rolled her eyes and muttered, "Crazy old hag."

I glared at her, but she was already headed back into the kitchen.

The old woman opened a battered handbag and took out a twenty, then tucked it under her water glass. Carefully she got up, using the table for balance. I rose to help her, but she shook her head. "Save your strength, dear. And don't you mind Sally, she's in a mood. Now, eat up."

"Thanks again," I said as she shuffled toward the door.

She tossed a wave over her shoulder. I took a quick scan of the room; everyone seemed occupied by their food, and the kitchen door was still closed.

Don't you dare, the little voice in my head admonished.

But I'd had even less cash in my accounts than I thought. No idea where I was headed yet, and I couldn't risk credit cards. I had to make every dollar count.

Deciding, I shoveled the last bite in my mouth, washing it down with coffee as I stood. Then I strolled out, casually scooping the twenty off the table as I went. *Fuck you, Sally. I'm in a mood, too.*

When I got back to my car, I frowned at the sight of a postcard under my windshield wiper. I pulled it off and examined it. It was a promo for cheap Vegas vacations, which still seemed like a stretch for the Waffle Barn's clientele. Hearing a commotion behind me, I hurriedly tossed it on the passenger seat and tore out of the parking lot.

I spent the night parked on a residential street, tucked in a sheltered spot out of view of the houses. Despite my exhaustion, I jerked awake every time headlights swept by, or a branch rustled, or an animal scurried past. I lay in the back seat clutching the Glock like it was a security blanket, heart pounding, seat belt clip digging into my back. All told, I'd probably only clocked three hours by sunrise.

I hadn't bothered brushing my teeth, so my mouth was mossy and tasted foul. My whole body was achy and sore, and my eyes felt like they'd been filled with sand. It had been a long time since I'd had to sleep in a car, and clearly I was out of practice. I couldn't afford a motel, though.

What else is new? I reminded myself. I'd been in this situation plenty of times in the past, and based on how things were going, I would probably find myself there again in the future. And I'd always survived. I just needed to come up with a destination, somewhere to regroup as far away from Agent Cabot as possible.

Still. This wasn't supposed to be happening again. I was an upright, taxpaying citizen now, expected to walk across a stage in cap and gown in two months. But despite my efforts to leave the past behind, it had caught up with me. Maybe it always would.

I sighed, then sat up and stretched. Yawning widely, I checked the news on my phone. There were more articles on Beau Lee Jessop, mainly regurgitations of what had already been reported. No mention of potential witnesses or people of interest, but that might change later today when I didn't show up for that interview.

I sighed and rubbed my eyes. It was so unfair. *How the fuck had the FBI found me?* Campus police had taken a thumbprint for my student ID, but I'd wiped down Bea's phone with my sleeve after using it, so it couldn't have been that. They must've found some trace of me in the cabin. Apparently Ski Mask wasn't as good at covering tracks as she thought.

Unless she set you up.

I chewed that over, then shook my head. Didn't make sense. I was too likely to rat on her if they picked me up.

As if on cue, my phone buzzed. UNKNOWN NUMBER: You okay?

I frowned; Ski Mask hadn't struck me as the type to give a shit. I typed back: how'd they find me?

She sent the shrug emoji. *Really?* Angry, I typed, could've used that heads up earlier.

A long pause. I'd almost given up hope of an answer when sorry popped up.

"Yeah, I'll bet," I muttered, although the apology seemed out of character, too. A woman with a golden retriever puppy on a leash was approaching the car. Seeing me, she slowed and crossed to the other side of the street.

That was my cue. I climbed awkwardly into the front seat and turned the car on, executing a quick three-point turn before heading back to the highway. I was starving again, and desperately needed to pee. But I wouldn't risk another restaurant until there was more distance between me and Johnson City.

I felt a familiar itch on the back of my neck, the one that meant someone was chasing me. My mom had always been adamant about paying attention to that itch; she had several cautionary tales about friends who got nabbed because they chose to ignore it.

I pulled into the first service station I saw and paid cash to fill the tank (thanks, Sally). While it gassed up, I used the truly foul bathroom as fast as possible, holding my breath the entire time. I grabbed a six-pack of Red Bulls and a bag of Corn Nuts for the road (corn is a vegetable, after all, so it passed as a healthy breakfast if you squinted).

I chugged half a Red Bull on the way back to the car. Climbing in, I discovered another text on my phone. "Look who decided to get chatty," I murmured, reading: Can help if u need it.

I scowled at the screen and typed, Help w what?

New ID.

Now, that was interesting. I did need one, the sooner the better. But how did Ski Mask know that? Because something had occurred to me during the long, dark night. I would've realized it sooner, if I hadn't been racing to leave my whole life behind. As far as she knew, I shouldn't have had any problem baring my soul to the authorities. Amber Jamison was a model citizen; I'd made sure of that when I assumed her identity. Even if Ski Mask had NSA-level computer skills, there was no trail to lead her back to the real me.

Which made this sudden interest even sketchier. Was it even her? Who else could it be, though? The FBI wouldn't bother texting, they'd just put out a BOLO and set up some roadblocks.

After a minute of debate, I replied, no thx.

If you change your mind, lmk.

"Hell no," I said out loud. I was perfectly capable of handling this on my own.

Although scoring a new ID was always a pain in the ass. The one I was using now had taken a month to sniff out (and a hell of a lot of whiskey shots in biker bars before I was pointed in the right direction). I didn't have that kind of time or resources. Which meant I'd have to go somewhere that churned them out en masse.

I popped a few Corn Nuts in my mouth and chewed them thoughtfully. New York was out—too expensive. Atlantic City could work, but I'd pissed off some dangerous people with long memories there. Which crossed off New Orleans and the riverboat scene, too. And don't even get me started on Miami. Unfortunately, the old me had burned pretty much every bridge this side of the Mississippi.

My eyes fell on the promo card peeking out from underneath empty snack wrappers. Huh. Vegas was known for generating IDs that withstood official scrutiny, and under the circumstances, that was something I desperately needed.

Drumming my fingers on the steering wheel, I mulled it over. Vegas was a big town, thronging with people. Easy to get lost in a crowd. Cheap, too. And I'd never been there, so the chances of stumbling across someone who wasn't a fan was minimal. Maybe it was time to say goodbye to this part of the country for good. I'd planned on heading to California for a fresh start after graduation anyway. Vegas could be my pit stop.

I did some quick mental calculations. It would be tight, but I had almost enough cash to make it there. And if necessary, I could make up the difference.

At least it was a plan, and it beat the alternatives. I rolled down the window to let the brisk morning air wake me up. Humming "Viva Las Vegas," I pulled onto the highway and headed west.

Thanks to higher-than-expected gas prices, I was down to my last twenty when I reached the outskirts of Albuquerque two days later. My car was running on fumes, so I followed signs off the highway to a gas station.

I pulled in and shut off the engine. It was a national chain, not a mom-and-pop operation. Cars occupied half the pumps: busy, but not too busy. There was a mini mart with a chain pizza place inside.

It was perfect.

I checked myself in the mirror and discovered that, sadly, I was still bald. New hair was just starting to sprout, giving me the unfortunate appearance of a newborn chick. My eyebrows were in better shape; I'd gotten better at penciling them in, and they gave me kind of a rockabilly vibe. At the moment, this was about as good as I could look.

Showtime.

I pulled on a ball cap and went inside. Making a beeline for the bathroom, I did a quick survey of the layout.

A middle-aged guy was working the main register; at the opposite end of the store, a pock-faced teen stood behind the pizza counter. A couple of hipsters were in the chips aisle, and a pregnant woman was filling an Icee cup by the freezer.

Honestly, I couldn't have asked for a better setup.

In the bathroom I spent an extra minute washing my hands, silently psyching myself up. Then I tightened the straps of my bra to create more cleavage, tied my T-shirt in a knot above my navel, and pushed open the door like I was going to war. I eased down the chips aisle, surreptitiously shifting my attention between the guys manning the registers at opposite ends of the mart. The middle-aged one was hard to read, and chatty; he was joking with Icee woman as she paid. He had smart eyes, which was always a bad sign.

Teenagers were unpredictable, though.

Mentally, I flipped a coin. Tails had it.

The kid at the counter couldn't have been more than seventeen. He grinned as I approached, exposing a serious need for a good orthodontist. "We got a special today," he said. "Two slices for the price of one and it comes with a Coke."

"Diet Coke count?" I asked, matching his grin. "Girl's gotta watch her figure, y'know."

"Sure, diet's okay. I mean, not that you need to diet." He flushed deep red.

Damn. This is too easy. I willfully suppressed a pang of guilt, reminding myself that it wasn't his money. This was a national pizza chain, and the owner was a renowned bigot who donated to anti-LGBT groups. Really, I was performing a public service. Jutting my hip out, I purred, "Two slices of pepperoni and the Diet Coke, please."

While he got it ready, I checked the room again. The hipsters were paying now, which nicely distracted the other attendant. No one else was in earshot.

"Here you go." The kid slid the box across the counter and handed me a huge collector's mug. "I gave you the SpongeBob one."

I put a hand to my chest. "SpongeBob's my favorite!"

"Mine too." His face had gone so red it practically matched his polyester uniform.

I slid my carefully folded twenty across the counter. "I've only got a hundred, can you break it?"

"Um, sure. I got enough." He was already pushing buttons on the register.

"So how long have you worked here?" I asked. "I haven't seen you before."

"Yeah, I just started a few weeks ago."

"Lucky me." I leaned forward and put my elbows on the counter. His eyes slid down to where my shirt gaped open, and his Adam's apple bobbed as he swallowed. "You got a girlfriend?"

"A g-girlfriend?" he stuttered. The drawer slid open. His hand shook slightly as he took the bill I'd left on the counter.

When he started to look at it, I grabbed his other hand and flipped it over. "You want, I can read your palm. My grandmother was a fortune-teller in the circus." I traced a line down the center of it. "Long love line. That's always a good sign."

Poor kid looked like he was about to have a heart attack. "The circus? Really?"

"Oh, yeah." I let go of his hand but held his gaze as I added, "My mom was a contortionist. That's why I'm so bendy."

"C . . . cool," he said, lifting the till and sliding my twenty underneath to join the larger bills. Inwardly, I breathed a sigh of relief. He wouldn't realize what had happened until the end of his shift, and by then I'd be in Arizona.

As he carefully counted out ninety-three dollars in change, I picked up the cup and played with the straw.

"Thanks." I withdrew a five and tucked it in the tip jar. "That's for you, for being so sweet."

I gave him a little wave, then sashayed over to the opposite register to get twenty dollars' worth of gas. The middle-aged guy looked over the rim of his glasses. "What, you're not gonna flirt with me?"

I smiled and nodded at his wedding ring. "Don't think your wife would appreciate it."

He guffawed. "Doubt she'd care. Drive safe, miss."

I tossed pizza boy a final wave as I pushed open the door. Another promo postcard had been tucked under my wiper; this one had a picture of a crappy-looking motel on it and promised *CHEAP ROOMS!* Apparently the Vegas tourism board had no issue killing trees to further their cause. I tossed it on top of the other one.

The gas seemed to take forever to pump; I kept waiting for one or both of the employees to charge out yelling, or worse yet, for a cop car to pull up. But five minutes later I was back on the road, headed west at sixty miles an hour.

I'd like to say that I felt dirty. After all, I'd used that poor kid, taking advantage of his raging hormones. But the truth was I felt amped up, riding a rush. I glanced at myself in the rearview mirror and muttered, "Just like riding a bike."

It's not my fault, really. My parents were small-time grifters (although, if asked, they'd claim to be Madoff-level masterminds). Growing up, I was a prop in most of their schemes to liberate marks from their money. By the time I turned eight, I was basically a pro myself.

So I started running my own scams in junior high. School was already a pretty patchwork affair, since I rarely made it through a semester without coming home to find our car packed with bags and my parents waiting impatiently. "Hop in, hon," my mom always said. "Time to blow this popsicle stand." And away we'd go, off to fleece the next group of suckers.

Until the day in tenth grade when I came home and the car had already left.

There was a note that read *Sorry kiddo, timed this one wrong* with a twenty-dollar bill on top, like some sort of tip.

I could've found them, probably—I knew their "friends" in a dozen different states, all short-term partners in their schemes. I also could've tried one of the more recent burner phone numbers.

Instead, I went into the kitchen and made myself a peanut butter and banana sandwich, then sat at the counter eating it contemplatively.

Technically I was fifteen years old, but in terms of street smarts and life experience I could probably have added a decade to that. I didn't hate my parents, but I didn't particularly like them, either. And I'd come to realize that they weren't very good scammers. If they had been, we wouldn't be racing away from every gig, sometimes well before the payoff. Plus, I was tired of playing the cancer patient/car accident victim in their cons. (Man, would they love my new look. In retrospect, I was shocked that they never shaved my head.)

As I sat there licking peanut butter off my fingers, it occurred to me that I could do so much better on my own.

So that was how I spent the next few years. Sometimes I worked with a crew, sometimes alone. My parents usually stuck to the Midwest (especially Ohio, my mother loved the Buckeye State), so I stayed east. After bouncing along the seaboard for a bit, I homed in on the South. The accent was easy enough to fake, and I could play any age from fourteen to twenty without too much trouble, depending on what was called for.

I'd always abided by a couple of rules, my own personal code.

I never stole from the little guy if I could help it. No one who couldn't afford the loss, especially old people. I liked it clean and quick; no long cons, where there was too much risk of getting caught.

And I never, ever resorted to force or violence.

It was going great until I made a big play for real cash. I was nineteen years old and thought I knew everything. Long story short, I made an error in judgment. And someone got hurt. Killed, actually. Not by me, but still. It was my fault.

That's when I swore I was done. Courtesy of a forged high school diploma, I went to community college, then Eastern Tennessee State. I majored in psychology, thinking it would enable me to put some of my less reputable skills to good use for a change, maybe even help some folks. I paid for my education with epically crappy work-study jobs and financial aid.

At times, the temptation to backpedal was almost overwhelming—one good scam would've covered at least a year's tuition. But I was determined to go straight. As time passed, the criminal part of my life started to feel like it happened to someone else.

And yet here I was, taking advantage of a teenager for quick cash. *It was an emergency*, I told myself, repressing a pang of guilt as I drove away. *That was the last time.*

Shit. I wasn't even good at lying to myself anymore.

CHAPTER SIX

WOMAN ON THE RUN

The iconic **Welcome to Las Vegas** sign glowed in the early-dawn light as I drove slowly along the Strip. At this hour, the sidewalks were populated by drunks staggering out of casinos and street cleaners mopping up after them. A year ago, I would've been giddy with excitement at the scale of it all. Instead, I drove past the Luxor pyramid and Caesars Palace with barely a glance, continuing until I hit a line of run-down motels.

A sign on my right tugged at my attention. Curious, I eased to the curb in front of a crappy motel named the Buggy Suites. It was oddly familiar. I dug through the detritus on the passenger seat and pulled out the postcards: the one tucked under my windshield in New Mexico had a picture of this motel on the front.

So was fate telling me to stay here? I frowned. In person the motel looked godforsaken, better suited to the set of a dystopian film. It was L-shaped, with two levels wrapped around a parking lot. The neon sign featured a covered wagon that bounced up and down. There was only one car in the parking lot, a total beater. Apparently it was the off-season, at least for this fleabag.

"What a dump," I muttered. Chewing my lip, I debated. Something about the place gave me the willies. As I watched, a guy in a white tank top with stains at the armpits stumbled out of a room on the top level, unzipped, and started pissing over the railing into the parking lot.

"Sorry, fate," I said, wrinkling my nose. "Not gonna follow you on this one."

But I desperately needed sleep. The past few days had been spent blearily mainlining bad truck-stop coffee while trying not to swerve into oncoming traffic. My lower back was tight from twelve-hour-daily drives, and my personal hygiene had consisted entirely of wet wipes. Now that I'd arrived, the thought of driving much farther was overwhelming. I wanted a shower, breakfast, and a reasonably comfortable bed, not necessarily in that order.

A half mile down the road, I hit pay dirt. The Getaway's neon sign advertised **VACANCY/$30/FREE HBO/WIFI/CLEAN ROOMS!** The latter didn't necessarily seem worth bragging about, but for thirty bucks a night, if they actually were clean I'd be pleasantly surprised. And it definitely looked like the type of place that accepted cash. I had sixty bucks left, enough for one night here and a couple cheap meals. If I made a score today, I could upgrade.

Deciding, I turned in.

The Getaway was U-shaped, with two floors of rooms lining a half-full parking lot. That, at least, seemed like a reassuring sign. Rubbing grit from my eyes and suppressing a yawn, I went into the office.

The clerk seated behind the battered reception desk looked like she'd stepped out of a 1950s sitcom. She was wearing a flowery housedress and had a peacock-blue scarf wrapped around curlers. Cat-eye glasses and bright red lipstick completed the look. "One night, hon?" she drawled, eyes still glued to a black-and-white movie playing silently on the mounted TV in the corner.

"To start, yeah," I said. "Cash okay?"

That got her attention. She gave me a once-over and cocked her head to the side appraisingly. "I run a clean joint here and I got rules. No guests."

It took me a second to figure out what she meant. "I'm not a hooker."

"Uh-huh." Her eyes narrowed. "Whatever you say, hon. I see any pimps or drugs, you're out."

I suppressed a flash of annoyance; apparently I looked even rougher than I thought. "I'm just here to gamble."

"Sure you are. Twenty-five a night if you're paying cash. Check-out's ten a.m. A minute after that, you pay for another day." She watched as I signed the register with one of my mom's old aliases, then slapped a key card on the counter. "Number nine. Park in front and keep your car locked if you value it."

"Thanks," I said, taking the card. She'd already turned her attention back to the television.

I shifted my car to the spot in front of number nine. The room was on the ground floor, next to last from the end. When I opened the door, a pungent wave of air freshener nearly knocked me back on my heels. I covered my nose and stepped inside, eyes watering. The only window faced the parking lot; I immediately opened it to clear out some of the stench.

The room itself was nothing to write home about, but miracle of miracles, the sign hadn't lied: it was clean. Or rather, as clean as possible, considering age and hard use. There was a definite noir motif, with framed movie posters on every wall. The industrial carpeting was a muddy, nubby brown; the queen bed was covered by a loud polyester comforter that definitely wouldn't hold up to scrutiny under a black light, and there was a wobbly-looking desk and chair in the corner with a matching dresser facing the bed. The bathroom would only fit one person at a time, and the shower stall was more like a coffin. But there was a paper seal over the toilet and no (visible) bloodstains, so all things considered, it was perfect.

I flicked on the AC to bat the heavily scented air around the room (and out the window, ideally), then moved my duffel bags and backpack inside and set them on the bureau (because if any place had bedbugs, it was probably a thirty-bucks-a-night dive). Plopping down on the bed, I pulled my sneakers off. Something tugged at the back of my mind; I pulled out my phone to double-check.

It was my birthday, and I'd completely forgotten. "I'm twenty-four," I said aloud to my small pile of worldly possessions.

They seemed unimpressed. I sighed and closed my eyes.

After showering I was torn between sleeping or eating, but days of microwaved gas station food had left me craving something that didn't have a five-thousand-year shelf life.

I followed signs to the Mega Luck buffet a block from the hotel, which promised all you can eat for seven dollars. I'll say this for Vegas: it doesn't cost much if you're willing to trade glittering casinos for buffets and skanky motels. I devoured enough food to last the day (and possibly longer, since I discreetly stuffed some fruit into my backpack), then made my way back to the motel.

I felt a spark of alarm when I saw a woman sitting on the curb in front of my room. She didn't look like a cop, though. This woman was small, with a massive pouf of curly black hair, heavy makeup, and a passing resemblance to Amy Winehouse. She sported a tank top, skintight shorts, and spike heels.

Definitely a working girl, which helped explain the desk clerk's suspicious nature.

"Got a smoke?" she asked when I was five feet away.

"Nope. Sorry."

"S'okay." She eyed me. "You staying here?"

"Just for the night," I said, digging into my pocket for the key card.

"Can't bring johns back here, y'know." She toyed with the strap of her heels.

Why the fuck does everyone think I'm a sex worker? Are there a lot of bald ones running around Vegas? "I'm a tourist."

She looked me up and down and smirked. "If you say so."

My stomach gurgled, then cramped so badly I almost doubled over. "Oh, crap."

"What?"

"Nothing. I just . . . I don't feel great." I flashed back on the buffet. "Probably shouldn't have had the shrimp."

Her smirk widened. "You coming from the Mega Luck?"

"Yeah."

"Well, shit, kiddo." She shook her head. "That place gives you the runs. Gotta go to Garden Court."

"Oh." Another cramp, alarmingly low in my intestines. I hurried past her and fumbled with the key card, swiping it over the pad three times before it glowed green.

"Good luck," she called after me as I clench-walked to the bathroom, letting the door slam shut.

After ten minutes of quality toilet time, I decided the worst was over. While washing my hands, I checked myself in the mirror above the sink. Granted, fluorescent lighting was no woman's friend, but I looked a hell of a lot older than twenty-four. And the sleepless nights hadn't helped. I looked haggard and hollowed out.

Oh well. It wasn't like I was here searching for love, not even if it was conveniently located right outside my door. (The woman on the curb had actually been pretty hot, all things considered. Probably out of my current price range, though.)

I staggered out of the bathroom and double-checked the window lock; my new friend was gone. Maybe she'd scored a date, although it was hard to imagine someone paying for sex at eight a.m. I pulled the comforter off the bed (because yuck), tucked the gun under my pillow (safety first), and collapsed onto the bare sheets.

The AC was decidedly lackluster, so the still super-stinky room was stifling. After spending the past few years in the South, you'd think heat wouldn't bother me, but Las Vegas's blistering weather was a special kind of hell. It was only April, for fuck's sake. Who would actually choose to live here?

I covered my eyes with one arm to block out the light and swallowed back bile. Hopefully by this afternoon I'd be able to stray far enough from a toilet to make an easy score. Then I'd get the hell out of here.

I awoke to a thumping bass line, loud enough to make the wall behind my head vibrate. I stretched, yawned, and checked my watch: six p.m.

"Crap!" I said, bolting upright. I'd lost nearly the entire day and had nothing to show for it except residual stomach gurgles and a headache from air freshener fumes.

And ironically, I was starving again.

I shuffled to the bathroom and relieved my bladder. After skeptically examining the bananas I'd taken from the Mega Luck, I decided E. coli was unlikely and horked them down. I took another quick shower and changed into fresh clothes while I mulled over options.

Without an accomplice, I was somewhat limited. And I didn't have anything to use in a melon drop or fiddle game. Barred winner was a possibility, but I'd have to spend money on imitation casino chips, and those might not be easy to come by. Trick rolling was risky (and icky); even though everyone was mistaking me for a sex worker today, I didn't want to deal with the kind of dude who went for a bald chick.

Probably best to just keep it simple and use my current pathetic state to my advantage. Time for a little sad dolly.

I locked my door and crossed the parking lot. Despite the setting sun, it was still hot as hell. But Vegas was waking up, like a nocturnal beast slinking out of its den. The street hummed with traffic, a steady stream of cars heading toward the tonier parts of the Strip. The sidewalks were packed, but not with the bachelorettes and conference attendees that I'd expected. Almost everyone shuffling along the cracked pavement was old, obese, or both. Some toted oxygen tanks. A few used walkers or rode powered scooters. There was no happy chatter, and no one made eye contact. It was depressing as fuck and made me want to shower all over again.

I checked the map on my phone; the Strip proper (at least the section with hotel names that I recognized) seemed to start about a mile away. I dreaded the thought of walking in this heat but couldn't afford to pay for parking, and looking sweaty and ragged could actually prove helpful. So I joined the stream of zombies shuffling toward the giant gleaming towers that loomed over the landscape.

By the time I arrived in front of the Sahara, I was wiped. I sat on a bench and swiped a hand over my forehead, trying to gather myself. I'd put on just enough makeup to look presentable (and, hopefully, not like a hooker). I was wearing a sundress and floppy hat to cover my baldness; I couldn't bring myself to play the cancer card again, it felt like tempting fate. As the sun began to set, the temperature dropped precipitously, making me wish I'd brought a sweater.

For a while I just sat and observed; ninety percent of pulling off a successful con was choosing the right mark. And in a place like this where people expected to be ripped off, it was even trickier than usual.

I had to admit, I was kind of excited for the challenge.

After about a half hour, by which point I was properly cold, I spotted him. Mr. Country Club was a middle-aged guy in a polo shirt and chinos. He had a tan line on his right wrist from a golf glove, a bulky platinum wedding ring, and a chunky gold watch. As I watched he lit a cigar and started puffing on it, checking his phone with his free hand. Then he strolled right toward me.

I held my phone to my ear and released a small sob when he was five feet away (crying on cue is one of my résumé skills). Mr. Country Club glanced up from his phone and frowned. I had wrapped my arms around myself and was rocking slightly, watching him from under my eyelashes. When he kept walking, I cried, "They took everything! I don't even have money for food! And my license, and my keys . . . the police said they couldn't do anything! They acted like it was my fault!" I raised my voice at the end to a full-blown wail.

Mr. Country Club stood a few feet away, clearly eavesdropping. "Yeah, okay," I said more quietly once I was sure I had his full attention. "But what about tonight? I mean, am I supposed to just sleep on the street?"

His watch was a Piaget, I noted. Even better. I rubbed tears away with the back of my free hand. "Okay, Mom. I love you, too. I'm so sorry about this, I know you can't really afford it."

Then I hung up and let out a small, hiccupping sob, staring at my sandals.

"You okay, miss?" I looked up and feigned surprise at finding him right in front of me. In response to my flinch, he stepped back and raised his hands. "Sorry, I couldn't help but overhear. Are you in some kind of trouble?"

Mr. Country Club had a slight Midwest accent—Ohio, if I wasn't mistaken. My mom would've loved that. I matched it, saying, "Thanks, I'm fine. I just . . ." I sniffled and wiped my face again. "I was robbed. I was using the bathroom, and—and—my purse was on the floor, and the person in the next stall just grabbed it! By the time I got out, she was gone. And the guards, and the police, they're acting like it's my fault!" I released another small sob. "Everything was in there! My license, credit cards, money . . ."

"Not your phone?" he asked, eyeing it.

I shook my head, thinking, *Well played, mister.* "I was looking at it."

"And you're here alone?"

"No. I mean, yes. I am now." I took a deep, shuddery breath. "I came with my boyfriend, but we had a big fight, so he left, and now I'm just trying to get home."

"Sure, sure." He rocked on his heels. "Where are you from?"

"Ohio."

"Thought I recognized the accent." He grinned, pleased with himself. "Grew up in Cleveland myself."

"Really?" I said brightly. "I'm from Cincinnati!"

"Great town."

I coughed lightly, as if the cigar was bothering me. Noticing, he held it at arm's length. "Sorry, bad habit. Drives my wife nuts, so I'm smoking out here."

"It's okay," I said in a muted voice. "Anyway, my mom is going to wire some money, but she said it probably won't get here until tomorrow. Hopefully it'll be enough for a bus ticket, but . . . well, she doesn't have much."

Mr. Country Club stood there looking irresolute, ash growing at the end of his cigar. I had to be careful not to push, let him think he'd arrived at it on his own. And pray that his wife didn't show up to check on him. I kicked my heels against the wall like a little kid, which might've been overkill, but it had the desired effect: his gaze softened. He pulled out a wallet and dug through it, then offered me two bills. "Here. This should help."

I waved him off. "Oh, thank you, sir, that's so sweet, but I couldn't possibly—"

"I insist," he said. "Had a good night at the tables, so they're comping our room. If Desert Pines didn't charge so darn much, I'd be making money on this trip."

I bit my lower lip and looked reluctant. "Are—are you sure?"

"Please," he insisted. "I've got a girl around your age. If something like this happened to her, I'd hope someone would help."

"You're a good dad," I said, heaving a deep breath as I accepted the bills. "She's lucky. If you give me your address, I can pay you back—"

Mr. Country Club was already shaking his head. "Don't worry about it. You just take care of yourself and get home safe."

I hopped to my feet. "Thanks so much again! I'll go check the bus schedules. Maybe there's one tonight!"

I threw him a little wave and practically skipped down the street. A block away, I ducked into a doorway to check the take.

Two crisp hundred-dollar bills. "Holy crap," I said aloud. "I am good."

The sound of slow clapping. I quickly tucked the bills into my bra and spun around.

The Amy Winehouse look-alike from the motel stood a few feet away. She'd changed into a skintight leopard-print dress and six-inch heels, and a cigarette dangled from her frosted pink lips.

"What?" I demanded.

"Guess you weren't lying," she said with a smirk, then came over and leaned against the wall beside me.

"About what?"

"You're not a hooker." She took a deep drag, then offered me one. I shook my head. "You're a con."

"Retired," I said.

"Didn't look retired to me." She grinned. "I had my eye on that guy. Shame you got to him first."

"Would've been a waste of your time. He's here with his wife."

"Aren't they all," she snorted.

I checked past her; it was never a good idea to stick close after hitting a mark. "I need to get going."

"Yeah." She tossed her cigarette toward the street. "Sahara's a wash, I'm headed to the Hilton. Wanna come?" Seeing my hesitation, she added, "It's good hunting. They got a big construction convention this week. Lots of guys with more money than brains. And no wives."

Two hundred bucks was a pretty good haul, but I'd need a lot more than that for new ID documents. And my motel buddy could probably steer me in the right direction for those, too. Deciding, I fell in step alongside her. "So what's your name?"

"Marcella," she said. "You?"

I fumbled for a minute, trying to remember which of my mom's pseudonyms I'd used at the motel. "Mary Ann," I finally said uncertainly.

She raised an eyebrow. "Bullshit."

"What do you mean, 'bullshit'?"

"I mean that's definitely not your name. But whatever."

She picked up the pace. I hesitated, then hurried to catch up. "You're right."

"None of my business," she said.

"I know, it's just . . . I'm kind of between names at the moment."

"Gotcha." Marcella laughed. "See, I've known a few Mary Anns, and you're definitely not one."

"True. According to a BuzzFeed quiz, I'm definitely more of a Ginger." I batted my eyes at her.

Looking bemused, she said, "Funny, I always get the Professor."

"Yeah?" I matched her pace, which wasn't easy; she made walking in ankle-breaker stilettos look easy. Casually, I asked, "Any chance you might know where to go for a better name?"

Marcella darted a glance at me. In the heels she towered over me, although she couldn't have been more than an inch or two taller without them. "Me? Nah. Dot'll know, though."

"Who's Dot?"

"Your landlady." She pulled out a lipstick and talked around it, adding, "Runs the Getaway."

I pictured the desk clerk and frowned. "The redhead?"

"Yeah. Dot's sort of the unofficial queen of Vegas. You need something, she can probably get it. But only if she likes you."

"Good to know." I was having a hard time reconciling the image of the woman in curlers with a queenpin, but there was no reason for Marcella to lie about it. I rubbed my upper arms; maybe I should spring for a souvenir sweatshirt, I was freezing my ass off. It would make me look younger, too, if I sized up. Marcella was wearing considerably less clothing, but she seemed fine. "Aren't you cold?"

"You get used to it," she said. "Word of advice: Dot doesn't truck with any of us working the Getaway, so keep it away from there."

"Doesn't seem like a great place for marks anyway."

"True." Marcella laughed. "Not too bad for johns, though."

"So where do you take them?"

"Place called the Buggy down the road." Off my reaction she cocked an eyebrow. "Know it?"

"No, I just drove past on my way in." I hesitated, then added, "Actually thought about staying there."

"Ugh, no." Marcella wrinkled her nose. "It's nasty. Gotta pay extra for clean sheets."

"Glad I chose the Getaway, then." I decided not to mention that soon I'd be trading up. If tonight was any indication, I could score a couple grand in a week, easy; then I'd be on my way.

"Dot would say that the Getaway chose you," she said, grinning.

"So she's kind of New Agey?"

"More like old school. She's all about fate and destiny."

"Really?"

"Yeah." Marcella cocked her head to the side. "You think that's bullshit?"

I shrugged, thinking about the promotional postcards. "Sometimes, I guess."

"Me, I'm a believer. What's your sign?"

"Um, Aries."

"Figures." She nodded sagely. "Fire sign."

Personally, I thought the zodiac was about as reliable as my parents. I was enjoying the conversation, though. In fact, I was pretty sure she was flirting with me. "How long have you been staying there?"

"Too long."

"Gotcha. Where are you from?"

"Everywhere, kind of."

"Yeah, me too."

"Really?" She grinned. "So tell me, Mary Ann. How'd you get off that damn island?"

"Easy," I tossed back. "I fixed the goddamn boat."

She laughed. We were coming up on the Hilton. A circular drive ringed by palm trees led to an Art Deco–style portico. "I'm gonna work the bar." Marcella pointed toward the entrance. "Careful of the cameras. Anyone catches you rolling their guests, they won't be friendly."

I looked to where she'd indicated and saw a camera tucked discreetly into an alcove. "Got it. Thanks."

Marcella grinned and blew me a kiss. "See you back at the hut."

"I'll have a coconut drink waiting, Professor," I threw back.

She laughed again, then sauntered toward the entrance. I watched her, feeling an odd tingling that I hadn't experienced in a long time.

"Well, shit," I muttered. "That's bad timing."

awoke the next morning to someone banging on my door. I jerked upright, heart pounding, then fumbled for the gun under my pillow. A pause, and then the pounding started again. In a shaky voice, I called out, "Go away!"

"Sorry, toots. It's ten thirty, either pay up or check out."

My shoulders sagged; it was just Dot the desk clerk/queen of Vegas. I tucked the gun away and stumbled to the bureau. Digging underneath, I ripped off the stash I'd taped there for safekeeping. I'd hit three more marks last night; none as good as the first, but I'd totaled four hundred bucks, which was not bad for a night's haul. I'd really hit my stride. My last mark had started crying a bit himself as I described my poor mother's hardscrabble life as a truck-stop waitress and the cruel, controlling boyfriend who had abandoned me on a whim.

Okay, maybe he'd been a little drunk, and I'd gone a bit overboard. But I definitely still had it.

I dug out a couple wrinkled twenties, taped the rest back, then went to the door and opened it a crack. Passing the money through, I croaked, "Here. Sorry."

Dot was dolled up in a black-and-white polka-dot dress with a frilly hem. Her eyes were dramatically lined and shaded behind cat-eye glasses, and her red hair was coiffed to within an inch of its life. She was gorgeous, like an even more voluptuous Jayne Mansfield. Hands on hips, she said, "So you're staying?"

I sighed; I hadn't planned on it, but moving seemed like a lot of effort, and the Getaway's distinct lack of security cameras was a definite plus. And either the deodorizer stench had dissipated or I'd grown used to it. Plus, if Marcella was right, Dot could help with my ID problem. "One more night."

"Okay, then. I'll bring back your change."

"No rush," I called after her. I shut the door and fell back against it, rubbing my eyes. I'd slept surprisingly well and still felt groggy.

I couldn't repress the niggling sense that my night's rest might've been less because of the accommodations and more because I always slept great after pulling a successful job. *It's just until you make enough to get to California*, I reminded myself. It was a cliché, but ever since I was a kid, I'd dreamed of living there. I'd fantasized in elaborate detail about an open-floor-plan two-bedroom/three-bath condo on cliffs overlooking a beach, with a couple of palm trees (and maybe a pool) thrown in for good measure. The plan had always been to earn my bachelor's degree, then drive west and embark on the next stage of my life, ideally at a UC grad school.

For the moment at least, that was on hold. But once I was sure the whole Johnson City mess was behind me, I could go back to being a law-abiding citizen.

After showering and changing, I went out in search of breakfast. Marcella was right, the Garden Court's buffet was a hell of a lot better than the Mega Luck. The place was filled with a higher class of clientele, too, in that most still had their teeth. Regardless, I avoided the shrimp.

While I chewed, I scrolled through emails on my phone. There was a (predictably) raging one from Joanie, demanding to know where the hell I was and whether I was coming back (and more importantly, if I was going to keep paying rent). *Nope*, I thought as I deleted it. Another from my thesis professor expressing concern that I'd missed our scheduled meeting.

I felt bad about that one. I'd liked the professor; she'd always been supportive and had promised to write a glowing recommendation letter for grad school. Not anymore. Sighing, I deleted it. This was so frustrating. Just two more months and I'd have had my first real diploma in hand. I'd worked my ass off for three years and was so close to that condo (or at least some approximation of it). And now, not only was I scamming people again, I was basically starting from scratch. I mean, I could fake a diploma; even nowadays, that wasn't impossible if you found the right people. But I'd tried to steer my life down a different path.

As if on cue, my mind showed me Stella. Reaching out for me as a pool of blood spread around her . . . saying my name, over and over. She'd looked so afraid . . .

I resolutely shoved it away, thinking, *I* am *going straight, just like I promised. This is just a little hiccup.*

I turned back to my inbox to distract myself. Aside from spam, the final message was from Agent Cabot, announcing in vaguely threatening terms that I'd missed our meeting, and he fully expected me to reschedule soon.

Delete.

As I finished off my (second) Denver omelet, I replayed the events of last night. It didn't take a psych major to figure out that working marks had felt good because it provided a sense of control. Being in a totally different environment, manipulating people . . . it made my abduction seem far away, at least temporarily (flashes of the van, the table, the apron . . . I shuddered and forced those images away, too).

Silently, I thanked Ski Mask again. She'd saved my life, and even though apparently that wasn't her main goal, it was more than I'd ever done for another person. On the long drive, something had occurred to me: she was probably an assault survivor, too. Capturing killers like Beau Lee Jessop probably worked as an antidote to feeling powerless: a kind of coping mechanism. Dangerous, but maybe it worked for her.

And conning marks works for you.

"Shut up," I muttered to my irritating inner voice, then drained my orange juice and left a decent tip. On the walk home, I mulled over the best way to approach Dot. The last ID had set me back about five hundred bucks, but that had been years ago in a rural area; new papers would probably cost at least twice that.

Only if she likes you, Marcella had said. Staying at the Getaway couldn't hurt, especially if I was a model guest. I decided I could manage a few more nights there; if nothing else, it would leave me with plenty of cash to start over in California. And the noir motif was growing on me; it felt appropriately Vegas.

Walking into the parking lot, I spotted Dot sitting at the patio set outside her office, holding an actual parasol over her head. I nodded to her and she called out, "Afternoon!"

"Hi," I said.

"Want to rest your dogs?" She gestured to the seat beside her.

Figuring this was as good a time as any to butter her up, I mustered enthusiasm into my voice and chirped, "Sure!"

I settled on the white plastic chair and tilted my head back, enjoying the sun. She tsked. "Hope you're wearing sunblock. Complexion like yours, you'll bake in a heartbeat."

Dot had a great voice, smooth and sultry. I couldn't place the accent, though, which was rare. "Yeah, I'm pretty bad about that."

"Trust me, hon. Start taking care of your skin now, it makes all the difference."

I nodded and suppressed a burp. "So, uh—"

"Oops, almost forgot. Got something for you," Dot said, folding her parasol and pushing to her feet.

"For me?" I asked, puzzled.

Dot had already vanished into the semidarkness of the office. A moment later she emerged, fanning herself with a thick manila envelope. "Someone slid this under the door last night."

I eyed it dubiously. There was no way anyone could've tracked the alias I'd used to register for the room; not even Ski Mask was that good. "How do you know it's for me?"

"See for yourself," she said, tossing it on the wire table.

Tentatively, as if it might detonate, I flipped over the envelope. In neat block letters it read: For Amber Jamison, Room 9. And in smaller letters beneath: (the bald girl).

Crap. It was practically God-like, the way Ski Mask kept finding me. She must have been tracking my phone. I should've switched to a burner back in Tennessee, but I hadn't seen her texts as a threat. *Like a fucking rube,* I scolded myself. Clearly I'd lost my edge.

"Not expecting that?" Dot asked.

"Not exactly," I muttered, my head spinning. *Why would she follow me? Back in Tennessee, she couldn't wait to get rid of me.*

What could she possibly want?

Dot settled back into her chair and drummed red fingernails on the table. "Aren't you gonna open it?"

I flushed and laid a protective hand over the envelope. "It can wait."

She eyed me. "Funny that you signed in as Mary Ann Massey."

"Yeah, um . . . Amber's my middle name."

"Oh, honey." Dot barked a laugh. "I'd expect a flimflammer to be a better liar."

Flimflammer? Seriously? "You've been talking to Marcella," I said, trying to repress my irritation.

"I like to get to know my guests," Dot said with a smirk. "Even the ones just passing through. And Marcella says you're sniffing around for new papers. Unless they're in there?"

I shrank down in my chair. Marcella was apparently the Getaway town crier. Which would've been helpful to know before I'd overshared with her. Mumbling, I said, "I seriously doubt there's anything in here I need."

Dot sighed dramatically. "So I got me a bald hustler who pays cash, gets mysterious packages, and needs a new name. That about sum it up?"

"Basically," I said. *Crap. If she's called the cops—* As if guessing my train of thought, Dot said, "Don't worry, toots, your troubles are your own. I don't narc on my guests."

"Good to know." My nerves were still humming regardless. I needed to get the hell out of here. Get a new phone. Regroup.

But dammit, I still needed new papers. And Dot was apparently my best shot for that. I had to risk it. Tentatively, I said, "So is Marcella right?"

"About new papers?"

"Yeah."

Dot tilted her head coyly. "I might know someone."

I relaxed slightly; this didn't feel like a setup. And I was comfortable with this kind of exchange; I'd been doing it most of my life.

Switching to business mode, I said, "I figure new docs cost about a grand, is that about right?"

"About," Dot conceded.

"Great," I said. "I can offer ten percent on top for you."

"Fifteen," she said cagily.

"Twelve," I said.

Dot tilted her head to the side. "Tell you what. Let me take a gander inside that envelope, I'll only charge eleven."

We both looked at the envelope lying on the table between us. Why was she so curious? *And what the hell is in here?* Maybe Ski Mask had gotten hold of FBI files on me. In which case, I couldn't risk anyone else seeing them. I shook my head. "No deal."

Her eyebrows shot up. "Well, well. Must be something pretty special."

"I don't know what it is," I said truthfully. "But it might be private."

"I see." Dot grinned. "Well, hell. Nothing I hate more than an unsolved mystery, but I like you, so eleven percent sounds fine. You prefer Amber or Mary Ann?"

"Amber," I said with a resigned sigh. No reason to overcomplicate things.

"Nice to meetcha, Amber. Takes about a week for a clean one, and you don't get to choose the name. That work for you?"

A week seemed like an eternity, but I said, "Sure."

An older couple limped toward the office. Dot held up a finger and said, "Back in two shakes."

She went inside to help them. I hesitated, but the suspense was killing me. So I slit the seal with a fingernail and peeked inside.

The large envelope contained two file folders. I pulled out the top one and cracked it open. I frowned: it looked like some sort of police file.

I flipped through the pages but didn't recognize any of the names, and it was clearly from the Las Vegas Police Department. I'd never even been here before, and as far as I knew, neither had my parents.

Weird.

Halfway through the file, I gasped. There was a photo of a naked woman lying in a bathtub filled with muddy-looking water. Her head was tilted at an unnatural angle and her eyes were open. There was a cord around her neck, and the porcelain side of the tub was streaked red.

She was definitely dead.

What. The. Fuck. Why would Ski Mask send me this? Was she trying to retraumatize me?

Despite the heat, I went cold. My heart pounded and my chest contracted until it was hard to breathe. I wanted to run, but it felt like even standing would make me pass out.

"You okay, hon?" Dot asked, but her voice sounded far away. I fumbled with the photo, trying to stuff it back into the folder.

But it was too late, she'd seen it. Dot slapped a hand down on it and said, "Why the fuck do you have a picture of Lori?"

CHAPTER SEVEN

THE LAS VEGAS STORY

couldn't have answered if I'd wanted to. My vision had gone black around the edges, like I was looking through the wrong end of a telescope. My mouth opened and closed, but I wasn't getting enough air. It felt like I was being pulled away from the parking lot and thrust back into that dark place . . . *the table. The smell of blood. The apron . . .*

"Hey, kiddo." Dot leaned in. "What the hell's wrong? You on something?"

I shook my head and gasped out, "Just . . . panic attack." I gripped the edge of the table and closed my eyes, trying to focus on my breathing.

"Panic attack, huh?" Her voice sounded like it was coming from the bottom of a well.

I managed a nod. I hadn't had one in years, but it was instantly familiar. My heart galloped, as if trying to break free of my chest. My breakfast rose up my throat and I staggered out of the chair, throwing up everything I'd just eaten in the parking space in front of the table.

"Oh, for Chrissake," I heard Dot say. "I'm charging extra for that."

I bent down, hands on my knees, struggling for air. I felt a hand press lightly on my back. "Listen. Close your eyes and breathe in for five, okay? I'll count."

That seemed impossible. The first breath, I only made it to two.

"Good," Dot said. "Now, breathe out for three counts."

I managed to do that. She guided me through until I could breathe in for five counts, hold for two, and breathe out for five. With each breath, I started to feel more in control. And more horrified by what had just happened.

Dot patted my back and said, "That should do it. Now, sit."

I straightened. *Shit.* What I'd intended to be a quick, easy exchange had taken a hard right turn. "Thanks. Um, I should probably—"

"I said park it, missy." Her tone didn't brook any argument, and if I refused, she might decide to call the cops after all. Sighing, I sat and tried to ignore the fact that my mouth tasted like puke.

Dot went to the vending machine beside the office door and punched in a code. A Coke slid out and she handed it to me. Gratefully, I took a few gulps, then wiped my mouth with the back of my hand.

Dot sat back down. Leaning in, she looked at me piercingly over the top of her sunglasses. In a low voice, she said, "I'm gonna ask again, and believe me when I say I've got the best bullshit detector in a town full of 'em." She jabbed the folder with her index finger. "Who gave you that, and why?"

"Honestly, I don't really know," I admitted. "Not why, at least."

"Try again," she said. "'Cause that girl there? Name's Lori Riffle. She lived in room seven until she got killed a few months back."

I felt faint again. "She was killed *here*?"

Dot shook her head. "Told you, I don't truck in that business, and the girls who stay here know it. Lori worked out of a dump down the road. That's where they found her."

"Wait. Was it the Buggy Suites?"

"As a matter of fact, yeah."

My head started spinning again. This was starting to feel way too coincidental. A girl was murdered at the motel I got a flyer for, two states away? Not for nothing, but it hadn't exactly seemed like a place with a big ad budget. "So they didn't catch whoever did it?"

Dot snorted and crossed her arms over her chest. "They didn't exactly try. So you're not a cop?"

"Me? Definitely not." I almost laughed, the concept was so absurd.

"But that right there is a police file," she said pointedly. "Even I can't get my hands on those. So why do you have it?"

"It's a long story." Anger was starting to supplant my terror. *What the hell is Ski Mask playing at?* Were these files on the killer she was tracking now? Did she expect me to help find him?

Had *she* left that flyer on my windshield?

If so, she'd made a serious mistake. At this point, I was ready to take what I'd already made and bolt for L.A. Someone there had to be able to produce good IDs.

But that meant starting at ground zero. And L.A. motels were definitely not renting rooms for thirty bucks a night. I drank more Coke to stall. It was a risk either way.

Dot was still looking at me expectantly. "So, toots?"

Fuck it. A hotel manager who rented to sex workers and dealt in fake IDs was unlikely to rat me out. And clearly, she had some sort of personal interest in this woman Lori. I sighed and said, "Last week this guy kidnapped me."

Her eyes widened. "For real?"

"Yeah. It was that serial killer they just caught, Beau Lee Jessop?"

Dot inhaled sharply, her eyes widening. I plowed ahead. "Anyway, he didn't have a heart attack like they said. This woman showed up and killed him. Well, not on purpose, her cattle prod was wonky." The words tumbled out. It felt good to tell someone about what had happened; I hadn't realized how much it had been weighing me down until now. "So she freed me, but the whole thing kind of . . . blew up my life, so I had to take off. That's why I need new papers."

Dot eyed me skeptically. "Why would that blow up your life?"

"Let's just say I had some issues with law enforcement in the past. Nothing violent, though," I added hurriedly, off her expression. "Just, y'know . . . cons."

"Um-hm." Dot's eyes narrowed. "Okay, so what's up with the file?"

"I have no fucking clue. The woman who rescued me, I guess she's good with computers. She tracked me down and texted me after, offering to help. But this?" I tapped the folder with one finger. "I swear I don't know why she left it."

Dot scrutinized me, clearly trying to gauge if I was full of crap. Honestly, it was a ridiculous story; I wouldn't believe it either. But after considering me for another moment, Dot pushed her sunglasses on top of her head and got to her feet. Jerking her head toward the office, she said, "C'mon, then."

Apparently following wasn't optional. Keeping my eyes averted, I slid the files back into the envelope and got to my feet. A blast of cold air washed over me as I entered the office. I'd been too zonked to notice much when I'd arrived, so as Dot rounded the front desk I looked around. Ferns were suspended from the ceiling in macrame holders. The standard rack of brochures occupied the far corner. Giant film noir posters like the ones in my room covered the walls, and a grainy movie played on the mounted TV. I watched an old car drive silently off a cliff, plunging into the sea. Kind of felt like an apt metaphor for my life right now.

"Back here." Dot waved me through another doorway. I hesitated, then complied.

Her back office was cozy. A small desk with an open laptop sat in the corner. Three walls were covered with more noir posters, interspersed with framed headshots of famous femmes fatales.

But the wall flanking the door was a different story. Newspaper clippings dangled from a giant corkboard, their edges fluttering in gusts from the air conditioning. *Great*, I thought. *She has a crazy board. Always a sign of mental stability.*

Dot settled her hip on the edge of her desk and motioned to the wall dramatically. "Sandy Gant was the first victim, killed at the Satellite about a month before Lori. Figured it was just a bad john, but then—" A shadow passed across her face. Dot shook her head as if to clear it, then pressed on. "Anyway, we figure there are at least three victims so far—"

"'We'?"

"I'm part of a group of citizen sleuths," she said proudly. "Y'know, like the gal who helped catch the Golden State Killer?"

"Uh-huh." I had no clue what she was talking about.

"We call ourselves the Fatal Femmes. Get it? Like femmes fatales, 'cause we're all into noir. We're not all women, though, so lately that's become a bit of an issue, some folks want to change it to—"

"Why are you showing me this?" I interrupted, feeling faint again. The headlines at eye level practically shouted at me: LOCAL

Sᴇx Wᴏʀᴋᴇʀ Fᴏᴜɴᴅ Dᴇᴀᴅ ɪɴ Bᴀᴛʜᴛᴜʙ. Sᴇᴀʀᴄʜ ғᴏʀ Mɪssɪɴɢ Gɪʀʟ ɪɴ Dᴇsᴇʀᴛ. Hᴇᴀᴅʟᴇss Bᴏᴅʏ Uɴᴄᴏᴠᴇʀᴇᴅ ᴀᴛ Dᴜᴍᴘ.

"Because we could really use those police files," Dot said, pointing to the envelope.

I frowned. "Use them for what?"

"To track down the killer," she said impatiently.

Christ, is everyone a vigilante serial killer hunter these days? "What about the cops?"

"Please," she snorted. "The cops couldn't care less about a few working girls."

"So . . . they were killed at the Buggy Suites, too?"

"Nope. Other side of town. But same MO. Bathtub, rope . . . it all matched. Cops won't even admit they're connected, though. We already tried, they said it was just a coincidence."

Dot definitely talked like someone who had listened to too many true-crime podcasts. Also, like someone with a personal stake. "That's a shame."

"Not surprising, though. You know how many people go missing here every day?" I shook my head, and Dot said with what struck me as a pretty inappropriate level of glee, "Five to seven. That's, like, two hundred a month. Nuts, right?"

"Um, yeah," I said. "Nuts."

"But your friend, the lady who saved you—"

"She's not my friend."

"Well, whatever she is. If she's looking into this, maybe we could work together." Dot's voice held the earnestness of a kid hoping to stay up past bedtime. I imagined how Ski Mask would respond to a group of "citizen sleuths" encroaching on her turf.

Then again, apparently she was in the market for help; why else would she have sent me this crap? And I was definitely not willing or able to provide it.

"One sec," I said. Dot watched as I awkwardly sifted through the files, avoiding the photos as much as possible. Dot was right, the other one was for Sandy Gant's murder.

Somehow, I'd wandered into another serial killer's hunting grounds. Was I some sort of magnet for them now?

He was here way before I was, I reminded myself. Based on the dates, this had been going on for months before Beau Lee Jessop even got started.

With feigned reluctance, I said, "Tell you what. I can give these to you *if* we cut a better deal on my new papers."

Dot hesitated, but I could tell I had her. She finally said, "Eight hundred."

"Total, no commission."

Dot pretended to be offended, but her eyes glittered. She obviously wanted the files badly. "You're asking a lot. And it doesn't seem like you want them anyway."

"True." I tapped my chin. "I could just shred them."

Dot gasped audibly. "Fine. Eight hundred flat."

Inwardly, I pumped my fist. "Great. And I'd love a room upgrade, too."

Dot laughed. "Well, damn. You're something else, you know that? Pay up front and you're on."

"Deal."

"Can't say I blame you. Number nine isn't my best, a rat died in the wall and the smell's not gone yet."

"A rat?" I felt like I might get sick again.

"Exterminator took care of the rest. I'll put you in twelve." Dot held out her hand and raised a perfectly arched eyebrow. I gave her the envelope, secretly relieved to be rid of it. "And if you hear from your friend again, let her know the Femmes are here to help."

"Will do," I said with a grin. All in all, this day had taken a turn for the better.

My phone buzzed in my pocket. Sighing, I checked it. Unsurprisingly, it was from my best bud UNKNOWN NUMBER and read: GO HOME AMBER.

Room twelve was a step up, literally. It was on the second floor, with an extra window looking out the back of the building (over an abandoned lot, which wasn't a huge improvement, but I wasn't about to complain). There was barely a whiff of the deodorizer that inundated the dead-rat room. It even had a bathtub, which all things considered, I now had mixed feelings about.

I set down my stuff with a sigh and rolled my shoulders, tilting my head to work out the kinks in my neck. "This is great, Dot. Thanks."

"Sure, doll." She pointed to the bed. "You got MagicFingers, too. Broken in every other room. I usually keep twelve unoccupied since it's my personal massage parlor."

"Uh, okay." I couldn't imagine getting a lot of use out of that personally, but who knew. I handed over two hundred dollars and said, "Down payment. I'll have the rest soon."

"This'll get you started," she said. "The rest on delivery. And same rules apply, yeah? Do your work somewhere else."

"Sure." Probably best not to point out that it would only be worth scamming Dot's clientele if I was desperate for cups full of quarters. Although those would come in handy for the Magic-Fingers. I nodded toward a second door by the bed. "What's that?"

"Goes to the next room. For families."

"You get a lot of families?" I said dubiously.

"You'd be surprised." She wiggled her fingers at me and said, "Ta!"

After Dot left, I double-bolted the main door and made sure the connecting one was locked, tucking a chair under the knob for good measure. Then I cracked the rear window to let in fresh air. I flopped down on the bed, eyed the MagicFingers, and said, "What the hell."

Three quarters later I felt relaxed and slightly nauseated; probably not the best idea to shake my insides when they'd just been turned inside out again.

Clicking on my phone, I stared at the most recent text. It seemed to glare back at me, as though Ski Mask's ice-blue eyes were right on the other side of the screen. *Go home?* What the hell was that supposed to mean? It wasn't like I even had a home to go back to. Maybe she'd seen me show Dot the envelope, and she was pissed. Well, it served her right for using an intermediary. She could've just slid it under my door, after all.

I really needed to get a new phone.

My finger hovered for a moment, and then I texted: GO FUCK YOURSELF. Which seemed like appropriate last words. Hopping back up, I dropped the phone on the bathroom tiles, stomped on it, took out the SIM card, and flushed it. I'd get a burner on my way out tonight.

Feeling slightly better, I fell back onto the bed, crossed my hands behind my head, and closed my eyes. I had a few hours to kill before the marks would be out. Might as well get some more shut-eye.

I had a banner night; turns out the trick was to hit the marks after midnight. The cheap wig I'd picked up didn't hurt, either. I used my "sad dolly" act on a particularly generous (and extremely drunk)

Texan in an honest-to-God ten-gallon hat outside the Venetian. He mixed up his twenties with hundreds, and I walked away with full payment for the ID.

Hell, I could probably net six figures a year if I stayed.

Until it catches up with you, I reminded myself. Every good grifter knew the risks of milking a place too long. Eventually, your luck always ran out. That was something my parents had never learned, and I'd be damned if I was going to repeat their mistakes.

Plus, I was going legit again. Although with every mark, the prospect of spending my days listening to spoiled rich people's "problems" as a psychologist sounded less and less appealing.

When I got back to my new and improved motel room, I celebrated with a few margaritas from a can, then crashed out hard a little after three o'clock.

Which made the pounding on my door at four a.m. all the more intrusive. Groggily, I opened my eyes and called out, "Go away!"

More pounding. I grabbed the gun from under my pillow with shaking hands and yelled, "I mean it! I'm armed!"

The pounding ceased. A long beat passed, and then a low voice said, "Let me in."

I frowned—it sounded like Marcella. I called out, "Hang on!"

Holding the gun down by my side, I checked the peephole, then unchained and unbolted the door. As soon as the lock slid clear, it burst open and Marcella staggered in, nearly knocking me over. She reeked of booze and her hair was a mess. She was barefoot, holding a pair of hot pink platform heels by the straps. "Whoa," she said, spotting the gun. "You weren't lying."

"Yeah." I put the safety back on.

"I should get one." She lurched past me and collapsed facedown on the bed.

"Um, did you need something, Marcella?" I asked.

She flipped over on her side with some effort, a maneuver that caused her black lace miniskirt to crawl up, exposing—well, pretty much everything. "You're a lezzie, right?"

She was slurring badly. If she threw up and stuck me with another smelly room, I was going to be so pissed. "You know, it's really not okay for straight people to say that."

"Who said I was straight?" She cocked an eyebrow at me. "Wanna fuck?"

I rubbed my eyes, regretting the margaritas; the cheap tequila had spawned an epic headache. "Let me get you some water."

"You think you're too good for me?" Marcella snarled, pushing back to her feet. Which might have had more impact if she hadn't promptly toppled over. "Shit. I'm fucking hammered."

"Yup. And even though that's definitely super hot, I don't sleep with people who might puke halfway through. Usually," I amended, remembering one particularly bad date.

Marcella glared at me, then abruptly spun and stumbled for the bathroom. The sound of intense vomiting issued through the open door. I'd officially desecrated two bathrooms in the Getaway Motel in roughly twenty-four hours, which might have been a record. (Although all things considered, maybe not. No offense to Dot.)

There was a loud flush, followed by a moan.

I tucked the gun underneath the mattress before going to help. Marcella was slumped beside the toilet, one arm draped across the bathtub rim. Her legs were splayed in front of her, and mascara was smeared down her cheeks. Her hair looked like she'd plugged her finger into a light socket. I crossed my arms over my chest and made a show of taking her in. "Now, this," I said, "is fucking hot."

She started cracking up. I laughed, too, for the first time in a long time.

Marcella swiped a hand across her mouth. "Can I use your toothbrush?"

"Absolutely fucking not," I said. "But I've got an extra. They came in a pack of three."

"Okay. Mind if I take a shower?"

I hesitated, then said, "Sure." There was nothing of value in the bathroom; if she wanted to steal my off-brand shampoo/conditioner, she was welcome to it. I wouldn't be needing it for a while anyway.

I rummaged through my suitcase for the extra toothbrush while the shower ran. When it shut off, I passed it through the door crack and said, "Here."

"Thanks, gorgeous." She shut the door. Sitting back on the bed to wait, I caught my reflection in the mirror. I was wearing my usual pajamas: boxer briefs and a plain tank top. My eyebrows had started growing back but they were patchy, and the sight of my baldness was still startling. It made my eyes look bigger, but still. Hard to imagine why Marcella was hitting on me, unless she wanted something.

I propped a pillow against the headboard and sat back against it, then grabbed the glass of water to have something to do with my hands. Sipping it, I realized I felt nervous, which was ridiculous.

The door finally opened and Marcella came out with one towel wrapped around her body and another around her hair. "Both towels?" I protested.

"Easy, bitch. I'll grab more from the maid cart, I know where Tina keeps it." Remarkably, Marcella barely seemed tipsy anymore. With her face scrubbed clean, she looked younger, probably around my age. And she was strikingly pretty. Her body was off the hook, too, all softness and curves—

Marcella laughed out loud and said, "Shit, Mary Ann. You really are gay."

I shifted uncomfortably. "Call me Amber. I wasn't perving on you. Just—"

"It's cool." She dug around in her purse and pulled out a vape pen. "You mind?"

I shrugged, and she put it to her lips and inhaled, holding it in for a few seconds before blowing out vapor. She offered it to me, but I shook my head. "I don't smoke."

"Good for you." She kicked her heels out of the way and climbed onto the bed, crawling until she was inches away from me. She wiggled her eyebrows and said, "How d'ya like me now?"

"I really need to sleep, Marcella," I said pointedly.

"Not me." She flipped over and maneuvered to sit beside me, shoulder to shoulder. "I only need a couple hours a night. Just lucky that way."

"Good for you." Her nearness was unsettling. I hadn't been touched by anyone in a long time; Johnson City wasn't exactly a haven for lesbians. "Did you need something, Marcella? Aside from a puke and a shower?"

She lolled her head toward me. "Dot said she told you. About Lori."

"Um, yeah." I frowned. "Did you know her?"

"We had kind of a friends-with-benefits thing going, y'know?"

"Sure," I said, recognizing the tightness in her voice. Obviously it had been a bit more than that, at least for her. Maybe that was what prompted this drinking binge. Or maybe she ended every night this way. None of my business, really.

A long pause, and then Marcella continued. "Dot said your friend is looking for the asshole who killed her."

"She's not exactly my friend." Jesus, the rumor mill in this place was truly extra.

"Doesn't really matter." Marcella's voice was thick as she added, "She'd still be gone."

I tried to come up with something comforting, but my mind was scrambled from exhaustion. Which wasn't exactly a great sign for my future as a therapist. "I'm really sorry."

Without meeting my eyes, Marcella fumbled for my hand and entwined our fingers. We sat like that for a while, not saying anything. Finally, she asked, "You mind if I sleep here?"

"Just sleep?" I quirked an eyebrow at her.

"Please, girl. You can't afford me," she snorted. "Even your toothpaste is shit. Turn off the light."

Honestly, I don't like sleeping with other people—actual sleeping, that is. I never have. It always feels awkward. And who wants to smell someone else's morning breath?

But for some reason, as I lay there listening to Marcella's light snores, I felt calmer than I had in a long time. And when I fell asleep again, I didn't dream at all.

CHAPTER EIGHT

DON'T BOTHER
TO KNOCK

I awoke to find Marcella gone. There was a stack of clean towels on the bureau, topped by a tissue with a lipstick kiss.

I smiled, then immediately checked where I'd stashed my cash and gun. I liked Marcella, but that didn't mean I trusted her.

Still, I'd slept amazingly well. It was nearly three o'clock, which meant I'd clocked twelve hours (albeit interrupted).

The AC was fighting a losing battle with the heat outside. I opened the blinds and blinked against the glare. At the edge of the parking lot a middle-aged guy was bent double, aggressively throwing up.

"Vegas, baby," I said, then went to take a shower.

My room phone rang. When I answered, Dot chirped, "Morning, toots. Need to get your beauty shots done today."

"Oh, okay." I sat back down on the bed. My stomach was grumbling. Thanks to last night's haul, I could afford something a little fancier than the Garden Court for breakfast. "What time?"

"Be ready in five."

I tried to protest, but she'd already hung up. *Crap.*

I brushed my teeth and threw on some clothes, then slumped down to her office.

"Morning!" Dot called cheerily from the back room. "Coffee's in the corner if you want some."

The machine had nearly a full pot and there was a beautiful plate of donuts beside it. "Thank God, I'm starving."

I gobbled down a cruller, chugged half a cup of coffee, then tucked into a bear claw. I was sitting in the wingchair trying to clean glaze off my fingers when Dot swept in from the back office. Today she sported a bright red kimono dress. Her hair was piled on top of her head and secured by an orange butterfly clip, and her makeup was impeccable as always. She tossed me a tube of sunblock, then started wrapping a scarf around her head. "I've got a convertible, you better put on extra."

"Thanks." My scalp was already itchy from the night before, so I'd opted to skip the wig. Obediently I started slathering sunscreen on my bald head, feeling the scratchiness of new hair growth. Dot's fabulousness was intimidating, to be perfectly honest. In my tank top and cutoffs, I felt like a film set gaffer who had stumbled across the star at craft services.

Dot tucked in the ends of her leopard-print scarf as she asked, "Didja sleep okay?"

"Great, thanks." I wondered if she'd seen Marcella slip out of my room. Not that it was any of her business, right? "Love the new room."

"Nice, right?" Dot eyed me, then touched the corner of her mouth. "You got a little something right here, hon."

"Thanks," I muttered, swiping at it with a napkin.

"No problem. Well, off we go!"

Dot's car was every bit as fabulous as she was: a monstrous teal convertible from Detroit's heyday, complete with swooping fins and seats like sofa cushions. Dot had donned white sunglasses that took up half her face; she was also wearing an honest-to-God trench coat despite the heat.

I was feeling considerably less impressive. I half expected the car to eject me on principle.

We cruised down the Strip drawing a fair number of stares. A few people catcalled; Dot threw them a queenly wave. In the bright of day, it was all a bit much. Vegas was a mad conglomeration of togas and pirates and fountains that shot water ten stories high. The air was saturated with desire and desperation as crowds surged between the monolithic casinos that stretched for blocks.

I found it exhausting. But Dot seemed right at home. "So are you from here?" I asked as we passed the Venetian.

"Born and bred," she said.

"Oh. That sounds . . . nice," I ventured.

She laughed. "Hardly. A girl my size? Let me tell you, it was no picnic when I was younger. But the great thing about Vegas? You can become whoever you want."

"Well, it suits you."

"I can't imagine living anywhere else." She glanced over at me. "What's next for you, if you don't mind my asking?"

I shrugged. "Not sure. West Coast maybe." *Better to keep it vague, for both our sakes.*

"Mm. Wouldn't mind going to Hollywood myself. But in a time machine, back to the Golden Age, y'know?"

"Sure," I said, mainly to placate her. I was fine with any version of Los Angeles that involved me making a pile of cash.

"Anyway, my daddy always said there's no bad places. Just bad people, and they're everywhere."

"Smart man," I muttered. I'd certainly come across my fair share of them.

"You should give Vegas a chance," Dot said, glancing sideways at me.

"Maybe." *Never*, I added mentally. I was going to stand at the edge of the ocean and sink my toes in the sand, let it wash away all the bad memories. I needed to utterly sever the last remaining ties to my past, and Vegas was the sort of place that would only keep reminding me of it. Plus, it was already clear that going legit here would be impossible; there was too much temptation. Might as well be a diabetic opening a candy store.

In a few minutes, we'd left behind the sprawling high-end hotels and casinos. Dot checked her watch. "Better be quick about this. I don't like driving around here after dark."

"Why not?" I couldn't see any difference between this stretch and where the Getaway was located, to be honest. All of Vegas outside the mega casinos seemed indistinguishable: a dismal procession of budget motels, buffets, bail bondsmen, and pawnshops.

"Naked City isn't a safe place for my baby," she said, patting the dashboard.

"Naked City?" I asked. "Because of the strip clubs?"

"Nah, most of those are over on Dean Martin." She waved a hand expansively. "In the fifties, this was all cheap apartments for casino waitresses and showgirls. They'd sunbathe naked to avoid getting tan lines. So everyone started calling it Naked City."

"That's actually kind of charming," I said.

"Nothing charming about it. Even the cops won't go here at night," Dot said darkly. "And good luck getting a cab."

That jibed with it being a good place to acquire a new identity, though. I'd gotten the paperwork for "Amber Jamison" off a survivalist who lived in a trailer deep in Appalachia. It had all been very *Deliverance*; to be honest, at the time I'd been pretty sure he was a serial killer.

.I shuddered involuntarily despite the heat.

"We're here!" Dot chirped, turning into a motel parking lot.

At first glance, it looked like any other budget dive, but the paint job was new, and its neon sign cheerfully blared **MAYHEM MOTEL** in a retro font. Rather than the usual promises of **FREE CABLE!** or **DAILY, WEEKLY, OR MONTHLY RATES!** (apparently no one officially copped to hourly), it read: **SO CLOSE, YET SO FAR OUT.** Every door was painted a different color, ranging from aqua to orange. The parking lot was newly repaved and filled with an assortment of hybrid hatchbacks and rental sedans.

"This place attracts kind of a different crowd, huh?" I asked.

Dot's face clouded over. As she turned off the engine, she sniffed, "Fucking Gen Z really is ruining everything."

"Um, I'm technically Gen Z," I said.

"I'll make an exception for you," she said charitably. "Just don't ever use the word 'woke' in my presence."

I grinned. "Deal."

"Jessie's good people," Dot said, hitting a button on the dash. With an ominous grinding noise, a giant white ragtop unfolded and lowered over us; Dot really wasn't taking any chances with her baby. "But in my opinion, she was a damn fool to go this way."

"She's the owner?"

Dot nodded. "Spent a wad of cash fixing it up to attract a younger crowd, even put açai bowls on the menu. Doubled the nightly rate, too." She clucked her tongue. "Hell, for sixty a night you can get a room at the Rio."

I eyed the nearly full parking lot. I didn't want to offend Dot, but this joint was a hell of a lot busier than the Getaway. "Seems like it worked."

"Here's the thing," Dot said, wagging a finger at me. "Sure, hipsters pay more than your regulars. But they're weekenders. They think it's fun to stay somewhere dangerous, off the beaten path, 'like the locals.'" Dot shook her head. "Then they get mugged, beaten, or, God forbid, killed, and suddenly that's it—they're never coming back, and you got nothing but one-star Yelp reviews to show for it. It's terrible to say, but Jessie's lucky the vic was a working girl. If it'd been some techie from out of town, well . . ." Dot shook her head. "That'd be it for the Mayhem."

"Wait . . . what?" I stared at her. "Someone was killed here?"

Dot flushed. "Oh, did I forget to mention that?"

"Um, yeah, you did." I glared at her. "I made it pretty clear that I didn't want to get involved. I'm here for a new ID, nothing else."

"Easy, toots. This is just one-stop shopping."

I crossed my arms. "Let me guess. Jessie's part of your group."

"The co-founding Femme," Dot said guiltily as she dug a familiar-looking envelope out from beneath her seat.

I groaned. "Seriously?"

"Two birds, one stone. Jessie makes the best IDs in town. Trust me, you won't be disappointed."

I sighed. It didn't seem like I had much of a choice. "Doesn't seem like the type of place that hosts working girls."

"Oh, honey, every place has working girls. Some just get the classier ones," Dot said. "This won't take long. Promise."

The front office was twice the size of Dot's, but even that wasn't enough to contain Jessie; she wasn't just a breath of fresh air, she was a goddamn gale-force wind. She was easily six feet tall and dressed in a flowing bohemian dress. By contrast, her face was done up in layers of severe goth makeup. Those two looks should have been raging against each other, but on her they were weirdly complementary. The tastefully potted succulents and framed Coachella posters positively paled in Jessie's presence.

She rose from a Herman Miller chair behind a low midcentury desk and acknowledged us with a curt nod. The conversation that ensued was a dizzying, rapid-fire exchange that went something like this:

Jessie (looking me up and down): Well, you're not a showgirl. Stripper or hooker?

Me: Are those the only options?

Jessie: Around here? Basically.

Dot: Ease up, Jessie. The kid's had a rough go of it.

Jessie: Must've if she's staying at your place. Listen, honey, I can match her rates, and you'd be with people your own age. Not a bunch of—

Dot: Are you seriously trying to poach her when I'm standing right here?

Jessie: Room comes with a VIP pass to the XS, too. Skrillex is there this week.

Dot: Just don't go more than a block in any direction if you value your life.

Jessie: Oh, like your little stretch of paradise is any different.

Dot: At least I didn't sell my soul to some Russian oligarch for a loan.

Jessie: It wasn't my soul he wanted, toots.

Me: Um, ladies? Maybe we could just talk about the—

Jessie (eyeing the folder): Those the files?

Dot: As promised. Seems like police tape didn't hurt business any. I'd think the Zoomers would be shitting out their avocado toast.

Jessie: Hardly. Reservations are up twenty percent. I can rent that room for twice as much once the cops let me open it up.

Dot: So where's the kid?

I was still trying to catch up as Jessie produced a walkie-talkie from within the deep folds of her caftan. "BJ," she barked. "Get your ass down to the office."

The unfortunately named BJ materialized a minute later. He was probably no more than nineteen. Tall but slight, wearing painfully tight black jeans and a T-shirt with a picture of a bone that stated: I FOUND THIS HUMERUS. He appeared equally terrified of both Dot and Jessie, and I couldn't say I blamed him. I was feeling a bit cowed myself.

"Explain how a street whore got into one of my rooms," Jessie said, sitting back in the chair and crossing her hands over her stomach.

BJ pushed thick-rimmed glasses back and said, "Yeah, um, there was a little mixup. I mean, I was—"

"Little shit was watching the desk while I went to the new Cirque show," Jessie interrupted.

"I hear it's good," Dot said.

"I preferred *Love*," Jessie sniffed. To BJ, she snapped, "Continue."

"Right, well, um . . . anyway, this girl comes in and she's dressed like a, well, like a—"

"Like a hooker," Jessie interrupted.

"Yeah, but I thought maybe just ironically, y'know? I mean, the girls here dress like that sometimes, it's kind of like a cosplay thing—"

"God help us," Dot sighed. "You should make flash cards to teach him the difference."

"If he wasn't my favorite nephew, he'd already be on a bus back to Stockton," Jessie snorted.

BJ appeared to be trying to sink into himself as they discussed him. I felt for him, and was also getting annoyed. "Um, is this going to take long?" I asked. "'Cause I thought we were just here to get my pictures taken."

All three stared at me as if I'd sprouted horns. Then Dot turned back to BJ. "What else?"

"She . . . um . . . she didn't have any credit cards, or she said she didn't. But she gave me cash for the full night," he said, throwing a pointed look at Jessie.

"Definitely a street girl," Jessie said.

"You're sure?" Dot asked.

"Absolutely." Jessie waved a hand at him. "Tell her about the guy."

I sighed; clearly I wasn't going to be dealt with until they'd both got their Nancy Drew on. I stomped to a chair in the corner and sat down, crossing my arms over my chest. Whatever. I had time to kill.

BJ cleared his throat again. "Yeah, so, I had to go check the ice machine right after I gave her the key, 'cause number six was bitching about it. So I got it working again—you have to hit the upper right corner, sometimes ice gets stuck up there and blocks the rest—"

"Christ, BJ. Dot doesn't care about the ice machine," Jessie groaned.

"Right, okay."

"And this was three nights ago?" Dot asked.

"I guess." BJ looked toward the ceiling, visibly doing math in his head.

"It was Thursday," Jessie confirmed.

"Wait, this *just* happened?" I blurted. Christ, Thursday was the night before I'd arrived.

"Yeah." BJ's eyes swept over me, pausing on my breasts. He reddened and continued. "I went to tell the girl in six that the machine was working again—"

"'Course you did. Hot little thing from L.A.," Jessie said. "So much for not hitting on the guests."

"I wasn't hitting on her!" BJ retorted with unexpected ferocity. Jessie raised an eyebrow. He took a deep breath, then continued. "I was knocking on six, and the door to five opened. The girl stuck her head out, she looked kind of freaked. I asked if something was wrong, and she just shook her head and closed the door again. But it seemed kind of off, y'know? The curtains were open a little—"

"So like a damn perv, he checked it out," Jessie interrupted.

"I just wanted to make sure she was all right! So, anyway, I looked in and saw a guy. She'd only rented a single, which meant she wasn't supposed to have guests—"

"Little shits try to sneak in," Jessie said with a nod. "Caught twelve of them in a room once. Claimed since they weren't actually sleeping there, just stowing their stuff, it shouldn't matter. I told them—"

"What was he doing?" I interjected, curious in spite of myself.

"The guy was just standing there looking at her. She was walking around the room, like she was nervous; I couldn't hear what she was saying. She wasn't naked," he added pointedly.

"What did he look like?" Dot asked eagerly.

"He was tall. Wearing long sleeves, which I thought was kind of weird because, you know, it was super hot out. Baseball cap." He shrugged. "Just, y'know, normal clothes."

"Did you see his face?" Dot pressed.

"Yeah, a little bit. White guy. Kinda old. He had a scar, right here." BJ drew a line across his cheek by his left eye. "He looked . . . tough. Not like the folks who usually stay here."

"Because most of our guests don't pick up street trash," Jessie growled. "You're right, Dot. I'm gonna make flash cards."

"How old?" Dot asked.

"Um, I don't know. Like, forty?"

Jessie swatted him on the arm. "You think forty is old?"

"Anything else? Could you see his eyes, or did he have a tattoo or something?"

BJ was already shaking his head. "Nope, that's it." He wrung his hands and stared at the floor. "I just keep thinking, maybe if I'd knocked on the door and said something, maybe—"

"Maybe you'd be dead, too, and my sister would be coming for my scalp," Jessie said, not unkindly.

"Who found her?" Dot asked.

Jessie sighed. "I did, the next morning when this moron told me what happened. Figured I'd haul her out myself. Instead . . ." She splayed her hands open, palms up.

"Dead in the tub," Dot said.

"Yup. Strangled and bloody."

"No fingerprints?"

"Whole room was wiped clean. Guy did a better job than my housekeepers."

Dot held up the envelope. "No fingerprints at the other scenes, either."

Jessie eyed it. "Right. Saw that on the file you uploaded."

I suddenly felt faint. "You uploaded the files to the internet?"

"Of course. How else was I supposed to share them?" Dot asked.

I put my head in my hands. I had absolutely no idea how easy it was to access the forum Dot and her Femmes used. But based on Ski Mask's uncanny ability to track me down, there was an excellent chance she'd already discovered that I'd shared her little gift.

Well, screw her. I'd done everything she'd asked: I'd waited to call the cops and hadn't told them about her. And I'd definitely never asked to be part of her fucked-up hobby. If she wanted to be pissed at me for sharing creepy files I hadn't wanted in the first place, that was her business.

"There was one weird thing," BJ said.

"Oh, just one?" Jessie snorted.

"Yeah," BJ said. "She told me her name was Krystal when she checked in, and that's what the cops said, too."

"And?" Dot asked.

"You and your conspiracy theories." Jessie rolled her eyes. "I swear, this generation."

"It's not a conspiracy theory if it's true," BJ said, setting his jaw. "Why would her necklace say 'Amber' if that wasn't her name?"

I went rigid. Dot's jaw dropped as she turned and met my eyes.

"She probably stole it off someone," Jessie said, waving a hand dismissively.

"She wasn't wearing it when she checked in," BJ said. "I swear. Maybe the killer left it."

I'd gone cold. This was officially too much of a coincidence. I could feel another panic attack coming on. Dot was already moving toward me as I bent down and put my head in my hands, struggling to control my breathing.

"Or maybe your memory is shit," Jessie retorted. Eyeing me, she asked, "That one okay?"

Dot had knelt beside me and was rubbing my back again. "Easy, hon, just breathe . . ."

The room fell silent. I kept my eyes closed and tried to tune everything out, gritting my teeth. I'd be damned if I was going to succumb to another panic attack in public.

"What?" I heard Jessie say. "What's wrong?"

"Maybe we should just get those pictures taken. We can talk about the rest of this later," Dot said.

"Suit yourselves." She snapped at BJ, "You. Back to work."

I heard the sound of the front door closing. I still felt strange, like I wasn't fully in my body. But Dot's hand on my back helped root me again, and I finally opened my eyes to see Jessie regarding me like I was some sort of freak.

"Sorry," I croaked.

"Well, Dot vouches for you," Jessie said, pushing off the desk to get up. "Guess that's good enough for me. Any interest in being a Stella?"

I sucked in a sharp breath and spat, "No!"

Jessie frowned. "What the hell, kiddo, it's a solid name."

"*Streetcar Named Desire*," Dot said. "One of the best."

"You're telling me. What I would do to a young Brando—"

"Just . . . anything else," I said, remembering Stella straddling me, her hair brushing my face as she bent to kiss me. Those same lips, twisted in pain as she screamed my name . . .

"All right, then, how about Dawn? I got one of those who's about your age."

"Sure," I said, sighing internally. Apparently I was doomed to a lifetime of stripper names.

"Good. Let's get your beauty shot taken."

'll say this for Jessie: once she got down to business, she was impressively organized and quick. She had a full photography studio set up in her back office. I was going to become Dawn Lamm of Caldwell, Kansas. (I didn't ask where the birth certificate and social security number had come from; frankly, I didn't want to know.)

Dusk was falling as we cruised back to the Getaway. I was grateful that Dot kept the top up; the heat faded quickly, and I shivered in my tank top.

Dot hadn't spoken since we got back in the car; she seemed preoccupied. "Sixty a night." She shook her head. "I don't know, maybe she's right."

I could tell she was trying to distract me from what had happened, and I appreciated the effort. But I couldn't stop obsessing about the necklace, the Buggy Suites postcard . . . on the face of it, there was no direct link to me. But once again I had that sense of being followed. Or hunted, which was worse. Trying to shove it to the back of my mind, I said, "For what it's worth, I think you'd kill it with the hipster crowd. Play up the noir theme and they'll go bananas." I didn't add that a fresh coat of paint and better carpeting wouldn't hurt, either.

Dot laughed. "Maybe. Sorry, just . . . things have been a little tight lately."

"So, is Jessie kind of your frenemy?"

"What?" Dot looked startled.

"I mean, you two kind of lit into each other back there."

She laughed. "That's just how we are. Jessie's got a heart of gold. She took me in when I was just a snot-nosed kid."

"Really?" It was hard to imagine Dot as a kid; I could only envisage a miniaturized version of her in kitten heels.

"Honestly, she did more for me than my own people. She was a big part of the reason I got into this business myself." She checked her watch again. "Ah hell, I promised Jim I'd be back a half hour ago."

"Who's Jim?"

"He's my fella." A genuine blush spread under Dot's rouge, and her lips perked in a shy smile.

"Got it," I said, trying to picture the man who could handle Dot. In spite of myself, an image of Marcella flashed across my mind.

Dot glanced sideways at me. "One tip, toots? Don't get too close, 'kay?"

"Meaning what?" I asked.

"Meaning . . . Marcella's a handful. Don't get me wrong, of all the girls, she's easily my favorite, but—"

"She's not my type," I protested uncomfortably, crossing my arms over my chest.

Dot laughed. "Oh, honey. One way or another, she's everyone's type."

I leaned my head back and watched the passing parade. We were driving through an older section of Vegas. Small casinos advertised five-dollar tables and free drinks. "I don't know how you live here. It's just so weird."

"There's a lot more to Vegas than what the world sees. Like I said"—she turned into the Getaway parking lot—"give it a try, you might like it."

"You seem kind of eager for me to stay," I said suspiciously.

"I like you, kiddo. And forgive my saying so, but you seem like someone who hasn't fit in anywhere else." Dot shrugged. "But maybe I'm wrong."

I didn't answer. She wasn't wrong.

Jim turned out to be a bear of a man, easily six-five and built like a tank. He was dressed in a loud Hawaiian shirt and had graying hair slicked into an Elvis pompadour. The minute I saw him, I couldn't imagine Dot with anyone else. He clearly felt the same because he was all smiles, leaning against the office doorjamb as he watched us pull in. As soon as Dot got out of the convertible Jim swept her up in a bear hug, causing her dress skirts to swirl around her.

When he released her, Dot put a hand to his cheek affectionately and asked, "Any problems, lover?"

"Nothing a plunger couldn't fix." With his low drawl he sounded like Elvis, too. Finally noticing me, he extended a hand and said, "Jim. Pleased to meetcha."

"Amber," I said.

"Right." He winked at me. "You got my Dot in a lather with those files."

"Well, that certainly wasn't my intent," I muttered.

Dot swatted his arm. "Stop. You working the Nugget tonight?"

"Got a show at nine." He wrapped an arm around her and nuzzled her neck. "Which leaves plenty a' time for—"

"Okay!" I said quickly. "Thanks again, Dot."

"Remember what I said!" Dot warned, wagging a finger at me.

"Right. Thanks." I watched as Jim basically carried her into the office, Dot giggling the whole time.

Must be nice, I thought. I'd never had a girlfriend for more than a few months; all my relationships had been turbulent, punctuated by more fighting than loving. Even with Stella, before she died (*before you got her killed*) things had already been heading in a familiar direction. Whatever made two people stay together didn't seem to be coded into my DNA; I had a unique knack for screwing things up. Studying psychology, I'd learned the appropriate terms for it: abandonment issues, splitting, avoidant attachment disorder. With parents like mine, the source was hardly a mystery.

But defining it didn't change anything. I'd been damaged even before the abduction, and was plainly in much worse shape now. Broken attracts broken, and that way lay disaster. Dot had nothing to worry about; Marcella was definitely not on my agenda. In fact, it was probably a good idea for me to avoid her from here on out.

"Hey!"

I turned to find Marcella framed in the doorway of her room, wearing a silk kimono that barely brushed the tops of her thighs.

"Um, hey," I said, stopping in place.

She lazily extended an arm up, propping herself against the frame in a way that accentuated her curves. "You busy?"

I hesitated, fighting past the sudden dryness in my mouth. Then

I crossed the parking lot to her. "Thanks for the towels." *Seriously?* I sounded like a moron.

Marcella cocked her head to the side and pursed her lips. "Stopped by your room earlier. You weren't there."

"I was out with Dot." I opened my mouth to say something about the dead girl but couldn't figure out how to bring it up. *Hey, did you hear another sex worker was murdered the other night, just like your friend?* seemed a little insensitive.

"Right. Jessie take care of you?" Marcella's hair draped down to her breasts in long curls. It was very distracting.

Self-consciously I ran a hand over my own peach fuzz and answered, "Think so. Guess I'm going to be Dawn now."

Marcella's eyes widened. "That's my mother's name."

"Oh." I nodded like an idiot. "Good name."

She slapped my arm and said, "I'm just fucking with you. You working tonight?"

"Probably," I said, feeling a bit nonplussed. *What is her deal?* "You?"

"Nah, it's my night off." She stretched languorously and asked, "Wanna go out?"

"Um . . ." I tried to come up with an excuse, but my mind had gone blank. Truth was, after the events of this afternoon, I was considering loading up my car and hitting the road. I didn't know what sort of game Ski Mask was playing, but she knew where I was staying. That was feeling more and more like a huge risk.

"C'mon, it'll be fun. I'll ask Dot to come, too. She'll protect you."

"I don't need protection."

"That's what you think." Marcella ran a finger along my cheek down to my chin. "See you later."

I stared at the door after she closed it. Then forced myself to march across the parking lot and mount the stairs to my room.

closed the door and fell back against it, suddenly exhausted. It was barely six p.m., but I could hardly keep my eyes open. I was starving again, too, so I dug a few energy bars out of my backpack and ate them on the bed.

Jessie had loaned me a different wig for the passport and license photo; Dawn Lamm was apparently a redhead, which might be a welcome change. She'd promised to have everything ready in a couple of days. I'd offered to pay more to have the job expedited, but she claimed there were constraints on how fast she could get it all in order.

I sighed. Would the wait be worth the risk? After paying half up front, I had four hundred bucks left. That wouldn't go far in L.A. or San Francisco, and it would be much harder to book a room with cash outside Vegas. I really needed that ID.

If I kept scoring a couple hundred a night, within a week I'd have enough for a decent start in California. Vegas was a big town, with a lot of hidey-holes. I could switch motels, make sure I wasn't followed. Lay as low as possible until the new papers were ready.

I felt an unexpected wave of sadness at the thought of saying goodbye to Dot and Marcella. *Stop it. You're being ridiculous.* I barely knew them. Once I left, they'd probably never think of me again.

I brushed crumbs off my lap, then grabbed the energy bar wrappers and got up to throw them in the trash. Feeling parched, I went to the bathroom for a glass of water. I guzzled the first cup, then refilled it twice; my thirst seemed unquenchable. *Dry heat*, I reminded myself.

Four glasses in, I was finally sated. I splashed water on my face, then wet my hands and ran them over my scalp. The circles under my eyes were slightly diminished, but I still looked like a refugee from a Dickens book.

Maybe that was why Marcella was only interested in sex when she was drunk.

I shook it off. It didn't matter. Bracing myself on the sink with both hands, I met my gaze in the mirror. "Just a few more days and you're done."

"Done with what?"

I froze. Whoever said that was close by—in my room. *Has the killer found me? Did I forget to lock the door?* I tried to scream, but all that came out was a strangled gurgle.

The only potential weapon in the bathroom was the plunger. I lunged for it, cursing myself for leaving the Glock in the other room. By the time I straightened back up, my uninvited guest was standing in the bathroom doorway.

"Gross," Ski Mask said, wrinkling her nose. "Put that down and wash your hands. We need to talk."

CHAPTER NINE

BEWARE, MY LOVELY

C hrist, you nearly gave me a heart attack," I said angrily, jabbing the plunger at her. "You ever hear of knocking?"

Just like last time, Ski Mask was dressed all in black and
carried a cattle prod. No balaclava, though, which was a bit of a
relief. She cocked her head to the side. "Cattle prod trumps plunger,
last time I checked."

I eyed it. "Thought you were getting rid of that thing."

"It's an upgrade." She swung it in a circle. "This one is almost a
full pound lighter. Amazing what they can do with carbon fiber these
days. I actually haven't had the opportunity to try it out yet." She
directed it back toward my chest. "Maybe I should do a field test."

I swallowed hard. First she sent me creepy files, then she turned
up in my motel room? Something was very off about all this. Especially since she came armed. Keeping the plunger ready by my side,
I said, "How the fuck did you get in here?"

"Key card cloning. You should always use the deadbolt."

"Yeah? Well, for someone who said they wanted nothing to do with me, you're turning into a serious stalker."

She cocked an eyebrow. "Which is precisely what I'd like to discuss. How did you track me down?"

"Track *you* down?" I shook my head. "You're one to talk. I switched phones, by the way. So good luck pulling that little trick again."

"What trick?" She looked puzzled.

"Oh, y'know. Texting me constantly, following me across the country. Sticking postcards on my windshield." I pointed the plunger at her again. "You want help with abandonment issues, you'll have to start paying me."

Ski Mask frowned. "Did you sustain a head injury during the abduction?"

"What? No. I mean, I don't think so." Her tone was really pissing me off; she was treating me like a whiny kid.

"Perhaps we should move this discussion into the bedroom."

"I'm comfortable right here," I retorted.

"Really?" She made a face. "It reeks of vomit."

I sniffed; she wasn't wrong. "Fine. But the plunger comes with me."

Ski Mask backed out and I followed, muscles tensed. If I had to, I'd plunge her face and bolt for the door. I perched on the corner of the bed closer to the exit, and she leaned against the bureau facing me. Seconds ticked by while I waited for her to start talking. She just sat there eyeing me, eyebrows raised. Finally, I asked, "So what's up with the files?"

"What files?"

"The ones full of murdered girls. Look, I didn't ask for them in the first place, so you've got no right to be pissed at me for giving them away."

She stared at me, then said, "I genuinely have no idea what you're talking about."

"That envelope you dropped off, with my name on it?" Noting her blank look I said, "Lori Riffle, Sandy Gant? Not ringing any bells?"

Ski Mask suddenly went very still. "Someone dropped off murder files with your name on them?"

I paused a beat. "Hang on, that wasn't you?" My head was spinning. "Are you gaslighting me?"

"No." She set the cattle prod on the bureau. "Start from the beginning. Why did you come to Vegas?"

"Because I need new papers, thanks to you."

"But I got rid of your prints."

"Not according to the FBI guy."

"What FBI guy?"

We stared at each other. I had a finely tuned bullshit meter, and it was telling me she wasn't lying. A pit yawned open in my stomach. "You didn't text to warn me about him?"

She crossed her arms. "I texted you precisely two times. Once to tell you that I'd removed your prints from the scene, and then yesterday, to tell you to go home."

"Uh-huh. So how'd you know I was here?"

"You told me to meet you here."

"No, I told you to go fuck yourself."

"After that," she said impatiently.

I tried to piece it together. "Did the text come from a different number?"

"Yes." I could see from her eyes that she was working it out with me.

"And? What did it say?"

"That you were staying here, and would like to get together if I was available." Ski Mask was chewing her lip. It was the most emotion I'd seen her express, which didn't help my nerves.

I barked a laugh. "And you thought that was from me? Lady, does that sound even a little like something I'd say?"

"It did strike me as overly polite."

"So just to clarify," I said slowly, "you didn't text to warn me about the FBI being on my tail. Didn't put Vegas motel flyers on my car. And you didn't drop off an envelope."

She frowned. "I believe I made it perfectly clear in our last encounter that I preferred we never see each other again."

"Yeah, you did." Which explained why the tone of the other texts had been so different. "Well, I never asked you to meet me here. And what . . . you just let yourself into my room?"

"It seemed prudent to take precautions." She leaned forward, regarding me intently. "Stick to the point. You said FBI guy. So it was one agent?"

"Yup."

"What did he look like?"

"Hell, I don't know. I was a little preoccupied with not getting caught." I paused and tried to remember. "He was kind of tall."

"Blond?"

"Maybe. He was wearing a hat."

"Did he give you a name?"

"Yeah, Agent Cabot."

She inhaled sharply, looking like I'd slapped her.

"What?"

The look on her face was unsettling; she'd been totally cool in Beau's basement, but right now she looked freaked out. Which, in turn, was freaking me out. "So the FBI is after you, too?"

"He's not FBI."

"What?" I stared at her. "Then who the hell—"

Her face had gone a full shade paler, if that was possible. She hesitated, then said, "He's a killer. I was looking for him here, months ago. Then the trail went cold. When I heard about the murders in Tennessee . . . well, there was a reason I thought they were connected."

"But they weren't."

"Definitely not. But he must have followed me there."

"To Tennessee?"

"Yes."

I stared at her. This was a lot to process. "So you hunt serial killers, and they hunt you back?"

"Just him." A beat, then she added, "And he's far more dangerous than Beau Lee Jessop."

"Well, that's just fucking fantastic," I said. "You're telling me I threw my whole life away and headed to Vegas because a serial killer asked me to?"

"Basically, yes."

Fuck. I started hustling around the room, gathering up my things. Dot could probably refer me to another motel that took cash; she'd be annoyed, but I'd let her keep what I'd already paid, and maybe add a little extra on top. The image of Marcella in her kimono breezed through my mind, and I thought, *So much for that.* Which, honestly, was probably for the best. "He showed up at my apartment. How the hell did he find me?"

"I don't know." She ran a hand through her hair, looking agitated. "He put postcards on your car?"

"Yeah, for a no-tell motel where one of the girls was killed." At the thought, a shudder ran through me. He'd touched my car. *He'd been inside my apartment.* Did he follow me back from the diner that first morning? I'd been pretty out of it on the bus; I'd barely noticed any of the other passengers. "His last victim was killed the night before I got here. She was wearing a necklace with my name on it."

Ski Mask's face went blank. For some reason, that was more alarming than anything else. But all she said was, "I see."

"You see what?" Shoving clothes into my duffel, I asked, "Could he have followed you?"

"Your backpack." Ski Mask was staring at it. "It was in Beau's van."

I froze, then picked it up and carefully set it on the bed, as if it were radioactive. I tentatively dug out a souvenir sweatshirt, baseball cap, a mushy apple . . . I wasn't even sure what I was looking for. The emptier it grew, the more frenzied I became, yanking things out and tossing them to the floor. "So this has nothing to do with Beau Jessop?"

"I'm certain that Mr. Jessop worked alone."

"What's that supposed to mean? Was there someone else there?" I flashed on that moment by her car. "You thought you saw someone in the woods, didn't you?"

Instead of answering, she extended a hand toward the empty backpack. "Give that to me."

Reluctantly, I handed it over. She ran her hand carefully along the outer seams, then turned the backpack inside out. Lint, old ChapSticks, and gum wrappers spilled onto the floor. She groped along the padding, then reached in and extracted a small electronic device from a slit in the very bottom of the bag.

I swallowed hard and whispered, "Is that . . . is someone listening to us right now?"

"It's just a GPS tracker." She held it up to the light. "Long range. You can buy these off the internet." She tossed it on my bed, and I recoiled as if it were a snake. I'd thought I was so clever, when I'd actually been leading a serial killer across the country this entire time. I mentally smacked myself; implanting the idea of Vegas with those postcards was a classic long-con move, and like an idiot, I'd fallen for it.

I sank down on the bed and put my head in my hands. "Why the fuck would someone do all that?"

"It would take too long to explain."

"Too long to explain? Seriously?"

Ski Mask abruptly went to the window overlooking the parking lot. Peeking out the blinds, she said, "This is serious, Amber. Your life is in danger."

"But . . . why? Why me?"

She sighed. "He's trying to get to me through you."

"That makes zero sense," I protested. "We spent what, an hour together? And I wasn't exactly your favorite person by the end."

"You definitely weren't," she said dryly. "But he doesn't know that. Besides, it's not about whether we like each other. It's more that I saved you, and he wants to punish me by taking that away."

I blew out hard. "Well, gee. Thanks for that."

She'd picked up the cattle prod again and was tapping it against her leg. "Would you rather I'd left you in that basement?"

"No, obviously." I massaged my temples; a panic attack and migraine were currently fighting for headspace, and I wasn't keen to let either of them win. *Just breathe*, I reminded myself. "So I'll switch motels, make sure I'm not followed."

She was already shaking her head. "He'll be expecting that."

"Then what?!" I threw up my hands, exasperated. "I didn't get away from one serial killer just to be murdered by another!"

"You won't be," she said dismissively. "I'll handle it."

"Handle it how?"

Ski Mask appeared to have regained her poise. "Trust me. I know what I'm doing."

Her confidence was oddly reassuring; of course, I desperately wanted to believe her. "How the hell are you so calm?"

"Years of practice." Pointing the cattle prod at me, she said, "Just stay out of sight for a few days. Here should be safe enough. Do you have a weapon? Other than a plunger."

"Yes." I made a mental note to keep the Glock on me at all times from now on. And I was changing motels, no matter what she said. Hell, I'd change zip codes. Best to put as much distance between me and another killer as possible.

"Good." She headed toward the door.

I scrambled to my feet. "Wait! How will I know when it's over?"

"I'll text."

"Okay, um . . . let me give you my new number." I had decidedly mixed feelings about that, but I could always switch to another burner.

She pulled out a smartphone, checked the screen, and said, "Is it 702-213-3131?"

I gaped at her, then double-checked to be sure. Yup, that was my new number. "How the fuck did you do that?"

"Wait for my text. Goodbye, Amber."

Then she opened the door and left. I hurriedly got up and locked it behind her, putting on the security chain and deadbolt for good measure. The panic attack was winning, and I preferred to ride it out in relative safety.

I collapsed into the desk chair, closed my eyes, and said, "Fuck."

A half hour later, the waves of terror had abated. I was lying on the bed trying to motivate myself to continue packing but couldn't even muster the energy to stand.

A knock at the door supplied the requisite burst of adrenaline. I sat bolt upright, grabbed the Glock, and shouted, "Go away!"

"Well, that's rude," Marcella said in her deep alto.

"Open up, buttercup!" Dot called out.

I groaned. This was the last thing I needed. Turning away from the door, I called out, "I don't feel well. I'll talk to you tomorrow."

There was a quick, whispered conversation. Then Marcella said, "Sorry, bitch, we're coming in."

"Seriously, I'm having a rough night." It still didn't feel real; how was it possible that my life just kept getting worse? Just an hour ago, I'd been feeling pretty good about making a fresh start as a redhead named Dawn.

Another knock, then Dot said, "Don't make me use my master key!"

"Fine!" I growled, rolling off the bed. "One sec." I threw the door open to find Dot and Marcella standing there with a small suitcase. Seeing my expression, their smiles faded.

"What happened?" Dot demanded. She'd changed into a black silk number edged with lace that was vaguely reminiscent of a flamenco dancer's dress. Marcella was wearing a plain white sundress, the most conservative outfit I'd seen her in yet. Her hair was swept up in a bun, and she only had a few touches of makeup on her eyes and lips. She looked amazing. They both did. But I didn't feel like dealing with either of them at the moment.

"Listen," I said. "I just got some bad news, so I think I should probably—"

"Christ," Marcella said, pushing past me and flopping down on the bed. "She's breaking up with us, Dot."

"The hell she is," Dot snorted. "Saddle up, hon. We're going out."

I was already shaking my head. "Hell to the no. All I want is to order a pizza, take a shower, and go to bed."

Marcella grinned wickedly. "I could be into that."

"Y'all can do whatever you want later." With some effort, Dot wrangled the suitcase onto my bureau. I swallowed hard, remembering the cattle prod that had sat there less than an hour earlier. "But first, Marcie and I are taking you out to see the *real* Vegas. Locals-only stuff."

"Wow, that's tempting," I said, even though in my experience, "locals only" usually involved some sort of harm to animals, followed by throwing up in a Dairy Queen parking lot. I hesitated, then added, "But I really have to finish packing."

"You skipping town?" Marcella asked with a frown.

"You can't leave!" Dot protested. "Jessie doesn't have anything ready yet!"

I examined my hands. "Yeah, I know."

"No refunds," Dot said sternly. "That's the deal, okay?"

"It's fine. Once I get settled, I'll send an address where she can mail them." Hopefully I wouldn't need my new ID before then. I'd spent the last hour thinking it over and had decided that my best bet was to put a few hundred miles between me and my latest serial killer. Forget finding a new motel; I'd stick to cash and sleep in my car. Los Angeles was a big place, with a lot of urban campers; it would be easy to get lost there.

Dot gaped at me. "But . . . why?"

Because someone wants to kill me. Again. I shrugged. "It's complicated."

"Complicated. Sure." Marcella eyed me. "Honey, I could give a shit, but Dot's got something special planned. So sit your pretty ass down and let her have her way with you. Tomorrow you can do whatever the hell you want."

I frowned. "Have her way with me how, exactly?"

Dot looked disconcerted by my attitude; still, she threw open the suitcase and said with a muted flourish, "Ta-da!"

"Oh, crap," I moaned, spotting compartments filled with eye shadow and makeup brushes.

"That's right, bitch," Marcella chortled. "Makeover time! We're gonna do something with this shit look you're rocking."

I closed my eyes. I would rather be digging into another platter of diarrhea food at that awful buffet right now. Hell, I'd rather already be in my car.

Although the prospect of getting back on the road turned my stomach. The killer was probably out there right now, watching and waiting. I should check my car for trackers, too; but what would I even look for? Somehow, I had to find a way to shake him, and it would have to be smart . . . which I didn't feel very capable of at the moment.

Ski Mask had promised to handle it. I wasn't the type to trust blindly, but of the two of us, at least she seemed to know what she was doing. So should I put my faith in her? Or would that just land me dead in a bathtub?

I squeezed my fists against my forehead. There was no easy answer.

"You okay, kiddo?" Dot asked with concern. "Need help relaxing again?"

I shook my head. I was too frayed to contemplate leaving tonight, that was certain. If I headed out in the morning, even with evasive maneuvers I could make it to California by nightfall. By this time tomorrow, I could be sitting on a beach.

And until then . . . it was unlikely that this creep would come after me in public, right? Maybe going out was actually the safest option. If I stayed surrounded by people, it would give Ski Mask time to do whatever she had planned.

"Please?" Dot asked, seeing my resolve weakening. "Trust me. It's going to be fantastic."

I sighed. "Fine. But there better not be any male strippers involved."

"Well, shit, there go all my plans," Marcella said, pouting.

Ouch!" I protested. "I just got my eyebrows back, could you leave them alone?"

"They need shaping. Now, stay still, hon."

"Easy for you to say," I muttered. Dot was bent low enough to offer me an expansive view of her cleavage, which I had to admit was not unpleasant. She smelled amazing, too, like strawberries and clean linen. Marcella was lounging on the bed, helping herself to the Prosecco that Dot had produced along with three vintage champagne coupes. It was turning into a regular girls' night, albeit an involuntary one on my part.

I sipped from my own glass, moodily reflecting on the fact that thanks to constrained gender roles, men never had to deal with this shit. Any self-respecting stag party would be on their second strip club by now, not sitting around a motel room. How this was supposed to be part of the fun was frankly beyond me, especially since Dot had spent the better part of an hour taking tweezers to the few parts of my body that had started sprouting hair again.

At least it was providing a slight distraction. I was only thinking of being murdered in between plucks.

"Almost done," Dot said, tongue touching her upper lip as she brushed yet another layer of mascara on me. "Okay. You can look."

Resigned, I turned to face the mirror, then did an actual double take. "Holy shit!"

"Damn," Marcella said approvingly. "Not bad. We could get fifty a pop for you, easy."

"Hush, Marcella," Dot said, throwing her a look.

"What? That's good money in this town."

I could barely speak. Dot had reshaped my eyebrows into perfect arches, penciling in the gaps, and highlighted my cheekbones and eyes with a dusting of shadow and contouring powder. There wasn't much she could do about my patchy hair aside from slicking it down, but still. I'd honestly never looked this good in my life.

"Well?" Dot asked anxiously.

Tears welled in my eyes. It had been a long time since anyone had been kind to me.

Marcella made a noise and said, "For Christ's sake, don't mess it up already."

Dot dabbed anxiously at mascara smears as I said, "Thanks, Dot. Really."

"Sure, hon." She leaned in and pecked me on the cheek, then rubbed away the lipstick mark with her thumb.

"And now, the pee-ass de resistance!" Marcella drawled, making it sound truly dirty. She motioned to a garment bag on the bed that I had barely registered.

"It's from the lost and found," Dot explained. "This little number turned up a few months back, and I held on to it. Obviously it wouldn't fit me, and Marcella didn't like it, but I figured . . . you never know. And, well—here you are!"

I unzipped the bag. Inside was a cocktail dress. Not the sort of thing I ever would've wasted money on, but I wasn't about to complain about free clothes. Especially when I saw the designer label; it had to be worth several hundred dollars. "Someone seriously left this here?"

Dot made a face. "Most of the stuff isn't nearly this nice. Now, put it on—we've got a show to catch!"

"A show?" I said dubiously.

Dot made a shooing motion with her hands. "Five minutes, Cinderella!"

Which was how I found myself getting snuck in a stage door behind Caesars Palace twenty minutes later. If my companions noticed me frantically checking the faces of everyone we encountered, they didn't remark on it. Not that I'd recognize the guy. All I had to go on was tall and blond, which described an alarming number of the men we passed.

Dot exchanged air-kisses with the security guard, then swept in like she owned the place. Marcella and I followed her through a warren of service hallways, emerging at a plain door. Dot grinned at us, then pushed it open.

I gasped. It was an enormous theater in the round, filled with tables encircling a stage. The place was nearly full. Dot wove through the crowd, leading us to a small table set right in front. It had a white tablecloth and a rose in a vase.

I pulled out a chair and sat, trying not to gape like some country hick. I'd only been to a theater once before, on a school field trip. And this place was huge; there were probably five hundred other people crammed into the cavernous space.

"What?" Dot asked.

"Nothing." I swallowed hard; I hadn't been around this many people since the attack, and the air felt close and hard to breathe. Panic stirred in my gut again, and I closed my eyes to fight it off. Was this safe, or had I made a terrible mistake?

"Hon? You all right?" Dot's voice sounded far away. "Maybe this wasn't such a great idea—"

"She'll be fine," Marcella cut in. I felt the press of her lips against mine; she pushed a small pill into my mouth with the tip of her tongue and whispered, "Swallow." Reflexively, I did, then thought, *Shit*.

As the lights went down, I leaned toward Marcella and hissed, "What was that?"

"Mama's little helper," she said with a wink.

"No, seriously," I protested, suddenly panicked. "You shouldn't have—"

"Shh." Marcella wrapped an arm around my shoulders and drew me into her. "Trust me."

"You'll love this," Dot said, patting my knee. "And it's the hottest ticket in town."

"Have a drink," Marcella whispered, handing me a glass of champagne. "It'll help."

Moodily, I gulped half the glass. The room was completely black, which should have helped since I couldn't see the crowd anymore but only served to increase my claustrophobia. The oppressive darkness was too much like that basement. It was cold, too; my arms spiked with goose bumps, and my heart raced. I half stood, ready to run.

"Easy," Marcella murmured. "Give it a minute."

A spotlight suddenly flared to life right in front of us, directed down at the center of the stage. *Like a lightbulb, dangling above a table.* My breath caught in my chest.

"Is she okay?" Dot whispered, waving a hand in front of my eyes. "Amber, sweetie? You all right?"

I'd gone rigid. *He's going to get me. This was a mistake, I should have left, should have run . . .*

"She's fine," Marcella said, rubbing my arm.

I barely felt her fingers; both of their voices sounded far away, on the periphery of my consciousness. I was laser focused on the shadows just outside that damn circle, waiting for a tall blond guy to emerge.

"She's not," Dot said, leaning in to peer at me. "Christ, she's white as a sheet. This was a bad idea. Let's—"

And then suddenly, there was a roar in my veins. Actually, it was more like . . . singing. Something small and warm wriggled to life in my belly, then stretched and sprouted throughout my bloodstream. The tingle extended through my arms and legs, soaring all the way up to the crown of my head. Every single one of my nerves started firing simultaneously . . . it was just this side of excruciating. All the breath I'd been holding in suddenly released, and I sagged into the chair.

With effort, I turned to Marcella and asked, "What. The. Fuck."

"Told ya." She winked. "Now, just enjoy the ride."

My head felt like it was perched on a swivel; I was keenly aware of every muscle moving it. I slowly shifted to look back at the stage. It wasn't scary anymore; now the spotlight looked warm, cheery. And out of nowhere came a cavalcade of performers. They fell from the ceiling and tumbled in from the shadows; some even emerged from the crowd around us and vaulted onstage. I gasped as they executed maneuvers that seemed to defy physics. It was like watching a dream—no, more like entering one. I felt like they were all there just for me, on a mission to strip my fear away, so that by the end I'd be whole and new again.

The rest of the night was a blur. At some point, I was onstage—at least I thought I was—embraced and supported by dozens of gentle hands, all working on me, rubbing me, telling me everything would be okay. I could see Dot in the audience, and Marcella . . . the entire crowd was looking at me warmly. It was hard to believe that I'd ever felt alone, because it wasn't true, I was surrounded by love, in fact I *was* love, and—

I was staring at the ground and everything hurt. Blearily, I raised my head: Dot and Marcella loomed over me, staring down with concern.

"Looks like she's gonna puke again."

"Christ, Marcella. I should kick you out for this," Dot growled. "What did you give her?"

"Just something to help her relax. Chill the fuck out."

"Well, if she keeps going like this we're gonna have to take her to the ER."

"You're the one who kept filling her glass," Marcella retorted.

I blinked, and my surroundings slowly clarified. I was sitting on a curb. There was an impressive puddle on the ground, which I suspected had something to do with me. I swiped my mouth with the back of my arm and said, "Where are we?"

"See? Told you she'd be fine," Marcella said. I felt her hand on my back, rubbing in small circles as she added, "You totally hurled on Dot's shoes."

"Twice," Dot growled, examining them. "They were my favorite pair, too."

My head felt like it had been stuffed with cotton. In fact, it was eerily reminiscent of how I'd felt after Leather Apron injected me with—

Another torrent of vomit. Marcella jerked her foot out of the way too late and yelled, "Fuck!"

"That's karma for ya," Dot said smugly.

I spit, trying to get the bad taste out of my mouth, but only succeeded in making it worse. "Do either of you have any water?" I asked, wincing as a stab of pain shot through my head. I really had to stop throwing up, this was becoming a thing.

Wordlessly, Dot handed me a bottle. I gulped half of it down, then stopped to make sure it would stay put. My head still hurt like hell, but the nausea eased slightly. I looked around blearily. "Where are we? Is the show over?"

"Oh, honey, the show ended hours ago," Dot said. "Then we went to a local spot—"

"The Tiki Hut," Marcella said. "Super cheesy, and the drinks are foul."

"You loved it, though," Dot said. "We had to pull you off the bar, you kept hopping up to dance—"

"And to stick your tongue down girls' throats," Marcella said. "You got a wild streak. Lucky I'm not the jealous type."

"They kicked us out when you started puking," Dot sniffed. "Lenny probably won't speak to me for weeks after what you did to his koi pond."

"Sorry," I muttered. I swigged more water until the bottle was gone. "That's why I don't do drugs," I said pointedly to Marcella. "They turn you into an idiot."

"A fun idiot." Marcella smirked.

"She's right, you were a hoot," Dot agreed. "Well, up until the last Scorpion Bowl. Things took a turn after that."

"What time is it?" I asked.

"Time to get you home," Dot said decisively. "Our ride should be here any minute."

As if on cue, a limo pulled up in front of us.

"That's not a cab," I pointed out.

"Told you Dot basically runs this town," Marcella said.

"Well, that's hardly true," Dot protested. "I just happen to have a lot of friends."

They each took an arm and pulled me up. I staggered slightly in the heels. My feet were throbbing nearly as painfully as my head. "Oh, crap," I said woozily. "How the hell am I supposed to drive to California?"

"First things first, you need to get some shut-eye," Dot said. "Now, listen, toots—you puke in Maury's car, I'll never forgive you, because he won't forgive me. Got it?"

"Got it," I said weakly.

Not ruining the interior of Maury's limo proved challenging. Thank God it was only a five-minute ride; any longer and I would've gotten Dot blackballed from any and all future car services. As it was I stumbled out, bent double, and promptly heaved up all the water I'd just drunk.

"Oh, dollface," Dot said, shaking her head. "You're a mess."

"Yeah. Probably better if you sleep in your own room," Marcella said, wrinkling her nose. "And maybe take a shower."

I started to nod, then frowned. "I need to stay with people, I think."

"Yeah?"

A tiny voice in my head was adamant that I stay away from my room, but I couldn't remember why. "Can't sleep there."

Dot and Marcella exchanged a glance. "I guess you can crash with me," Marcella said reluctantly.

"You're the one who dosed her," Dot said crisply. "Seems only fair."

"Just for a few hours." I winced; every word elicited a fresh stab of pain. "Quick nap, then I'm heading out."

"Sure you are." Marcella chortled. "Listen, I got the perfect thing for a hangover—"

"No more drugs!" Dot snapped, jabbing a finger at her.

"I was talking about burritos. Jesus, chill."

My stomach lurched again. "Don't. Mention. Food."

"The pair of you, I swear." Dot sighed and shook her head. "You need any help, hon?"

"Um, I need my toothbrush." I peered dubiously at the stairs to my room. Maybe relocating had been a mistake. They were cast in deep shadow, and it was hard to suppress the sense that something ominous waited at the top. But I really needed to get the taste of puke out of my mouth. "Would you guys mind waiting while I grab it?"

Another look was exchanged. I wanted to tell them what was going on, but that would require remembering more than scattered images, none of which made sense. A woman in a ski mask, a girl in a bathtub, a koi pond. I felt simultaneously drunk and high and hungover, which hardly seemed fair.

"Well, I ain't got all day," Marcella said, shooing me. "Get on it."

"Okay." Drawing a deep breath, I wobbled across the parking lot, intently focused on putting one foot in front of the other. The first rays of dawn tinged the sky, making my head pulsate worse than ever. I would've thrown up again, but there was nothing left; at this point, I wouldn't have been surprised to see actual organs come out.

Gritting my teeth, I made it to the stairwell. It took an eternity to totter up, one step at a time. In the background, I could hear Marcella and Dot having a whispered conversation, probably about what a nutcase I'd turned out to be. At the top I paused, feeling like I'd just summited Everest. Once I caught my breath, I staggered toward my room.

There was a bundle of laundry outside my door. Which was super weird, because it was way too early for the housekeeper.

As I got closer, I realized there was a dark puddle extending from the laundry to the ledge.

The bundle suddenly shifted. Vacant eyes stared up at me, and a hand reached out . . .

I screamed and stumbled back. Turned and tried to run, but forgot I was wearing heels and found myself falling instead. A hard *CRACK* on the side of my head, and everything went black.

CHAPTER TEN

THE DAMNED
DON'T CRY

woke up in a hospital bed. Kind of. It was made of metal, and an IV bag hung from a stand next to me, but I was surrounded by dozens of disembodied heads.

I raised my head and winced as a sharp stab of pain shot from my forehead and reverberated through my skull. "Fuck!" I hissed through clenched teeth, falling back to the pillow.

There was a clack of heels as Dot hurried in. "Easy, hon. Dr. Aboud said you need to stay put."

"Who said what?" I slurred, head throbbing. I was going to strangle Marcella for giving me that pill.

"Dr. Aboud. He's excellent, really." Dot glanced back at the door—her gorgeous dress had a weird pattern on it now, like it had been smeared with an alarming amount of—

"Is that blood?" I asked.

Dot looked down. Her hands moved reflexively to smooth her dress, but she stopped an inch from the fabric. "Not yours, sweetie." She was much paler than usual, which made the rouge on her cheeks stand out alarmingly.

"Whose—"

"You're just supposed to rest," she said, patting my shoulder soothingly. "Dr. Aboud said it's a bad concussion, but you'll be good as new with a few stitches. He's going to do them as soon as, well . . ." She tapped a bit too forcefully as she looked toward the door again.

"Ow." I brushed her hand away. "What's going on? And where the hell are we?" For the first time, I became aware of urgent voices on the other side of the wall. One of them sounded familiar. "Is that Marcella?"

"She's fine, hon. She's just helping out in the next room."

"Helping with what?"

"Helping Dr. Aboud with your friend."

"My what?" Everything she said left me more confused. "I don't have any friends. I mean, aside from you two." I put a hand to my forehead; it felt sticky. "What happened?"

"I honestly don't know." Dot settled herself carefully next to me. I realized the bed was actually more of a worktable, and a damn cold one at that. I was still only wearing a thin slip of silk that barely qualified as a dress, and the room was freezing. I shivered, and Dot pulled the thin cotton blanket over my shoulders. "I can try to find another blanket, they must be around here somewhere—"

"I'm fine," I said, although my teeth were threatening to chatter. "Tell me what's going on."

A male voice in the next room barked orders, which made Dot start wringing her hands again. "Lord, this night," she sighed. "All right, well . . . we were waiting for you, like you asked, and then you screamed bloody murder. Marcella ran up to check on you, then she screamed, too, and when I got to you all—"

The person on my doorstep, I realized. I pointed at her dress. "Whose blood is that?"

"Your friend, she's . . ." Dot looked down at her dress again. "Dr.

Aboud is doing his best, but maybe I should've taken her to the hospital after all. I thought we were doing the right thing, but now I just don't—"

A cry from the other room, sharp and loud. "Oh, dear," Dot mumbled. "Poor lamb. She made us promise not to call the police or take her to the hospital."

I only knew one other person in Vegas. "Shit. Ski Mask." I remembered a pile of laundry moving, an outstretched hand, turning to run and tripping in those damn heels . . . then, nothing.

Dot cocked her head to the side. "Ski Mask? She said her name's Grace."

"Tall, blond, bitchy?"

"Oh, yes. She reminds me of Lizabeth Scott in *Dark City*. Except for the blood." Dot looked dazed. "There was a lot of it, everywhere. I'm going to have to use bleach on the walkway. I should probably call Tina to warn her—"

Grace. It was a little weird to know her name now. And a little irritating that she'd immediately shared it with Dot but hadn't told me. Not that that was important right now. "So she's bleeding?"

"Badly. I've seen some things, trust me, but this . . . nothing like this."

Dot's makeup was smudged, and her curls were a mess. She looked absolutely distraught. And it was all my fault. I was the one who'd quite literally brought this to her doorstep. I should have explained everything to her last night, then left. "I'm really sorry, Dot."

She took my hand and forced a strained smile. "Don't you dare apologize. I'm just so glad you're okay. Do you want some Advil?"

Another horrible, strangled sound from next door. "What's going on in there?"

"Dr. Aboud is operating. Grace told us to bring you both somewhere safe. Nowhere official, though." Dot gnawed her lip. "I shouldn't have listened. I should have just gone straight to the hospital."

The wig stand directly across from me had an unsettlingly real face and bore more than a passing resemblance to my third-grade teacher, Mrs. Clarkson. I was really not digging the vibe in here. "So where are we?"

"Nowhere official," Dot said, waving a hand at our surroundings. "Dr. Aboud was a surgeon in Syria but couldn't get licensed here, so he sells wigs and does this on the side. He helped my friend Rina with her gallstones. But this, well . . ." She started wringing her hands again. "I could still call 911. Should I call 911?"

I wanted to answer, but my brain felt like it had been stuffed with wet wool . . . just like that awful night in Beau Lee Jessop's basement. I'd involuntarily done more drugs in the past two weeks than in the rest of my life combined.

I lay back on the pillow, closed my eyes, and tried to orient myself. Marcella was okay. Ski Mask was actually named Grace (or at least that was what she'd told Dot), and she was being treated by a surgeon who also owned a wig store. I was hurt, but not too badly. A bubble of completely inappropriate laughter formed on my lips and I forced it back down; it came out as a strangled gurgle instead.

"Are you okay? Do you need something?" Dot asked anxiously. "I can get ice chips—that's what you give people, right?" She scanned the room. "There must be ice chips here somewhere."

She's in shock. "I'm fine," I said. "But can you check on Grace for me?"

"Right, okay." Dot nodded. "I can do that. I'll just go"—she looked warily at the doorway—"out there. Marcella is helping, I had no idea she'd be so calm under pressure. People can surprise you, can't they?"

"They can," I agreed. "Like, I'm super surprised that my head feels like a bowling ball filled with hammers. Otherwise I'd go check."

"Right." Dot was still nodding like a crazy person. "Out there."

She clearly was loath to do it. "Is Grace dying?"

"No! I mean, maybe. I don't know." Dot bit her lip again. "I just— I don't like blood. And there's a lot of it."

"Okay." I drew a deep breath and carefully pushed up to my forearms. The room wobbled, but that was to be expected. It would stop in a minute. I just needed one—

"Amber!" I heard Dot yell as the room went black.

T his time when I woke up, a bright light was shining in my eyes.

"Dammit," I groaned. "This has got to stop happening."

"How many fingers am I holding up?" a heavily accented man's voice asked.

"Two," I said, squinting at them. "Three if you count the thumb."

"Why wouldn't the thumb count?"

"Because it's just different, okay? Now, lose the light, it's making my headache worse."

"Good to see you still got your charm," Marcella said. I shifted my head to find her standing by my right shoulder, smiling down at me. Which would have been more comforting if she didn't look like she'd just stepped off the set of a horror movie. Her white dress was caked in even more blood than Dot's, and there were streaks of it on her arms and face.

"This one is fine." The light clicked off. Dr. Aboud was a slight man in bloody surgical scrubs. He was younger than I'd expected, probably midthirties, and had kind eyes. I could absolutely picture him as the lead on a medical drama; he projected competence and weariness in equal measure. "I'm going to check the other one again, then I'll be back to do the stitches." He rapped my arm with the penlight. "Do not move, understand? If you pass out again Dot might have a heart attack, and there is no room for another patient."

"Got it," I said. "How's Grace?" They exchanged a look. Something went cold inside me. "Is she dead?"

"She's resting. It's too soon to say." Dr. Aboud's voice was clipped and careful. "But she's young and healthy. The cut was deep, but no major organs were affected. All things considered, she is very fortunate."

"He was amazing," Marcella said, taking my hand and squeezing it. "I mean, damn, you should've seen it. I'm a little in love right now."

"I'm a married man," he said, frowning.

"All my best customers are," Marcella said. "I'll give you my number."

"That won't be necessary," he said stiffly before practically fleeing the room.

"I would seriously do him for free," Marcella said. "That was awesome. I should've been a surgeon. I'd look super hot in scrubs, too."

My thought processes were still sluggish, but I was pretty sure he'd said *cut*. "Was Grace stabbed?"

"Dot didn't tell you?"

"I think she was too freaked out." I looked at her. "She said you screamed."

Marcella settled on the corner of the table and rested a hand on my shoulder. I could feel its warmth through the blanket. "When I saw you on the ground you looked dead. Like, really dead. And then your friend—"

"She's not my friend," I interrupted. "Why does everyone keep calling her that?"

"Well, your whatever. She said it was the same guy who killed Lori." Marcella's face clouded over. "And that we couldn't go to a regular hospital. Bossy bitch wouldn't even let Dot call Jim to help. So we got you in Dot's car—"

"Oh, no," I said, picturing blood all over Dot's pristine upholstery.

Marcella waved a hand dismissively. "No worries, we know a guy who can get blood out of anything. So Dot drove us here. I held a towel to Grace's side the whole time, she was bleeding like crazy and you're supposed to apply pressure, right? I took first aid when I was a Girl Scout, I remembered that part."

"You were a Girl Scout?" For some reason, that was the strangest thing I'd heard yet.

"Oh yeah. Still got the uniform, too. I'll put it on for you sometime." She threw me an entirely inappropriate wink, then continued. "Anyway, Doc checked you out and said you were fine, and he asked me to help with her." Marcella's cheeks were flushed; she seemed positively giddy. "You are fine, right?"

"My head is killing me."

"Mine too. But this shit sobered me up quick." She eyed my forehead. "I can clean the blood off. Probably make it easier to stitch you up."

Marcella went to a side table stacked with boxes of medical gear. She grabbed gauze and a bottle of antiseptic, then brought them back to the table. As she snapped on latex gloves she joked, "Not what I usually use these for."

"Funny."

She shook the bottle, then poured a liberal amount of antiseptic onto the gauze. "This is gonna sting."

"Great." I winced as she dabbed the right side of my forehead. "How bad is it?"

"Not too bad. Probably won't even scar," she said. "Your friend's bikini days are gone, though. Shame, 'cause she's got a tight little tummy."

I frowned, not loving the thought of Marcella appreciating Grace's body, even under these circumstances. *That's what you're focusing on?* I chided myself. A particularly sharp pain made me cry out.

"Don't be a baby," Marcella ordered.

"Your bedside manner sucks," I grumbled. While she kept working, I distracted myself by trying to figure out what the hell had happened.

Apparently Ski Mask/Grace hadn't done a great job of "handling it" after all. Which was ominous. Especially since the guy she'd been tracking stabbed her right outside my motel room door. Had he come there looking for me? I pictured a huge man lurking in the shadows outside my room with a knife and a rope. *If I hadn't gone out last night, if I'd been alone in my room . . .* I started to shiver uncontrollably, envisioning all sorts of nightmare scenarios.

"Cold?"

"No, I'm fine. Just . . . freaked out."

"Yeah." Marcella drew her hand back. I'd never seen her look so serious. "So that's the chick who saved you?"

"Yeah."

"You knew she was here?"

I nodded, then instantly regretted it as pain shot through my skull. "She showed up in my room last night, right before you guys came."

Understanding dawned on her face. "So that's why you were gonna skip town."

"Yeah, basically." After a beat I added, "She said someone was trying to kill me."

"Why would someone want to kill you?" Marcella frowned.

"To get to her." Catching her expression, I added, "Apparently it's complicated."

Dr. Aboud reappeared in the doorway and asked, "How's my other patient? Ready for stitches?"

"Oh, absolutely," I muttered. "Can't wait."

A half hour later I was stitched up, rehydrated, and could stand without passing out or puking. Under protest, Dot helped me limp to the next room. Stabilizing myself with both hands on the metal table, I stared down at Grace.

Her room was larger than mine and had fewer wigs. It looked more like an operating suite, with plastic sheeting on four sides, battered oxygen tanks, and a swiveling overhead light. The floor was littered with blood-soaked towels and gauze.

Grace was covered in blankets and had an IV coming out of her arm. She looked small and pale, but other than that she just seemed to be asleep.

"Sure you're okay, hon?" Dot asked worriedly. She stood behind me, probably braced to catch me if I passed out again.

"I'm fine," I answered, although in truth I was pretty woozy. Dr. Aboud had given me meds before suturing; combining those with whatever drug was still in my system was probably not medically recommended. The pain was gone, though. "Has she woken up yet?" I asked in a low voice.

"I don't think so," Dot murmured. She seemed much calmer; I suspected Dr. Aboud had given her something, too. "Doc said she'd be out for a few hours at least."

"Right." I frowned as my legs started to shake. "Maybe I should sit down."

Dot hurriedly grabbed a folding chair from the corner and eased me into it. "You should be resting."

"I'm fine," I repeated, shifting closer to the bed. "Better than her, at least."

It was strange to see Grace reduced to this; I'd mythologized her into some kind of superhero. She looked small and helpless, which unnerved me even more. When she'd said she'd take care of the threat, it had actually gone a long way toward tempering my fear; after all, she was the expert, right?

Without her, I didn't have a chance. I flashed back on the "Amber" necklace and shuddered involuntarily. The killer knew where I was staying. I wasn't in any condition to drive. And I doubted Dr. Aboud would be keen to host me here indefinitely.

Dot pulled a chair up next to mine. "You gave me a hell of a fright."

"Sorry," I said, distracted.

"Not your fault, kiddo." She smiled ruefully. "All of this . . . it's not really like the movies, is it?"

"No," I agreed. "It's not."

"I guess I always assumed I'd rise to the occasion, y'know?" Dot examined her hands. "I guess I'm not much of a heroine."

"Are you kidding?" I reached over and put my hand on top of hers. "You saved a total stranger. That was badass."

"Yes, well." She offered me a wan smile. "Thanks, toots. I appreciate that."

We sat in silence for a minute. The clock over the door read seven thirty. Less than twelve hours ago Dot had been doing my makeup; it felt like an eternity had passed since then. Poor Dot. All she'd wanted was to give me a nice night out, and look how I'd repaid her. "You should go home."

"I will in a bit. Just want to make sure she's out of the woods first," she said, nodding at Grace.

As if on cue, a groggy voice from the bed grumbled, "For Christ's sake, what does it take to get some sleep around here?"

"Hey!" I scrambled to her, nearly tripping over the IV stand. "You're awake!"

Grace squinted, taking in the room. "This better not be a hospital."

"It's not," Dot assured her.

"Good." Grace's eyes were remarkably clear, considering the fact that she'd just undergone surgery. "How did we get here?"

"Dot drove us," I said.

Grace tilted her head to look at her. "You're the redhead. Where's the hooker?"

I felt a flare of rage. "A thank-you would be nice. They saved your life."

Grace rolled her eyes. "I was never in danger of dying."

"A stack of bloody towels would disagree," I retorted.

"Not to mention my car," Dot muttered.

Grace had the gall to look annoyed. "Focus, Amber. I need you to walk me through how we got here, step by step."

"You need to explain some things first." I crossed my arms over my chest.

"We don't have time for that."

"Sure we do. 'Cause you're not going anywhere unless you want to bleed out. And this time, I'll let you."

"Me too," Dot said.

Grace sighed heavily. "Okay. But be quick about it."

"Let's start with why you came back to my room. Did you track him there?"

Grace was frowning. "I was nowhere near your motel."

"Yeah, you were. Bleeding on my doorstep."

She closed her eyes. "Crap."

"'Crap'? That's all you have to say?" I snapped.

"Shut up." Grace brought a shaky hand to her temple. "I need to think."

Dot had flushed bright red. "I don't much care for your friend, Amber."

"We're not friends," Grace and I said in unison. We glared at each other.

"So," I said. "Guess you didn't do such a great job handling it, huh?"

"He surprised me," Grace muttered. "Goddammit, I was so close."

"That's not exactly reassuring," I said, heart sinking. I'd really been counting on her to fix this. And now she was in worse shape than me. I sank back in the chair. *What am I going to do now?*

Eyeing my forehead, she asked, "What happened to you?"

I put a hand to it defensively. "When I saw you, I ran—"

"You ran?" She raised an eyebrow.

"I didn't know it was you, and there was blood, and I freaked out a little. So I hit my head—"

Grace scoffed.

"Yeah, I know. Stupid. Almost as stupid as getting stabbed."

"That was beyond my control."

"Sure it was." Her attitude was really starting to piss me off. "Then Dot and Marcella did exactly what you asked and took us to a doctor in a wig store when they should have called 911 on your ass."

"This is a wig store?" Grace craned her head, examining her surroundings.

I ignored her and forged ahead. "Maybe show some real

gratitude. Because I gotta say, I'm tempted to just roll you outside and leave you there."

"Amen, sister," Dot agreed.

"You don't understand," Grace said, irritated. "He left me outside your room to send a message. You're part of the game now."

"I'm . . . what?"

"What game?" Dot asked.

Grace pushed up to her elbows. "Tell the doctor to ease off the morphine. I need to be ready."

"Ready for what?"

She fixed her eyes on me again and said, "For when my brother comes to kill you."

S orry, what?" My head was still swimming, which might explain why the words coming out of Grace's mouth made absolutely no sense. "Your brother?"

"Yes, my brother. Try to keep up." Grace was struggling to sit. "He drugged me and took me to your motel, probably hoping to make me watch while he killed you. But apparently you weren't there."

"Hang on." I could feel bile rising up my throat again. "Your brother, like an actual family member, is the serial killer you've been tracking?"

"It would be helpful if I didn't have to explain everything twice."

"There was a serial killer at my motel?" Dot looked faint, too.

"Yes."

Slowly, I said, "So if I hadn't gone out last night . . ."

"You'd most likely be dead."

I collapsed back in the chair, trying to process that. How long had he waited for me to come back? Had he actually been *inside* my room?

I shuddered. No way I was ever going back there now.

"It was smart to stay out in public," Grace said. "Perhaps I haven't given you enough credit."

"Gee, thanks." I felt oddly calm, all things considered. Maybe my body had run out of adrenaline. "So why didn't you tell me last night that your *brother* was the one after me?"

"It didn't seem relevant."

"Not *relevant?*"

"Honestly, Amber." Grace tried to sit again, then winced. "You're wasting time. Now, shut up and let me focus."

The urge to slap her was almost overwhelming, despite her weakened state. Instead, I rubbed my temples with my thumbs. "Trust me, I don't want to talk any more than you do. I've got a concussion and I'm hungover as hell. But if I'm going to be murdered by your brother, I'd really like to know why."

"Because he's a psychopath," Grace said. "Obviously."

"Pretty coincidental, your brother turning out to be a serial killer when hunting them is your hobby."

Grace had awkwardly managed to push herself up to a forty-five-degree angle. The strain of the effort showed on her face, but I didn't move to help her. She closed her eyes and exhaled deeply. "He's the reason I do it. I've always been hunting him—just him. I find the others by accident."

I blinked at her. "Seriously?"

Grace put a hand to her side and groaned. "Are you sure that man has a medical license?"

"So your brother . . ." Dot said faintly, ". . . is a serial killer, and he knows who we are, and where we live?"

"I doubt you're in any danger, if it helps. Amber is the one he's after." Grace cocked her head to the side. "Although I can't actually guarantee that; this situation is entirely unprecedented. Now, where the hell are my clothes?"

I put a hand on Dot's arm. She'd gone stiff, and her lower lip trembled. "Easy, Dot—"

"We'll call the police," Dot said. "They'll send a SWAT team—"

"A SWAT team for a con artist, a hooker, and a motel clerk? Unlikely," Grace scoffed. "Besides, there's no proof that he did anything."

"There's you," I pointed out. "We'll report the stabbing."

"I'll deny it."

"What is wrong with you?" Dot cried.

Grace paused and looked at her. "I understand that this is a lot to absorb—"

"You think?" I scoffed.

"—but my brother is brilliant and extremely dangerous. The police can't handle him."

"Neither can you, apparently," I said, gesturing to her wound.

"I almost had him," Grace said in a low voice, as if trying to convince herself. She shifted her legs toward the side of the bed, huffing with pain.

The eerie sense of calm was sticking with me; probably not a good sign, but at least it provided some emotional distance. A lot of things were clicking in my mind; mainly, an understanding of why Grace would engage in such a dangerous "hobby." Serial killers usually exhibited signs in childhood; had she witnessed those?

Grace eased one leg over the side of the bed, then gasped. I sighed. "Give it up, you're not going anywhere. Chill before you pop a stitch."

"We're not safe here."

"He could've killed us back at the motel, right?" I swallowed hard, imagining that scenario. How hard would it have been for him to overpower three unarmed women in a deserted parking lot? But he hadn't done that, which meant something else was going on. "But he didn't, so I figure we've got a little time. Right?"

"Possibly," Grace acknowledged after a beat.

"Fantastic. Now, lie the fuck back down."

Grace glared at me but carefully eased back against the pillows.

"Now," I said. "Answer our questions—all of them—or I'll smother you with a pillow. I've heard this is a great place for desert burials."

"I know the perfect spot," Dot chimed in.

"Is that supposed to scare me?" Grace snorted. "Please."

I eyed her, almost impressed with how blasé she seemed. "I get that you saved me, and for some bizarre reason that makes me a target." I glanced at Dot. "But Marcella and Dot should be fine, right?"

"Honestly, I don't know." Grace sounded tired. "Possibly. His behavior has been increasingly erratic lately."

"'Erratic'? You mean, aside from killing people?"

Grace shrugged. "I used to be better at predicting what Gunnar would do. But this?" She waved a hand toward her torso. "It's . . . unusual."

Gunnar, I thought. Apparently her folks were really into *G* names. "So he's escalating."

"Evidently," she said dryly.

"And this is the first time he's tried to kill you?"

"Gunnar would never kill me."

"Well, according to the doctor, he came close."

"He said you almost bled out," Dot chimed in.

Grace frowned. "I doubt that. Gunnar would've been watching to make sure I survived."

Her certainty was unnerving, and I definitely didn't like the way she said her brother's name. There was an undercurrent of affection there, which made me wonder exactly what their relationship was.

Looking shaky, Dot sat back down. "I can't believe this is happening."

Maybe I was in shock, too, because even this revelation didn't have much of an impact. I felt oddly distant, like I was participating in the conversation from a remove. I ran a hand over my head, forgetting that my entire scalp was a contour map of pain. Wincing, I mulled over everything she'd said. "So if we just stay away from you, he'll leave us alone?"

"Not anymore." Grace shook her head. "Once he's marked you, that's it." Seemingly as an afterthought, she added, "Sorry."

"'Sorry'?" I had to resist the urge to throttle her. "Well, fuck that." I turned to Dot. "We can handle this. We'll call the cops, maybe they'll put us in protective custody or something."

"Someone in private security owes me a favor," Dot said. "I can call him—"

"You really don't get it," Grace said. "All those other assholes I caught don't even come close to Gunnar. No one can protect you."

Again, a hint of something that sounded suspiciously like pride in her voice. "So what do we do?"

"'We'?" Grace cocked an eyebrow.

"Hell yeah, we. I don't plan on dying because your brother thinks we're friends."

"Me either," Dot said.

Grace was silent for a minute, staring up at the ceiling. Then she said, "I suppose I do owe you a debt."

"You think?" I said. "Plus you might've noticed that you're not exactly mobile right now."

She scowled. "I can manage."

"Desert. Grave," I said, leaning in.

"I really don't care for you."

"You're not my favorite person either. But I won't let anything happen to Dot or Marcella. And neither will you." She didn't answer. I leaned over and hissed, "This is the part where you agree to act like a goddamn human being."

"Fine." Grace sighed heavily. "I will come up with a plan."

"Fabulous." I clapped my hands together, enjoying her flinch. "So what next?"

She made a face. "Obviously we need to get the fuck out of here. Discreetly."

"I think I can help with that," Dot said slowly.

OUT OF THE PAST

The boy and girl sat on a branch, peering through leaves at the dog.

"Bet it finds another one," Gunnar said through a mouthful of licorice. He was tall for a ten-year-old—they both were. Over the summer they'd become all legs, coltish and wobbly. They took after Mother with their golden hair and ice-blue eyes. Not Father, who was on the short side, slight and dark. The main difference between the twins—at least externally—was Grace's long hair.

"Isn't that where we put Poppy?" Grace asked with concern, leaning forward carefully. The tree was technically the neighbor's, although the branch they sat on dipped into their backyard. They'd climbed it ever since they could remember, sneaking through a hole in the fence behind their shed. The branches started low, which made the bottom ten feet easy climbing. As the years went on, they become adept at scaling to greater heights. They now sat nearly thirty feet above ground, straddling a thick branch, a plastic tub of Red Vines balanced between them.

"Yeah." Gunnar grinned wolfishly at her, his teeth stained red by the candy. "I bet there are only bones left."

She scowled at him. "Shut up."

"You shut up."

A bark from below caught their attention. They watched as the dog strained at its leash, sniffing a spot on the ground. The officer holding him waved, and one of the hazmat-suit people lumbered across the yard toward him.

"It's just Poppy," Grace said angrily, fighting back tears. "I wish they'd leave her alone."

"Maybe not." Her brother bit into another Red Vine. They watched as the man started digging, cutting through the sparse grass of their backyard. "Maybe he put one in there with her."

Grace watched him warily. Gunnar's eyes were bright, and dots of color flushed his cheeks. He was four minutes older than her, which shouldn't have made a difference but for some reason did. She always followed his lead, whether that meant stealing a tub of candy or climbing a tree to watch police tear up their backyard. He was the one who invented all of their games, including his favorite (and her least), Catch Me. It was a mix of hide-and-go-seek, truth or dare, and tag—and she always lost.

He'd also come up with the language they used to communicate, which they spoke now even though no one could overhear. "Father wouldn't," she said stubbornly.

Gunnar just shrugged. "She was just a stupid dog."

Grace didn't answer. Poppy had died young, and suddenly; they'd only had her a few weeks. They'd found her lying on her side in the backyard, wheezing and panting. The worst part had been the desperation and fear in her eyes. Grace had thrown up. Gunnar bent in closer to watch.

That was when they were seven. Even then, Grace knew better than to ask for another dog.

Gunnar nudged her, grinning as he bit into another Red Vine. The smell was making Grace nauseated. "Ten bucks they find one in there."

"You're disgusting," Grace muttered, scooting back until she was pressed against the tree trunk. She wanted to climb down, but there was nowhere else to go. There were people all over their house, and Grace didn't have any friends aside from Gunnar.

The dog sniffed, then barked excitedly at the newly overturned dirt. Two hazmat suits peeled off from the dozen milling around other holes and trundled over. There were now nine craters pocking their backyard, like the remnants of a detonated minefield. It made Grace think of the moon. She'd spent hours lying on that lawn staring up at the sky. She and Gunnar had picnics, caught fireflies, and camped out on warm summer nights. And all that time, this was what lurked beneath them. The thought made her shudder.

At least she hadn't known. Gunnar's window faced the backyard. Had he ever watched Father dig one of these holes? Had he seen what was buried there? Watching him now, she wondered.

His entire attention was fixed on the new hole, where one hazmat suit took pictures while another laid a tarp beside it.

"It'll be pretty funny if they count Poppy," Gunnar said.

"No it won't. We should get back to Mother." Grace tossed her half-eaten licorice over to the neighbor's side of the fence. Not that Mother had probably even noticed they were gone. She'd taken something to "calm her nerves," and consequently was still asleep at her friend Nancy's house even though it was midafternoon. Although *friend* was a strong word; the only thing they had in common was a shared loathing of other neighbors. Maybe that was enough for friendship when you were a grown-up.

Since the day before Grace and Gunnar had been ensconced in Nancy's downstairs rec room, which was really a basement with a washer/dryer at one end and a pull-out couch at the other. The bed creaked and smelled faintly of mold. They'd spent last night lying there not speaking. She was pretty sure she hadn't slept at all.

"I'm not going back there," Gunnar declared now.

Grace snorted. "We have to."

"Who's gonna make me?" Gunnar said.

"There's nowhere else to go."

Her brother didn't have any friends either. He claimed to prefer it that way. "We don't need anyone else," he'd say sometimes, with a ferocity that flattered and frightened Grace.

"Don't you get it? We can go anywhere," he said, kicking his heels against the lower branch.

"You're being ridiculous," Grace said, switching to English as she turned away. The police dog was nosing the ground intensely again, this time in front of the rosebushes Father had planted last summer. Their mother had always disparaged his "gardening fetish." Months would pass when the grass would go to seed, and then Father would show a sudden interest in cultivating tulip bulbs along the rear fence, or rosemary bushes under the kitchen window. After a few weeks of watering the plants, he'd abruptly lose interest. As a result, most of their yard was a wild tangle of weeds and half-dead plants. Occasionally Mother muttered about getting a gardener, but nothing ever came of it. Father had always said it was a waste of money.

Which made sense now.

"Do you think they'll let us get the rest of our stuff?" Grace asked, watching as they started digging away at a tenth spot. She'd been sitting here for hours, and the branch was becoming increasingly uncomfortable, the bark rough through the thin fabric of her khaki shorts. As the intruders uprooted the only rosebush that kept producing flowers, her eyes welled up. It felt like they were stripping her bare. She wanted to be anywhere else. Even Nancy's gross basement.

It hadn't even been a full day since their life imploded. Right before dinner Father had been marched out in handcuffs by grim-faced men in navy windbreakers. He was still wearing work clothes: light gray suit pants and a stiffly starched white shirt, his tie and jacket already carefully hung in the upstairs closet. Mother just stood there silently, a hand covering her mouth like she was trying to hold words in. Grace and Gunnar hadn't even been allowed to go to their rooms alone; two FBI agents walked them upstairs and watched as they stuffed a change of clothes and their toothbrushes into backpacks. Even though she hadn't slept with it in years, Grace grabbed her stuffed elephant.

"They have to let us back in. It's still our home," Gunnar said.

Grace turned that over in her mind. Would she still want to live here? Would Mother? Probably not. Gunnar wouldn't care—nothing ever seemed to bother him, really.

Father is never coming back, she realized, watching them carefully lift a large, dirt-covered trash bag out of the closest hole. Apparently it was heavy, because they struggled with it.

"That's not Poppy," Gunnar noted.

Grace couldn't speak. It had suddenly dawned on her that their lives would never be the same again. They couldn't go back to school—things had been bad enough before, when they were just the weird twins. But now it would be so much worse.

Maybe Gunnar was right, and they should leave. There were only two more weeks of summer vacation; they'd have to figure something out before school began. She racked her brain; other than Nancy, they didn't really have family or friends. It had always been just the four of them. But she had a dim memory of a large house inhabited by a sharp-beaked woman who smelled like dead flowers.

"We'll go live with Grandmother in Boston," Grace said, looking to him for approval.

Gunnar nodded slowly. "Boston. Could be cool. Definitely better than here."

"Anywhere is better than here," Grace said fiercely.

She must have spoken too loudly, because one of the hazmat suits looked up and spotted them. Pointing, he yelled, "Hey, kids! Get down from there!"

"Busted." Gunnar grinned. He flipped the guy off, then turned and deftly shimmied down the trunk, yelling, "Catch me, Grace!"

Grace followed, scrambling from limb to limb. Her brother was already halfway to the street by the time she caught up.

CHAPTER ELEVEN

YOU CAN'T ESCAPE

A casual observer might have found it odd when a uniform delivery truck backed up to the service entrance of a wig supply store. Odder still that five minutes after it departed, a series of other delivery trucks followed: catering and florist vans, office supplies, even a cable truck.

Had that same puzzled observer attempted to follow even one of those vehicles, they would have been led on a meandering tour of the Strip, forced to wait outside the guarded service garages of various hotel/casinos as the vehicle was waved inside. Each stop lasted only minutes before the truck glided back out, headed to the next destination.

No one else gave the trucks a second glance—after all, they were part and parcel of life in Las Vegas, the nickel beneath the gold plating, the cogs that kept everything spinning as smoothly as a roulette wheel. Effectively invisible to the revelers stumbling past en route to their next gambling/booze/sex/drug fix, which was precisely as intended.

Only one of those locations mattered, however: the Strat. The hotel was a slim needle that jutted out of the desert, topped by a SkyPod with four thrill rides. Though it towered above the city, the hotel was on precarious footing, becoming less desirable with every glistening new addition to the Strip.

Still, it was a major step up from the Getaway.

Dot, Marcella, Grace, and I rode there in a refrigerated food delivery truck, shivering under a stack of blankets. "No one would follow a reefer truck," Dot had declared as we slid Grace in on a makeshift stretcher.

I was less certain but didn't say anything. At least it wasn't a florist delivery van. But despite the blankets, by the time we arrived at the Strat, I was pretty sure I was going to lose a couple of toes to hypothermia. Even Dot was uncharacteristically quiet.

Grace actually fell asleep. I was tempted to kick the stretcher to wake her up—she had gotten us into this mess, the least she could do was suffer through the ride with us. But I managed to restrain myself. Dr. Aboud had dosed her with extra morphine, so it wasn't entirely her fault.

The door finally slid open, revealing a docking bay. Our driver was a burly, middle-aged man in coveralls. Dot gave him a big hug after he helped her down and said, "Thanks, Stan. You're a prince."

Stan nodded, looking embarrassed. "Gotta be at the Mirage in twenty, so better make this quick."

I hopped down after her. The garage was blessedly hot; it was like stepping from a fridge into an oven. I rubbed my arms and tried to stamp feeling back into my feet. Marcella sauntered over to a pillar. Leaning against it, she pulled out her vape pen. She and Dot were still in their bloody clothing. Thank God the docking bay was empty, because we were definitely a strange group.

I tapped Grace's foot to wake her. "Can you get out on your own?"

Grace tilted her head up. Grimacing, she eased herself off the stretcher to the lip of the truck. Spotting the waiting wheelchair, she declared, "I'm not using that."

"Then you can crawl to your room," I snapped. I desperately wanted a warm shower and a hot meal. Dr. Aboud had scrounged up stale tortilla chips, but they hadn't made a dent in my hunger.

I really hoped that Grace's crazy brother didn't go after him, too. She'd said it was unlikely, but who knew; it felt like I infected everyone I came in contact with, however briefly. *Or more accurately, she does*, I thought, glaring at Grace, who was grumbling as Stan eased her into the wheelchair. Erring on the safe side, Dr. Aboud had agreed to head out of town for a few days. Avoiding Marcella's eyes, he'd mumbled something about making it a belated anniversary trip for his wife.

Which just left Dot and Marcella. Thanks to Grace's general vagueness regarding how much danger they might be in, we'd decided they should take precautions.

"You're sure you'll be safe with Jim?" I asked Dot for the hundredth time.

"Don't you worry, hon. Jim's a Marine. He served two tours and has a black belt."

"Of course he does," I said. "He's the perfect man."

Dot managed a laugh. "I'll tell him you said that, he'll be tickled." She abruptly threw her arms around me and squeezed so hard I practically choked. "You take care. We'll figure something out, you'll see."

"Sure," I gasped.

Releasing me, she turned to Marcella, who was already waving her free hand. "Uh-uh. I stink."

"Oh, shut up," Dot said, grabbing her anyway.

"Service elevator is that way," said Stan, nodding to the right. "Candy's waiting with your room keys."

"Thanks."

Dot climbed back into the truck and wrapped a blanket around her shoulders again. As she waved, Stan rolled the door shut and returned to the driver's seat. The three of us watched the truck trundle away, destined for a few more stops before dropping Dot at the Golden Nugget, where Jim was waiting. I said a silent prayer for her safety, even though I generally didn't believe in that sort of thing.

The next ten minutes were a blur. The highly efficient Candy ushered us into the service elevator and snuck us into three adjoining rooms on the eighth floor.

"I can do it," Grace snapped as I tried to wheel her into the first room.

"Suit yourself," I said, letting go of the handles. The chair rolled forward and smacked the doorframe. Wincing, Grace wheeled in and let the door slam behind her. I turned in time to see Marcella's door shut, too. She'd scoffed at going into hiding until she realized it came with a temporary housing upgrade.

"If you need anything, just call down and ask for me," Candy said, handing me a key card. "I can comp up to fifty bucks in room service for each of you. But leave the minibar alone, I can't cover that."

"Got it," I said.

"I'll see what I can do about clothes, too," Candy said, eyeing my dress.

She hurried back down the hall as I scanned the key card. Stepping inside, I gasped, "Holy crap!"

The room was easily three times the size of my Getaway motel room. Hell, it was twice the size of my old apartment. Floor-to-ceiling windows lined one wall, offering a sprawling view of the Strip. I could see all the way out to the low hills in the distance.

On my left, a king-sized bed occupied one side of the room. To the right was a full sitting area, complete with a couch and two armchairs. A massive TV was tucked in the wall above a gas fireplace. Straight ahead of me, two chairs flanked a round café table.

Awestruck, I went to the windows. From up here, Vegas looked like a completely different place. Clean, even. And quiet, thanks to the double-paned glass.

It was honestly one of the nicest rooms I'd ever seen, and definitely cost a lot more than what I'd been paying. Self-consciously, I tugged at my soiled dress. Dot must've pulled some serious strings to arrange this.

Despite the circumstances (or maybe because of them), I suddenly felt giddy. No worries about touching the comforter here. Momentarily forgetting my headache, I charged across the room and vaulted onto the bed, sprawling my arms and legs out wide.

The bathroom was equally impressive. There was a giant white bathtub, double sinks, and a walk-in shower with four nozzles. I stripped off my dress and set the water to scalding, then spent an inordinately long time scrubbing every inch of my body. I even carefully washed my scalp. (Dr. Aboud said to keep my stitches dry, but they were covered with a waterproof Band-Aid, and honestly, it was worth the risk.) When I finally felt clean, I cocooned myself in the thick white robe and terry-cloth slippers provided by the hotel. If this was how rich people vacationed, I was all for it.

I flipped through the room service menu, mentally calculating what combination of food offered my budget the most bang for the buck. After ordering, I plopped down on the couch and flicked on the TV to distract myself while I waited.

Only five minutes had passed when there was a knock at the door. I frowned; the food couldn't possibly be ready yet.

It had to be someone else.

I'd used the bolt and metal swing bar; was that enough to keep someone out?

Conversely, only a truly polite serial killer would bother knocking, right?

Heart in my throat, I tiptoed over to the door and squinted through the peephole. Marcella stood there in a matching robe and slippers. Relieved, I threw the bolts and opened the door. "Hey."

"Can I come in?" Marcella asked, sounding uncharacteristically shy. Her curls were wet, face scrubbed clean.

"Yeah, sure." I stepped aside and she sidled past me.

"Mine's the same," she said, taking it in. "Just opposite. I mean, my bed's right on the other side of the wall from yours."

"Oh," I said, wondering what I was supposed to make of that information. Picturing her just a few feet away would certainly be distracting later when I tried to sleep.

Marcella seemed as out of place in the room as I felt. I motioned to the couch and she sat down gingerly, as if it were mined with a pressure sensor.

"So . . . you okay?" I asked.

She grinned at me. "You kidding? I've never stayed somewhere this nice in my entire life."

"Me either." I perched on the other end of the couch. "Sorry it's only for a couple nights."

Marcella shrugged. "Dot's gonna ask Jessie if I can crash at the Mayhem after they kick us out. Y'know, just in case."

"Yeah, she said." I picked up one of the sofa pillows and wrapped my arms around it. "Listen, I just wanted to say that I'm really sorry. For, y'know, getting you into all this."

"No big deal," Marcella said, tracing the paisley pattern on the couch with one finger. "You figured out who killed Lori. That's more than the cops ever did."

"Well, not exactly," I said. "That was courtesy of serial killer hunter Grace, who apparently knew all along."

"Yeah." Marcella eyed me. "What's her deal anyway?"

"Honestly? I couldn't even begin to guess." I shook my head, then winced.

Noticing, she asked, "How's your head?"

"Better," I said, although it still felt like someone was rapping the inside with a mallet. Gravely, I added, "This was actually all part of my elaborate plan to get a nicer hotel room. So, mission accomplished."

Marcella laughed. "Your plan, huh?"

"Oh, absolutely."

"You make any other plans?" Marcella asked, leaning forward on her elbows. "Just so I can be ready, y'know?"

"I ordered food," I said tentatively. "I mean, unless you already ate."

Marcella cocked her head to the side. "Depends on what you got."

"A little bit of everything." On cue, there was another knock at the door. "Hang on."

Five minutes later we'd made a serious dent in the room service spread. I dipped another mini egg roll in sauce and tucked it in my mouth, closing my eyes in pleasure. "Oh my God. It feels like I haven't eaten in days."

Marcella's mouth was too full to answer, which cracked me up. She grinned around her egg roll. The TV was showing the hotel's promotional video on a loop. She drained her water and nodded to the screen. "You know, when I first moved here, I thought I'd end up in one of those shows."

I eyed the row of beaming showgirls dressed in pasties, a ridiculous amount of plumage, and not much else. "Really?"

"Yeah, really." Marcella threw me a sharp look. "Why?"

"I didn't know you were a dancer."

"I was on the dance squad in high school," Marcella said defensively. "Wasn't bad, either. Too short to be a showgirl, but figured maybe a magician's assistant or something like that."

"Huh." I was having an extremely hard time picturing Marcella smiling while a guy pulled quarters out of her ear. "So what happened?"

"The usual. Waited tables and auditioned. Never got the part. Got older. Started getting high. Got fired. And then . . ." She gestured expansively. "I became a street ho."

"Don't say that," I said, shifting uncomfortably.

"Why not?" Marcella nudged me with her foot. "I'm not ashamed of it. Well, not usually." She narrowed her eyes. "Are you?"

"No," I said, squirming. "I just don't think of you that way."

"Really," she scoffed. "So how do you think of me?"

"I don't know. You're smart. And funny. And hot," I said, flushing.

Marcella cocked an eyebrow. "Hot, huh?"

"Definitely." Even without makeup her eyes were huge and luminous. Her hair had dried into a halo around her face. The robe had fallen open slightly, showing more than just cleavage.

Following my eyes, she smirked and pushed back her plate. Then she got up and sashayed to the closet, throwing open the doors with dramatic flair. "For my next trick," she announced in a deep voice, "I will magically open . . . the minibar!"

"What? No. Candy said—"

"Fuck Candy. What's she gonna do?" Marcella hunkered down and pulled out a handful of tiny bottles. She brought them back and carefully lined them up in front of me. "Vodka, whiskey, or tequila?"

"I probably shouldn't drink. I mean, I still have a concussion, and the doc gave me meds—"

"Amber." Marcella bent and put her hands on my knees, which made her robe gape open. I valiantly tried not to look. "There's a fucking serial killer after you. Let's have a goddamn drink."

"You know what? You're right." I grabbed a bottle of tequila, and she took the whiskey. We clinked, and then I downed mine in a single gulp. She did the same, then tossed the bottle over her shoulder. It landed on the couch as she said, "Ta-da!"

Several bottles later, we'd somehow made our way to the bed. I lay on my back, staring up at the ceiling. Marcella was propped against the padded headboard, sipping gin. Watching her, I slurred, "You would've been an awesome magician's assistant."

"Right?" she agreed.

"I think you could've been a showgirl, too."

"Yeah?"

"Oh yeah. I mean, your body is banging."

Marcella laughed. "You're drunk."

I waved a tiny bottle in a giant circle. "True. And you know what?"

"What?"

"Fuck serial killers." Marcella snorted with laughter. I sat up and said earnestly, "No, I mean it. What the fuck is wrong with these guys? Who wakes up one morning and is like, 'Hey, you know what? I think I'll put on a leather apron, kidnap a girl, shave off all her hair, paint her blue, then kill her.'"

Marcella put a hand to her mouth and her eyes widened. "Oh my God, is that what happened to your hair?"

I touched my head, which oddly didn't hurt anymore. "Yeah. But joke's on him because *zzzt.*" I mimicked getting shocked by a cattle prod, which sent Marcella into hysterics. She tossed me another bottle. "Fuck serial killers."

"Yeah! Fuck 'em." We clinked again. I tipped the bottle into my mouth, only to discover it was empty. "Crap."

Marcella frowned and shook hers upside down. "Did we drink them all?"

I looked at the fallen soldiers littering the room. "Yup. Candy is gonna kill us."

"She's gonna have to get in line!" Marcella chortled. Which shouldn't have been funny, really, but we roared with laughter.

There was a loud banging on the far wall, and Grace's muffled voice said, "Will you shut the fuck up? I'm trying to sleep!"

Marcella and I goggled at each other, and then we collapsed in giggles again. I fell back on the bed. My stomach hurt from laughing (and too many egg rolls). "Shit. I ate too much."

"Me too." Marcella rolled over to face me, propping her head on her hand.

Her robe was basically just a suggestion at this point, both breasts fully exposed. My throat went dry. "I should probably drink some water."

"Mm," she agreed. She rolled to grab a bottle from the nightstand, then shifted back until she was inches away. "So how badly does your head hurt?"

"Um, not too badly, I guess." I took the water from her and swigged, even though thirst was no longer at the top of my mind.

"Did you hurt anything else?"

"Well, I scraped my knees," I said, swallowing hard. "And my left elbow—"

"Poor baby. How about this?" she asked, sliding her hand inside my robe. She trailed the backs of her fingers along my stomach, making my skin tingle.

"That feels okay," I said. Other things were starting to feel pretty good, too. "I think—"

Marcella interrupted by pressing her lips to mine. She tasted sweet, making me self-conscious of my own breath. But when I tried to pull back she kissed me more forcefully, prodding my lips open with her tongue. Putting her hand behind my head, she gently drew my ear to her mouth, nibbled on it, and said, "Let's see what else can feel better."

We lay side by side facing each other. I hadn't closed the blinds, so the wall of windows glowed with reflected neon light. The dull throb in my head had started up again, but I didn't care. I felt weightless. Relaxed. Marcella had released a tension I hadn't even known I was carrying.

"That was—"

"Awesome. Yeah, I know." Marcella ran a finger down my side, raising a line of goose bumps. "I'm a pro, remember?"

She said it lightly, but I detected sadness in her voice. "What are you thinking about?"

"Nothing."

"Yeah?" I cupped her chin with my hand, forcing her to meet my eyes. Gently, I asked, "Is it Lori?"

"What? No." She shook her head vigorously.

"Because I'd totally get it if you felt weird. I mean, I don't know if you've been with anyone else since—"

"Seriously? I've been with dozens." She sounded bemused.

"Right, but not like this."

"Like what?"

"Like, just for fun," I said awkwardly. I was getting better at reading her and could see that prickly side rearing up again.

A long beat passed. Then she said more quietly, "We weren't like that. Me and Lori. I mean, I loved her, but we were more like really good friends who fucked sometimes, you know?"

"Sure," I said, although I didn't. I hadn't been good friends with any of my sex partners, to be honest. Not that I'd ever given them much of a chance.

"I just can't stop thinking about how she must've felt. I mean, she was all alone." Marcella raised her eyes to meet mine. "What was it like? I mean, for you?"

"Um . . ." I shifted uncomfortably. It felt like bringing up memories from that night would taint everything, but the need in her voice was clear. "Yeah, I felt really alone. I think the worst part, though, was realizing that no one would miss me." I took her hand. "Lori knew you would. That probably helped."

"Yeah?"

"Yeah."

I stroked her fingers. The psychology major in me knew this was just a response to our shared trauma. We were both lonely, scared, and in need of comfort, like two people clinging to a life raft. Still, it felt like more. *Stop it*, I told myself.

Maybe Marcella was thinking the same thing, because she abruptly drew her hand back. "I'm wiped."

"Me too. We should get some sleep." I found the water bottle at the base of the bed where we'd kicked it and gulped some, then handed it to her. Between us, we drained it. I set it on the nightstand and said, "Well, good night."

"Night."

I turned away from her and closed my eyes. I could hear her breathing behind me. It sounded like she was still awake, too. In the dark, her voice was small as she asked, "What's gonna happen?"

"I don't know," I said. "I guess we'll figure it out tomorrow."

"Yeah." So low that I barely heard her, she added, "Didn't think I'd live this long anyway."

I lay there for a long time, staring into the dark. What she'd said, and the way she'd said it, broke my heart. I finally flipped over. Marcella was out cold, lips slightly parted, hair spread like a fan across the pillow.

Fuck it, I thought, climbing out of bed and groping for my robe.

I had to knock increasingly louder until Grace finally opened her door. She gazed at me blearily, leaning heavily against the jamb. Instead of a robe, she had on actual pajamas. *Where the fuck did she get those?*

"We need to talk," I said.

"No."

"Yes," I insisted, pushing past her. The bedside lamp was on. Her room was the same as mine, although considerably neater. Even her room service tray was tidily stacked, and the wheelchair was backed against the wall by the bathroom. I sat in one of the armchairs and crossed my arms over my chest.

"Five minutes," Grace said. "And I'm fucking lying down for this." She eased herself onto the couch, clearly in terrible pain.

I wanted to help, but she'd probably bite my head off again if I tried. Once she was settled, I said, "This is all your fault."

"Yes, you've mentioned that," Grace said. "Can I go back to bed now?"

"I mean it," I said. "The only reason Dot and Marcella might be on your brother's radar is because you showed up at the motel."

"That wasn't exactly my choice."

"Doesn't matter."

We glared at each other.

"Are you done?" she asked.

"Nope. I wanted to make sure you aren't going to bail on us."

Her eyes shifted toward the wheelchair. *That bitch*, I thought. She *had* been planning to ditch us. "I swear, if you're not here in the morning I'll go to the cops and tell them everything. About you, your brother, Beau—all of it."

"They won't believe you," she said.

"Maybe not, but I've got witnesses."

At that, her frown deepened. "That would be a mistake. If Gunnar isn't pursuing them now, that would certainly convince him to."

"But he might be after them anyway."

"As I said, I have no idea. Possibly." She sighed deeply. "Go back to bed. We can talk about this in the morning."

"We're talking now," I said, remembering the fear in Dot's eyes as the truck door slid down, and the resignation in Marcella's. "Because here's what's going to happen. I'm guessing you stay somewhere safe when you're not stalking your brother?"

"Stalking?" She raised an eyebrow. Off my look, she reluctantly said, "Yes."

"Great. You and me are going there together. We'll stay until you're better."

"I'm not bringing you with me," she snorted.

"Yes, you are. Because I'm going to help you catch your brother."

"Really." Grace rolled her eyes. "You."

"Yes, me."

"I've been trying for years," Grace said disdainfully.

"Right, but you've been doing it alone. And now you've got me."

"And you've proven *so* useful thus far."

I leaned in close and lowered my voice. "I'm guessing you dug into my past?"

"Yes, I did," she said. "Oddly, there wasn't much there. Except for your untimely demise in a car crash five years ago."

I allowed myself a moment of self-satisfaction; it clearly bothered her that she hadn't been able to find out more about the real me. "Well, you should know that I can be pretty damn useful."

She eyed me. "I doubt any of the skills you possess are relevant."

"You're not really in a position to argue. Besides, what've you got to lose?"

"My privacy?" Motioning to her side, she said, "This will take weeks to heal."

"Yup."

"I don't need a nurse."

"You sure about that?" I leaned toward her again. "How, exactly, are you getting home? You can't even sit up."

She opened her mouth, then closed it again.

Smugly, I said, "So here's the plan. Dot will get us out of Vegas— even you have to admit that today was pretty damn impressive."

Grace grudgingly inclined her head.

"And she and Marcella will lay low while we figure this out."

Grace rubbed her temples with her thumbs. "This is insane."

"Yeah, well, like I said. You don't have a choice. Oh, and I need some cash for the minibar."

Everything came together faster than expected. Marcella was right; Dot was basically the queen of Las Vegas. Apparently everyone in town owed her a favor, or liked her enough to help for free. By midafternoon, it was all settled. While Dot crashed with Jim, Jessie would manage the Getaway for her (although I suspected she might banish poor BJ there). As planned, Marcella would stay at the Mayhem. And Dot promised to have found a safe, untraceable way out of town for Grace and me. "Don't you worry, hon," she'd said on the burner phone Candy had dropped off (along with clothes, although me and Marcella didn't bother wearing them). "I got it all squared away."

She refused to say anything else, insisting on keeping it a surprise. I would've been more adamant about the details, but Marcella was climbing up my leg at the time. Which was kind of the theme of our day. We watched TV. Ate Marcella's fifty bucks' worth of food. And had so much sex I lost count.

It had been a long time since I'd been with anyone—I'd practically become a nun since starting college.

But it was like Marcella reached inside me and threw a switch. Every touch, every kiss, every sensation was heightened. The intensity of it was almost painful. I couldn't get enough of the curve of her breasts, the softness of the skin on the inside of her thighs, the way she threw her head back and moaned when I found just the right rhythm. In my experience, the first few times with someone were all wrong moves and awkwardness; I could never get out of my own head, wondering, *Is this okay? Does she really love this, or is she just pretending?*

But somehow, I could sense what Marcella wanted. It was amazing and unsettling. I completely lost track of time, barely even noticing when the sun set and cast the entire room in a pink glow.

Late that night, there was one moment when we were kissing, and Marcella pulled back and looked in my eyes. The outside lights illuminated her face, and it was as if I was seeing right into the heart of her.

I'd never felt that before. Honestly, I wasn't sure I wanted to feel it again. It was too much for a person to contain, too much emotion, too much everything.

Afterward, Marcella crashed out hard, one leg flung over mine. I should've been exhausted, but my pulse was racing and my skin still buzzed. Plus, I had a psychopath after me, so, you know—lots to consider.

But in that moment, I was mainly freaked out by my emotions.

As the first rays of dawn tinted the room mauve, I got dressed as quietly as possible and snuck out.

Terrible, I know. I didn't even leave a note.

I paused at the door, taking in Marcella's still form on the bed. I mouthed *I'm sorry* before easing it shut behind me, wincing at the loudness of the latch clicking into place.

I rapped lightly on Grace's door. When no one answered I had a moment of panic, convinced that she'd abandoned us after all.

But a minute later Grace wrestled it open. She was sitting in the wheelchair fully dressed in jeans and a white T-shirt. Taking in my outfit, she said, "Christ, our clothes even match."

"Keep your voice down," I hissed.

She threw a glance at my room, then smirked. Wheeling down the hallway toward the elevator, she said, "Guess I'm not the only bitch in town."

As we took the service elevator down to the sub-basement, I silently prayed that a lifetime of devouring noir plotlines had adequately prepared Dot for today.

Grace grudgingly let me push her through the bowels of the hotel, down dark hallways that only the housekeeping and maintenance staff ever saw. We waited in the laundry room for a full hour. The air was hot and humid, and the constant rumble of a dozen machines made quiet conversation impossible. Not that either of us was up for a chat.

"Well, this is taking fucking forever," Grace finally grumbled. "I'm starving."

"Shut up," I said, even though my stomach was complaining, too. *There's probably a buffet upstairs*, I thought longingly. *With an omelet station, and waffles, and—*

The door flew open. Instead of another housekeeper who eyed us questioningly, Jessie swept in wearing a flowing caftan, an honest-to-God turban, and huge sunglasses. She towered above us looking like a refugee from one of Dot's films.

"What the actual fuck," Grace mumbled under her breath.

"My thoughts exactly." Jessie tossed a huge canvas tote toward us. "Change into these."

I pulled out what seemed like an endless length of fabric. "Seriously?"

Grace was equally nonplussed. "If I'm getting carted out in a truck again, why the fuck do I need to change?"

"Because this time," Jessie said with a flourish, "we're going out the front."

T his is ridiculous," Grace mumbled.

"I don't know. I think it's kind of genius," I said, trying but failing to repress a grin as I pushed her down the hallway. "It's a good look on you, too."

"Shut up, the pair of you," Jessie hissed. "This only works if you act the part. So try to seem less . . . young." She paused in front of the double doors that led to the casino. "Now, remember. Keep your heads down until we get to the shuttle bus."

Accordingly, I hunched my back. I was wearing a caftan in alarming shades of neon, a floppy sunhat that had seen better days, and an enormous pair of cheap sunglasses that basically covered the top half of my face. The look was completed with garish lipstick and circles of rouge on my cheeks.

Under protest, Grace was wearing a polyester pantsuit in the ugliest shade of brown I'd ever seen, a white wig, and sunglasses that made mine seem dainty in comparison. She'd refused makeup, but the grim set of her lips aged her anyway.

Jessie pushed open the doors and we entered the main floor of the casino. Even at this early hour, half the slot machines were occupied by people who either started early or had never left. The craps, roulette, and blackjack tables were at about a quarter capacity.

Scanning the room, I saw that Dot had, once again, come up with the perfect plan. Most of the crowd was elderly, and we blended right in.

Still, it was hard not to feel like hidden eyes were observing us.

"This'll never work," Grace muttered. Still, she'd caved forward in the wheelchair, making it look like she had a dowager's hump. Her hands were tucked under a ratty lap blanket.

If I hadn't known better, I would've sworn she was eighty years old. I shuffled forward slowly, acting as if the wheelchair was taking a great deal of effort to push.

"Stop your yammering, Mom," Jessie chided loudly. I had to bite my cheek to keep from cracking up.

We made our way across the casino at an excruciatingly slow pace. Other senior citizens shambled around us, cups of coins gripped in liver-spotted hands. It was like being an extra in a really depressing zombie flick. The wheelchair creaked as I maneuvered it forward. It actually wasn't the easiest thing to push across a carpeted floor; a trickle of sweat slipped from under my hat and slid down my face.

"Would you like some help?" someone asked brightly at my elbow.

I stiffened. *Oh God, is it him? Of course, anyone with sense would see through these shabby disguises.*

Slowly, I turned to find a guy my age. He was wearing a huge, fake grin and a Strat uniform with the name tag *BRAD*.

"We're fine," Jessie snapped, swinging her purse to shoo him away.

Brad frowned at her. "Sorry, ma'am, just trying to help—"

"Don't give him any money," Grace croaked. "He'll just spend it on drugs."

At that, Brad looked affronted. "Apologies for disturbing you, ladies. The Strat likes to offer the highest level of—"

"Where's the shuttle?" Jessie barked at him.

"Um, right out front," he said. "At the curb."

"Going to Harrah's," Grace mumbled. "Better luck there."

"Well, I hope you have a lovely day," Brad said stiffly before turning on his heel and heading back to the help desk.

As soon as he was out of earshot, I said under my breath, "That wasn't him, was it?"

Grace scoffed. "If it was, you'd already be dead."

"Thanks, sunshine."

"Shut your traps, both of you," Jessie said without moving her lips. We continued to inch forward. It seemed as if the door was getting farther and farther away, but we eventually emerged at a porte cochere.

I was glad for the sunglasses; the desert sun was already glaring and hot. The rayon tent I was wearing didn't help; I could feel the stage makeup melting. Thankfully, it only took a few minutes for the courtesy shuttle to arrive. It lowered a ramp for the wheelchair, and the driver descended to help us on.

The shuttle bus was empty. Jessie patted the driver on the shoulder as we pulled away from the curb and said, "Thanks again for this, Chuck."

"No problem," Chuck said. "Don't get many folks at this hour anyway."

Yet another part of Dot's plan. I marveled again at her ingenuity. "Where are we going?" I asked, moving up to sit behind Jessie. Grace was still slumped forward in the wheelchair; she might actually have fallen asleep.

"You'll see," she said.

"I'm really not a big fan of surprises anymore," I said. "Besides, won't it seem suspicious if we don't go to the other casinos?"

"Nah, my shift is over anyway," Chuck said reassuringly. "We're pretty much headed to my last stop."

Despite what he said, the paranoia was hard to shake. I scanned the few other cars on the road, wondering if one of them was following us. To distract myself, I asked Jessie, "So how long have you known Dot?"

"Since she was a snot-nosed brat hanging around the Sands," she said with a snort.

I vaguely remembered Dot talking about her childhood over Scorpion Bowls at the Tiki Hut, and miraculously some of it had stuck. "Right, she said her dad was a comedian and her mom was a showgirl."

"Mm," Jessie said. "Degenerate gambler is more like it. And her mom took off when she was a toddler. She basically grew up in that motel she owns, she tell you that?"

I shook my head.

"Her old man left her there every night while he worked, and by 'worked,' I mean pissed away every dime he made. She's obsessed with those old films because they were the only thing that kept her company." Jessie sighed. "When his liver finally quit, she had to work off his debt by cleaning rooms at the Getaway. Eventually made enough to buy the place, and there you are."

"Wow," I said. "The way she described it sounded a lot more—"

"Glamorous?" Jessie smiled. "That's Dot for you. She sprinkles fairy dust on everything. You can take that off, by the way," she said, nodding to my caftan. "Won't be needing it from here on out."

With relief, I peeled off the heavy dress. "Um, about Marcella . . ."

"We'll get her squared away. Don't worry." Wryly, she added, "The hipsters will be thrilled by the authenticity she adds to the Mayhem's ambiance."

"As long as she's safe," I mumbled, feeling another pang of guilt.

"They'll be fine." Jessie patted my hand in a surprisingly maternal gesture. "Dot's family, I'll take care of her and Marcella. You just worry about yourself. And watch out for that one," she added in a lower voice, eyeing Grace. "I don't like the look of her at all."

"Don't worry. I'm a pro at taking care of myself."

"I can tell." Jessie grinned at me. "You got 'survivor' written all over you, kid."

While I appreciated the sentiment, I wasn't feeling like much of a survivor at the moment. More like prey. If Dot hadn't befriended me, I'd probably already be dead. Which was a grim realization. "I feel awful about dragging them into all this."

"Can't say I'm thrilled about that." She appraised me, then added, "But Dot's a big girl. If she hadn't wanted to get tangled up in this, she wouldn't have. I gotta respect that."

The shuttle slowed, then stopped in front of a metal gate at a small airfield. Seeing the sign on it, I frowned. "Hang on, does that say—"

"Excellent," Grace said approvingly, craning forward to peer through the windshield.

Jessie nodded. "Dottie pulled out all the stops for you."

She really did, I thought. Dot had done more for me in the past week than anyone else in my entire life. Including my parents. And to thank her, I'd inadvertently put her life in danger. We hadn't even had a proper goodbye.

It struck me that I might never see her again. A wave of sadness washed over me.

Noticing, Jessie said, "None of that, now. And don't worry, your stuff is inside."

"It is?" That was almost the most surprising development of the day. "But he might've been watching the room."

"Dot had Tina wrap everything in double bags and toss them in a dumpster. A friend picked them up from there. Trust me, they were careful."

"Great," I said, thinking, *My stuff was in a dumpster?* Gross, but I wasn't in any position to complain.

Chuck pulled to a stop and said, "Here we are."

We were facing a bright red helicopter with **GRAND CANYON HELITOURS** emblazoned on its side. The rotors were already slowly spinning.

"No way anyone is following you in that," Jessie said smugly.

"Uh-huh." I felt faint. Obviously I should be grateful—I mean, a helicopter? How rock star was that?

If only I weren't terrified of heights.

I descended to the tarmac and stared at it apprehensively. Jessie pressed a set of keys into my hand. "There's a car waiting on the other side, courtesy of one of Jim's leatherneck buddies. Dot left some cash in your bag. Oh, and here's your new ID. Bit of a rush job but it's some of my best work, if I do say so myself."

"Thanks," I said, taking the keys and a thick envelope from her. "Really, I can't tell you how much—"

"Of course, darling." She blew me a kiss. "Now, take care and don't die."

While we'd been talking, Chuck had helped Grace off the shuttle bus and into the back of the helicopter. She sat dead center, looking bored. Jessie waved to me from the shuttle bus steps, and then the doors swung shut and it chugged away. I resisted the temptation to run after it.

Drawing a deep breath, I eyed the helicopter warily.

"For Christ's sake, hurry up!" Grace yelled.

I wasn't about to give Grace more ammunition to mock me. Bending nearly double to avoid the rotors, I clumsily ran toward it.

As promised, there were two garbage bags in the back on either side of Grace. That cheered me considerably; I really hoped they smelled. The pilot was wearing a baseball cap and aviator glasses; he motioned for me to put on a set of headphones. Grace was already wearing hers, looking as if she spent every day flying around in a death trap.

The pilot's voice was overly loud in my ear. "It'll be a quick trip. Buckle up."

I scrambled to fasten the complicated seat belt, as if anything would save me if we suddenly tumbled out of the sky. As the last clasp clicked into place, the whine of the rotors grew piercingly loud. I gripped my knees and reconsidered the value of prayer.

We swooped up astonishingly fast. I squeezed my eyes shut, but that only made the motion sickness worse. Steeling myself, I opened them.

"Wow," I breathed. We were circling above the Strip. The tip of the Strat's spire was level with us, and the other casinos sprawled around it: I could see the Luxor pyramid, the Eiffel Tower, the Statue of Liberty. Light shimmered off tall glass towers, casting rainbows. It was so bizarre and beautiful I forgot to be terrified.

Minutes later we were cruising past the Hoover Dam. I leaned over to peer at it. In my ear, the pilot said, "Thought I might as well give you the nickel tour."

He grinned at me, and I smiled back. Grace's voice in my ear said, "How much farther?"

I threw her a look, which was wasted since she was staring straight ahead.

"Nearly there." The pilot sounded as nonplussed as I felt.

Five minutes later, we alit in the parking lot of a deserted office park. The only car in sight was a battered blue minivan. A guy with a buzz cut leaned against it, arms crossed. The pilot nodded toward him. "That's your ride."

Carefully, I climbed out. The guy trotted over and shook my hand. "Name's Pete!" he yelled over the rotors.

"Thanks for doing this!" I yelled back.

Pete nodded, then helped me load the bags in the minivan before going back for Grace. He got her settled in the passenger seat with some effort. "See ya," he said, tipping an imaginary hat at us before jogging to the helicopter and climbing in.

I shaded my eyes to watch as it ascended, hovering over the trees. It executed a slow spin and tilted back the way we came. Within seconds, it was out of sight.

From behind me, Grace snapped, "So are we going to spend the whole day in this godforsaken place?"

She really was unbelievable. Turning to her, I said, "A lot of people just went to considerable lengths to help us. You could've shown some appreciation."

"Yes, I particularly enjoyed the clothing donation," she said, gesturing to her pantsuit.

"Don't knock it. Wash-and-wear isn't a bad idea for stabbing victims." My stomach growled again. "God, I'm starving."

"You'll have to wait. There won't be a restaurant for miles."

"So we'll stop at a gas station. Or better yet, a McDonald's."

"Fast food? Absolutely not," Grace said with horror.

"Tell you what. If we pass a Four Seasons, I'll pull in there instead." I slid the side door shut and went around to the driver's seat.

The interior of the minivan more or less matched the outside: cracked leather seats, a sticky steering wheel, and the fug of old cigarette smoke. Still, there were fewer miles on it than my junker. And it would be a lot easier to sleep in. I hoped Dot got a good price for my car. It was the least I could do to repay her.

There were two disposable cell phones in boxes on the dashboard. I tossed them in the back and picked up the map Pete had helpfully left. "Any idea where we are?"

"About thirty miles northwest of Vegas." Grace tilted her seat back and closed her eyes. "Get on the 15 South."

I peered around the office park. There was no sign of a highway anywhere. Not that she seemed to care. Irritated, I asked, "Then what?"

"I'll tell you when we get closer," she said.

"Fabulous," I muttered, flicking on the radio. "I just love a road trip."

CHAPTER TWELVE

L.A. CONFIDENTIAL

Worse traveling companions than Grace must exist. I could've been stuck with a gassy dog, teething baby, or car full of mimes. But two hours into the drive, I probably would've welcomed all three.

Every time I turned on the radio, she reached over and flicked it off. "I need silence," she said. "To think."

"Yeah, see, I'm trying *not* to think about how your brother wants to murder me." I obstinately flicked the radio back on and cranked the volume. "Besides, I'm the driver. Which means I control the radio."

Grace sighed elaborately, then nodded toward a sign for the next exit. "Pull off here."

"Primm?" I furrowed my brow. "You live here?"

"Service station," she said with a jerk of her chin. "Gas up. I'll pay inside."

"With cash," I said.

Grace threw me a scathing look. "Obviously. I've been doing this for a long time, you know."

"And look how well that's going for you," I muttered as we pulled up to the pumps. Grace limped toward the mini mart before I could stop her. "Get junk food!" I called after her. "Something spicy!"

By the time I'd topped off the tank, she was shambling back with a plastic bag dangling from her wrist. Without a word, she went to the driver's side.

"Um, what're you doing?" I asked.

"Driving. I need to take some precautions."

"No one's following us," I said. "Can you even drive?"

"I'm feeling much better," she said stiffly, although the tightness around her eyes indicated otherwise.

"It's a bad idea."

"Do you want me to save your life or not?" she asked, cocking an eyebrow. When I didn't answer, she climbed in and made a big show of adjusting the seat. I got in the passenger side like a sullen teen. She tore out of the lot before I'd even had a chance to put my seat belt on. As I fumbled with it, the traffic light turned red. Ignoring it, she took a sharp left and swung onto the 15 North.

"What the fuck!" I yelled. "Are you trying to get us killed?"

"Get comfortable," Grace said. "We'll be doing a lot of that over the next few hours."

"I did not survive a serial killer to end up dead on the highway."

"Stop whining. I have a perfect driving record." She reached over and flicked off the radio.

"Hey!"

"Driver controls the radio, right?" She smirked.

Swearing under my breath, I grabbed the plastic bag and started riffling through it, then moaned. "Sparkling water and pistachios? And what the fuck . . ." I dug a small bag out. "Sunflower seeds?"

"I know, it was the only real food they had," she sniffed. "I was really hoping for some almonds."

"You suck at road trips, you know that?" I grumbled, bracing myself against the dashboard as she skidded across four lanes of traffic to exit the freeway, leaving angry horns bleating in our wake.

Despite the fact that Grace drove like we were in the final lap of the Indy 500, I managed to crash out. When I awoke, the sun was tilting toward the horizon. We were in a huge line of cars, nothing but taillights as far as I could see. I sat up, blinking sleep from my eyes. "Where are we?"

"Pasadena," Grace said without looking at me.

"Really?" I leaned forward and peered out the window, thinking, *California!* Sadly, it was too dark to see palm trees. In fact, this stretch of highway looked as depressing as any other. But I still felt giddy.

I grabbed the plastic bag of snacks and peered inside. Grace had made quite a dent in the pistachios. I cracked one open and popped it in my mouth. As suspected, it tasted nothing like a Dorito. "So how much farther until we stop for the night?" I asked, trying to imagine sharing a hotel room with her. I was guessing it would be very different from my nights with Marcella.

"No stopping. We're almost there." The circles under Grace's eyes were more pronounced, and her hands gripped the steering wheel. It was pretty obvious she was in pain.

"Why don't you let me drive again?" I offered.

Grace shook her head. "No need. We'll be there in ten minutes." Eyeing the traffic, she said, "Maybe twenty."

"Be where?" I asked, confused.

"My place."

I gaped at her. "You live in L.A.?"

"Yes." She glanced at me. "Why, is that surprising?"

"A little. I just figured you for something more exotic. Like an island. Or an underground lair."

"Sorry to disappoint."

We inched forward. Honestly, we'd probably moved faster playing old ladies in the casino. "So why L.A.?" I asked to fill the silence. "You a big fan of beaches?"

Grace guided us toward an exit onto the 110 freeway. "Good access to multiple airports. Lots of ways in and out. Relative anonymity."

"Really?" I asked.

"Absolutely," Grace said. "People live behind gates here. They rarely interact with their neighbors. Everything can be delivered, so if you choose not to leave your house, you don't have to. It's much easier to hide than it would be in a small town."

"That sounds . . . depressing."

"More depressing than an island?" she scoffed. "Out in the middle of nowhere, trapped with no easy exit route? Honestly, Amber. We've got to work on your survival skills."

"I've survived pretty damn well so far, thank you very much," I said, bristling. "And in my experience, small towns can be ideal. People are more trusting there."

"True," she said. "Far too trusting of serial killers with delivery vans, in my experience."

"Yeah, well, you're the one who got herself stabbed," I retorted.

Without responding Grace turned onto a quiet block lined with palm trees. I resisted the urge to press my face to the window. Los Angeles! From Tennessee, it had felt as far away as the moon. "Can we swing by Disneyland as long as we're here?" I said, only half-joking.

"Surviving Gunnar will require upping your game considerably," Grace said. "So, no."

So: Grace's house.

Pretty much what I'd expected, actually. It was set back from the street, behind a huge gate nestled in an impenetrable twelve-foot hedge. The driveway was short, leading straight into a garage. Which was, of course, immaculate: not even an oil stain on the concrete floor, and the walls were lined with white cabinets.

That pretty much set the tone for the rest of the house: spotlessly clean, absolutely zero personality. No artwork, no photos, not even a refrigerator magnet. Open floor plan: the dining room, living room, and kitchen were one big, blank expanse. White couches, white rug, white walls . . . I've seen hospital rooms with more pizzazz.

"Wow, this is . . . white," I said, dropping my duffel bags on the floor.

"You can take the guest bedroom. It's up the stairs on the right." She looked at my bags pointedly. "Don't forget your luggage."

"Right. Guest room." I lugged my bags upstairs. There was a short hallway with a door at either end. I turned right and opened the door onto—you guessed it, more white. The bed had a padded white headboard, white duvet, white sheets. The rug was ivory. Still, aside from the Strat, it was pretty much the nicest bedroom I'd ever stayed in. Feeling self-conscious, I dropped my duffels in the closet and went into the bathroom to relieve my bladder.

The bathroom was equally nice: bathtub, separate shower, double sink . . . if this was the guest room, I couldn't even imagine what hers looked like.

I looked longingly at the shower, but it seemed a little weird to wash up when Grace was probably waiting downstairs. Instead, I splashed water on my face and examined myself in the mirror. The nasty lump on my temple was morphing into shades of purple and green, nicely framing the ugly black stitches. I had scrapes on my cheeks from the concrete. And my lips were chapped, thanks to an excessive amount of kissing the other night.

The smile inspired by that memory quickly faded when I thought about how pissed Marcella must've been when she'd woken up alone. She'd probably never speak to me again. Not that it would be an option anyway, with Gunnar running around.

If anything happened to them . . .

Stop it, I told myself. Dot knew Vegas better than anyone, and certainly better than Grace's psycho brother. They'd both promised to stay out of sight, and he had no way to connect them to either the Nugget or the Mayhem. They'd be fine. I was probably still his main target anyway.

I opened the bedroom door and heard a shower running. "Rude," I muttered. Not that I'd expected Grace to be the perfect hostess, despite her airs. I flounced downstairs to check the fridge for something other than pistachios.

Inside were dozens of yogurt containers, the labels perfectly aligned. The next shelf had boxes of unopened soy milk, also in a meticulous row. Below that, eggs, then a drawer of root vegetables. She didn't even have any cheese.

"For fuck's sake," I muttered. "She might as well be a serial killer." The cabinets were equally disappointing: cans of high-end vegetarian soup, pasta, organic tomato sauce. Nothing with preservatives or additives, or anything that added flavor. I plucked an apple from the fruit bowl on the counter and munched it resentfully. The first order of business was going to be securing something truly disgusting to put in my body. Anything with a shelf life of at least fifty years.

The water was still running in her bathroom when I went back upstairs. Well, if she was going to avoid me, I'd do the same. I ran a bath, found a bag of fancy lavender salts in the vanity, and dumped them all in. Then I sank into the tub and lay there until my skin pruned.

When I finally went downstairs an hour later, feeling somewhat human in a pair of clean shorts and a T-shirt, Grace was sitting at the dining room table eating—who would've guessed it—a yogurt. There was a laptop open in front of her. She didn't even look up as I came in.

"Want to order something for dinner?" I asked.

"There's pasta if you're hungry. Or soup."

"I saw," I said moodily. "Can't we order Chinese?"

"I don't think my stomach could handle it," she said, waving her spoon in a circle. "Thanks to the giant hole in my torso."

"Oh, right." I felt like a jerk. "How is it?"

"Painful. The meds wore off an hour ago." She tucked the spoon in the yogurt carton and pushed it away. "I assume you found everything you need?"

"Yeah, thanks. It's a nice room."

She nodded, then said, "It's been a long week. I'm going to bed."

And with that, she went upstairs.

After her bedroom door shut, I went over to her computer and tapped a button to wake it up. Password protected, of course. Sighing, I went to make myself some pasta.

As a small act of rebellion, I ate in front of the television, although I kept the volume low. I flipped through channel after channel, but nothing held my attention. I finally settled on a home improvement show and settled down under a white blanket.

Someone was banging on the door. For a second, I thought I was back at the motel; I squinted at the unfamiliar silhouettes looming in the dark, momentarily perplexed. *Right*, I thought. *The guest bedroom in Grace's house. Her ice palace. Her fortress of solitude.* I snorted at my own stupid joke.

The knocking was getting louder. It was weirdly regular, like someone was systematically thumping their fist against it.

I bit my lip—*What if it's Gunnar? Can he get in?* But the front door was reinforced metal, with three impressive deadbolts; I'd checked the entire setup myself after dinner. Grace also had a fancy alarm system that made me afraid to crack a window.

Bang! Bang! Bang!

Bleary-eyed, I got out of bed and fumbled for the light. It practically blinded me, and I kept my eyes squeezed shut as I groped for the doorknob and opened it.

The hallway was still dark. Grace's bedroom door was open, but her light was off. The banging noise was coming from there, not downstairs, I realized. The clock above the landing read 3:22 a.m.

"Christ, Grace," I called out, marching to her room. "What the fuck are you—"

My breath caught in my throat. A shadowy figure knelt on the floor at the foot of Grace's bed. He turned to face me, his features concealed by the brim of a baseball cap. He was holding a hammer in one hand, and beneath him . . .

Everything in me seized up—heart stopped, breath caught in my throat, it was like that terrible night playing out all over again. Grace lay on the ground in front of him, arms splayed out to the sides, eyes contorted with pain. Her fingers were wriggling, but she wasn't moving her hands—because she couldn't, he had nailed them to the ground.

Grace's head swiveled toward me. Her mouth opened impossibly wide and she screamed, "Amber, run!"

It felt like I was moving in slow motion. I pelted down the stairs, nearly tripping on my pajama bottoms, missing steps along the way and barely righting myself with my hands. Within seconds I was at the front door, desperately trying to unbolt all the locks—*how the fuck had he gotten in if the door is still bolted?*—but it was too late. He caught hold of the back of my T-shirt and yanked, hauling me off my feet like I weighed nothing. I kicked and flailed, but he dragged me back upstairs. All I could think was that we'd failed, Grace was right, we'd never had a chance—

I awoke to the feel of someone's hand on my shoulder. I sat up fast, scrambling backward as I slapped it away. In the dark, it took a moment to register Grace's pale face.

"Easy, Amber," she said, holding up both hands. "I was just waking you up. You were screaming."

I looked around, trying to get my bearings. I was still in the living room; I must've fallen asleep in front of the TV. A cashmere throw was twisted around my legs, and my back was pressed against the far end of the couch. "Sorry. I—I had a nightmare."

"Obviously," Grace said. Her eyes narrowed. "About my brother?"

I nodded. My heart was still hammering, and my throat was so dry it was hard to swallow. "I need a glass of water," I croaked, disentangling myself and staggering clumsily to my feet.

Grace watched as I poured one and sucked it down. After a moment's hesitation, I refilled the glass and drank it more slowly. As the rush of blood in my ears abated, my pulse started to stabilize.

"Better?" she asked.

"Yeah. Sorry I woke you."

"Oh, I wasn't asleep," Grace said. "I was working."

"Working on what?"

"If it puts your mind at ease, I installed a special alarm system," she said, dodging the question. "Movement anywhere on the property triggers a silent alarm. If someone comes within five feet of a door or window before I disengage it, metal shutters slide down."

"Seriously?" I went over to check the windows. She wasn't lying; I could see the glint of metal tucked into the frame. It seemed a bit extreme, but based on what she'd said about her brother, metal shutters sounded pretty damn good. And bonus—they'd also come in handy in a zombie apocalypse.

"Plus, there's a panic room off my closet with enough supplies to last a month," Grace added.

"Wow," I said. "So I just run there if the alarm goes off."

Grace's brow furrowed. "Hm. I suppose."

"What, I'm not welcome in your damn panic room?" That was pretty insulting. Although a relatively fast, violent death might be preferable to spending a month with her in a confined space.

"It's irrelevant, because no one is getting in without my knowledge."

"Unless your brother is also a computer whiz," I muttered darkly.

"It's possible. Honestly, I have no idea," Grace said thoughtfully. "Gunnar is brilliant. And incredible with languages—he could pick a new one up in a few weeks. He's quite charming when he sets his mind to it, too."

"Great," I said. "Those are definitely the traits I look for in a serial killer. It's so much better than being murdered by a dull idiot."

Grace sniffed. "You asked."

"I asked if he was good with computers. Just in case he could, I don't know"—I gestured to the doors and windows—"mess with your security system."

"Oh, no." Grace laughed. "Trust me. The NSA couldn't crack that encryption code."

"If you say so." It actually was comforting, though I'd never admit it. Despite her (many) faults, Grace did seem to excel at computer stuff. I still had no idea how she'd tracked me.

"So what are you working on?" I asked again.

Grace sighed heavily. "I thought you wanted to get some sleep."

"Plenty of time for that, right? I mean, it's not as if we're going anywhere while you're still bleeding." I motioned to where her shirt showed fresh dots of red.

Grace frowned at the stain. "Dammit. The stitches keep popping."

"Probably because you're supposed to be lying in bed."

"You're right," she said wearily, surprising me. "I've got butterfly Band-Aids in the cabinet above the stove. Can you get them?"

"Sure." Like the fridge, the cabinet was insanely organized; there was actually a mini cabinet *inside* the cabinet with small pull-out drawers, each labeled. I opened the one marked BUTTERFLY BAND-AIDS and grabbed four.

"Thank you," Grace said as I handed them to her. She leaned back against the cushions and pulled up her shirt, wincing as she peeled back the thick square of gauze on her abdomen.

"We should probably replace that, too," I noted. "Is gauze in the same place?"

She nodded. I brought it back, along with some rubbing alcohol and cotton pads. "You need some help?"

"I've got it," she said, carefully cleaning the wound. This was my first time actually seeing it: it was a nasty slash about two inches long, an inch in from her side. The black stitches were ugly and slightly crooked.

"Aboud's sewing skills aren't anything to write home about," I said awkwardly.

"He was rushed," Grace said. "It's actually not a bad job. I've had worse."

"Worse?" I asked dubiously. "When?"

"You asked to see what I'm working on?" she said, pressing the fresh bandage into place and taping it. "It's in here."

Grace hobbled toward what I'd assumed was the laundry room. She held her wrist to a small panel beside the door; a light turned green and a lock clicked. I stared at her. "Did you just unlock that with your hand?"

She held up her wrist. "It's a biometric chip that controls locks."

"Yeah, that's definitely some next-level shit," I muttered, following her. No big shocker that she was part robot, though.

Inside was two hundred square feet chock-full of crazy. One wall was covered by a gigantic map of the United States, the kind you might find in a kid's room. But this one was pocked with colored pushpins; nothing in Alaska or Hawaii, but there were some in nearly every other state.

Opposite the map was a computer geek's wet dream: a long row of monitors, towers, and keyboards. Pushed against the wall in between was a free-standing whiteboard on wheels that was covered with some sort of code.

Instead of carpet, the floor was padded with thick black gym matting. There was a rack of dumbbells, a practice dummy, and other things I couldn't identify. "Wow," I said, going over to the map. "All you're missing is newspaper clippings and string."

"Yes, it is a bit analog," Grace said, as though *that* was what was weird about it. "But it enables me to see everything simultaneously."

I leaned in to examine North Dakota: three yellow pins clustered together, and a blue one at the northern edge of the state. "So what do the different colors mean?"

"Blue means I'm fairly certain Gunnar wasn't involved but can't rule him out completely. Yellow means, well—the yellows are him."

"Christ, really?" I stepped back to take in the entire expanse.

A hell of a lot of the pins were yellow, easily half of them. I tried to count how many, but before I even got close, Grace said, "Two hundred and fifty-three."

I goggled at her, momentarily speechless. "Two hundred and fifty-three *people*?" I finally managed to choke out. "Holy shit. That doesn't seem possible."

"I know, it's impressive. The only person who comes close is Harold Shipman, a British doctor suspected of killing over two hundred of his patients. But that was years ago, before computer tracking."

"'Impressive' isn't the word I'd use," I muttered. Once again, her attitude was unnerving; it almost seemed like admiration. I eyed her, wondering what her relationship with her brother had been like before all this.

"Two hundred and fifty-three victims, in this day and age?" Grace tilted her head. "I'm not saying it's good, it's just not easy to accomplish. Of course, he varies murder methods, and unlike Mr. Jessop, never kills in a garish way. That would attract too much attention."

"Garish" is one word for it, I thought, repressing a shudder. "Then how do you know it was Gunnar, if he's so good at covering his tracks?"

"Yellows are confirmed within a five percent margin of error."

"Confirmed how?"

"The computer algorithm I told you about," she said, "I'd explain it, but it's a bit complicated if you're not well versed in such things."

I rolled my eyes. "Whatever. Nerd."

Ignoring the jab, she added, "I actually think he's been exercising some restraint. Over the course of seventeen years, Gunnar could have done considerably more damage."

"Seventeen *years*?" I tried to run the math in my head. "He must've started when he was just a kid."

"He killed my best friend when we were sixteen," Grace said woodenly.

"Oh, that's— I'm so sorry," I said, trying to wrap my head around the fact that Grace ever *had* a best friend.

"It was ruled a riding accident, so I didn't realize until much later. Otherwise, I might've been able to stop him then."

I didn't answer, mainly because I didn't know what to say. My suspicions were right; Grace hunted her brother out of a sense of guilt. I leaned in to examine a cluster of yellow pins in Las Vegas. There were three of them, and one green pin. "Is that—"

"Yes. The most recent murders."

So one of those yellow pins was for Lori, Marcella's friend with benefits. I swallowed hard. "What's the green one mean?"

"Greens, he didn't kill." Off my blank look, she added, "That's you."

"Oh," I said faintly. I ran my eyes across the map again. "How many of those are there?"

She looked at me for a moment before saying, "One."

THE UNKNOWN MAN

Goddammit!" BJ grumbled. Just his luck, the can of Coke had gotten stuck. The Getaway's stupid vending machine had eaten three bucks already, and there was no way Aunt Jess would pay him back. He kicked the machine again, which did nothing to dislodge the soda but painfully stubbed his big toe. "Fuck!"

"Need a hand?"

Startled, he turned to find a tall, bearded guy in aviator glasses smiling down at him. *Shit.* He'd catch hell if either Dot or Aunt Jess found out he'd sworn in front of a guest. "Sorry, man. Just this fu—" Catching himself, he amended it to "This darn machine always jams."

"I can see that." The man stepped forward to examine it. Then he drew back his fist and BJ flinched, thinking for a split second he was going to hit him. Instead, he punched the side of the vending machine.

The Coke slid free and landed in the drawer. BJ clapped. "Dude, nice!"

The man grinned. "Had one just like this at my old job. Pain in the ass, amirite?"

"Totally." BJ retrieved the soda, but before he could pop it the man put out a hand to stop him.

"Probably best to wait for it to settle, yeah?"

"Yeah." BJ set the can on the table. "Uh, sorry. You need a room?" The man's sunglasses reflected his image back, which was slightly disconcerting. He spotted a piece of spinach lodged in his teeth and reached up to surreptitiously dig it out.

"I'm good, thanks." The man smiled again. There was something weirdly familiar about him, but BJ couldn't place it. Leaning in, the guy said, "Actually, I'm looking for a girl I used to know. She worked that corner."

BJ followed his pointing finger to where a hooker in a miniskirt and fishnets was smoking a cigarette. "Oh, yeah, um . . . I don't really know the girls over here. I can hook you up in Naked City, though. There's this girl Bambi and man, she is un-fucking-believable."

The guy chuckled and said, "Thanks, but it's not like that. She's an old friend, I just wanted to say hi."

"Oh, sure, I'm not really into that scene either. I mean, if you gotta pay for it . . ." BJ's voice trailed off. The guy was regarding him with a familiar expression of bemusement. Seeing it, BJ felt a flare of rage. Vegas was supposed to be different, a place he could reinvent himself. But no matter where he went, people still thought he was an asshole. Maybe he should just go back home.

"Naked City, huh?" the guy finally said.

"Um, yeah. I'm just, like, temping here. I usually work at the Mayhem."

"The Mayhem?" The guy cocked his head to the side. "Haven't heard of it."

"It's a hell of a lot better than this dump," BJ said. "I'm watching this place as a favor for a friend of my aunt's." Belatedly, he remembered Aunt Jessie's mysterious orders not to "blab Dottie's business all over town." Well, what did she expect? She and her stupid murder groupies always acted like what they were doing was so important, when no one else gave a shit. Drama queens, every last one of them. Especially Dot. "You should check it out."

"Thanks, I will." The man reached out his hand. "Nice to meet you, BJ."

"Yeah, you too." BJ shook, trying not to wince—the guy had a serious grip.

It wasn't until later, when he was sitting in the office smoking a joint, that he wondered how the guy had known his name. But that was the same moment he popped the soda, and it sprayed all over him and (more importantly) the papers stacked on Dot's desk.

"Fuck!" he exclaimed, frantically mopping at the mess with his shirttail. Which of course was precisely when Aunt Jess dropped in to check on him. She stood there, terrifying as always with her hands on her hips, surveying the mess and the smoke. And he was on a bus back to Stockton by nightfall.

Nursing his wounded pride, BJ decided that Aunt Jess could go to hell. He'd hated that job anyway. As the Greyhound's gentle rocking lulled him to sleep, BJ hoped that the cool bearded guy had managed to find his friend.

CHAPTER THIRTEEN

JIGSAW

In a movie, this would have been the part where they put in a slick montage scene: me and Grace doing martial arts, constructing a scale model of our brilliant plan, walking hand and hand through the park . . .

Just kidding. That last one is obviously from a very different type of film.

Instead, we quickly settled into a routine. Grace spent the bulk of her time in what I'd dubbed her "Serial Killer Suite" (SKS). After the first week, I periodically heard her beating the crap out of the practice dummy. She didn't ask for any more medical assistance, so I assumed she was healing just fine (although every morning I listened at the door for a full minute until the sound of typing convinced me she hadn't bled out in her sleep).

Meanwhile, I spent my days on the couch binge-watching every television show ever made. Seriously, I could've gotten a PhD in sitcoms by the end. The efforts to distract myself were only partially successful; in the middle of laughing at a dumb joke, I would flash back on that green pushpin and start panicking. The truth was, I had no clue what it would take to stop Grace's brother. If she'd been chasing him since they were teenagers, what chance did I have? Especially if she kept shutting me out. And despite my boasts to her back at the Strat, I wasn't sure that anything in my life had truly prepared me for this.

For a change of pace I'd sit in her small backyard, which was surprisingly charming; it even had an orange and a lemon tree. Aside from that, neither of us left the house. Forget Disneyland; at this rate, I wouldn't even get to see the Hollywood sign, and that was less than a mile away. Not that I was really up for crowds at the moment.

Every time it felt like I was climbing out of my skin, I'd pound on the door to her SKS.

"What?" she'd ask with irritation.

"Anything I can do to help?"

"No," she always replied. At which point I'd generally make faces and rude gestures at the door before stalking back to the couch.

It was maddening. Aside from daily check-in texts from Dot and Marcella (Dot's were always elaborate and newsy, while Marcella just copied and pasted not dead yet over and over), I had virtually no human interaction. By the end of two weeks, I'd resorted to watching *Saved by the Bell* while imagining a far superior queer version where Kelly and Jessie got hot and heavy.

And then one day, I awoke to find the house empty.

I did a full circuit to confirm it, since Grace didn't have much of a personal presence to start with. But there was no sound coming from either her bedroom or the SKS. She wasn't in the yard, either, and the nondescript sedan she kept in the garage was gone.

"Fuck me," I muttered, moodily crunching one of the Pop-Tarts I'd ordered off the internet. Where the fuck had she gone? If she'd abandoned me to go after her brother alone . . . well, actually, that wouldn't have been the worst thing. Still, it would've been nice if she'd left a note.

By the time I'd finished my second cup of coffee, though, I was thoroughly pissed. How dare she act like I was nothing but an irritating houseguest? Thanks to her, my life was in danger again, and she'd completely shut me out. I was stuck here alone, and I was officially out of shows to binge. It would serve her right if I went snooping around to entertain myself.

My eyes drifted over to the electronic pad next to the SKS door. The indicator light was a solid red. I got up and went over to examine it, then ran my hands over the hinges and grinned.

Ten minutes later, thanks to the hammer and screwdriver I'd found in the garage (in carefully labeled drawers, natch), the door's hinges were off and I was inside the SKS. So much for technology.

I tapped at her keyboard and a password window popped up on the center monitor; knowing Grace, it was unlikely I'd be able to crack it. I examined the map wall, but as far as I could tell, there were no new pins to explain her sudden departure. She hadn't left any addresses helpfully lying around, either.

Sighing, I plopped down in her swivel chair. It was every bit as comfortable as it looked. I spun in a slow circle, examining the contents of the room. The top of the whiteboard was covered in some sort of code, with alphabet letters below bizarre symbols. The bottom half had a list of flower and plant names, followed by what seemed like surnames. I examined those for a minute, then gave up. Maybe Grace did word puzzles in her spare time.

If I were Grace, where would I hide something? "It's my house," I said out loud. "So I'm probably not going to be too paranoid about locking stuff up. I'd keep most of it on my computer anyway, 'cause I'm such a nerd."

Not everything, though, I thought. Pushing off the armrests, I went to examine the whiteboard more closely, rolling it away from the wall.

Jackpot. The back side was corkboard, covered with carefully organized news article printouts: not dissimilar to Dot's crazy wall. Most of the stories were old, going back nearly twenty-five years. The earliest were all about a serial killer: Gregory "Gruesome" Grimes. I hadn't even been born when he was captured, and I'd heard of him. I vaguely remembered watching a gory reenactment documentary on him during one of my insomnia bouts last year. Grimes was definitely in the serial killer top ten list along with Bundy, Dahmer, and Gacy. And like Gacy, he'd kept his victims close to home, burying them in his backyard while his young family slept inside.

But Grace would've been just a kid when he was caught, so why the interest? It was perplexing. I sifted through the other articles, which were organized in groups. A bunch of them were about Grimes's victims: fifteen women, all between the ages of twenty-five and thirty, mostly prostitutes. His trial had landed him in America's worst prison, the supermax in Florence, Colorado. Honestly, there wasn't much that I hadn't learned from the TV documentary.

The other stuff didn't seem at all related. A piece from the *Tennessee Sentinel* about the riding death of Rose Abernathy, age sixteen. Must have been the best friend Grace told me about, the one her brother killed. A lightbulb clicked: *that's* why Grace had decided to check out the murders in Johnson City; it was only a few towns away. She'd probably assumed her insane brother was revisiting the scene of an earlier crime to taunt her. So apparently I had Rose to thank for my survival.

Another article was from a year later, about the disappearance of a boarding school kid the day of his graduation; could that have been Grace's brother? I frowned and squinted at the picture; if it was Gunnar, I couldn't detect a family resemblance. The most recent article memorialized a cop in Oregon who had been killed while making an arrest in a motel parking lot; that one was from four years ago.

I stepped back, feeling more confused than ever. How did any of these things intersect? Grace was clearly not a sentimental person, so there must be a reason she'd printed these out and posted them.

I found more answers in her bedroom closet, thanks to my trusty hammer-and-screwdriver door-opening method. In a file box tucked on the top shelf of her closet, I finally found the kind of personal items that were missing from the rest of the house. I grabbed it and brought it into my own room, genuinely nervous about how she'd react to finding me going through her stuff.

It was a bonanza. Considering how much crap most people haul around, there wasn't much, but the things she'd saved finally helped put the pieces together. Exhibit A was a birth certificate for Grace Cabot Grimes. Father: Gregory Grimes.

Holy shit.

So Grace's dad was a serial killer, too, and he'd buried his victims' bodies in her backyard when she was just a kid. That would definitely mess you up. And, apparently, make you follow in his footsteps. I shuddered. No wonder Grace was such a cold person; it was kind of remarkable she hadn't turned out to be a killer, too.

Cabot was the name her brother had given me when he had been pretending to be an FBI agent; that was why she'd reacted so strongly to it back in my motel room. I wondered if she still went by that; all this time together, and I had had no idea what her surname was.

A noise outside made me jump. I hurried to the window; the thick hedge partially obscured my view of the street, but I could make out a gardener maneuvering a lawn mower onto his truck bed. Coast was still clear—for now.

I quickly rifled through the rest of the stuff. A photo of Grace in a graduation gown standing stiffly between two snooty-looking older women in pearls, and a high school diploma from the same school where the kid had disappeared on graduation day. Grace said her brother killed the people she got close to, so maybe this had been a boyfriend? I scoffed; that was even more inconceivable than Grace having a best friend. He was probably someone important to her, though.

The diploma from MIT was the least surprising thing I found.

I sat back and tried to make sense of it all. Given this new information, the fact that Grace's brother had turned out to be a serial killer wasn't all that shocking; it explained her sociopathy, too. That was a lot of trauma to process at a young age, and the women in the graduation photo with her didn't exactly look warm and fuzzy. Mother and grandmother, I was guessing.

Keeping my ears pricked for the sound of a car pulling into the garage, I kept putting the pieces together. By lunchtime, I'd basically memorized everything I'd found: trust papers for a Grace Cabot (of course she was a trust fund kid, that explained how she could afford to run around chasing her brother). Shedding the last name Grimes was understandable, too; even if her dad hadn't turned out to be a psycho, it wasn't exactly a great last name. A web search for Grace Cabot didn't turn anything up at all; she must've used that MIT degree to wipe herself from the internet.

I'd just set the file box back in her closet when my phone buzzed. I fumbled for it, nearly sending it shooting across the room in my eagerness to answer. A slight pang of disappointment when I recognized Dot's number. Grace had been gone for hours; it would've been nice of her to check in. Sighing, I answered.

"Hey, toots," Dot chirped. "Just wanted to hear you for a change."

Despite the forced cheer, I could hear the strain in her voice. "Hey, Dot. How's it going?"

"Oh, you know me." A beat, and then she asked, "So, any idea how much longer I'll be shackin' up with Jim?"

I sat down with my back against Grace's bed. "Sorry, I'm not sure. Hopefully not too much longer, though."

"Gotcha. And how is the ice queen?"

Good enough to ditch me. "All healed up, I think. Not that she's sharing."

Dot laughed. "Well, color me surprised."

"Actually, Dot," I said as something occurred to me, "do you think you and your group could look into something for me?"

"Sure, honey." Her voice brightened considerably. "The Femmes are always happy to help. Is it about . . . you-know-who?"

"I think so, yeah," I said. "I need everything you can find out about Gregory Grimes. Especially his kids. A few other things, too. I'll email them to you."

"This have something to do with Grace and her brother?"

"Maybe," I hedged.

"The plot thickens. You got it, kiddo. Honestly, I'm happy for the distraction."

"Great. Um . . . how's everyone else doing?"

"Oh, you know." Dot sighed. "Marcella is putting Jess through her paces, that's for sure. But we're hanging in there, dollface. Don't you worry about us."

After hanging up, I carefully put everything back the way I'd found it and reattached the bedroom door. Then I went downstairs for a well-deserved snack.

FALLEN ANGEL

already told you, Chrissy, I don't blame you. I blame that sorry sack of genes you divorced." Catching her reflection in the plate glass window, Jessie adjusted her turban. Then frowned as, through it, she saw the door to number eighteen open. A sleazy-looking guy in a tracksuit emerged and hustled down the stairs, checking back over his shoulder as if someone might be chasing him.

"*Goddammit!*" Jessie muttered. "What? No, I'm not swearing at you, Chris. Listen, I already agreed to give BJ another shot. But he screws up again, it's on you, got it?"

Jessie hung up without waiting for a response. She marched upstairs, huffing slightly as she reached the top. Maybe her doctor was right, and it was time to start Lipitor. Either that or add another tango class a week—

She rapped on the door. "Marcella! Open up."

No answer. After a long pause, she barked, "I saw Buddy just now. Told you to keep that shit out of my house, didn't I?"

Still no answer. Jessie sucked her teeth. She was half tempted to throw this girl out on her ass, even though it would piss Dot off.

Honestly, how much was a person supposed to shoulder? Bad enough she had to take back her waste-of-space nephew. She sighed and muttered, "I am too old for this crap."

Digging a master key out of the folds of her kimono, she unlocked the door. As soon as she spotted Marcella, she said, "Aw, hell."

The kid was sprawled on the floor by the bed, arm still tied off and the rest of her kit scattered beside her. Her head lolled to the side, eyes closed. Jessie hurried in and knelt to check her pulse. Then she dug Narcan nasal spray out of another pocket, inserted the tip in Marcella's nose, and pressed the plunger. Sitting back on her haunches, she muttered, "C'mon, kid."

Jessie held her breath as a full minute ticked by. Then Marcella's eyes popped open and she drawled, "Fuck!"

"My thoughts exactly." Jessie stood and put her hands on her hips. "You want to kill yourself, do it somewhere else."

"Fine. I'll go," she slurred, struggling to get up.

Jessie kicked her with one foot. "Sure. And then you'll turn up dead in a tub, and Dot'll roast me on a spit." She sighed. "Didn't your friend text you?"

"She's not my friend," Marcella growled.

"Whatever. She told Dot this should be over soon." Jessie winced at the piles of dirty clothes and takeout containers littering the carpet. She was going to have to get this rug professionally cleaned. Nudging Marcella again, she said, "No more pushers. Got it?"

No response. Jessie bent low to meet her eyes, waiting until Marcella mumbled, "Got it."

"Fan-fucking-tas-tic." Jessie waved a finger at the mess. "And clean this crap up before it brings critters."

Jessie pressed a hand to her lower back as she descended the stairs. Instead of more tango, maybe it was time to give Pilates a shot. Her eyes narrowed at the sight of her nephew skulking away from a cab. "You! Waste of space! Stow your crap and run to the market, we're out of avocados."

BJ immediately started protesting. Squabbling, they went into the office.

Neither of them noticed the SUV parked across the street or the man in the driver's seat watching them through binoculars. After they vanished inside, he trained them back on the upstairs window.

CHAPTER FOURTEEN

I WAKE UP SCREAMING

Shortly after dawn the next day, I jerked upright on the couch at the sound of the garage door grinding open. I'd gone to bed late and slept fitfully, snapping awake at the slightest sound. It was almost as bad as my drive cross-country; in spite of Grace's assurances, I didn't feel at all safe here. And nothing I'd discovered over the course of the past twenty-four hours had allayed those fears. If anything, it had made them worse.

At least, largely thanks to Dot, I finally had some answers. I hurriedly scrambled into the SKS as the garage door creaked open.

I could hear Grace moving through the house, making disgusted noises (probably thanks to the pile of dirty dishes stacked in the sink). When she finally appeared in the doorway, I was braced for her wrath.

"What are you doing in here?" she asked, her voice even icier than usual.

"Just chillin'," I said, repressing a yawn.

"Get out," Grace said, crossing her arms over her chest.

"You know, it only took five minutes to get in." I nodded at the lock on the door. "Didn't even need a fancy implant. Where were you, by the way?"

She didn't respond. I saw her eyes narrow as she spotted the changes I'd made to her massive wall map. As she stomped across the room to it, I thought, *Here we go.* She stood in front of it, hands opening and closing in fists. "What the fuck did you do?"

"Oh, that?" I said casually.

She spun on me. "You've ruined years of work."

"Look, don't beat yourself up. You were on the right track. But I figured it out."

"Figured what out?"

"The pattern." She glared at me. I crossed my arms and matched her gaze. Winning staring contests was another of my résumé skills.

Finally, her eyes broke off. She waved at me. "Get out."

"C'mon, admit it. You're a little curious."

"I mean it," she said. "This little experiment is over. I don't need your help."

"Well, if you insist, then fine. I'll lay it out for you," I said, brushing past her as I went over to the map. "The pattern starts back here, right after you graduated from high school, right?" I pointed at the pushpins on the board that I'd linked together.

"Is that . . . floss?"

"Yeah. Only string I could find. You need more, by the way." The floss looped from pushpin to pushpin, making it look like a drunkard's macrame project.

"Jesus," she said. "You are insane."

Ignoring her, I pressed on. "I get why you were so obsessed with that weird code." I waved toward the whiteboard. "Where'd it come from anyway?"

A beat, then, "It's not a code, it's an alphabet. Gunnar and I made it up when we were kids."

"Kind of a twin language. Sure, I've heard of those."

"I never told you we were twins."

"Didn't have to. I figured it out," I said blithely. Plus, Dot had done a deep dive into the Ohio state birth certificate database and uncovered one for Gunnar Cabot Grimes, born four minutes before Grace. "Anyway, you figured out that where he was leaving the bodies was a code, right? In each city, they formed one of those symbols." I pointed to the board.

Grace was still staring stonily at me. After a beat, she shrugged. "Yes."

"And once you decoded a few of those symbols, you realized that they formed a word." It had been a serious thrill when I finally realized what the deal was with the whiteboard: symbols on top, flower names below. It'd felt like cracking that famous mathematical proof no one has solved for centuries. "The words were all flowers: rose, tulip, that sort of thing. Right?"

"Some were plants," Grace said grudgingly.

I drew a deep breath and dropped the bomb. "Exactly. The plants your father buried his victims under."

She stared at me, agape. It had taken a good chunk of last night for me to put that together, but as I matched the last names written on the whiteboard to the news articles, it had suddenly clicked. Gunnar was taunting Grace by referencing their father's pattern. "How did you—"

"Oh, I'm not done," I said smugly. "Because you missed something. See, you've been too micro about this. There's a bigger pattern here." I waved at the floss linking the pushpins on the map. "It's kind of like Google Earth, okay?"

"I'm familiar with Google Earth," she said dryly, recovering some of her poise.

"Right, so . . . the pattern you found with the victims? That's, like, the city level. But if you pull out further, there's a bigger pattern that you missed."

"And you found it."

"Yup." It was probably wrong to feel victorious about what I'd discovered; we were talking about literally hundreds of victims here. But still, when I'd realized what I was looking at last night, I'd actually whooped out loud.

Part of me kind of understood the appeal of this game they were playing. Which was disturbing in and of itself.

"Well?"

I stepped closer to the board to explain. "Instead of looking at the individual victims, you need to look at *where* and *when* they were killed. These were the earliest, right?" Dot had helped with this, too, linking the clusters of murders for me with assistance from her Fatal Femmes network.

In spite of herself, Grace looked intrigued. "Yes, I believe so."

"Okay. So he started in Tulsa." As I spoke I traced my finger along the floss connecting the pin clusters. "Then he went to Shreveport, Wichita, Fort Worth, Fayetteville, and Springfield. See the pattern?"

"No," she said curtly.

"Next," I forged ahead. "He makes a big jump, which kicks off the next pattern in the Northeast. Starting in Albany." I ran my hand along the lines. "Same pattern."

"You're seeing things that aren't there," she said dismissively.

"No, I'm seeing something you missed." Triumphantly, I went over to the whiteboard and grabbed a dry-erase marker. With large strokes I drew the symbol I'd found, then presented it with a flourish.

Ⅱ

"The Gemini symbol," she said flatly. "So?"

Based on her reaction, she was distinctly underwhelmed. Undeterred, I continued. "So based on this, he's about halfway through the latest pattern."

Grace sighed and rolled her head forward, rubbing the back of her neck with one hand. Tiredly, she said, "You think this means we might be able to predict where Gunnar is going next."

"Exactly. So maybe instead of just sitting around waiting for him to, y'know, *kill* a bunch of people, we can get ahead of him." I held the dry-erase marker out like it was a mic and dropped it. "C'mon, admit it. You're impressed."

"It's an interesting theory," she conceded. The skepticism in her voice was clear, though.

"It's the right theory," I retorted, feeling nonplussed. I hadn't expected a parade, but a little appreciation would've been nice.

"Maybe." Grace ran a hand over her face. "Look. I've been driving all night, and I'm starving. I need to eat—"

"Driving where?" In my excitement, I'd almost forgotten that she'd abandoned me to go off God knew where.

"None of your business," Grace snapped.

"None of my business?" My voice rose to match hers. "Listen, lady. The only reason I'm even here is because you put a bull's-eye on my back."

"Not intentionally."

"Does it matter? I've been out there twiddling my thumbs while you do—what? Stare at a computer screen and try to decipher some weird code you made up when you were a kid? And meanwhile, you missed this." I gestured to the wall. "Back in Vegas you called this a game, which is fucking sick, by the way, and news flash—you're losing."

"Fuck you."

"No, fuck you, Grace Cabot Grimes."

Grace's brow darkened, and she stepped toward me. I braced, ready to be slapped, pushed, or worse . . .

Instead, her eyes rolled up in her head and she crumpled to the floor.

SCENE OF THE CRIME

Hilda grimaced at the sight of a used condom wrapper peeking out from under the bed. That was the fourth one she'd found in this room alone. Making a face, she used a napkin to scoop it into the bucket beside her. She really needed to find a better job, in a real hotel. Odila claimed that Caesars Palace was hiring summer help; maybe she should head over after her shift to try her luck.

Hilda did a cursory wipe of the bathtub and scrubbed congealed toothpaste off the sink, grumbling the entire time. As if she didn't have enough to worry about, she'd caught her son's girlfriend sneaking out of his bedroom the night before. She was at her wit's end. The fight they'd had last night played on a loop in her head: her screaming about teenage pregnancy, him yelling back that they were careful and she was a prude, that he got straight As, so she didn't have the right to say anything . . . he wasn't wrong. But ever since Joe turned fifteen, he'd gone from being the sweet boy who told her everything to this sullen stranger who barely spoke to her. Tears threatened, and Hilda swallowed them back. She knew plenty of people who had it worse. Kids in jail, kids having kids . . . she'd assumed she'd never have to worry about those things, not with her child. He was too smart, too gentle. But that was before he met Cassie.

Cassie. Thinking of a few choice names for *that* girl, Hilda gave the toilet bowl an extra-vigorous swish, then flushed it and struggled to her feet. Her dream had always been for Joe to go to college. She'd worked too hard, for too long, for him to just throw that away. She cast a final glance around the bathroom: good enough. The manager always said she was too thorough anyway. Maybe Caesars Palace would appreciate that.

Still stewing, Hilda pushed her cart to the next room and knocked, calling out, "Housekeeping!"

No answer. She opened the door and stepped inside, then her shoulders sagged. This was the worst yet. Junk-food wrappers everywhere, and needles . . . what was wrong with people? She'd be in here for a half hour at least. And of course, there was no tip in sight.

Sighing, Hilda started with the bed, stripping the sheets and shoving them in her bin. As she swiped the vacuum cleaner back and forth across the industrial carpeting, her determination solidified. The rooms at Caesars might be just as bad, but it attracted a higher class of clientele, and if Odila was telling the truth, she'd earn three times the tips. She'd need that soon enough. Joe was weeks away from getting his driver's permit and had already been making noise about buying a used car.

By the time Hilda was ready to tackle the bathroom, it was nearly her break. Thanks to her latest diet, lunch was just string cheese and a hard-boiled egg, but even that would be an improvement over the chalky smoothie she'd choked down for breakfast.

Bathroom first, she decided. After dragging the cart across the room, she locked the wheels and gathered up the cleaning spray and sponge. Then she turned around and screamed.

CHAPTER FIFTEEN

THE LONG MEMORY

F or fuck's sake," I hissed, dropping down beside Grace. Her chest was rising and falling, so she was still breathing. I wasn't exactly first-aid certified, though, so aside from that, I had no idea what to check. Tentatively, I tapped her cheeks. "Hey, Grace? I don't know what to do. Grace?" I bit my lip. Had something happened to her out there? Maybe Gunnar caught up with her again? She didn't seem to be bleeding . . . but should I call 911?

I glanced around the room; EMTs would probably not be very understanding about the crazy wall. I could drag her into the living room . . .

Grace moaned something. I leaned down closer to hear as she mumbled it again. It sounded like "Juice."

I raced into the kitchen and sloshed juice into a glass, spilling about an equal amount on the floor. Skidding in my socks, I hurried back in. Awkwardly, I lifted her head and said, "Hey, can you drink this?"

I poured it slowly into Grace's mouth. Some slipped out the

sides, and for a second I was afraid she was going to choke . . . then she took a good gulp. It took a few minutes, but she managed to drink it all. Finally, her eyes opened and focused on me. "Welcome back," I said. "Diabetes?"

She shook her head and mumbled, "Just low blood sugar."

I blew out a breath. "Well, shit, that was scary as fuck. Can you sit up?"

She nodded and I helped her, propping her against the leg of her desk. Then I sank back on my haunches across from her. "More juice?"

"In a second." She closed her eyes and tilted her head back. I watched her for a second, feeling useless. It was funny; in my head, I'd built Grace up to be practically superhuman. But between the stabbing and this . . . her fallibility was honestly unnerving. Maybe it would've been smarter to just head out on my own while she was gone; I'd already made it to L.A., had new papers and some cash. Why not just take my chances?

The weird thing was that it hadn't even occurred to me.

Grace extended an arm and said, "Can you help me up?"

Obligingly, I hauled her to her feet and maneuvered her into the swivel chair. Her color was looking slightly better, but she still seemed wobbly. "Can I get you something?"

"I need food."

"Yeah, sure. I can grab something."

Without opening her eyes, she said, "I'm sorry if I scared you. That hasn't happened in a very long time."

I stared at her. "Holy shit."

"What?"

"You actually apologized for something."

"Yes, well . . . I won't be making a habit of it." She smiled thinly and tried to push out of the chair. "I think I can make it to the kitchen for a yogurt."

"The hell you will," I said, horrified. "Sit your ass back down, I'm making pancakes."

Despite the limitations of Grace's pantry, I managed to whip up some surprisingly decent pancakes.

"So what do you think?" I asked, digging into my third.

"I need to examine it more closely. But you might be right about the pattern."

My fork froze en route to my mouth. "I was talking about the pancakes."

"Oh. They're fine." Grace dipped a bite in maple syrup and tucked it in her mouth. Her table manners really were impressive; I felt like an ape in comparison. "I'll examine the data to see if it holds up. If it does, I might be able to build a new predictive algorithm off it."

"So basically what you're saying is that I'm awesome." I shifted another pancake onto my plate.

Grace watched with disgust as I lathered on a thick layer of Nutella. "It's honestly remarkable that you still have all your teeth."

"Good genes," I said thoughtlessly, suppressing a burp. Internally, I smacked myself. I'd never been proud of my family's business, but at least it wasn't mass murder. "Sorry."

"For what?" She looked genuinely puzzled, then laughed. "Yes, I suppose my genes aren't the best, all things considered. How did you find out about my father anyway?"

"Internet search," I lied. After a beat, I added, "Sorry. Must've been tough."

"Yes, it was." Grace stirred her coffee.

"We can't pick our families. Mine weren't exactly great, either."

"Ah yes, the infamous Jamisons of Tuscaloosa." She arched an eyebrow. "It's curious. Despite the fact that you talk incessantly—"

"Hey!"

"I actually know very little about your past. Ironic, isn't it?"

I eyed her. We'd been together long enough now for me to recognize her tells; that little line between her brows meant something was really bothering her. I felt a pang of guilt for digging through the file box in her closet; I knew a lot more than she thought. But this didn't seem like the best time to bring that up. "This really bugs you, doesn't it?"

Grace shrugged. "I don't like being at an information deficit."

"Ah yes, an information deficit," I intoned. "The worst of all possible fates."

Her mask slid back into place. "Thanks for the pancakes."

She started to get up; I put a hand on her arm to stop her. "Look, you're right. The truth is, we're a lot alike." Off her look I said, "With some things, at least. Neither of us likes talking about our past, right?"

"No, I suppose not."

"But the one advantage we've got is that there are two of us. And maybe if we shared information, it'd help us come up with a plan. To get a handle on how Gunnar thinks, I need to know more about how you two grew up." I drew a deep breath. "And in exchange, I'll tell you why I became Amber Jamison."

Grace examined me. "You're serious."

I nodded. "Deadly. But it requires mass quantities of booze."

She rolled her eyes. "It's not even nine a.m."

"You have someplace to be?" I cocked an eyebrow at her this time. "No? Then show me where you've been hiding the good stuff."

G race produced a giant bottle of vodka from the garage freezer (which was literally the only place I hadn't checked for alcohol) and added a tiny splash to her orange juice. I, on the other hand, kicked things off with two shots just to oil the gears.

As I was pouring my third, Grace started to talk about the day her dad was arrested. Her face remained oddly blank, like she was sharing something completely mundane. Apparently she and her twin watched a team of CSI agents dig up their backyard, uncovering more than a dozen trash bags filled with his victims. *A therapist would have a field day with that*, I thought.

The rest of her life was straight out of a Danielle Steel novel. The following week they moved to Boston, staying with a rich, crazy grandmother who didn't like kids. There was no further contact with their serial killer dad; in fact, no one in the family ever mentioned him again. Their increasingly distant, withholding mother shipped them off to separate snobby boarding schools (Grace went to a horsey school in Virginia, Gunnar to a boys' school in Connecticut).

"He hated it," Grace said. "It was the first time in our lives we'd ever been separated, and that was bad enough. But the school turned out to be ghastly, practically a military academy. Gunnar was miserable there."

"Mm," I said, sipping orange juice (I'd realized that unless I wanted to pass out and miss this rare opportunity, I'd better slow down). "But were there any other signs growing up? I mean, did Gunnar set fires or hurt animals or anything?"

"Well, he did like to rip the legs off mice and watch them drag themselves around."

"Um, yeah, I'd say that counts," I said, feeling sick.

Grace added a bit more vodka to her drink; she was doing that more and more as the story progressed. "And we had a dog for a few weeks, Poppy. She died suddenly, and I always wondered . . ." She shook her head. "You have to understand how close we were; our parents were very old school, they thought children should be seen and not heard. Neither of us really had anyone else.

"Looking back on it later, I realized that Gunnar must have poisoned every other relationship I'd ever had. For instance, in kindergarten I made my first real friend. But she suddenly started avoiding me and told everyone that I'd wet the bed at our sleepover." Grace pursed her lips. "Gunnar insisted on retaliating. For a week he stole her lunch and peed on it. At the time, I thought he was just being protective. But later—"

"You think he scared her off."

"Most likely, yes. He always said that we had each other and didn't need anyone else. Apparently he meant it."

"Apparently," I agreed. It was textbook narcissism. Gunnar viewed Grace not as another person but as an extension of himself. Seeing her interact with anyone else threw him into a rage, which caused him to lash out. "But that changed when you went to boarding school. You started to make friends again."

Grace nodded. "My roommate Rose. She was smart, funny, and an amazing rider. I adored her. And I started neglecting Gunnar."

"Neglecting him how?"

"I didn't answer his emails right away. I spent the summers with Rose instead of going back to Grandmother's house. I basically abandoned him."

"You still feel guilty about it," I noted.

She cocked her head to the side. "If you start psychoanalyzing me, this ends now."

"No, it's just—you sound like you're blaming yourself, but the truth is that unless you did exactly what Gunnar wanted for the rest of your life, the end result would have been the same."

"Perhaps," she acknowledged.

"Definitely," I said. "Guy sounds like a total control freak."

"Yes, you could say that." She swirled her drink, gazing into it as she continued. "Anyway, Rose died in what was officially declared a riding accident when we were sixteen. I'd already transferred to Choate at that point, but we were still close. I was devastated."

"I'll bet."

"And then I started dating Mike. We were together for all of senior year. Both of us were going to college in Boston—"

"Let me guess. Harvard."

She gave me a look. "MIT, actually."

I feigned surprise. "So Harvard wasn't nerdy enough for you?"

"Do you want to know the rest, or should I stop now?"

"Sorry." I waved a hand. "Continue."

"Well." Grace stared off into the middle distance. "The day of our graduation, Mike never showed up. We were all frantic, his parents and friends and I searched everywhere." Her voice hardened as she continued. "Gunnar offered to help us look. I thought that was out of character at the time, especially since we hadn't really been speaking." She issued a sharp laugh. "I even thanked him before he left. After we finally gave up for the night, I went back to my dorm room and found Mike's mortarboard sitting on my bed."

I swallowed hard, picturing it. "I'm so sorry. That's horrible." The pancakes were starting to churn in my stomach; all this talk of serial killers was wreaking havoc on my digestive tract. "Um, did they . . . was he ever found?"

"I found him." Grace's face still displayed no emotion, frozen as a mask. But she poured straight vodka into her glass and knocked it back. "There was something written on the inside of Mike's mortarboard: 'Catch Me.'"

"'Catch Me?'"

"It's a game Gunnar made up when we were kids. One of us would leave clues for the other to follow, a sort of scavenger hunt. As we got older, the boundaries expanded until we were playing all over town."

"So Mike's mortarboard was like your invitation to play." I was fascinated in spite of myself. Which was probably better than sitting here horrified, but still. Hundreds of people were dead because a serial killer's fucked-up kid was trying to get his sister to play with him. Freud would have had a field day with these two.

Grace pushed her plate back and sighed. "Anyway. When I saw that, I just knew. I drove back to our old house in Ohio and found Mike precisely where our father buried his first victim." She met my eyes and added, "There was a Gemini symbol marking the spot."

I stared at her. "Holy shit."

"Holy shit, indeed. I've been after Gunnar ever since."

"Except for college," I pointed out.

"I knew I needed to build my proficiency in order to be more effective. It was a calculated risk." She paused, then added, "As far as I can tell, he went dormant until I graduated."

The same way he waited for us to get Grace help, rather than just murdering us in the Getaway parking lot, I thought with a shudder.

I took a moment to process that. "And before Vegas, had you ever caught up to him?"

"Three other times. The last one was Portland, Oregon." She fell silent, staring moodily into her empty mug.

The dead cop. Final mystery solved. I swallowed hard. "And what, Gunnar escaped?"

Grace nodded. "I thought the local police could handle it, but they didn't understand how dangerous he was. So yes, he got away. After killing one of the officers."

"Which is why you don't like to involve the police."

"Yes."

"So back when you were kids," I said thoughtfully, "when Gunnar played this game, was he all in? Like, almost too intensely engaged in it?"

"Yes, exactly."

"And he usually won?"

Another long beat, then she said, "He always won."

That's not exactly reassuring. I ran a hand through my hair, which was nearly a half inch long now and getting scruffy. "And basically, for the past seventeen years, you've kept playing. He runs, you chase him."

"Basically, yes." Rubbing her temples, she said, "Your turn."

"What?" I was still going over everything she'd said, turning it over in my mind. Talk about a fucked-up codependent relationship. Usually when damaged people like this tried to hurt each other, they didn't leave literally hundreds of bodies in their wake. "Sorry, this is just a lot."

"Enough stalling." Leveling her gaze at me, she asked, "What are you hiding, Amber Jamison?"

"Fine." I topped off my glass, regretting the fact that I'd agreed to this quid pro quo. I hadn't told this story to anyone, ever. I'd done everything possible to block it from my own mind. Which didn't really work. Not a day went by that I didn't think of Stella.

I pulled my knees to my chest, wrapped my arms around them, and started. "So, my parents were grifters. Kind of shitty at it, though. I was pulling scams with them my whole life, and then they dumped me, and I went out on my own. Small-time stuff, just enough to get by."

I was silently praying for an earthquake or tsunami to strike, anything that would prevent my having to share the next part. I was already getting terrible flashbacks of gunfire and screaming and blood, so much blood—

"Amber?"

"My name's not Amber," I said in a small voice. "It's Emily. Emily Austin."

Her voice was gentler as she said, "Okay, Emily. You don't have to tell me."

"No, I do." I drew a deep, shuddery breath. "I have to tell someone."

So I did. I explained how this girl I was dating came up with a huge score, one that would set us up for years, maybe even the rest of our lives if we were smart. And boy, did I think I was smart back then. I was sick of all the nickel-and-dime gigs, and deep down probably needed to prove to myself and everyone else that I was better than the parents who had abandoned me.

The best part was that it was a two-woman con, no need to bring in anyone else. A variation on "Pig-in-a-Poke," a grift I'd been pulling since before I lost my baby teeth. The more Stella talked about it, the more excited I got. This was it, the "one last job." Then we'd retire to an island somewhere and spend our days sipping mai tais and fucking.

"You can leave out some of the details," Grace interrupted.

"Sorry. Got carried away." I cleared my throat, debating how another shot of vodka would mix with the pancakes. Not well, but I didn't care. I tossed one back, then said, "Anyway, Stella had been scoping out the mark for a while. He was a real dirtbag who built condos, sold them to people who couldn't really afford them, then kept raising the HOA fees until they definitely couldn't pay their mortgage. He'd kick them out and resell the unit to some other sap."

"So basically, another con artist."

"Basically. But *I* never robbed anyone who couldn't afford it," I said defensively. "And I never kicked anyone out of their house."

"Understood. Continue."

"Okay, so this was Florida, where what he was doing was perfectly legal. By the time I got there, Stella had laid all the groundwork. She was beautiful—" My voice caught as I remembered the way her eyes sparkled when she got excited. "Guys were tripping over themselves for her. She had this asshole on the hook, he thought she was some trust fund bitch—no offense—"

"None taken," Grace said, waving a hand.

"Anyway, her cover was that she had a bad coke problem and had blown through her money, so she was selling everything off. Including her yacht." I paused. For a minute it felt like I was back there, watching Stella standing in the bow, wind blowing her long hair back. I'd never said it, hadn't even admitted it to myself at the time, but I'd probably been in love with her. "Anyway, she agreed to sell it to him for five hundred grand cash. Told him it was important that her parents not find out, or they'd be pissed at her."

Grace's brow wrinkled. "Didn't she have to prove it was her boat?"

I waved a hand. "We had fake documents drawn up, and frankly, the guy was an idiot. He barely even glanced at them."

I noticed that his bald spot was already burning. His wedding ring glinted as he bent over the papers, barely able to tear his eyes away from Stella's cleavage long enough to sign. I was dressed in white pants and a navy shirt with the boat's name embroidered on it, trying not to stare at the duffel bags a few feet away, the ones Stella had already opened to confirm the contents. In my mind over and over, an endless chorus of five hundred thousand dollars five hundred thousand . . .

"Thanks for the boat, sweetheart. Should we go below to cele-brate?" he said around his cigar, leering at Stella.

That was when the yelling started. I turned and saw two guys with assault rifles running down the dock toward us. One of them started firing.

Stella stood up to see better, and the first bullet spun her around . . .

"I'm confused."

I frowned at the interruption. "Confused by what?"

"How did you even get on the yacht?"

Irritated, I said, "We took jobs on it a couple weeks earlier. Made sure the rest of the crew was ashore for the day, then invited him on board. Okay?"

"It still seems implausible."

"It's a con!" I said, throwing up my arms. "The key is choosing the right mark. They need to be just dumb enough to buy it."

"Then who was shooting? His bodyguards?"

"See, that's the thing," I said. "What we didn't know was that this guy had some side hustles, storing drugs and guns in empty condos. I found out later that he'd screwed over some pretty scary people."

"I see." Grace examined me. "I take it your friend didn't make it."

For once, her chilly reserve was actually helpful. It anchored me in the present, providing some distance from that terrible day. "Stella was standing right behind him, so she got the worst of it."

"And you?"

"I, uh . . . I dove off the ship." I squirmed. It was not my finest moment, but pure instinct had kicked in. The last thing I'd seen as I'd gone over the edge had been Stella's hand reaching out for me, her eyes pleading. Then, *Splash!*

I swam like hell. Didn't come up for air until I was a hundred yards out, and by then the boat was on fire . . .

Grace frowned. "I still don't see why you changed your entire identity. Her death wasn't your fault."

I mimed picking up a phone. "Yeah, hello, Officer? So my friend and I were robbing this guy, and then these really bad dudes who work for a cartel showed up and shot at us and oh, yeah, I'm a witness, so they're probably still after me."

"But—"

"Look, I panicked," I said angrily, jumping to my feet. "I was young and scared and I've never had a great relationship with law enforcement. And I just wanted to put it behind me. So I changed my name and started over. I even went straight. But it didn't matter, because I'm right back where I started, with a different asshole trying to kill me."

I was breathing hard, hands curled into fists. Grace looked startled by my outburst. She held up both hands placatingly. "It's okay, Amber. Emily. I'm sorry. Okay?"

My stomach was roiling, and pancakes and booze don't play well with bile. Turning on my heels, I ran to the downstairs bathroom. I splashed water on my face, fighting to quell my heaving insides. I really did not want to puke again.

When it felt like I'd regained control, I eased down to the floor, resting my head against the wall. Even worse than the memories was the guilt. Because I hadn't even told Grace the worst part. The thing that made me hate myself every time I remembered it, the real reason I'd decided to shed my old life and never look back.

As the shock of the water hit me and I started swimming away, I wasn't thinking about Stella. What popped into my mind was *Shit. I forgot to grab the cash.*

Deep down, that's who I am. And sure, I had a crappy

childhood, but that's not really an excuse. I'm the bitch who worried about money when her girlfriend was bleeding out.

That part, I'll never confess to anyone. Not in this life or the next.

A knock on the bathroom door. "Emily?"

"Just call me Amber," I said in a ragged voice.

"Okay, Amber." A pause, then Grace said, "Can I get you something? Water, maybe?"

I closed my eyes. What I really needed was a nap. But I called back, "Water would be great."

While I waited, the revelations of the past few hours tumbled through my tired, inebriated brain. Zodiac symbols and secret alphabets and so many bodies. At the end of the day, Grace and her brother were just a couple of bored rich kids playing an elaborate game with other people's lives as chits. And deep down, maybe neither of them wanted it to end.

I woke up a couple hours later in the same position. My head was pounding, my mouth tasted like ass, and both legs were asleep. Gingerly, I got to my feet. There was a glass of water on the lip of the sink. I drank it in two gulps, then followed the sound of tapping keys back to the SKS. Grace was sitting at her desk again. Without looking up, she said, "Feeling better, Emily?"

"I told you Amber was fine." My stomach growled, and I tried to remember if there was any pancake batter left. "What are you doing?"

"I've double-checked your work, and the theory seems plausible. I'm working on the predictive algorithm we discussed to pinpoint where Gunnar might go next."

I resisted the urge to break into a victory dance; under the circumstances, it seemed like poor form. But something had shifted in our relationship. We weren't friends, exactly, but Grace's tone no longer defaulted to dripping disdain. Which was progress. "Like you said before, I'm totally awesome."

She didn't look up, but a smile tugged at her lips. "Yes, well. You're not entirely unhelpful."

"I'll take it."

Her computer pinged, and she frowned. I leaned over her shoulder to peer at the screen; one of the lines was blinking. "Is it done already?"

"No. That's one of the 911 alerts."

My heart skidded to a stop. "You mean—"

"There's no guarantee it's him." She tapped a key, and the transcript of a conversation popped up onscreen. I skimmed it quickly, the key words leaping out at me: *Vegas . . . bathtub . . . prostitute . . .*

"Wait, did this . . . is it happening right now?"

"Within the past few hours. There's a lag, it has to complete transcription before the algorithm can catch it. The call came in . . . three hours ago."

"So it happened last night?" *Marcella.* My knees wobbled, threatening to give out. I eased myself to the floor, frantically trying to dial Dot's number.

She answered on the first ring. "It's not her."

I released a breath I hadn't even realized I was holding. "You're sure?"

"Positive. I was about to call you, hon, but wanted to talk to her first. Marcella is fine."

"Thank God." I closed my eyes, trying to will my stomach to settle. "So who was it?"

"Some poor girl who worked out of the Super 8 on the North Strip."

My eyes immediately went to the map; that was exactly where

Grace had expected to find the next victim. I looked at her. "The place you got jumped, was it the Super 8?"

Grace was eyeing me with concern. Slowly, she nodded. "It was. Gunnar is still in Las Vegas."

"Fuck," I said. "Listen, Dot, I don't want to freak you out—"

"Too late for that, toots." She sounded tired and defeated. I felt awful; what had I dragged her into?

"Listen, just hunker down. I've got a plan."

"Yeah?"

"Yup," I lied. "Won't be much longer."

"Well, that's good to hear." Dot didn't sound relieved, though. Her voice was thin and taut.

"Could you do me a favor? Find out everything you can about this murder. Safely, okay?"

"You got it. And don't worry, I'll get Marcella to stay put, too. Even if I have to tie her to a chair."

I hung up and stared at Grace. She'd already turned back to her screen. "This is actually a fortunate turn of events."

I frowned. "Another woman is dead."

"Yes, but now we know for certain that he's still in Las Vegas. For the moment at least."

Grace's voice had gone flat again, and she seemed to be avoiding my eyes. Was she hiding something?

Where the hell *was* she yesterday anyway? It wouldn't have been hard to drive to Vegas and back in that amount of time.

I felt a sudden, intense urge to get the hell out of there. I'd spent weeks with this person, and it still didn't feel like I could trust her.

But then, I wasn't trusting by nature. And really, what alternative did I have? Marcella and Dot needed me, and to help them, I had to rely on Grace. Trying to sound casual, I asked, "Where did you go anyway?"

"What?"

I grabbed the back of her chair and spun her around to face me. Leaning in, I asked, "Where were you?"

She looked bemused. "Are you asking if I drove to Vegas and killed someone?"

"Yeah, basically."

"Well, I didn't."

"Then where were you?"

"It had nothing to do with Gunnar." She crossed her arms over her chest. "It was personal."

"Personal?" I guffawed.

"Yes. I do have a life outside this, you know."

"Not that I've seen." I sighed. "Look, I want to trust you, but you haven't exactly made it easy."

"Well, that's a shame, Amber. I honestly don't know what more I can do. I saved your life—"

"And endangered it," I interrupted.

"I took you into my home, and all you've done in exchange is break into my personal spaces and accuse me of things." She cocked her head to the side. "Let's be honest. If I wanted to kill you, you'd be dead."

I squirmed. There was an unerring logic to that. But something still felt off. "Why am I the only one?"

"The only what?" Her voice was steely again; so much for progress.

"The only person you've saved."

A long beat passed before she said, "It was the first time I had the opportunity."

"Really?" I crossed my arms in front of my chest. "You said you spent weeks watching Beau. I'm guessing you do that with all of them. Are you telling me there was never a chance to rescue someone else?"

Grace turned the chair to face away from me again. "It's not a perfect science."

"Meaning what?"

"Meaning, no, I was unable to get there in time to save anyone else."

I didn't believe her. I opened my mouth to say so, then shut it again. Because it occurred to me that I was alone, in her house, and she was in much better shape than me, blood sugar issues aside.

Besides, she had rescued me, right? Maybe she was telling the truth, and she'd usually gotten there too late. My eyes landed on the wall map again, all those yellow pins. Clearing my throat, I said, "We need to stop him."

"Obviously." She pushed off the arms of her chair. "I'm going to pack."

"What, right now?" My arms dropped.

Grace strode past me. "My wound is healed and we know where Gunnar is, for the moment at least. That killing was the final data point."

"Data point?" I parroted dumbly. *She wants to go back to Vegas. Where he's waiting, to* kill *me.*

"He finished the symbol." She went to the whiteboard and pointed at a backward *K*, which had the letter *R* beneath it. "Usually once he does that, he moves on."

"Well, we still need a plan," I protested. "I mean, you don't know exactly where he is, right?"

Grace sighed and rubbed her neck with one hand; she looked tired, drawn. "Fine. What do you suggest?"

I looked at her, startled. "Are you really asking?"

"I really am."

After a moment's hesitation, I swallowed hard and went back to the wall map. Scanning it, I thought grimly, *We're going to have to add another yellow pin to Vegas.* I drew a deep breath to steady myself and said, "So this is a game. Gunnar uses your made-up alphabet to write a letter in each city, and those letters form a word referring to where your father buried his victims. While also drawing a giant Gemini symbol across the country. And he's been doing it for years. That's . . . ridiculously complicated."

"Yes, well. Gunnar was never one to keep things simple."

Grace was absent-mindedly rubbing her side, where he'd stabbed her. Something occurred to me. "Before Vegas, did he ever hurt you?"

A pause, then she answered, "Yes."

"But not as badly, I'm guessing?"

"This is the second time he's stabbed me."

"Really? Where was it last time?"

"In the leg." She paused, then added, "He was just trying to slow me down."

Right. Totally normal, I thought. "So you weren't hurt as badly?"

Grace shrugged. "He threw the knife from a distance, so it wasn't very deep."

"Which means he's escalating the attacks on you." My eyes widened. "You're the real victim!"

"I think two hundred and fifty-four people would be inclined to disagree," she said dryly.

"No, I mean—to Gunnar, you're the only *real* victim. Think about it. You've literally spent your entire adult life doing exactly what he wants you to do—chase him. He's completely controlled you. And you've let him."

Grace stared at me, her face blank. She opened her mouth as if to say something, then closed it again. Finally, shaking her head, she muttered, "I didn't ask for therapy."

"Well, you're getting it. Because this is nuts." Suddenly, I froze. *Of course.* I felt like an idiot for not realizing it before.

"What?" Grace asked.

Not even her glare could diminish my excitement. "We're doing this all wrong."

"That's such a valuable insight. Thanks."

"I mean it. This is a game, right? And frankly, you've been losing. So there's only one way to win."

"Exactly!" Grace said with exasperation, throwing up her hands. "By catching him!"

"No." I shook my head. "By changing the rules."

CHAPTER SIXTEEN
THE SET-UP

This is a terrible plan." Grace was leaning against the guest room doorway, watching me pack.

"You've made your opinion clear," I snapped. "But unless you've come up with something better, we're doing it." I finished shoving my belongings (including the Glock—thank God Dot had managed to retrieve that) into my duffel bag. "We'll have to stop along the way for a few more things."

Grace, of course, had already finished packing. "Gunnar will never fall for it."

I sighed and straightened. "Even if he doesn't, what's the harm? I mean, otherwise we just sit around waiting for him to kill someone else. At least in Vegas, we'll probably be closer to his next stop."

"I think you're putting a lot of faith in a motel manager," Grace grumbled.

"Hell, yeah I am," I said. "Because this whole lone-wolf, go-it-alone thing hasn't worked out so well for you, has it? The one thing

Gunnar definitely won't be expecting is numbers. And in Vegas, we get that."

"Maybe."

"Definitely." I zipped my bag closed.

The past few hours had been a whirlwind of activity—well, on my part at least. Grace had spent them sulkily packing up enough electronics to stock a Best Buy.

Which was fine, because I had come up with, if I do say so myself, a phenomenal plan.

Grace prattled on about what a genius her brother was, but they'd been raised in what sounded like a pretty posh family, complete with boarding schools and trust funds.

Which meant that deep down, they were soft. Grace was losing this "game" because they thought too much alike; they *were* too much alike. Not that I'd ever tell her that.

Whereas I was a survivor. No one had ever handed me anything, I'd had to take it on my own. Consequently, I brought a whole other skill set to the table. I knew how to navigate the real world in a way that neither of them could possibly grasp.

Besides, all this nonsense about secret alphabets and symbols forming patterns within patterns; I mean, really? That was some serious rich-people bullshit.

I zipped the duffel bag shut and slung it over my shoulder as I stood. Grace was glaring at the wall as if it had just mouthed off to her. Without meeting my eyes, she asked, "What if it doesn't work?"

Her brow was crinkled with worry, which for her constituted a positive outpouring of emotion. "It will," I said with forced confidence. "He won't be able to resist."

"And if he does?" Grace pressed.

"Keep an eye on your algorithms, and if he pops up somewhere else, you have my permission to drive there and go cattle-prod crazy."

"Your permission?" Grace arched an eyebrow.

"*Until* then," I said, forging ahead, "we follow the plan. Which means it's time to put on your big-girl panties. Now listen, this is important. Did you pack the turkey jerky and mini pretzels?"

THE TRAP

@**Ashleyk212** OMG did u hear they found ANOTHER sex worker dead um hello #SerialKillerInVegas

@**Ladyjanesdomain** Srsly if u needed any proof that #womenslivesdontmatter maybe call LVPD and ask why no one is talking about the 5 WOMEN FOUND STRANGLED IN MOTEL TUBS

@**itchyscratchykitty** #FEMICIDE is REAL people what does it take to get FBI involved oh right they don't care bc #sexworkers #women

@**JennyinLA** Guys I'm like totes freaked rn it turns out they found a girl dead in her room last night IN THE SAME MOTEL I'M STAYING IN um hello TripAdvisor #nostarreview

@**Keri_will** LV Safety Alert: Stay away from the Buggy Suites Motel they found two prostitutes ded there strangled in tubs #BatesMotel #LeavingLasVegas

CHAPTER SEVENTEEN

NO QUESTIONS ASKED

We didn't exactly sneak into Vegas under cover of night, but we did travel the last ten miles in the back of an honest-to-God tour bus courtesy of Jim. It deposited us inside the service entrance at the Golden Nugget Hotel/Casino. I could barely contain my excitement as we rode the elevator up to the fifth floor, where Dot was waiting in our suite.

Sadly, the hotel was a step or two down from the Strat (although according to promotional posters in the elevator, there was a glass waterslide through an aquarium tank filled with sharks, not that we'd get to enjoy that). I tried to hide my disappointment when Dot opened the door to reveal a somewhat lackluster room decorated in varying shades of brown and gold. Per usual, Grace was much more direct, saying, "I suppose I've seen worse."

"It's perfect, Dot," I said, drawing her into a hug and casting a warning look over her shoulder at Grace. The entire suite was smaller than the room I'd shared with Marcella, but it was spotless and plenty big for what we needed. "Thanks."

"I did the best I could," Dot said, clearly miffed. "You're registered under a false name, so there shouldn't be any way to find you . . . I can't even count how many favors I'm gonna owe folks after this."

"It'll be worth it, I promise," I said.

Dot had visibly wilted over the past few weeks. Her exquisite makeup job didn't quite conceal the dark circles under her eyes and a pronounced tightness around her mouth. Even her brassy hair seemed more subdued. Still, she was beaming. "I'm chuffed to see you, dollface. I got everything set to go, you just say the word."

Grace was already at the desk, arranging monitors and other equipment in a replica of what she had at home. Which seemed like overkill, but she'd explained that my plan required more computing power than an internet café could provide. Plus, privacy.

I followed Dot to the plush couch and pulled up the app we'd decided to use. In the past, I'd always avoided social media; it was way too easy to be tracked through it thanks to facial recognition software. But going viral was a critical part of my plan, and the posts I'd come up with were pretty convincing, if I did say so myself.

Skimming them, Dot snorted. "Ha! Love the hashtags."

"Thanks."

"How many of these are there?"

"I wrote something like three hundred," I said. "And then Grace made some bots—"

"Social bots," Grace interrupted. "Algorithms designed to mimic human behaviors."

"Yeah, they're pretty cool," I said. "We set it up—"

"I set it up," Grace interjected.

Dot and I exchanged a look, and then I continued. "The great and powerful Grace set it up so that each gets shared under a fake account, then another picks it up, and another . . . until hopefully real people start tweeting about it."

"Like an election, but with a serial killer," Dot said brightly.

"Exactly. So if we get enough traction, Gunnar will see reports that a fifth victim was found at the Buggy Suites. We can follow him from there."

"You sure he'll take the bait?"

"He won't," Grace said curtly.

"He won't be able to resist," I said, cutting her another look. "Another killing, matching his MO? It implies that there's a copycat, and he'd hate the idea of someone stealing his thunder." I was banking a lot on this, but in my gut, I knew it would work. What I wasn't saying was that he'd most likely suspect that his twin had decided to take a more aggressive role in their game; that would be incredibly intriguing for him.

I'd decided against sharing that theory with Grace, for obvious reasons.

"Well, here's hoping," Dot said, smoothing her skirt.

I scrolled through my phone, checking trending hashtags. None of ours had popped up yet, but we'd only kicked off the cyber assault after entering the city limits a half hour ago. I had no idea how long it took to go viral, but if it didn't happen soon, I'd have to goose the posts a little.

The Vegas police department was going to freak out when they heard rumors of a nonexistent fifth victim—but any denials they made played right into our hands. And maybe creating a fake victim would prevent someone from becoming one in real life. At least, that was how I'd justified it to myself.

"Thanks again for all your help with this, Dot," I said.

"Honestly, toots, anything to stop looking over my shoulder." Dot patted my knee.

"Um, so is Marcella coming?" I said with forced nonchalance.

Dot frowned. "She's on my naughty list, to be honest. Been quite a handful for Jessie. Three times now she tried to bring dates back to her room at the Mayhem."

Hearing that made my stomach flip; I tried to tell myself it was because Marcella was being reckless, not that I was jealous. That was her job, after all. But Grace had been persuaded to cover any monetary losses racked up by Dot, Jessie, and Marcella during all this. That argument had happened early in my stay at Grace's fortress of solitude, and she'd initially resisted. But as I'd pointed out (repeatedly), if they were in danger, it was only because they'd saved her life. And they shouldn't be penalized for that. "Didn't you get the money we sent?"

"I sent," Grace muttered from where she was connecting a power strip.

"Sure did. Jim was pretty tickled, he's always wanted a Bitcoin."

"Then why is she working?"

"Why does Marcella do anything?" Dot sighed. "She's also not happy that you left without saying goodbye."

"Right." I picked at a stray thread on my jean shorts. "I figured."

"But," Dot continued brightly, "she promised to cool it while you're here. And if you need help with anything, she's in. For Lori."

"Great." Even though I only had myself to blame, being ghosted by Marcella hurt. "If everyone does their part, it should be perfectly safe."

"Nonsense," Grace snorted. "It's not safe at all."

I threw her an exasperated look. I mean, sure, dealing with a super-smart, extremely lethal serial killer was never going to be as safe as a kiddie ride at Disneyland. But those weren't one hundred percent safe either. Just, like, ninety-nine. "It'll be fine, Dot. But if you want to back out, I'll understand." I mentally crossed my fingers because the truth was, without Dot's help, the whole plan was roundly fucked.

"Well," Dot said slowly, "I gotta admit, when you first called, I wasn't exactly jazzed." She adjusted her glasses and smiled at me. "But I trust you. You're a smart cookie."

"Thanks, Dot," I said, touched. I wasn't used to people trusting me. "Did you find out anything about the woman who was killed at the Super 8?"

Dot clucked. "Poor lamb. McKayla Nichols, only nineteen years old. There's finally some talk about starting a task force."

"Oh, that's helpful," I said, perking up. "It should give the hashtags a boost."

"So what do we do now?" Dot asked.

"We wait," Grace said, sitting back from her monitors and scowling. "And hope that Amber doesn't get us all killed."

"Just ignore her," I said, trying to sound reassuring. There was doubt in Dot's eyes, though; hopefully it wasn't mirrored too blatantly in my own.

HER KIND OF MAN

I t had been an unusually busy shift, and the line of people waiting to return rental cars was still five deep. Kim checked the time on her monitor: five more minutes until she could clock out. She forced a smile at the exhausted-looking mom standing in front of her whose three kids were currently smearing chocolate all over the waiting area.

"There you go, ma'am. Have a nice flight."

"With these little monsters?" the woman scoffed, wheeling her bag toward the door as she waved for her kids to follow.

"I told you when I got the car that I didn't want any goddamn insurance!"

Kim looked over at the next station, where her friend Tess was currently dealing with what they privately referred to as express-holes: people who thought they had a God-given right to berate anyone in the service industry. This one was a prototypical example: middle-aged, white, and sunburned, with a T-shirt straining against his gut and a set of golf bags beside him.

Tess smiled thinly back at him. "I do apologize for the confusion, sir. Things have been a bit hectic today."

"Where's your manager?" The guy peered past her, as if she were hiding him somewhere.

Tess and Kim exchanged a look; no one earning minimum wage deserved this shit. Smoothly, she replied, "I can get him for you, sir, if you just step to the side."

"Oh, hell no. I was waiting for a frickin' half hour already, I'm gonna miss my flight."

"If you'd like, sir, I can give you the number for customer service—"

He was already walking away, waving his receipt as he called back, "I'm tweeting about this shithole!"

"To all twelve of his followers," Kim said sotto voce.

"Right?" Tess agreed.

"Ladies, allow me to apologize on behalf of all boorish white guys." Kim's eyes widened as the next customer stepped to her window: he was tall, blond, and H-O-T. When he lowered mirrored sunglasses to reveal gorgeous blue eyes, she practically swooned. Smiling at her, he tucked them in his pocket.

Tess kicked her under the desk, which served to break the spell. "Um, g-good afternoon, sir. Did you enjoy your time in Las Vegas?"

"Sadly, it wasn't as productive as I'd hoped," he said with a small shrug.

Kim caught herself nodding like an idiot. "And everything went well with the rental, Mr. . . ."

"Keats," he said. "Like the poet."

"He's one of my favorites," Kim said, brightening. Hot *and* smart. That was definitely hard to find. "I'm studying English at UNLV."

"Really?" He leaned both elbows on the counter. "Well, it's a shame I'm leaving. It's so rare to find someone who knows their Romantic poets."

"Um, yeah—" Kim was interrupted by a tap on her shoulder. She swiveled to find Jordan standing there, which meant that technically, her shift was over.

"I can wrap this up for you," Jordan offered, eyeing Keats greedily.

Kim frowned. "That's okay, I got this."

"Suit yourself." He started logging into the terminal on her left, chatting away as usual. Kim silently willed him to shut up, but Jordan wasn't the best at reading social cues. "Hey, did you hear? Another girl was murdered last night. That's two in two days. They think it's a serial killer."

"Seriously?" Tess exclaimed.

Jordan nodded. "Apparently he's killed five so far, but the mayor has kept it quiet so people don't freak out."

"Typical," Tess said, shaking her head.

Kim was trapped between them as they started jabbering about a bunch of sex workers being murdered in motels. She threw an apologetic smile to Mr. Keats, but he'd shifted his attention to them. "Sorry, what happened?"

Tess showed him her phone screen. "It's all over Insta."

Kim bit her lip in annoyance. Typical of Tess to try to elbow her way in. This was just like that time Michael B. Jordan came through with his entourage, and Tess practically crawled over Kim to lure him to her window. She was the one with a boyfriend, too, not that you'd know it.

"It's probably nothing, sir. The LVPD always issues warnings for serious threats . . ." Kim's voice trailed off as she realized she'd lost his attention completely. He'd taken Tess's phone and was intently scrolling through it.

"You can put your number in while you're at it," Tess said, batting her eyelashes.

He handed the phone back. "Maybe I'll stay a few more days. Seems like my luck might be changing after all."

Which seemed like a super-weird thing to say. Kim frowned. "Are you sure, sir?"

"I'll take the same car, if it's still available."

Kim hesitated, then voided the return. After he left, Jordan turned to her and said, "I'm sorry, did he just decide to stay *because* there's a serial killer here?"

"It's always the hot ones," Tess said, shaking her head.

Kim didn't answer. She was already logging off, ready to go home and take a long, hot bath. She really needed to find a job where there weren't so many assholes and weirdos.

CHAPTER EIGHTEEN

CRY OF THE CITY

I think this is it," Dot said at five thirty, checking her phone.

I bolted upright on the bed where I'd finally lain down, exhausted from worrying that the plan was a bust. Everything revolved around piquing Gunnar's interest enough to make sure he stuck around Vegas. If our posts didn't start trending, and he left, the rest of the plan would fail, too. Wherever he popped up next, we wouldn't have access to Dot's resources, and we'd basically be starting from ground zero. Which would be bad, to say the least.

Grace had been on her computer for hours, tweaking the posts. Meanwhile, I'd been compulsively monitoring social media sites, checking trending hashtags and praying. It had gone slower than I'd hoped. Apparently a serial killer in Vegas barely got anyone's attention, especially on a day when, as luck would have it, a celebrity had a total meltdown in an airport.

But around two p.m., our hashtags had finally started gaining traction. I'd watched as the campaign took on a life of its own, with reposts, comments, and a slew of emojis that I didn't even know existed (the knife and bathtub were particularly tactless). Suddenly, there were hundreds of responses, then thousands. "Is it enough, do you think?" Dot had asked nervously.

"Sure," I'd said, trying to sound confident.

"Only if my brother follows social media," Grace had muttered. Her mood had not improved; if anything, the success of my plan seemed to be irritating her.

But finally, we appeared to be in business.

Dot scanned through her texts. "Fred thinks he just checked into the Buggy."

"I knew it," I said smugly. Dot had asked local motel managers to keep an eye out for someone matching Gunnar's description. Over the course of the day we'd had a few calls that didn't pan out from overly excited (and probably bored) moteliers. But I was counting on the fact that Gunnar wouldn't be able to resist a return to the Buggy Suites if he thought another murder had occurred there. His curiosity would have gotten the better of him. Turning to Grace, I said, "You owe me fifty bucks."

"We don't know it's Gunnar," Grace retorted.

"Fred's sending a photo from his security cams," Dot said. "Hang on . . ."

She held up her phone. Grace and I leaned in to examine the picture, which was taken from above at an angle. "Wow, that resolution actually isn't bad."

"If there's one thing Fred knows, it's cameras," Dot said. "I hear he's got some in the rooms, too. Bit of a perv."

"So is it him?" I demanded.

Grace was staring at the photo. The man in it was tall and wore a baseball cap, his face shifted slightly right. The camera had captured most of his features, but it was hard to tell if the line on his cheek was a scar or a shadow. Grace expanded the image, zooming in.

"Well?" Dot asked.

"It's him," Grace said stonily.

I tried to force some bravado into my voice, despite the tremor suddenly shimmying down my spine. *Gunnar is less than a mile away.* "Like I said, fifty bucks. I take cash or Venmo."

"I'll put it toward your room and board."

"He's checking into room seven," Dot said with a shudder. "That's where Lori died."

"Did he ask about the other murder?" It was funny; we'd posted so much about it, I almost had to remind myself that no one else had actually been killed.

"He wanted to know about the crime tape on five. Fred told him there was an accident, but everyone was fine."

"Which is exactly what a sleazy motel owner would say if he didn't want to scare off a guest," I said with satisfaction. Fred had (thanks to a cash incentive from Grace and considerable arm twisting from Dot) put crime scene tape on room five earlier that day. "Is Fred freaking out?"

"Oh, definitely," Dot said. "But he's always a little off. I think it would be hard for anyone to tell the difference."

"Okay," I said, clapping my hands together. "So phase one is a resounding success."

"He's here," Grace said grudgingly. "Which is impressive."

"Impressive?" I cocked an eyebrow. "Why, Grace, I never. Did you just give me a compliment?"

"Luring him was never going to be the hard part."

I pointed at her. "Love the positive attitude. Time for phase two of Operation Fuck Gunnar."

Operation Fuck Gunnar was pretty basic, actually. It hinged on Grace's ability to hack security cameras and Dot's extensive network of motel owners, sex workers, junkies, and the rest of Vegas's seedy underbelly. A few local Fatal Femmes had enlisted, too, apparently unable to resist the chance to participate in an actual manhunt.

The first objective was to locate, then track Gunnar. Thanks to extensive television viewing, I knew that standard procedure for an FBI tail was three cars; they'd hand a target off to each other regularly, so the suspect wouldn't get suspicious when he kept seeing the same sedan in his rearview mirror.

My plan multiplied that exponentially. We had literally dozens of people signed on to follow Gunnar. Like I told Grace: thanks to Dot, Vegas gave us a numbers advantage. My plan wasn't risk-free, but everyone had been given explicit instructions to keep them as safe as possible:

-Don't get within twenty feet of the target; this was strictly surveillance.

-Text frequent updates to Dot's phone.

-When Dot said to, peel off. She'd make sure the next person in the chain picked up the trail.

-If at any point the target seemed to be on to them, get the hell out of there.

This was the part that had been tough to set up, but while we'd been preparing in L.A., Dot had coordinated her network. "I didn't tell them what he is, exactly," she'd confided over the phone. "Just that he's a real dirtbag we need to keep tabs on."

And apparently that was enough, because when Gunnar went for a stroll after checking into his murder motel, the text updates flooded in.

"Jackie says he's heading down West Harmon," Dot announced, chewing on a fry from room service. The table by the window was filled with plates; we might've gone a bit overboard, binge-eating our stress.

"Great," I said, leaning over the map of Vegas on one of Grace's monitors. "So what's in that direction?"

Dot shrugged. "Everything. The entire Strip, basically."

"Where's he going?" I mused.

"You're breathing on me," Grace complained, pushing me back.

"Listen, I know you've got mixed feelings, but it's time to get with the program," I said in a low voice so that Dot wouldn't overhear.

"Oh, crap," Dot said.

"What?" I asked.

She was staring at her phone screen with what appeared to be actual terror. Slowly, she raised her eyes to meet mine. "He just went into the wig store."

"Wait, what?" I said. "I thought Aboud was out of town!"

"He got back last week. Said he couldn't keep the clinic closed for that long. He promised to keep the shop locked today, though . . ." Dot was wringing her hands.

"Shit!" All the food I'd eaten was rising up my throat; if something happened to Dr. Aboud, I'd never forgive myself.

Grace was already on her feet. Resolutely, she strolled to the closet and pulled out a large duffel bag. "Time to cut your little plan short," she said. "I'm going after him."

"Wait!" Dot yelled, holding up a hand as she read a new text. "Jackie just saw him walk back out."

"That was a message," Grace said. "He knows we're watching him."

"Have someone else pick him up," I said, trying not to panic. "Is anyone close?"

"Dougy Deuce. Great guy," Dot said, checking her Find My Friends app. She cocked her head to the side. "Bit of a drunk, though."

"Okay. Did Dr. Aboud get back to you yet?"

Dot shook her head, looking worried. "He was only in there for a minute, though . . ."

"That's all it takes to kill someone," Grace said ominously.

"You're not helping." I jabbed a finger at her before turning back to Dot. "Have someone check on Dr. Aboud."

While Dot tapped away at her phone, I went over to where Grace was sorting the contents of her giant duffel bag.

"What?" she asked without looking up.

"You promised to stick with the plan," I said sternly.

Grace glared at me. "Do you know how hard this is? He's so close."

"Trust me, I know." I squatted beside her. "But charging down the Strip with a cattle prod won't solve anything. Like you said, he already thinks this is a trap."

"Exactly!" Grace said, exasperated. "So what are we waiting for?"

"I'm guessing he's intrigued," I said. "You've never made the first move before. Gunnar doesn't know whether or not the murder was real, and he's testing the waters, trying to draw you out." I put a hand on her arm. "Don't let him. Not until it's on our terms."

"Dr. Aboud is okay," Dot announced with relief. "Says he came in asking for directions to Circus Circus."

"Huh. Seems a little lowbrow for him." I looked at Grace. "Any connection?"

"We weren't exactly circus kids." Grace sat back on her haunches, staring into the depths of her bag. She wasn't suiting up, though, which was a minor victory.

"Well, there's no guarantee he's actually going there," I said.

"He's not," Dot announced. "Well, not exactly. Dougy says he's going into the RV park behind Circus Circus."

"Classy," Grace muttered.

I bit my lip; this was not a great development. We'd been counting on him staying in the parts of Vegas that teemed with people and surveillance cameras, many of which Grace had already tapped into. An RV park hadn't been on our radar. "Tell Dougy not to follow him. What's it like?"

"The RV park?" Dot shrugged. "Big. Filled with RVs."

"Lots of ways in and out?"

"Definitely." Dot sighed. "I can try to get people positioned at the exits, but it's kind of open there. Not a lot of places to lurk, if you know what I mean."

"Right." I rubbed my temples, thinking. I hadn't expected our plan to go off flawlessly, but I'd figured it would take more than an hour to fall apart. I turned to Grace. "I bet the RV park has security cameras. Can you get into them?"

"Yes," she acknowledged. "Or I could just go over there."

"Why don't we figure out what he's doing before we run in there half-cocked?"

"Your 'plan' has already gone off the rails," Grace said.

The worst part was that she wasn't entirely wrong; now that we were in it, this was all much more dangerous and terrifying than I'd thought it would be. I hated the fact that we were asking people to put themselves in harm's way. And Gunnar had already made unexpected moves, throwing a wrench into the works. Not great, considering that everything would only get more complicated from here on out. More treacherous, too. I could sense my control of the situation slipping away; I had to keep Grace on board, because without her the whole thing failed.

"Please, just . . . hang in there. If it gets worse, we'll go right to plan B, okay?"

Grace examined me for a moment, as if weighing my resolve. I met her gaze levelly. Finally, she issued a small nod. "Fine. But if we lose him—"

"We won't, if you access those cameras," I said pointedly. Making a face, she skulked back to her chair. I turned back to Dot, who was perched on the edge of the couch, staring intently at her phone. "Hey, Dot? Have Dougy pass Gunnar to someone else, he's probably doubling back to see if he's being followed."

"Already done. Diamond works that corner anyway." Dot's phone pinged again. "Okay, Diamond says he came back out the same way."

"Tell her not to follow, either," I said, thinking that Diamond sounded like she fit squarely in his victim profile. "Can someone else pick him up?"

"Sure. I'll get Skeeter on it."

"Lovely." Grace leaned back in the desk chair. "We're entrusting our fate to a guy named Skeeter."

"Skeeter is actually nonbinary," Dot sniffed.

I gnawed on a nail. Maybe I'd overestimated myself, or underestimated Gunnar. He obviously suspected that something was up. But we were committed now. Turning to Dot, I said, "Tell everyone to let us know as soon as he goes into a casino."

———————

Gunnar led Dot's constantly shifting surveillance team through most of the Strip—I'll give him this, the guy was definitely in shape. He'd walked miles by eight o'clock. He went into coffee shops and came back out without buying anything. He strolled through the Fremont Street Experience, a five-block vaulted pedestrian mall that just happened to be almost directly across the street from our hotel room. I basically had a heart attack thinking he'd somehow figured out where we were, plus I had to physically block the door to keep Grace from charging after him. He spent a full ten minutes staring at the giant water fountain in front of the Bellagio.

"Still checking for a tail," Grace said.

"Doesn't matter," I said. "We counted on that." Thanks to the shell game Dot had set up, more than three dozen people were tracking Gunnar through the city. While some probably weren't very subtle, their sheer numbers should throw him off. I mean, sure, you'd recognize one, two, or even three people. But thirty?

If I was wrong, though, and one of Dot's people got hurt, she'd never forgive me. Hell, I'd never forgive myself. Putting so many people at risk was terrifying. There was a lot riding on this.

I was pacing again. Over the past few hours, I'd walked miles, too. At regular intervals Grace snapped at me to sit the fuck down, but I couldn't stay still. The knowledge that Gunnar was so close, at times just blocks away, gave me a serious case of the jitters.

Dot had been uncharacteristically quiet all day. Granted, she didn't have a lot of time to chat, since the texts poured in nonstop. But when one of her contacts reported that Gunnar was in a diner eating a full lumberjack breakfast, she patted the couch beside her. "Have a seat, hon."

"I can't," I said, going over to the window to peer out. The desert sun was sinking, but the glass was still hot against my palms. By contrast, our room was frigid as a meat locker; apparently Grace's precious equipment required arctic temperatures to work properly.

"I got my friend Jean watching him, she's a waitress at that dive. And you're giving me vertigo," Dot said firmly. "Park it."

Reluctantly, I settled on the couch beside her. She'd kicked off her kitten heels and tucked her feet beneath her. The frames of her reading glasses were the same shade of purple as her pumps, and she'd draped a cashmere sweater with pearl buttons over her shoulders to combat the cold. For some reason, the more nervous I got, the calmer she became.

"Why aren't you more freaked out?" I asked, jiggling a knee; constant motion seemed to be the only way to calm my nerves.

"Well, I usually reserve weekends for tracking serial killers," she said airily. "But for you, I was willing to make an exception."

I issued a sheepish laugh. "So is Jessie still looking after the Getaway?"

"With help from that idiot BJ." She sighed and brushed a piece of lint off her dress, avoiding my eyes. "Not that there's been much to look after. Only a couple of rooms booked lately."

"Oh," I said. "Is that normal?"

She shrugged. "Been on a downswing for a while."

"Sorry, Dot. Really. It's my fault."

Dot laughed. "No, doll. If anything, this made me realize it might be time to try something else for a while. Maybe even take a trip with Jim. Y'know, I've never had a proper vacay."

"Still, I bet you regret ever meeting me."

"Well, I'll admit it got a smidge more exciting than expected." Dot patted her hair. "But then again, this is pretty much the most interesting thing that ever happened to me."

"Most dangerous, too," I said.

"Oh, I don't know about that." She laughed. "Someday I'll tell you about my stint at the Copa Room."

I forced a smile. "I wish it was under better circumstances, but I'm still glad I met you, Dot. You're pretty much the best friend I've ever had."

"Ah, honey. That means a lot," she said, rubbing my knee. Glancing toward the desk, she leaned in and asked, "So there wasn't much bonding between the two of you?"

"Hardly."

"Marcella will be happy to hear that. She wasn't delighted that you were shacking up with a hot blonde."

I snorted. *Hot* wasn't a word I'd ever associate with Grace. I mean, she was attractive, I suppose. I'd thought so the first time I saw her. But she was like one of those woolly mammoths they found sealed in a block of ice: inaccessible.

Which actually did kind of make her my type. I curled a lip involuntarily at the thought. Grace caught me staring and snapped, "What?"

"Nothing," I muttered, looking back out the window. The setting sun made the shimmering hotel towers look like molten silver.

Dot's phone pinged. "Okay, he's on the move again. And Jean said he tipped ten percent." She shook her head. "What an asshole."

I leaned back against the couch cushions and closed my eyes. My plan hinged on Gunnar engaging in Vegas's primary pastime: hanging out in a damn casino. But if he didn't, well . . . at some point, I might have to launch plan B. The very thought of it made me shudder.

An hour passed. More room service came and went. Dot splayed across the couch, wearily relaying information from the constant texts streaming in. I lay on the bed, exhausted but too keyed up to sleep. Grace was still tapping away at her computer, occupying herself by hacking into every possible security camera in a two-mile radius. "Casinos are still a no-go," she announced as I wheeled our dinner cart back into the hallway. "They've got better security than the NSA, I won't be able to hack any in time."

"Fabulous," I muttered. Not having eyes inside the casinos wasn't ideal, but then again, Gunnar hadn't actually entered one yet. And our plan had compensated for that possibility with Dot's network of volunteer trackers.

The next stage of the plan required getting someone close to him anyway. Which I, for one, was not looking forward to.

"That's weird," Dot said.

I sat up. "What?"

"He's back at Circus Circus."

"The RV park again?"

"Nope." She looked up, eyes glinting as she said, "He went into the casino."

Grace's posture went rigid.

"Right," I said, trying to inject some confidence into my voice. "Guess it's time for phase three."

"Phase three is a mistake," Grace warned. Her computer monitors had shifted to a view of the driveway outside Circus Circus; I watched a family of four clamber out of their minivan and struggle with luggage.

"And yet we're doing it anyway," I said with forced cheer.

Dot set her phone down and stretched her arms above her head. "I've got a cocktail waitress keeping an eye on him. But you better get moving—who knows how long he'll stay."

THE SUSPECT

Liz expertly dodged the hand that was reaching out for her ass, automatically tilting her wrist to steady the drinks tray. As she eased through the press of the crowd (not bad for a Thursday), she kept an eye on the guy sitting at the bar facing away from her. His back was a broad expanse; clearly, he knew his way around a gym. Dot said he was trouble, though, which was good enough for her.

He sipped something clear from a tumbler; vodka tonic maybe, or just seltzer. Even if Dot hadn't clued her in, something about him would've struck her as out of place. Liz prided herself on the ability to read auras, and he wasn't putting out the right kind of energy. Everyone else was either keyed up or sad, flashing varying shades of orange, yellow, and blue; she couldn't get a clear read on him, though, and was tempted to get closer. *Stay twenty feet away*, Dot had said, but that seemed silly. There were hundreds of people around, what could he possibly do?

"Hey, sweetheart, bring me a margarita?" She turned to find an old guy wearing layers of gold chains at her elbow. "Rocks and salt."

"Of course, sir." Liz smiled thinly as he patted her rump, making a mental note to tell Johnny to water it down. Jingling and chimes to her right as a slot machine started spitting out quarters. Suddenly, the guy at the bar jerked his head up, so fast it made her gasp. She realized he was reacting to a PA announcement. She cocked her head to listen. ". . . Grimes, there's a call for you. Please pick up any house phone. Gunnar Grimes . . ."

Strange name. Definitely fake, Liz thought to herself. She watched under her lashes as he slapped a five down on the bar, then headed to the old-fashioned phone bolted to the wall by the cashier windows. Seemingly unconcerned, he picked up the receiver.

Liz really wished she could hear what was being said.

"Hey, where's that drink?"

Without making eye contact, she chirped, "Coming right up, sir!"

The man held the receiver away from his ear, as if the person on the other end was shouting. Then he brought it back in, listening closely. Liz found herself mesmerized; what was happening here? She should've asked Dot for more details.

After a moment, he hung up the phone and turned, locking eyes with her. Liz took a second too long to react; her heart hammered in her chest as they stared at each other. Then he walked straight toward her.

Startled, she took a few steps back. The tray tilted, and the empty glasses started to slide off. Too late, she adjusted. One glass fell, shattering on the floor and sending a spray of shards in every direction. Liz bent to gather up the larger pieces. A set of feet paused beside her. Slowly, she looked up.

"Need a hand?" The guy was standing above her, looking down. From this vantage point he was absolutely huge. Liz swallowed, hard. "No, sir, I've got it."

"You sure?"

She nodded quickly. He shrugged, then moved past her.

Liz fell back on her high heels. She'd never seen anything like his aura before; it had been a deep, dark green, almost black. "What the hell does that even mean?" she muttered to herself.

"It means I'm firing your ass if you don't get a move on," barked someone behind her. Liz winced, then shifted to see Karen the beverage boss glaring down at her.

"Sorry, I just—"

"I've got a hundred girls who want this gig," Karen growled. "John says he's had a margarita waiting on you. Better get to it."

"Yes, ma'am." Ducking her head, Liz hurried to the bar. She'd text Dot in a bit, when that bitch Karen wasn't watching her like a hawk.

CHAPTER NINETEEN

CALLING DR. DEATH

H e's on the move," Dot said excitedly, nearly dropping her phone in her excitement.

"Which exit?" I asked, hurrying over to the bank of computers.

"West, by the parking lot." Dot looked up at me. "He took the bait!"

"Looks like it." Inwardly, I heaved a sigh of relief. The fact that Gunnar had heard his name over the PA system and picked up the phone was a victory in and of itself.

Now I just had to hope he'd follow our trail of clues. Grace had said his favorite part of Catch Me was the scavenger hunt; I was counting on that still being the case. A friend of Dot's who worked the switchboard at Circus Circus had played "La Marseillaise" over the house phone; it didn't take a genius to figure out that referred to the Paris Las Vegas Casino. If I was right, he'd make a beeline for it. I bent over Grace's shoulder to scan the security feeds. "Got him?"

She pointed at the center screen; in the corner of the frame I saw a man strolling down the sidewalk, heading away from the camera. He was wearing dark clothes and a ball cap, same as earlier. "That's the Battlefield Vegas surveillance cam," Grace said. "Right next door." There was an undercurrent of emotion in her voice, too, but her expression was stony as ever.

"All right." Trying to repress a quaver, I said, "I guess it's time."

"Sure you're ready, hon?" Dot asked.

"Yeah, I've got this." I couldn't summon much conviction, however. The plan that I'd hatched three hundred miles away suddenly felt much riskier. Especially since I'd assigned myself the most dangerous role.

"Very convincing," Grace noted.

I glared at her. "Again, not helpful."

Still staring at the screen, she said, "I think this is a mistake. There are too many contingencies."

"No, there aren't," I retorted. "The plan is simple, which is exactly why it's going to work."

She turned to face me, crossing her arms. "And when it doesn't?"

"Then we try yours." Which I sincerely hoped would *not* be the case, because what Grace had come up with was significantly more dangerous.

"Wait, there's another plan?" Dot frowned. "What is it?"

"Not important, because we won't need to use it."

"Unless just one thing goes wrong," Grace said, holding up a finger. "And everything goes to shit."

Dot looked concerned. "I don't know, Amber, it is starting to sound awfully complicated. Maybe we should call the cops? Jessie's cousin might be able to help—"

"No cops," Grace and I said in unison.

Dot sighed. "Fine. But you be careful."

"Always." After a beat, I added, "Still no word from Marcella?"

"Not since she texted this morning, promising to stay put at the Mayhem." Off my expression, Dot said, "Don't you worry. That girl can take care of herself."

"I guess." Trying to put it out of my mind, I checked my reflection. "How do I look?"

"Perfect," Dot exclaimed.

"Perfectly ridiculous," Grace grumbled.

I ignored her. I might not have been a mistress of disguise, but with my close-cropped hair and slender figure (the yogurt-and-soup diet had stripped off a few more pounds, to my dismay), I could pass for a guy my age. Accordingly, I was wearing baggy jean shorts slung low to expose boxer briefs and a button-down shirt over a white tank top. A chunky gold chain, oversized men's watch, Vans, and mirrored sunglasses completed the look. Dot had helped by slightly shadowing my cheeks and upper lip. I patted my pocket to make sure the device was still there, then turned in a full circle. Yup, I definitely looked like a scrawny Vegas asshole. Hopefully it would be enough to fool Gunnar.

"He's going to see right through that," Grace said.

"Why don't you shut the fuck up, toots?" Dot said sweetly, which set Grace's mouth in a tight line. "Now, honey, remember, if it starts to go south—"

"Your friend Daryl will be watching for my signal. Got it." I turned back to Grace. "You know what to do?"

After a beat, she nodded.

"Great." I did a final check in the mirror, trying to quell the panic burbling in my belly. Once I stepped out that door, there was no going back. I could see Dot and Grace flanking my reflection. They both looked concerned. "Don't worry. I got this."

"Sure you do," Dot said.

"Don't get yourself killed," Grace added.

And on that reassuring note, I drew my shoulders back and opened the door, ready for battle.

Forty minutes later I sat at a Caesars Palace bar, nursing a beer and trying not to look like I was climbing out of my skin.

I totally was, though. The adrenaline I'd been running on all day had shot up another notch—it felt like I'd been mainlining espressos (which also happened to be true). Anyway, my hands were shaky, which wasn't helping to sell the whole "chill dude" vibe I was aiming for.

"Breathe," I whispered.

"Sorry?" asked a woman at my elbow who was waiting for her drink.

"Um, nothing," I said, faking a deep voice that sounded like I was gargling marbles. Unsurprisingly, she gave me a strange look and shifted down the bar.

I checked my watch again: almost ten thirty p.m. This was taking longer than expected. I had to fight the urge to text Dot or Grace again; Grace had threatened to throw her phone in the toilet if I bothered her one more time, and Dot probably had her hands full tracking Gunnar via text. I tried to guess which of the guys in my general vicinity was Dot's buddy Daryl; whoever he was, he was good, I couldn't even feel his eyes on me.

Unless he wasn't actually here.

I shoved that thought away. If Dot's network had proved anything today, it was that they reliably went above and beyond the call of duty. We genuinely couldn't have done this without them. I loved the thought of Gunnar Grimes, super-scary serial killer, being sent on an elaborate scavenger hunt through Vegas.

At every stop, he'd been paged to the house phone and played a recording. At Paris Las Vegas, Pavarotti sent him to the Bellagio; then "Walk Like an Egyptian" (my personal favorite) led to the Luxor . . . by the time we were through, he'd have gone through a half dozen casinos. Which hopefully would produce the desired effect.

Based on my research, serial killers were control freaks to the nth degree. They didn't just *want*, they *needed* to manage every aspect of their environment. They tended to be meticulous Type A assholes, following set patterns.

Even though Gunnar was smart enough to vary murder methods, I was betting that everything leading up to the moment he killed was heavily choreographed. Incorporating the code he and his twin invented when they were kids, using murder locations to write a zodiac symbol . . . this guy was no improviser. Hell, Grace had lost her shit when I put the soy milk back in the wrong spot in her fridge. I'd bet cold hard cash that her brother was the same, especially when it came to this.

So being led around by the nose had to be driving him nuts. Part of me wished I could've watched it in person.

My heel tapped out a staccato beat on the stool's footrest. The last update from Dot placed him at the Venetian, the fourth stop of six. Which meant he'd be coming my way soon.

You can do this. I waved the bartender over and ordered a shot, figuring a little liquid courage never hurt anyone. While I waited, I mentally reviewed the plan again.

There are very few things that will get you detained at a Vegas casino. You can chain-smoke, strut around in your underwear, hell, they don't mind if you bring a loaded Uzi, as long as you're dropping cash.

The one thing they don't allow?

Cheating.

Do that, and a bunch of thugs escort you somewhere for a private conversation. Dot had assured me that Caesars Palace was old school that way. One of her many buddies was a pit boss named Linc who helpfully provided us with something he'd confiscated a few weeks ago, the very latest in cheating technology. The Remote Jackpotter looked like a car key fob, but apparently if it was activated near certain slot machines, they started to spew change.

Every casino in town was on the lookout for them. And according to Linc, the consequences for possessing one were severe.

I had one job: get close enough to slide the device into Gunnar's pocket, then alert casino security that I'd heard him bragging about beating the system. I had no doubts as to my ability to play this part convincingly.

Getting close to him, though: that was what scared me.

It wasn't a long-term solution, obviously, but casino security would helpfully keep Gunnar occupied for an hour or two while we set the final trap. It solved a lot of problems in one fell swoop; if a casino didn't want you to leave, you weren't going anywhere. Grace and I would make full use of that time, basically gift-wrapping him for the Las Vegas police. By the time he was released, there would be a slew of cops waiting to take him into custody. Grace had serious doubts about that part of the plan, thanks to what had happened in Portland. I reminded her there was a big difference between one cop on his own and a SWAT team. And the best part was that we wouldn't be directly involved, and could go on our merry way once he was in custody.

I chewed on my drink straw, keeping an eye on the room. It wouldn't be long now. Grace should already be handling her part of things.

My phone rang, and I frowned; we were supposed to stick to

texts. I dug it out: Dot. The minute I heard her voice, I knew it had all gone to hell.

W hat do you mean he disappeared?" I asked, plugging a finger in my ear to drown out the din; I could barely understand what she was saying.

Dot's words tumbled out at the same rate my heart was pounding: way too fast. "Corey had him at the Venetian. He saw Gunnar take the call that was supposed to send him to the Rio, but then he didn't leave. So Corey asked them to page him again, and this time he just walked right out of the building, and by the time Corey caught up—"

"We lost him?" I said, suddenly hyperconscious of the crowd surrounding me. Gunnar could be ten feet away and I wouldn't be able to see him. I hurriedly left the bar, checking back over my shoulder as I went down the nearest hallway to hear better.

"Corey's pretty sure he got in a taxi. Hanna's waiting at the Rio, but if he doesn't show, what do you want to do?"

My stomach roiled. I should've known that Gunnar's interest wouldn't remain piqued this long; I should've stuck to just a few casinos. I'd been too obsessed with throwing him off balance, and now he might've slipped the net. I squeezed my eyes shut, trying to think. In the background Dot was saying, "Amber, can you hear me? Hon, what do you want me to do?"

I drew in a deep, shuddery breath. "Let's assume he's sticking to the plan. Have Hanna keep watch at the Rio. How long should it take him to get there?"

"This time of day? Ten minutes. Maybe fifteen."

"Okay. So if he doesn't show by"—I checked my watch—"eleven thirty, tell everyone they're off the hook."

"You mean—"

I drew a deep breath. *Fuck.* "Yeah, we go to plan B." *Just like Grace wanted.*

"You didn't seem too happy about plan B," Dot said with concern. "Is it dangerous?"

"Um, no, not really," I lied. "Just . . . it's Grace's plan."

"Oh, dear." She sighed, and then asked, "Is there anything I can do to help?"

"You've done so much already, Dot. Just keep me posted on what happens at the Rio, and try to relax, okay?"

"All right, kiddo." Without any conviction Dot added, "I'm sure it'll work out fine."

I hung up. A cocktail waitress in a skimpy toga strolled past, carefully balancing a tray of shots. I scooped one up and tossed it back, coughing as tequila slid down my throat. It was looking increasingly likely that I wouldn't survive the night, so I might as well get a buzz on.

Almost immediately, my phone vibrated again. I frowned. *What now?*

It was a text from my old pal UNKNOWN NUMBER. Probably just Grace, letting me know she'd finished up.

The picture that popped up was tiny, with terrible resolution, so it took a second to make sense of what I was seeing. The photo was taken close-up at a strange angle. A woman, lying in a bathtub.

It was Jessie. And she looked dead.

CHAPTER TWENTY

I'LL GET YOU FOR THIS

My hand went to my mouth and I almost dropped the phone. "No," I whispered.

Jessie's goth makeup was smeared, and her wig was askew. Her mouth gaped open, lips parted, as if she were in the middle of speaking. But her eyes gazed past the lens at nothing, blank and devoid of life.

The walls around me started to throb ominously; I ducked into a corner behind a potted plant to catch my breath. *No,* I chastised myself. *Do not fall apart.* It didn't make any sense. Jessie and Marcella had promised to lay low, safely holed up in the Mayhem. So what happened? Had Gunnar found them? But how?

Had he killed Marcella, too?

That fucker. I'd been scared all day. Terrified, even. Now all of that was supplanted by rage. I was going to kill him myself.

Dot. Shit. Jessie wasn't just her best friend, she was basically her surrogate mother. She was going to be crushed by this.

Another text popped up. Hands shaking, I opened it.

No body, just a photo of the Getaway's sign.

I didn't even have time to feel relief before my phone chimed again.

Struck by an overpowering sense of dread, I sank to the floor, my back to the wall, knees to my chest. A few people looked at me oddly, but I didn't care.

I clutched the phone to my heart, trying to mentally prepare myself. *Please don't let Marcella be dead. Please.*

A flash of her grinning at me in the dark, the softness of her hand against my cheek. *Why didn't I do more to protect her?*

I wanted to run back to the Nugget and collapse in Dot's arms. I wanted to bolt, get the fuck out of this entire mess, just walk away without looking back. But I'd come up with this entire plan. It was my fault that good people were dying. And now I had to finish it.

I counted down from ten in my head. Then, with shaking hands, I opened the text.

It was another close-up, of Marcella this time. Her face filled the frame. There was duct tape across her mouth, her hair was wild, and her eyes were wide with terror. But she was clearly alive. I let out a shuddery breath, hating myself for feeling relieved about that when Jessie was dead.

I tucked the phone in my pocket. My hands were shaking again, more from anger than fear. So. That fucking psychopath was holding her hostage, trying to lure me to the Getaway. I wanted to scream. Grace had been right—there were holes in my plan large enough to drive a semi through. It had gone sideways, just like she'd predicted.

I pushed up the wall until I was standing. My legs felt odd as I stumbled to the restroom down the hall. It felt like I was on a moving train, jostling and shaking. I quickened to a trot as bile rose up my throat, hurrying into a massive bathroom filled with dozens of stalls. I threw open the door to the nearest one and bent double, throwing up all the room service I'd stress-eaten that day.

"Christ, drink much?" a girl at the mirror said with disgust.

"Seriously. Gotta pace yourself," her friend agreed. "And this is, like, the ladies' room, dude."

I slammed and locked the stall door and hovered over the bowl for another minute, heaving until there was nothing left. Then I flushed and sat down on the seat, head in my hands, remembering how Jessie had patted my hand and promised to take care of Dot and Marcella.

She and Marcella should've been in the hotel suite with Dot. I should've made certain they were safe before forging ahead. I'd been cocky and overconfident, and as a result, an innocent had ended up dead.

Just like last time, the voice in my head whispered.

I fought back nausea as Stella's panicked face flashed through my mind. I shook it off. There wasn't time for ghosts from my past.

It was too late for Jessie. But I still had a chance to save Marcella.

Not much of one.

I stared at my phone screen, trying to decide what to do.

Should I call the police? Have Dot reach out to Jessie's cousin on the force? Surely he'd be motivated to get the guy responsible?

Maybe too motivated. If it came down to taking out a serial killer or saving the life of a sex worker, which would the cops focus on?

I already knew the answer. In that scenario, Marcella had almost no chance of surviving. Her life was in my hands. And this time, I wasn't going to run away.

I wasn't an icy vigilante hacker like Grace.

I wasn't a supervillain like her brother.

I was just a hick with a shitty childhood. A petty criminal. A psych student turned victim. A twenty-four-year-old college dropout who only had two friends in the entire world.

No one very impressive at all, really.

But I'd be damned if I was going to let this asshole win.

"Fuck this guy," I said out loud.

"Yeah, girlfriend," someone piped up from the next stall. "You tell him."

"I will," I said. Screwing up my courage, I unlocked the door and went to the sinks. Ignoring the stares from girls who were fixing their makeup in the mirror, I washed my hands and rinsed my mouth out. Then I straightened, nodded at them, and put on my sunglasses.

Gunnar Grimes had fucked with the wrong person this time.

A text from Dot pinged as I sat in the back of the cab. I bit my lip and checked it: All good, hon?

Yup. I hesitated, then sent another one. If you don't hear from me in an hour, call the cops.

You got it. Where do I send them?

I hesitated. If I told Dot I was headed to the Getaway, she'd freak out. I needed her to stay safely holed up at the Nugget.

Of course, if plan B failed, I probably wouldn't be alive in an hour. I typed I'll lyk, then scheduled an automatic text. Unless I canceled it, in sixty minutes she'd receive the photo of the Getaway.

I sincerely hoped it would never get sent. I hated keeping this from her, but couldn't stomach the thought of putting anyone else at risk. If something happened to her, or Jim, or any more of her friends, I'd never forgive myself. She'd suffered plenty for the kindness she'd shown me. I already knew that I'd be haunted by Jessie, and I only had room in my life for so many ghosts.

Be careful kiddo.

I typed in a thumbs-up, which seemed a little frivolous all things considered, but my hands had started to shake and I didn't trust my ability to type actual letters. I closed my eyes and leaned against the cracked headrest. I was a minute away from the Getaway and had no idea what I was walking into.

Of course Gunnar had holed up at the same place he'd dumped his sister after stabbing her. He needed to exert control over his surroundings and probably also took pleasure in the fact that it had briefly served as a safe haven for me.

What an asshole.

The cab started to pull into the Getaway Motel lot. I launched forward and said frantically, "Not there! Can you please park on the street, a little farther up?"

The cabbie gave me a strange look but shrugged and eased to the curb. The neon sign for Dot's motel was flashing **CLOSED**, so at least that much had gone to plan. Every room was dark.

Except for number twelve.

My old room. The curtains glowed, and the door was ajar.

"You know, there are better places," the cabbie said. He was an older guy with nicotine-stained teeth and greasy hair. "Thursdays, they got a real deal going at the Nugget."

I barked a laugh, and he looked at me like I was crazy. Which wasn't totally wrong. "Thanks. I actually love this place."

I gave him a big tip; what the hell, after tonight I might not need money anymore. And technically it was Grace's cash anyway.

Then I did a final check to make sure I had everything. Wished

I'd thought to grab a bottle of water, because my throat was dry and still tasted of vomit. *Too late now.* And really, thirst was the least of my problems.

I checked my phone again: still nothing from Grace. I sent another text: just got here. where the fuck r u?

Then I closed my eyes again and said a short prayer.

"You okay, kid?" The cabdriver sounded concerned.

Treat it like they do, I told myself. *Like it's just a game.* "Yeah, I'm good." Drawing back my shoulders, I stepped out of the cab and into the furnace of the night.

CHAPTER TWENTY-ONE

SHADOW OF A DOUBT

Sticking to the shadows, I eased across the parking lot to the stairwell. The curtains in all the rooms on the ground floor were closed. I held my breath as I slipped past them, half expecting someone to jump out. I'd dumped the sunglasses and baseball cap in the planter at the end of the parking lot. It was tempting to lose the shorts, too; with the waistband hovering around my hips, they didn't exactly make for easy movement. But I wasn't planning on doing a lot of hand-to-hand combat. And I needed someplace to keep the Glock.

Gotta love Vegas. Apparently nobody was concerned about armed angry drunks, which worked to my advantage.

I held the Glock in both hands as I eased up the stairs. My heart was pounding, breath ragged with fear. It was hard to believe that I was voluntarily walking into a trap set by another serial killer.

And Marcella might already be dead.

No. He'd keep her alive, at least until I showed. I knew it in my gut.

Plan B was classic Grace: it involved confronting Gunnar when he was alone. But now, the fact that he had a live (hopefully) hostage complicated things immensely. I'd hated this plan from the get-go; it was exponentially more dangerous than mine. One mistake and Gunnar would kill us both. Or worse, just me. He'd disappear, Grace would pursue him. And around and around they'd go. Me, Jessie, and Marcella would just be collateral damage.

Fuck that, I thought, feeling another flare of rage. The weight of the gun was reassuring in my hands. If I was going out, I'd take him with me.

As I reached the top of the stairs, a police car raced past, sirens blaring. I seized the opportunity provided by the noise to hurry forward, hunkered low. The curtains up here were all drawn, too, including the ones in my old room. I paused a few feet from number twelve. The door was cracked, like he was waiting for me.

It was strange to be back; it had been weeks since that awful night when I'd found Grace bleeding on the walkway. Even in the dark I could make out a large dark stain on the concrete. I should've left once we got to L.A., just driven until I ran out of road. If I had, Jessie would be alive right now, and Marcella would be safe.

Don't think about it. Focus.

I swallowed hard. Drawing a deep breath, I braced to charge into the room . . .

A shadow appeared against the curtains: someone was coming. I fell back a step, aiming at the doorway. Panic swelled in my gut, and I fought to control my breathing. This was it.

A hand appeared and pushed the door all the way open. The man who leaned out was a larger, male version of Grace: blond hair, blue eyes, clean-shaven square jaw. At the sight of me, he broke into a wide smile. "It's you!" Stepping all the way out, he added, "Well, this is a pleasant surprise. Come on in!"

This had been my bogeyman for weeks; seeing him in the flesh, up close for the first time, I almost quailed. Even though he was less physically imposing than Beau Lee Jessop, he was far more terrifying in every other way. *He's killed almost three hundred people.* I kept the gun steady on him, aimed at the center of his chest. Trying to sound like I wasn't shitting myself, I said, "Thanks, I'm good right here. Where's Marcella?"

"Who?" Gunnar leaned against the doorjamb and crossed his arms over his chest. He was still grinning, like this was a delightful surprise. Instead of the Tyvek suit and rubber gloves I'd expected, he had on dark jeans, a black T-shirt, and sneakers. Honestly, I thought he'd be more intimidating. But aside from the scar on his cheek, he just looked like a normal guy.

Which was probably how he'd gotten away with it for so long.

"Where. Is. She," I repeated, jutting my chin up. I couldn't see a weapon, and we were five feet apart. Even I couldn't miss from this distance if he rushed me.

"Are you really going to insist on talking out here?" he asked, cocking his head to the side; the movement was eerily familiar. It was unsettling how much he and Grace moved and spoke alike, even after all these years.

"Yup," I said through gritted teeth.

"All right, then. We haven't been formally introduced. I'm Gunnar—"

"I know who you are," I spat. "Where's Marcella?"

His brow wrinkled. "I honestly have no idea what you're talking about."

"Did you kill her? Like you killed Jessie?"

He had the nerve to widen his eyes and look affronted. "What? Of course not. Are you okay? Because you seem a bit agitated."

My arms were starting to shake from the effort of holding the gun out straight. "Get on the ground."

"Here? Absolutely not." He wrinkled his nose in distaste.

"I mean it," I said. "I'll shoot!"

Gunnar rubbed his forehead with one hand—the motion startled me, making my finger tighten reflexively on the trigger. "It appears that my sister has told you some untruths about me."

"Untruths?" I was having a hard time getting a handle on this conversation; it wasn't going at all as I'd expected. For one thing, I thought I'd be dead by now. "Like the fact that you're a serial killer? And she's been chasing you for years, trying to stop you?"

He gaped at me for a second, then burst into laughter. I took another step back, keeping my eyes locked on him the entire time; he was just trying to distract me, he'd probably charge forward to overwhelm me . . .

"I'm sorry," Gunnar said, shaking his head. "I know it's not funny, it's just— I can't believe that's what she said." His gaze narrowed as he added, "Or that you believed her."

"Why wouldn't I believe her?"

"Because." Gunnar's features settled into a more serious expression. "You have it all backward. Grace is the killer."

CHAPTER TWENTY-TWO

CAUSE FOR ALARM

Bullshit," I snorted.

The sound of giggling below. Out of the corner of my eye, I saw a group of girls in heels teetering past the parking lot entrance. Thankfully, they didn't take notice of us.

"We really should continue this conversation inside," Gunnar said. "If someone calls the police, they'll find you holding an unarmed man at gunpoint."

"And then they'll search the room and find Marcella," I retorted.

Gunnar had the nerve to look peeved. "If you think there's someone else here, then by all means, come check for yourself." Seeing my hesitation, he added, "I couldn't possibly get to a weapon before you shot me."

"For all I know, you have guns stashed all over the room. And maybe on you, too."

He turned in a slow circle and lifted up his shirt to show me a (credit where it was due) pretty ripped six-pack. No gun, though.

And the T-shirt was tight, I'd definitely see a holster. "See? I'm unarmed."

"Pull up your pants legs," I ordered, gesturing with the gun. "Slowly, from the thighs."

Sighing elaborately (again, so much like Grace), Gunnar tugged at the denim, exposing first one ankle, then the other. No weapon stashed on either. "Satisfied?"

I bit my lip. Going into the room was dangerous. But if someone called the cops and Marcella wasn't here, I might never find her. Plus, police involvement definitely wasn't part of this stage of the plan. I just needed to stall him. "Fine. Back up slowly—and I mean like you're barely moving at all—and keep your hands on top of your head."

Gunnar complied, slowly inching into the room. The lights were all on inside. It was a little weird to see someone else's stuff in the room I'd stayed in. There was a small black suitcase tucked in the corner. The bed was made. He'd pulled down the comforter, same as I had, which was wise. Otherwise, the room was empty. Following my gaze, he said, "I told you, I'm alone."

"Stand against that wall while I check the bathroom." I directed him to a spot right next to the outside door. It was a risk; he could always bolt.

But maybe that wouldn't be the worst thing. Now that I had him here, I wasn't a hundred percent certain what to do. Grace was supposed to be with me. She was the expert, after all.

But he said Grace is the killer. I snorted. *Impossible.*

I edged across the room, keeping the gun on him the entire time. When I reached the bathroom door, I chanced a quick peek inside. The shower curtain was open, and the door was all the way against the wall.

There was no one inside. Nothing but a neat Dopp kit hanging from the towel bar.

Crap. Where was Marcella?

Gunnar was holding his head like he was starring in a migraine commercial. "Do you mind if I lower my arms?"

"I do," I said.

"Well, they're getting tired. What if I just keep them visible, like this?" He crossed them over his chest.

"Hey!"

"Relax, please. I'm assuming you've had some practice with that?" He nodded at the gun.

"A lot," I lied.

"Then what are you worried about?"

I debated, then said, "Fine."

"Excellent." He settled back against the wall, crossing one leg over the other like we were chatting at a cocktail party. "So let me guess. You met Grace when she 'saved' you from some terrible situation. The only contact after that was sporadic at best, perhaps some calls or texts? And just when you'd put her out of your mind, my sister showed up with an elaborate story about how I was the epitome of all evil."

I didn't answer, but that was pretty fucking spooky. My arms ached; I definitely wasn't in "hold a gun at shoulder height indefinitely" shape. Widening my stance, I said, "I came after you on my own."

"Did you? Or did she point you toward me? My sister can be very convincing."

"Just so I've got this straight . . . according to you, she's the real killer. And what—you've been chasing her?"

"Since we were teenagers."

"Uh-huh." *Ridiculous.* "She could've killed me a dozen times over. Hell, she could have left me to die the night we met."

"But that wouldn't have been enough," Gunnar insisted. "This is all a game to her. It's what she does. Grace finds some impressionable young girl—"

"I'm a woman, not a girl. And I'm definitely not impressionable," I scoffed.

"Fine, someone young. And she takes them under her wing, probably spins an elaborate story about how she's a renegade serial killer hunter—that's all part of her pathology. She'll kill people—sometimes a half dozen of them—and blame it on me."

"That's ridiculous."

"No, it's insane. She's a psychopath, and a very unique one. I suppose she told you about our father?"

I hesitated a beat, then nodded.

Gunnar cocked his head to the side. "That part, at least, is true. And it had a terrible impact on both of us. It's why I became a psychiatrist, specializing in criminal pathology." He paused, then continued. "Grace became a killer. But it wasn't enough for her to take victims. She needed to be seen as a savior first, the true hero. That's where people like you come in."

I had to admit, he sounded a hell of a lot saner than Grace. And he did have a psychiatrist vibe, right down to the condescension in his voice. "So say that's all true. What happens to the impressionable young girls?"

"Eventually, she tires of them." He lowered his eyes. "Usually, I arrive too late."

Apparently timing wasn't a strong suit for either of them. I sifted through what he was saying. "Why were you at my apartment in Tennessee?"

"Was I? That's interesting. I was interviewing any girl who matched the Pikachu victim profile, since based on the scene, I knew one must have escaped. Mr. Jessop's cell phone showed that he was in that area recently, so I extrapolated that the final victim might have been abducted there. I probably talked to a few dozen girls who looked like you before the task force shut down."

I frowned. There were some definite gaps in that explanation. "So you pretended to be with the FBI?"

He shrugged. "No pretending, I'm a consultant for them. I was already in Johnson City working the case. The circumstances we found Beau Lee Jessop in made me suspect Grace was involved. It was her classic setup; everything had been wiped clean. Then she sent me a picture of you in the parking lot of this motel. That's the sort of thing she does, to taunt me. For her, this is—"

"Just a game?"

"Exactly!" He nodded vigorously. "I came here hoping that this time, I could finally stop her before, well . . ."

"Before she kills me, according to you." My arms were full-on trembling with fatigue. I was starting to feel a quiver of uncertainty. *What if I've read this all wrong?* Had Grace been conning me this entire time? No way. I wasn't that much of a sap.

"Wait—" He frowned. "How did you know I was here?" He looked genuinely concerned, which was discomfiting.

"You texted pics of my friends. Including the one you killed."

Gunnar's eyes went wide and his body stiffened. He stepped forward and peered out the door. Startled by the sudden movement, I stumbled back, nearly falling onto the bed. I waved the gun wildly and growled, "Stay still! I mean it, I'll shoot!"

Gunnar held out his hands and quickly shifted back to the wall by the bureau. Earnestly, he said, "Please listen, this is extremely important. I didn't contact you."

Bullshit. I couldn't believe he actually expected me to fall for this nonsense. "Then why was your door open?"

"I'm waiting for a pizza! Plus, the room smells."

I eyed him. "You're lying." (Not about the room smelling, though. Some recent guest had left a distinct funk.)

"Believe what you want. But we should lock that door." He appeared visibly agitated.

"I bet you'd like that," I said, but doubt was niggling at me. The adrenaline pumping through my system was clouding my thought processes at the worst possible time. I was missing something, I could feel it—I needed time to sort through everything he'd told me. Because I had to admit, some of it rang true. There was the way that Grace looked at me sometimes, that gleam in her eyes when she talked about the killings. And how she'd warmed up in L.A., to the point of confiding in me . . . in retrospect, that definitely seemed out of character.

When she'd realized I was in Vegas, why had she bothered contacting me? If she'd been careful, I never would've known she was here. I would've gotten my documents and gone on my merry way none the wiser. Hell, if she hadn't shown up bleeding on my doorstep, I'd probably already be lounging on a beach in California. Could her stab wound have been self-inflicted? I wouldn't put it past her.

And where *had* she disappeared to the other day? She'd never told me. Another woman was killed during the only window when Grace could've done it . . . that was a hell of a coincidence to swallow.

Gunnar is brilliant, Grace's voice said in my head.

Maybe. But his twin was just as smart. Could she be equally dangerous?

"You didn't freak out tonight when you saw me." I waved the gun. "Why not? I could've been here to rob you."

"I've been studying that picture Grace sent for weeks. I recognized you immediately, despite the . . ." He motioned toward his chin to indicate stubble. "But I couldn't find you anywhere. I finally broke down and registered here as a guest, hoping to draw Grace out. The fact that you managed to find me seemed serendipitous."

"You're lying," I said uncertainly.

"I can prove it." He nodded toward the nightstand. "The picture is on my phone. I can show you her texts, too."

"Stay still," I warned.

"If you insist." If Gunnar was lying, he was damn good at it; my bullshit meter wasn't going off at all. And he did look pretty damn stressed; his eyes kept cutting to the open doorway as if the devil himself was about to appear.

"So why are you staying in my room?"

He raised an eyebrow. "Your room?"

"I was here a few weeks ago."

"Honestly, I had no idea. I gave the desk clerk an extra twenty for the best room. He said it was this one."

Well, he wasn't wrong about that. Dot had said the same thing. I frowned. "No one's supposed to be staying here."

"Yes, the young man told me that, too. I believe that's why he charged me double the listed price."

He had answers for everything. And on the face of it, most of them actually made sense. My voice faltered as I said, "But someone saw you check into the Buggy Suites."

"The what?" He raised an eyebrow.

"Another motel down the road. I saw a picture of you on their surveillance cameras."

"I see. But you didn't know what I looked like, did you? Not until now."

He was right, this was my first good look at him.

Grace had identified him. And I'd taken her at her word.

In fact, everything I knew came from her. Once she'd shown up, I'd shifted my entire game plan. She'd said her brother was fixated on killing me and wouldn't rest until I was dead. And after feeding me an elaborate backstory about her lifelong pursuit of her brother, she'd spent long hours alone in her SKS planning . . . what?

This?

But she hadn't wanted my help—I'd talked her into it (or had I?). She'd complained and dragged her feet every step of the way. I'd thought she was just being her usual obstinate self, but what if it was something else?

After all, that was a classic long-con move. The key was tricking the mark into thinking the whole thing was their idea.

I was reeling. Suddenly, all the events of the past month—hell, even my abduction by Beau—took on a whole new light. And she easily could've planted the tracker and the postcards. *What if I've been wrong about everything?*

"Don't blame yourself. My sister is a master manipulator." Gunnar sounded genuinely sympathetic. "She's been honing this methodology for years. It would be more surprising if you hadn't fallen for it."

I swallowed hard. "And why should I believe you? I mean, it's not like you have actual proof."

"Did she have proof?"

"No," I admitted.

"That's a bit curious, don't you think? Considering how much time you've spent together? I'm guessing it was a few weeks at least, that would fit the pattern."

I thought back to her map with the yellow pins. What if those were actually *her* victims? A sort of trophy room?

"Oh, no," Gunnar gasped.

"What?" I demanded, but I'd also caught movement out of the corner of my eye.

"Hello, Gunnar," Grace said from the doorway.

CHAPTER TWENTY-THREE

FOR YOU I DIE

*F**uck.***

Grace stood in the doorway dressed all in black. She'd also brought a gun and was pointing it at her brother.

Gunnar had shrunk back against the wall. He looked terrified. If he was faking, it was an impressive performance.

I backed toward the bathroom so I could see both of them but kept the Glock aimed at Gunnar.

"Hello, Grace," he said, then cleared his throat. "Long time."

"Fuck you, Gunnar."

Grace's expression was hard to read. Everything Gunnar had said ran through my mind. There was no way to cover both of them with the gun at the same time. But was I aiming at the wrong person? "I thought you didn't like guns."

"I made an exception," Grace said curtly.

"Amber, you have to believe me," Gunnar pleaded, looking terrified. "She'll kill us both."

"Ignore everything he says," Grace said without looking at me.

She was laser focused on her twin, and her gun hand was steady. In contrast, I was shaky with fatigue and filled with doubt. I cleared my throat and said, "Marcella isn't here. We need him to tell us where she is."

"She's already dead," Grace said coldly.

"What?" My stomach dropped. I stared at her. "Why would you say that?"

"Because there would be no reason for him to keep her alive." There was something different about Grace; it reminded me of when she showed up in Beau's kill room. Like she was in her element. Almost like she was enjoying herself.

My head was spinning. What if Grace had made sure my plan would fail? She could have hired some random guy to lead us around Vegas, pretending to be Gunnar. She could have sent me those texts.

She'd been in the hotel with us all day, but that didn't necessarily prove anything. According to Dot, she'd left the hotel room right after me, and I'd sat at the Caesars Palace bar for an hour. Could she have killed Jessie and kidnapped Marcella in that time frame? She'd known exactly where to find them. Was this her real plan all along?

Gunnar held up both hands toward her placatingly. "Please, Grace, let her go. This is between you and me."

"Enough, Gunnar." Grace stepped fully inside and said, "Amber, close the door."

She still hadn't looked directly at me. I hesitated. The thought of being trapped with the pair of them gave me a really bad feeling. For all I knew, they were actually a brother/sister killing team. At this point, I'd believe almost anything. "Maybe I should just, uh, leave you two kids to hash this out," I said, edging toward the door. "I'll go try to find Marcella."

Finally shifting her gaze, Grace frowned at me. "What's wrong?"

"Nothing. I just . . . I mean, it looks like you've got this handled." I eyed the door. Grace still blocked it; could I get past her?

"Interesting that she won't let you leave, don't you think?" Gunnar said.

Grace's eyes narrowed. "What have you been telling her?"

"The truth, Grace."

"She wouldn't believe your lies," Grace said dismissively. When I didn't respond, she threw me a funny look. "Right?"

"Um . . ." I was about three feet from the door now, closer to her than Gunnar. I'd lowered my arm slightly to give it a rest, pointing the gun at the space in between them.

"Are you fucking kidding me?" Grace said with exasperation. "Honestly, even you can't be that stupid."

"Well, it's not as if you won me over with your charm offensive," I retorted. "And he made some pretty good points."

"Christ." Grace shook her head. "Fine. If you want to leave, go."

Well, moment of truth and all that. One (or both) of them had a vested interest in keeping me in this room.

Time to find out who.

I swallowed hard and gripped the Glock with both hands as I sidled sideways toward the door.

"Take your time," Grace said impatiently. "It's not like we're in a hurry."

I'd been keeping an eye on Gunnar, but her comment made me shift to glare at her. "Seriously, you are such a—"

A couple of things happened before I could finish that sentence.

1. There was a hard yank on the back of my shirt, so forceful that I was actually lifted off my feet. *Fuck*, I thought as I went airborne. *It is him.*

2. Grace's eyes widened and her mouth opened. I saw her shift the gun, re-aiming, but I had (like an idiot) stepped into her sightline.

3. As I flew backward, my gun hand jerked up—

4. I landed hard on the ground and pain shot up my tailbone, causing my whole body to clench reflexively—

5. Including my trigger finger—

6. And the gun went off with a *Bang!*

Grace staggered backward clutching her chest. I stared at her dumbly. In my shock, it took a second to grasp that I'd shot her. She looked down at the hole in her shirt, dazed. Then she raised her eyes to meet mine and said thickly, "You bitch!"

As if in slow motion she fell out the door, collapsing on the landing outside.

For a moment, the world stopped.

Then I scrambled to my feet, staring out the door. Grace was lying there, not moving. Her head had fallen to the side; her hands had gone limp. The gun lay next to her where it had fallen.

Gunnar was on my left. He was hunched forward, breathing hard, hands curled—

His head swiveled toward me. The mask slipped, and I shrank away from the pure rage contorting his features. He looked like a man possessed. "You killed her."

"I—I didn't mean to," I said weakly. "I swear."

The Glock had dropped between us—like an idiot, I'd let go of it as Grace reeled. Gunnar followed my eyes. As I dove for the gun, his left foot lashed out and kicked it under the bed.

I scrabbled forward and frantically groped under the bed (Christ, it was filthy under there, and dark. I couldn't see it, couldn't see anything at all . . .)

A yank on my ankle made me yelp.

Gunnar dragged me out from under the bed. I kicked at him and screamed. I clawed at the carpet, tearing up tufts of it, but there was nothing to grab hold of—

"Fucking help!" I screamed. "Someone help! Fire!" It was just like before, that feeling of choking helplessness. The strange time shift, where everything was happening fast and yet really fucking slowly at the same time—

Another *bang*—I jerked my head around. But it wasn't a gunshot this time; Gunnar had kicked open the door to the adjoining room. *For families. You'd be surprised.* He hit the switch as he dragged me over the threshold and the room flooded with light.

With what seemed like superhuman strength, Gunnar lifted me off the ground by the ankle and hurled me toward the bureau.

I landed hard on my hip bone and the back of my head smacked the bottom drawer, making me cry out. I gasped for air as he charged forward and bent low, bringing his face inches from mine. Gunnar looked like a different person, teeth bared, eyes crazed. "Not a sound," he spat, then pointed across the room. "Or I swear I will rip her apart."

I followed his finger—Marcella was lying on the floor by the bathroom. She was barefoot, in a tube top and ripped miniskirt. Her face was puffy and red, like she'd been crying. There was a dark bruise on her cheek, and her hair was tangled and wild. Her arms were behind her back and she was bound at the ankles and knees with the same duct tape that covered her mouth.

Our eyes met. I couldn't tell if she was relieved to see me, or disappointed that I'd managed to get caught, too.

Couldn't blame her for that.

Gunnar paced back and forth in the space between the door and the bureau. He was agitated, tugging at his hair like a madman. Gone was the "psychiatrist" with the composed demeanor. Seeing him in this state, it was hard to believe that I'd ever doubted Grace.

Stupid, stupid, stupid, I chastised myself.

Gunnar stopped suddenly and looked at me with raw hate. "You killed my sister."

I frantically dug through my bag of tricks—he was a psychopath and a narcissist, there had to be a way to use that—but my head hurt, and sheer terror made it hard to think. "You—you told me she was the killer," I stuttered. "It's your fault."

Which was clearly the wrong thing to say, because Gunnar lunged down and grabbed me by the neck. He hauled me up, choking, until we were eye to eye. So close that spittle sprayed my face, he said, "You fucking little bitch. I am going to make this worse than you can imagine. I am going to dismantle you both piece by piece. It will take days. Weeks. You will beg for death."

I tried to scream but he was crushing my windpipe, cutting off my air. Past his shoulder I could see Marcella trying to struggle to her feet, but she was too tightly bound. "You . . . can't . . ."

He cocked his head to the side and slightly eased the pressure on my larynx. "You sad waste of space. You think you can tell me what to do?" He tossed me on the bed like I weighed nothing. "You were dead the minute Grace walked into that basement. You just didn't realize it."

The cold, clinical way he said that should have sent me straight into another panic attack. Because there was truth in it; I'd been living on borrowed time, maybe since Stella. But once you accept that you're going to die, there's nothing left to be afraid of. And maybe pissing him off would speed things up, because that whole "dismantling" thing sounded pretty painful. Rubbing my throat with one hand, I croaked, "Grace hated you."

He frowned. "Nonsense. You can't hate someone who's part of you."

"She wanted you dead. She said she'd kill you herself."

He seemed to forget me for a second. "Grace was the only one who understood," he said, as if something had suddenly struck him. "Without her, the game is over."

I subtly shifted to meet Marcella's eyes. She looked exhausted and terrified. She tried to say something, but her words were muffled by the tape. Carefully, I pushed up to my elbows. My voice was as raspy as a pack-a-day smoker's when I said, "Just following in Daddy's footsteps?"

His eyes flashed. "Father was an amateur."

"Grace thought it was pathetic, the way you copied him."

He lunged at me, snarling, "That's a lie!"

"It's not," I said, fighting the tremble in my voice. He was inches away, face flushed with rage. "She—she said it was embarrassing, that you weren't even good at it. She called you sloppy."

He straightened abruptly and ran a hand through his hair, making it stand on end. "Bullshit," he hissed. "She'd never say that."

Emboldened, I continued. "She said you only got away with it because you were lucky."

"Lucky? No one else even comes close." Leaning in, he added, "You know how many?"

I shrugged. "A dozen?"

"I'd killed that many by the time I was twenty," he scoffed. "I've expunged hundreds of useless drains on society. Like that one." He waved dismissively at Marcella. "Addicts, whores, illegals. They're so irrelevant, they're not even missed."

Marcella growled at that. I shot her a warning look, then said, "If you say so."

"You don't believe me?"

"I mean, it just seems pretty unlikely, killing that many people and getting away with it." I drew a ragged breath, then added, "Kind of a waste, too, if Grace didn't know."

"She did know. She had to." His face fell. "You've ruined everything. Now I'll just be playing against myself. If only—"

Sirens in the distance. His head tilted to listen, and then he said, "Time to go. The response time is slow, but they eventually investigate gunshot reports."

"Just take me," I begged. "Leave Marcella. Please! I'll do whatever you want, I swear!"

Gunnar had already moved around the bed to Marcella. He pulled open the bedside table drawer and withdrew a huge hunting knife. Kneeling down, he severed the tape binding her ankles and knees. Glancing up at me, he said, "You were right, by the way. I do have a room at the Buggy Suites. We'll go there now, quickly and quietly. If either of you tries to run, you will regret it."

Tears slid down Marcella's face. I tried to signal with my eyes that she should run, there was no way he could catch both of us, and if anyone was going to survive, it should be her—but that was a lot to convey with a glance, and she simply looked confused.

He yanked Marcella to her feet and turned back to me, keeping a firm hold on her right arm. "Get up."

I struggled to get off the bed, feeling resigned. Marcella was staring at me—our eyes met. Seeing what she was about to do, I nodded.

Marcella drove her head into Gunnar's sternum and stomped on his foot. With a grunt he let go, and she stumbled around the bed toward the open door. As she passed I reacted, even though I was thinking, *He's too fast, there's no way this will work—*

I shoved Marcella hard toward the open door between the rooms and screamed, "Run!"

Marcella flew through it, hands still bound behind her back, chest forward like a runner crossing the finish line.

At the same time I did a donkey kick, slamming my foot into Gunnar's hip. He staggered sideways, falling into the dresser, just missing me as he swung the knife in a broad arc. The mirror mounted to the bureau fell down and shattered. I launched myself back across the bed on all fours like a monkey and ended up on the floor by the bathroom, exactly where Marcella had been moments before.

Gunnar straightened, knife still grasped in his hand. Droplets of blood peppered his arm where tiny bits of glass glinted. He looked wildly at the door Marcella had run through—she was gone, I could hear her bare feet pounding along the walkway outside.

I sagged with relief. Marcella was safe. At least I wouldn't be responsible for another person's death.

Just my own.

Gunnar's face darkened. He crossed the room in two long strides and lowered the knife to my neck. I felt a trickle of blood where the tip of it nicked me. "That was very, very stupid," he said quietly. "You should have run, you fool."

I swallowed hard. "Yeah, well, I'm kind of known for being foolish."

"Actually, she's famous for it," said a voice from the doorway.

Gunnar whipped around. Grace stood there in all her glory, legs in a wide stance like a goddamn superhero. Sounding almost wistful, she said, "Goodbye, Gunnar."

Then she shot him three times.

CHAPTER TWENTY-FOUR

CONFESSION

Okay, so I haven't been completely honest. Force of habit.

Plan B wasn't entirely Grace's idea. I mean, I'm not a total idiot.

I knew all along that someone with a compulsive need for control might not follow our little wild-goose chase indefinitely. If Gunnar had gone along with it, great. Plan A would have landed him squarely in a prison cell. Because while he cooled his heels in a casino's holding tank, Grace would've been busily planting evidence at the Buggy Suites. Apparently over the years she'd collected things from Gunnar's crime scenes—an entire black case full of them. (I'd found that creepy as hell when she showed me. Almost as if she'd been taking trophies, too.)

After that, an anonymous tip to the cops, combined with helpful assists from more of Dot's friends (including a sex worker willing to claim that Gunnar had tried to kill her), would seal the deal. They'd find a motel room chock-full of serial killer trophies and overwhelming evidence that said killer had decided to try his luck at Caesars Palace.

It wasn't foolproof, but it should've been enough for even the most incompetent detective to connect the dots.

Well, we all know how that went. So plan B was a combination of Grace's usual "storm in without a real plan" and my lifetime's worth of experience with human behavior and con jobs.

I was pretty sure that Gunnar would try to lure us to the Getaway (Grace and I had another fifty-dollar bet riding on that). After all, he'd dumped Grace there. And he knew that the rest of us had a connection to it. So if things broke that way, all I had to do was show up and get a confession out of him. Thanks to the spy camera concealed in my enormous tacky gold necklace, it would be recorded. Grace would provide backup, and if we needed more leverage to get him talking, we'd stage the shootout. I'd predicted that losing Grace would catapult him into a state of extreme agitation. (That was the riskiest part for me, and I wasn't thrilled when things broke in that direction.) I'd use his agitation to get the confession, and then Grace would pop back in and hold him at gunpoint. We'd still be able to leave him gift-wrapped for the cops.

No one was supposed to get hurt.

But he went after Jessie and Marcella, which was not part of either plan. I'd been forced to improvise on the fly. Sadly, in at least one regard, I'd failed horribly.

"Why the fuck were you even here? You were supposed to be at the Mayhem," I said plaintively, staring down at Jessie. She lay in the bathtub of room eleven, her long legs dangling gracelessly over the side. The black cord Gunnar had used to strangle her was still wound around her neck.

Marcella stood at my shoulder scratching her arm—I was pretending not to notice the fresh track marks there. She looked wrecked, still barefoot, her face streaked with tears. She'd just reached the edge of the Getaway's parking lot when I'd yelled for her to come back (earning some odd looks from passersby). She'd returned to the room reluctantly.

I'd gently removed the tape binding her hands and rubbed her arms to get circulation back in them. She barely seemed to be listening as I explained everything that had happened; I chalked it up to shock. She was the one who showed me where Jessie was. Now I said, "I'm really glad you're okay. When he sent that picture of you—"

"It's my fault," she interrupted.

"What?"

Marcella was shaking her head hard, as if trying to dislodge something. "Jessie knew I was here. She came to get me."

"But—why?" I frowned. "You knew this was going down today. You were supposed to stay at the Mayhem."

Marcella started crying. Plaintively, she wailed, "I was stressed, I just needed a little fix."

I gaped at her. "And you couldn't get it there?"

"Not for trade." Marcella swallowed hard. "My dealer works this corner. I knew it would only take a few minutes. But then *he* showed up and so did Jessie, and he just . . ." She buried her face in her hands and turned away.

"Jessie came here looking for you," I said slowly.

Marcella nodded, and my stomach dropped. I could picture Jessie finding Marcella's room at the Mayhem empty and realizing where she'd gone. She must have rushed to the Getaway to help her, the same way she'd saved us.

And she'd paid with her life. All because Marcella wanted a dime bag.

I felt a wave of disgust. I couldn't even bring myself to look at her.

Marcella grabbed my arm. "I'm sorry. God, Amber, I'm so, so sorry."

Her voice was trembling. I tried to muster some sympathy, but I just felt empty. Wrung out. She stood at my shoulder crying, her breath hitching.

Staring down at Jessie, rage swelled inside me. How dare she cry. She should be the one to have to tell Dot. She should have to beg for forgiveness.

You're hardly one to judge, I reminded myself. After all, I had someone's death on my conscience, too. And it wasn't like Marcella had wrapped the rope around Jessie's throat. Staring at a spot on the wall above the tub, I forced myself to say, "It's okay. You made a mistake."

Marcella whimpered. I wrapped an arm around her shoulders, and we stood there in silence.

"I should go check on Dot," she finally said. I nodded, still not meeting her eyes. She brushed her lips against my cheek and whispered, "Thank you for saving me."

"I should have saved you both."

"It's not your fault, either."

I didn't answer. I couldn't. I was frantically swimming, my lungs screaming for air, bullets pocking the water around me. Muted screams and gunfire everywhere. I already knew that no matter what I said, Marcella would carry this with her for the rest of her life.

She stepped away and my arm dropped to my side. I heard the soft pad of feet across the carpet. Grace murmuring something. A door closing.

When I turned around, Marcella was gone.

Grace was standing over her twin. Gunnar was splayed out, arms flung wide, blood staining the carpet around him. His mouth and eyes were still open.

The gun was tucked back into Grace's shoulder holster. Her face was blanker than usual.

I went over to her. "You okay?"

She lifted her gaze to meet my eyes. "He's dead."

"Yeah." Killing him technically hadn't been part of the plan. Although if I was being honest, deep down I'd known it would end like this. And I wasn't exactly torn up about it—the world was a much better place without Gunnar Grimes in it. It was hard to get hung up on the whole "he deserved his day in court" bullshit, too, when all too frequently I'd seen how compromised "justice" could be.

Still, having another person die in front of me had been hard.

"My chest is killing me," Grace said accusingly.

"That makes sense, since I shot you." I sat carefully on the bed, wincing as my bruised tailbone protested. "What took you so long? He almost gutted me."

"I could barely breathe for five minutes."

I shrugged. "It's a training bullet. The guy at the gun shop said it wouldn't do any real damage."

"Well, he was wrong."

"You're standing here, aren't you?" I knew she was just arguing to distract herself.

"I suppose I should be grateful you didn't shoot me in my stab wound." She cocked her head to the side, eyeing me. "For a minute there, I thought you believed him."

I shifted uncomfortably. "About you being the killer?"

"Yes."

"I was just stringing him along," I said defensively. "Like we planned."

Seemingly satisfied with that, she turned back to him.

I gingerly rubbed my throat, glad she seemed to accept that. Because the truth was, I really had been ready to bail. In the moment, if Grace had turned out to be the killer, I wouldn't have been surprised. I checked my watch. "It's been ten minutes. We should get a move on." I looked around the room. "Should we wipe it down?"

"Are your gloves still on?"

I checked them. My hands were disgustingly sweaty inside the fleshy-looking latex, but there were no visible holes. "Yup."

"Then we're fine." Her nose wrinkled. "This place is a petri dish, they'll probably find hundreds of prints." For someone who had just killed the brother she'd devoted her life to pursuing, Grace appeared remarkably chill. If she felt anything at all—sorrow, relief—she was doing a great job of hiding it. But then, it was Grace.

The rage toward Marcella had quickly abated. Now I felt nothing, not even relief. *Maybe you're a sociopath, too.* I forced the thought away and looked around the room again. "Do we need to do anything else?"

"No," Grace said, but she still didn't move, she just stood there staring at her brother.

"Grace," I said gently. "We should go."

"Yes, of course." A pause, and then she said, "Just one more thing."

Grace bent low to whisper in his ear. Faintly, I heard her say, "I win."

DEADLINE-U.S.A.

BREAKING NEWS:

LAS VEGAS SUN TRIBUNE

MOTEL HOMICIDE VICTIM

A SUSPECTED SERIAL KILLER

There have been a series of extraordinary developments in the investigation of recent murders at the Getaway Motel on South Las Vegas Boulevard. Due to an anonymous tip, Gunnar (Cabot) Grimes and local businesswoman Jessie Lee Whitton were found dead on the premises in the early hours of May 5.

Along with Mayhem Motel owner Ms. Whitton, Grimes was initially thought to be the victim of a robbery gone wrong. However, it has now become apparent that Grimes was responsible for the death of Ms. Whitton. It was also revealed that Grimes was the son of notorious serial killer Gregory Grimes, who is currently serving a life sentence for the murders of fifteen women. The senior Mr. Grimes is being held at the supermax prison in Florence, Colorado, where the Federal Bureau of Prisons houses terrorists, serial killers, and drug lords.

The FBI has uncovered evidence that like his father, Gunnar Grimes was also a serial killer—and quite possibly one of the most prolific in the history of the United States, if not the world.

Police Chief Victor Martinez of the LVPD said at today's press conference that they have confirmed a link between Mr. Grimes and the deaths of four Las Vegas sex workers over the past several months. "We're also now certain that Mr. Grimes was responsible for the death of Ms. Whitton, who as a valued member of our community will be terribly missed." An unidentified eyewitness who survived the ordeal provided testimony confirming that chain of events. Chief Martinez also indicated that the FBI is investigating possible links between Mr. Grimes and several other murders nationwide over the past two decades. He declined to elaborate, referring questions to FBI Special Agent in Charge Jean Patrick. Agent Patrick said she would comment when more details have been confirmed.

When interviewed, the Getaway Motel's owner, Dorothy "Dot" Roux, explained that on the night of the murders, the motel had been closed for minor renovations. "He must've broken in," she said. "We're a very family-friendly place with a noir theme and some of the best rooms in Vegas. I'm shocked, shocked that something so horrific happened here."

Ms. Roux also expressed sadness at the fact that her close friend Ms. Whitton was Grimes's final victim. "Jessie had the biggest heart," Ms. Roux said, visibly distraught. "She was like a mother to me."

According to Frederick Hall, manager of the Buggy Suites Motel a half mile from the Getaway, Mr. Grimes had in fact rented a room there on the afternoon of May 4. When interviewed by phone last night, Mr. Hall said, "There was a s—ton of evidence in that bastard's room." He also went on to express his dismay, saying, "I can't believe I talked to a f—in' serial killer."

Chief Martinez said that there will be more information shared during tomorrow's press conference.

A memorial for Ms. Whitton will take place at local watering hole, the Tiki Hut, on Sunday, May 21. In lieu of flowers, the family asks that donations be made to the Project Garbo Foundation.

CHAPTER TWENTY-FIVE

THE LAST MILE

The FBI was never able to determine who sent the anonymous video in which Gunnar Grimes confessed to committing over three hundred murders. Despite the jumpy camerawork, most of the confession was clearly audible, although a few sentences dissolved into static; the techs assumed this was due to the cheap nature of the camera's microphone. Also, the shooter's face had been carefully blurred out.

The video had clearly been tampered with and would never have held up in court. But the sheer volume of additional evidence would've sent Gunnar Grimes away for the rest of his natural life.

Since he was already dead, everyone agreed it was a moot point. As the FBI sorted through the jewelry, clothing, and other items found in his motel room, they were able to start offering closure to the families of dozens of victims, including some who had only been thought missing.

A few of the Bureau's computer science agents started a private pool, betting on which hackers could have done such an elegant editing job (not to mention routing the video through dozens of servers). Most had money on a foreign group like Fancy Bear in Russia. A few made some headway in retracing the video's path but eventually gave up. No one would ever win that kitty.

When the FBI interviewed her, Dot explained that her friend Jessie had been managing the Getaway while she took a vacation (which was true, sort of). She claimed to know nothing about how Gunnar Grimes got into room twelve (also true), or who the shooter might have been (total lie).

I'm sure that Dot executed this performance flawlessly; she'd been positively starry-eyed at the prospect of it.

She watched now as I packed my car. Turns out that Jim had just stored it for me, which honestly was a relief. I really couldn't have afforded a new one, and the beater van was still back in L.A.

We were in the parking lot of the Mayhem. Jessie had left it to Dot in her will, which shocked the hell out of poor BJ. He'd headed back to Stockton in a huff after the memorial.

Dot had felt conflicted about taking it over, but me and Jim managed to convince her that something good should come out of all this. Dot certainly deserved it.

So I stayed there while everything got wrapped up (the Getaway held too many bad memories). Dot was right, though: the constant clamor of millennials and Gen Zers put a bit of a damper on the Mayhem. Sitting at a corner table during the continental buffet every morning, I found that their chatter grated on me. I wanted to shake them and tell them to wake up. Scream that the world was a cold, cruel place full of tragedy and suffering and danger.

Yup. I'd become that person. Get off my damn lawn.

"Sure I can't talk you into staying?" Dot asked again. The toll of the last month showed around her eyes; losing Jessie had hit her hard. Although that blow had been slightly mitigated when Jim proposed. He got down on one knee in front of Dot's convertible at the Drive-In Las Vegas, with *The Blue Dahlia* screening in the background. The ring was a gorgeous emerald in a vintage setting; it was still new enough that she kept unconsciously playing with it. I smiled, watching her twist it around her finger again.

Surprisingly, for a hot minute I'd actually considered staying. After all, it wasn't like I had a single friend anywhere else, and there were bound to be plenty of people in Vegas who could use a shrink. Since the FBI wasn't actually after me, I'd gotten in touch with my former professors and arranged to finish classwork virtually; I'd be done by the end of the summer. Really, I could have done that from anywhere. (I kept the new documents Jessie had made for me, though. Couldn't hurt to have a backup ID, even though I hoped to never need it.)

But every time I thought about setting down roots in Vegas, I got twitchy. "Sorry," I said ruefully. "I just need to find somewhere that feels like home."

Dot nodded. "I hear you, toots. Well, come back and visit anytime. I'll set you up with my best room free."

Neither of us mentioned the other reason I was leaving. Dot had installed Marcella as the temporary manager of the Getaway, and the thought of seeing her on a regular basis made me squirm. I had a lot of conflicting feelings about her, and about us.

As if reading my mind, Dot said, "Marcella will be fine."

I slammed the trunk shut. "Yeah." I hesitated, then added, "Are you sure it's such a good idea, putting her in charge?"

"Letting the cat watch the canary, you mean?" Dot looked bemused. "You think she'll take advantage?"

"It's just—I don't know if she can help it."

Dot sighed. "Honey, I know addicts. Hell, I was raised by one. But what happened to Jessie shook her up. She's going to meetings now, just got her first chip."

"That's great," I said, unable to keep the doubt from my voice.

Dot laid a hand on my arm and smiled. "Everyone deserves a second chance. Jessie would've wanted it that way. Besides—" She cocked an eyebrow. "You're no stranger to that, are you?"

"What do you mean?" I asked, thinking, *Shit. Did Grace say something?*

"Aw, honey." She pulled me into a hug. "You got second chance written all over you."

I hugged her back, trying to commit her reassuring scent to memory. When Dot released me, she pecked me on both cheeks and said, "You better skedaddle before traffic picks up."

"Right. Thank everyone again for me. Especially the Femmes."

"Will do. Let me know if you ever hear from that Grace."

"It's doubtful."

"You never know. Sometimes people surprise you."

"She's always been good at that," I muttered, although I didn't believe for a second that I'd see Grace again. After we returned to the hotel suite at the Nugget, I'd slept until nearly one in the afternoon. When I went to check on Grace, her stuff was already gone. True to form, she hadn't even left a note. Or the hundred bucks she owed from our bets.

Which honestly was fine by me. I'd had enough of her to last a lifetime. But Dot had developed a strange affection for her; I think she still thought of her as some sort of honorary Fatal Femme.

I turned to go, then stopped. "Um, could you tell Marcella that I said goodbye? And that, well . . ."

"I think she already knows," Dot said with a smile. "But I'll tell her anyway. Now, you take care. And remember, you'll always have friends here."

There was a lump in my throat as I climbed into the driver's seat. I backed out carefully, navigating between the electric cars cluttering the parking lot. Then I threw a final wave to Dot before turning west toward California. I had a long drive ahead and wanted to make it by nightfall.

Having had my fill of Los Angeles, I'd decided to start in San Francisco. I pictured a lot of fog and rain but really had no idea what to expect. That was part of the fun, though.

After a few hours, I stopped to refill my tank at a desolate gas station with a shabby mini mart. I was leaning against my car as it fueled up, munching on a Dorito, when my phone buzzed with a text. I frowned; it was a new burner, as far as I knew only Dot had the number.

I took it out of my pocket and almost dropped the chips when I saw UNKNOWN NUMBER.

"How the hell does she do that?" I said, grinning as I unlocked it.

The text read: I was starting to think you were going to stay in that hellhole.

"God, she is *such* a bitch," I said fondly. The person at the next pump gave me a strange look. I ignored them and typed, nice of u to say goodbye.

While I waited for a response, the latch on the pump clicked. I wiped Dorito dust off my hands and went to unhook it from my car. Then I sat in the driver's seat, curious to see if she'd respond. *I'll give her five minutes*, I decided, checking the time on my phone.

I waited, tapping a finger on my thigh: nothing. I was getting ready to pull out when another text chimed. Sighing, I threw the car back into park.

Did you get my present?

"Present?" I muttered. "What fucking present?" The concept of Grace giving me a gift was boggling. I answered, r u fucking with me?

I could practically picture her eye roll when I read Check your trunk.

A horn honked behind me—in the rearview mirror I saw a guy in a pickup waiting impatiently for my pump. I waved in apology and drove to a spot next to an old pay phone.

Feeling peevish, I went to open the trunk. My duffel bags were looking seriously the worse for wear after their exciting journey. I'd just repacked my stuff that morning after washing everything in the Mayhem's attached laundromat, so I was fairly certain there was nothing but clean clothes stuffed inside. Still, I halfheartedly dug through them, wondering what the hell Grace would even consider to be a present. Another cattle prod, maybe? I definitely would have spotted that right away. I had no idea what I was looking for.

Nothing here, I finally typed. Knew u were messing w me.

Check where u left my gun.

Grumbling, I dug around the spare tire. (Suffice it to say that my trunk, like the rest of my car, was considerably dirtier than Grace's. And stickier.) My fingers brushed against paper. I pulled out a small envelope and held it up to the light: there was something solid inside. I slit it open with a fingernail and dumped the contents into my hand. Out tumbled a small black device branded TREZOR that looked like a car key.

If she'd gotten me a car, that would've been helpful to know *before* I drove away from Vegas. I swiped a hand across my sweaty forehead. I'd just come through Death Valley without air conditioning. I was hot and tired and still had a long road ahead. I was definitely not in the mood for more of Grace's games. I was half-tempted to toss whatever it was in the trash can a few feet away. Instead, I wrote, what is this?

About three million dollars.

"Holy shit!" I yelled, nearly dropping the phone. I lunged to catch it, almost dropping the key in the process. I juggled both for a second, looking like a complete lunatic.

The phone rang. I carefully tucked the key in my pocket and picked up. "Um, are you fucking crazy?"

"You're welcome."

Grace's clipped voice was so familiar, it sparked an (unexpected) involuntary grin. I could practically picture her sitting in the SKS. Had she taken the pins off the map? I'd bet that wall was already repainted white. *Focus, Amber.* "I'm serious. What is this?"

"It's a hardware wallet."

"Uh-huh. What's that?"

An audible sigh of exasperation. "I took the liberty of going through my brother's things while I was leaving the evidence," she said. "I was curious about how he'd been accessing his money, and—it's a bit complicated to explain—"

Of course it is, I thought. *Christ, she still treats me like I'm an idiot.*

"—but I discovered where his funds were and converted them into cryptocurrency. I'll send the access code in segments, of course, for security. Don't lose them, or the wallet will be useless."

"O-kay," I said. The device felt inordinately heavy in my pocket; I double-checked to make sure there were no holes it could slip through. "I'm just super confused right now."

"Of course you are."

"Because," I continued, annoyed by her tone, "it's not like I'm your favorite person. I mean, are you really just giving me this?"

I eyed pickup truck guy as he walked back to his car from the mini mart; it suddenly felt like this conversation should be happening somewhere much more private. I swallowed hard and lowered my voice. "Why aren't you keeping it?"

"I'm already quite comfortable, and you certainly need it more. For new clothes and a decent haircut at the very least." A long pause, then Grace added, "I know it might not seem like it, but I am grateful."

I waited for her to continue, but there was only silence on the other end of the line. Still, from Grace, that had practically constituted an outpouring of emotion. "So you're saying I'm rich now?"

"Comparatively, yes."

It started to sink in. *Holy crap.* I could pay back my school loans, and wouldn't even have to work. I could compensate Dot for everything she'd done. I could send some to Marcella, too—or maybe give it to Dot to pass along when she was ready for such a windfall. I could—

"Amber?"

"Yeah?" I said, feeling dazed.

"Drive safely. And find a napkin. You have Dorito dust on your cheek."

I jerked my head around, scanning the lot. There was a security camera aimed down at me from the corner of the mini mart. I grinned up at it. "I knew you liked me."

"Don't get emotional. This doesn't mean we're friends."

"'Course not. Because we're *best* friends, right?" I might've been wrong, but it felt like she was smiling.

"Part of the deal is that you leave me alone."

"Sure. See you at Thanksgiving."

A click as the call disconnected. I waved at the camera. Then I gave it the finger and turned away.

ACKNOWLEDGMENTS

This is all Jandy Nelson's fault.

I honestly thought I was done with writing. I'd always been dismissive of writer's block; I felt it was for dilettantes. As a working author, I reasoned, I couldn't afford to swan around moaning about my inability to write. I had bills to pay.

And then, it happened to me. No opening ideas, no plot points, no characters whispering in my ear, just . . . nothing. It was devastating.

So, after much swanning about and moaning, I set my sights on a new career and applied to clinical psychology programs. My work with LGBTQ+ foster youth had inspired a desire to learn more about developmental trauma so that I could someday help these amazing young people more effectively. I started taking undergraduate psychology classes at community colleges (which was one of the very few silver linings of everything moving online during the pandemic). And to distract myself from the general awfulness of this global tragedy, I lurked on Twitter. Turns out that every day, my friend Jandy was urging people to treat noon as "magic hour," when we'd all sit and write.

The first time I saw her post, I thought it was sweet but impractical. Who could write under these challenging circumstances? I resolutely went back to my (sorry) attempts to bake bread from scratch.

The eighth time, I was annoyed. Obviously, anyone who could manage creativity during all of this was better than me, and that was profoundly irritating.

ACKNOWLEDGMENTS

The twentieth time, I thought, *What the hell.* I'd been mulling over the striking similarities between authors, therapists, and con artists, in that they all earn a living off an ability to read people. Consequently, I sat down and wrote about a psych major/former grifter who was trapped in the back of a serial killer's van.

From the beginning, I wanted something fun and sexy that nodded to the noir films and books I love. (Speaking of which, tip of the ol' hat to the amazing movie titles I borrowed for chapter headings.) I wanted it to be female-driven, starring women who used what are traditionally considered "feminine" strengths—their smarts, their instincts, their ability to form relationships. And I wanted them to be complicated, flawed, but redeemable.

Did I already say fun? I really wanted it to be fun (and yes, I realize that's a strange thing to aspire to with a book about serial killers). We all definitely deserve some serious fun and laughs and glitter and rainbows after suffering through the past couple of years.

Anyway, all of that is to say: thank you, Jandy. Without your gentle prodding, I'd probably just be shopping for therapist-appropriate cardigans, tortoiseshell glasses, and wraparound scarves right now. (I still am, but I've got this going on, too. Booyah.)

Thank you to my phenomenal agent. I was so lucky to wrangle Stephanie Kip Rostan into my corner. The fact that she sends back what I thought were completed manuscripts with copious notes explaining why "it's not quite there yet" is what makes her the best in the game. And she is always right. Repeat after me: Steph is always right. The final version of this book is entirely due to her unerring talent for homing in on the best and worst bits.

I'm also incredibly lucky that the manuscript caught the eye of the immensely talented Danielle Dieterich at Putnam. I've been in this business for a long time now (I won't admit to exactly how long for fear of dating myself), and it is such a delight to be working with someone as highly competent, intelligent, and driven as Danielle. It's been my best experience with an editor, and that's saying something. Plus, she's a fellow Wesleyan grad. Match made in heaven, as far as I'm concerned.

And what a fantastic publisher I landed! Thank you from the bottom of my heart to everyone at Putnam who helped make this book what it is. From cover design to copyediting (which was so meticulous I was genuinely gobsmacked) to sales and marketing, this is a crack team. You can run a con with me anytime.

I'm also delighted to be working with the exceptional Jasmine Lake and her team at UTA. I know what a rare gift it is to have a book receive such strong support, and I'm so grateful.

Thanks also to everyone in the MAP program at AULA for keeping me sane in a zany world. Only you could make me laugh during a discussion of the *DSM*. When people shine through Zoom, they're beyond dazzling IRL. Love to you all.

I managed to talk my way into the best traineeship in town. The good people at the L.A. LGBT Center do incredible, lifesaving, and affirming work in the face of tremendous obstacles. So please give it up for them. Love is love, people. Human rights belong to all humans. Support trans kids, because standing up for children is always the right thing to do. Climbing off my soapbox now . . . but seriously, lives are literally at stake. Join the fight for them.

I'm grateful to have such extraordinary friends; it's an embarrassment of riches. Leslie Margolis, Madeleine Roux, Erin Austin, Colin Dangel, Caroline Egan, Mindy McGinnis, Diem Ha, Bonnie Zane, Jasa McCall, Betsy Brandt, Kate Stoia, Jessica Postigo, Lisa Brown, Joe Loya . . . the list goes on. Raising a virtual glass of wine to all of you. And a real one the next time we meet in person.

And, of course, to you, dear reader! Thank you for coming on this adventure. I have been so blessed to have readers, booksellers, and librarians champion each and every one of my book babies. And I am eternally grateful for it. I'll sign copies for you anytime.

Finally, of course, to my family. My amazing parents, who inspired my love of writing, and who weathered this storm with their usual grace, grit, and New England stoicism. My sisters, who have had to deal with my lifelong carping and dramas, and yet remain my closest confidantes. Hold a seat for me at Bodhi Spa.

As always, I saved the best for last. I was already a huge germaphobe who carried hand sanitizer around before there was even a whisper of a strange new virus, so this was my worst fears realized. I absolutely could not have survived this pandemic without my family. They supported me through all the fear and anxiety, and even managed to make me laugh when I only felt like crying. Through poker nights, hikes, and many binged TV shows (so very many—literally, all the TV), they were my true shelter.

You also have my brilliant son to thank for a major plot twist. We were on a (masked) walk, and I was griping about being stuck, and he said, "What if we think Grace is the killer?" *Boom*. I tell you, this kid. He's something else. I can't wait to see where life takes him, because the world is lucky he came along.

And of course, Kirk. My best and truest partner in crime. Finding each other after decades apart will always be one of my life's true miracles. Who knows how things would've turned out if fate hadn't forced us apart when we were young? But I do know how fortunate I am to have you by my side for the rest of this crazy ride. Love you always, sweetheart.

Aw, hell. I always promise myself this isn't going to turn into the novelist's version of an Oscars acceptance speech: just row after row of names that, let's be honest, you don't care about unless your name happens to be included. Oh well. I'd apologize, but if you've read this far, it must not be bothering you. So, thanks again for joining me. See you in the sequel.

—MICHELLE